SHATTERED MOMENTS

IRINA SHAPIRO

Storm

This is a work of fiction. Names, characters, business, events and incidents are the products of the author's imagination. Any resemblance to actual persons, living or dead, or actual events is purely coincidental.

Copyright © Irina Shapiro, 2014, 2024

The moral right of the author has been asserted.

Previously published in 2014 as *Shattered Moments* by Merlin Press LLC.

All rights reserved. No part of this book may be reproduced or used in any manner without the prior written permission of the copyright owner.

To request permissions, contact the publisher at rights@stormpublishing.co

Ebook ISBN: 978-1-80508-655-0
Paperback ISBN: 978-1-80508-656-7

Cover design: Debbie Clement
Cover images: Shutterstock

Published by Storm Publishing.
For further information, visit:
www.stormpublishing.co

ALSO BY IRINA SHAPIRO

A Tate and Bell Mystery

The Highgate Cemetery Murder

Murder at Traitors' Gate

Wonderland Series

The Passage

Wonderland

Sins of Omission

The Queen's Gambit

Comes the Dawn

The Hands of Time Series

The Hands of Time

A Leap of Faith

A World Apart

A Game of Shadows

The Ties that Bind

ONE

VIRGINIA JUNE 1626

Alec gratefully shut the door on all the noise coming from downstairs—the squealing of children, the crashing of crockery from the kitchen, and the agitated voice of Valerie as she tried in vain to bring some order to the proceedings. Despite the addition, the house was still bursting at the seams, especially since Kit and Louisa were permanently in residence with their children, as well as Charles and Annabel. They'd lost their house in Jamestown to a cousin who inherited the estate on the death of Annabel's brother, Tom. Annabel was still seething at the injustice of this, claiming that her son should have inherited, but the law didn't quite see it that way. The entire estate went to Wesley Gaines, her father's first cousin, who proved to be a closer male relative than a nephew. Wesley, who was a widower, offered to share the house with Charles and Annabel, but Annabel refused to stay, seeing the man as a usurper and a cheat, despite the fact that he'd done nothing wrong in the eyes of the law.

Another pot went crashing to the floor as Cook's piercing voice ordered Harry and Robbie out of the kitchen under the threat of being made to wash dishes. Alec smiled when he heard the stomping of feet and then the slamming of the door as the boys ran for their lives, probably to catch frogs at the pond, which was a favorite pastime. A wail promptly erupted as little Tom tried to follow and was scooped up by Valerie and carried upstairs for his nap.

Strangely, Alec couldn't hear the girls, which was alarming. Evie was probably doing something unspeakable to poor Millicent, who went along with anything her older cousin wanted to do just to be a part of things. It had never been that chaotic when their own children were small, but then again, there had only been the two of them and they were further apart in age. The memory of Finn and Louisa as children cut through Alec like a knife, the pain of their loss still as fresh as ever. He prayed for Louisa's soul every single day and begged God to forgive him for not being a good enough father and not doing something to prevent the path Louisa had chosen. Alec had no idea what would have happened had she survived Tom's birth, but now both men who were at the heart of the tragedy were dead as well, the only reminder of that terrible time the little boy who regarded Alec and Valerie as his parents and was too young to understand that his own parents were gone and that the scandal of his birth had died with them.

Alec thanked God Finn was still alive, but not seeing him every day or being able to write was agony, eased only by their sporadic visits to the future, which they disguised from the rest of the family as visits to Finn's grave. Everyone believed that Finn had been killed by Indians, so Alec and Valerie could never tell the truth or share the joy of Finn's marriage or the birth of his lovely daughter the previous April. Alec longed to hold baby Diana in his arms and see her green eyes, so like Finn's, peering at him, but he had to wait until the next time they were able to get away for a few days to visit their son. She'd probably be walking by then and saying some words.

Alec glanced at the window to see if it was noon yet, then

poured himself a tot of brandy despite the early hour. He deserved it, he reasoned, simultaneously berating himself for being weak. He glanced at the ledger and pushed it away in disgust, knowing that he couldn't possibly face the numbers just yet. The plantation was doing very well and the shipments from the Caribbean were supplementing their income nicely, especially since they started shipping cane liquor on the advice of Valerie and Louisa. They called it rum and promised that it would be a prized commodity once people got a taste for it. They were correct, as usual, their knowledge infallible. Alec was just considering a refill when a knock on the door stayed his hand.

"You wanted to see me, Uncle Alec?" Genevieve advanced into Alec's office shyly, always conscious of her place within the family despite Alec's frequent assurances that she had equal rights to everyone else. She still saw herself as the unwanted orphan, not the beloved niece and cousin who held a special place at the heart of the family. Having spent her young life at the convent of Loudun, she still couldn't quite believe that her dream of finding her mother's family had come true and that her mother's alleged suicide just after her birth, which marked Genevieve as a bastard and a child of a sinner, had been disproved by her uncle, the slate wiped clean, and her mother's remains now resting at the convent cemetery, where she would have wished to be buried.

Genevieve slowly advanced into the room, always expecting to be reprimanded as she had been at the convent, but Alec never had any cause to be stern. Genevieve was the sweetest, kindest girl, who dedicated her life to serving others and making herself as useful as possible by helping with the children and pitching in with the chores.

Alec wanted to speak to her about her future, but he had to proceed carefully, fully aware that Genevieve might take his concern for a desire to be rid of her.

"Sit down, Jenny." The children had given her the name, unable to pronounce *Genevieve*, and he liked it. It was more affectionate, he thought, more loving, and it helped to breach the formality that Genevieve had been so used to at the convent. He was still trying to get her to call Louisa and Kit by their Christian names, but she invariably always chose *Lord and Lady Sheridan*, acutely aware of their social standing and fearing to offend them with unwelcome familiarity, which they constantly assured her was not the case.

"Any chance you might help me with the books?" Alec asked, his voice full of hope. Genevieve had a real head for numbers and although he hated to exploit her, he hated doing the books more and more with each passing year, finding himself without patience or hope of getting the figures to balance. He believed himself to be a savvy businessman, but as soon as he opened the ledgers, all the numbers seemed to change places, 879 becoming 789 before his eyes, making it nearly impossible for him to do the sums correctly. Maybe he needed spectacles, but that likely wasn't the case since he'd battled this problem since he was a child. Valerie told him he had something she called dyslexia, but he secretly thought it was a made-up word, and he was just impatient and careless as the result of his hatred of mathematics.

"Of course, Uncle Alec, it will be my pleasure," Jenny answered with a smile. She knew exactly what he was up to. "You don't even have to ask; I'm always happy to help."

"You are a godsend," Alec replied, sighing with relief before plunging into the real reason for the summons. "Jenny, I know you've been happy here with us this past year, but I can't help but worry about your future. A girl your age should be wed by now, with children of her own. Isn't there anyone who's caught your eye?" Alec winced when he saw Genevieve tense, her fingers digging into the cushion of her chair, her eyes darting around the room in a desperate effort to avoid his gaze.

How could he convince her that all he wanted was her happiness?

"No, Uncle Alec," she mumbled, her gaze eyeing the door with longing. "There's no one."

"Oh, come now. I saw you smiling at Roddy Parks. He's a fine-looking young man with good prospects, and he holds you in high regard."

"He is, but he's not Catholic." Genevieve looked at Alec, her lovely green eyes begging for understanding. "I cannot marry someone who isn't Catholic."

Alec nodded. That had been a problem for her since moving to Virginia. With Catholics being thin on the ground, and having grown up in a Catholic convent, Genevieve was very devout and wouldn't entertain the idea of sharing her life with someone who didn't adhere to her faith. She went to church services with the rest of the family, since not attending the Anglican Church was tantamount to treason, but Alec also held his own services at home for the Catholic members of the household.

"Yes, I understand," said Alec, giving up on Roddy Parks. "I felt very much the same before, but Charles married Annabel, and Louisa married Kit, and they manage to keep their religious differences from getting in the way of their relationships. Do you think you might be able to do the same?" *Not a chance*, he thought as Genevieve shook her head stubbornly.

"I'm sorry, Uncle Alec, but I simply couldn't, and if my husband were Anglican so would my children, and I simply couldn't bear that. It's a Catholic or nothing, I'm afraid."

She lowered her eyes demurely, but Alec knew that beneath that shy exterior was a will of steel, so he chose not to argue. His sister had run away when their father tried to marry her off and Genevieve might do the same if she thought Alec might try to exercise his power over her. This he would never do. All he wanted was for the girl to be content and live her life to the full.

Taking care of other people's children would not be enough to bring her emotional fulfillment, but if she chose to remain unwed, then he would gladly take care of her for the rest of his days and make sure she was well provided for after his death. She was free to choose her own fate, and he wanted to make sure she knew that.

"Jenny, you are free to choose your path. I only want you to be happy."

"I'm happy right here with you all," she replied, giving him a crooked smile. Alec was about to smile back, but it turned into a grimace as a sharp pain tore through his side, making him double over. He tried to hide his discomfort from Genevieve, but it was too late.

"Uncle Alec, what is it?" Genevieve was on her feet, helping him to a chair, her face full of worry. This wasn't the first pain of its kind. They were growing in intensity and coming more frequently these last two days, leaving Alec breathless, sweating, and trembling. "I'll get Aunt Valerie." Genevieve was already out the door before Alec had a chance to protest. He didn't want to worry Valerie any more than she already was, but it was too late as he heard her running up the stairs.

"Alec! What is it?"

"I'm perfectly well, really. It was nothing." He smiled at her, removing his hand from his side and pretending that all was well.

"Doesn't look like nothing," she grumbled. "You need a doctor."

"I don't want a doctor," Alec protested. "He'll just bleed me again and tell me that I need to be purged of ill humors."

Valerie was about to protest when Alec went white, his hand flying to his side again as he gasped with pain. Cold sweat broke out on his forehead, his eyes glazing with suffering as he panted and doubled over, moaning. Valerie froze with fear, noting the location of his hand. It was on the lower-right side of his stomach—appendix. She was no doctor, but she knew the signs. It was either that or some kind of intestinal blockage, which no seventeenth-century doctor could operate on without killing the patient.

"Come, let me get you to bed. Jenny, would you be so kind as to get a hot-water bottle for your uncle? That usually seems to help."

"Of course." Genevieve sprinted out the door as Valerie helped Alec to his feet and walked him slowly to the bedroom. He groaned as he reclined on the bed, his hand still pressed to his side, his face ashen.

Alec began to breathe a little easier when Valerie pressed the hot-water bottle to his side. His normal color was returning, and his legs stopped twitching as the pain ebbed away and he relaxed against the pillows. Alec was so rarely sick that Valerie didn't take the pains seriously at first. Everyone got a stomachache from time to time, especially when the diet wasn't varied and consisted mostly of meat and bread. People of the seventeenth century had absolutely no concept of nutrition and many suffered from chronic constipation, scurvy, and dehydration, since they didn't consume enough liquids, and the ones they did imbibe were all alcoholic. Even children drank beer and ale in large quantities since the water was often unclean and full of harmful bacteria, especially if it came from the area surrounding Jamestown. Many of the first colonists had died from drinking the putrid water, so people erred on the side of caution and avoided it.

Both Valerie and Louisa tried to keep the family healthy by forcing them to drink water from the well, which was safe and clean, in lieu of beer and ale, especially the children. They taught Cook to add as many vegetables as she could to every dish and spent countless hours foraging for wild strawberries, blueberries, nuts, and mushrooms to supplement their diet.

Thankfully, everyone still had their teeth, and their skin was supple, not dry and sallow like many people who lived in town and rarely ate a vegetable.

Valerie put a hand on Alec's forehead to check for a temperature, but he was cool to the touch, which was a good sign.

"Does it hurt anywhere else?" she asked as she watched his face. She knew he didn't want to worry her and might not be truthful.

"No, it's just my side, and it comes and goes," Alec replied, taking her hand in his and kissing her palm in a futile effort to calm her down. "I'm much improved. Can I go now? I have ledgers to balance."

Valerie was about to inform him that he wasn't going anywhere when there was a knock on the door, followed by Louisa's worried face. She glanced at Alec, then turned her attention to her sister. "Val, can I see you outside, please?"

"Don't move," Valerie warned Alec as she followed Louisa to the parlor. She knew what Louisa would say. They'd had this conversation only last night, but Valerie hadn't been receptive, probably because she was still in denial. But now things had changed.

"Val, you have to get him to a hospital. If it's his appendix, it might rupture, and he could die. There's no other choice." Louisa gave Valerie a stern look. She was right, of course, but there were so many obstacles to taking Alec to a hospital in the future.

"How can I pull it off?" Valerie moaned, fixated on all the details of such an undertaking.

"Easy. I will take you in the trap to where Williamsburg will be, and you will use the time travel device to transport yourself there. You will take him to the nearest hospital. No one will give you a second glance; they'll just assume you work at Colonial Williamsburg and still wearing your costumes. They are duty-bound to help him." Louisa smiled at Valerie, pleased with her plan. She'd obviously given the matter some thought since last night.

"Lou, but what about insurance? Money? We might have to stay for a while. I can't sell enough valuables to pay for a surgery. They'll want his medical history as well, and his social security number, address, and billing information." Valerie wrung her hands in agitation, already knowing that they would go no matter what.

"Just tell them he's British and give a phony address in London. Brits don't have a social security number and their medicine is socialized, so no insurance. Just wing it. Everything else will fall into place. You have no time to lose. Get some things together and I will take you right now." Louisa was already heading for the door, ready to bring the trap around.

"What will you tell everyone about our absence?" Valerie called after her, but Louisa waved her hand dismissively.

"I'll think of something, now quit stalling and go."

TWO

WILLIAMSBURG, VIRGINIA JUNE 2010

The Emergency Room was full of people, children crying, and adults suffering in silence as they waited to be seen to by the busy doctors, who were frequently appearing through the double doors to take in the next patient. Valerie was grateful to see that Alec didn't have to wait. He was shown right into an examining room, his strange garb not raising any eyebrows in Colonial Williamsburg. There was a young man two rooms down who was wringing his tricorn in his hands as a nurse stitched a cut on his leg, a woman dressed in a gown and linen cap sitting next to him and mumbling words of comfort. Nope, they weren't out of place at all. The nurse handed Alec a hospital gown, not noticing his look of astonishment at the flimsy garment as she took his blood pressure.

"Let me do the talking," Valerie whispered as a young, Asian doctor walked into the room. Alec opened his mouth to protest, but Valerie jumped right in, describing the symptoms and anxiously following with her eyes as the doctor began his examination. His face remained impassive as he took Alec's pulse, listened to his heart, and told him to breathe in and out as he pressed the stethoscope to his back. Alec remained quiet and did as he was told, but Valerie could see the confusion in his eyes. He couldn't understand why the doctor was checking things that weren't troubling him.

The doctor finally asked Alec to lie back and began to palpate his stomach. Alec tensed as the doctor pressed on the left side, but nearly jumped off the examining table as he moved to the right side of his abdomen. Alec moaned with pain and turned his face from the doctor in embarrassment, but the doctor hardly noticed. He pressed again, gentler this time, but his face was now tense, the eyes alert, watching Alec's reaction.

"I'm sending you for a CT scan, an ultrasound, and a full blood workup," the doctor told Alec. "However, I'm fairly certain that your appendix is severely inflamed and will most likely need to come out. Do you have any questions?"

Alec shook his head miserably. Valerie knew he had a million questions, but he didn't want to appear ignorant in front of the doctor, so he remained silent. The doctor patted him on the shoulder as he left to order the tests.

"What's a CT scan and an ultrasound?" Alec asked quietly as soon as the doctor left.

"Don't worry. They don't hurt. They will just look inside your stomach to see if it's really the appendix before performing the surgery." Valerie smiled at the panicked expression on Alec's face.

"How will they look inside my stomach?"

"These tests allow them to see inside without cutting you open. The CT scan is like an x-ray," she explained, belatedly realizing that Alec had no idea what an x-ray was.

"And if it is the appendix, they will cut me open?" Alec gasped, already jumping off the examining table and trying to reach for his clothes.

"Oh, no, you don't," Valerie said as she deftly plucked Alex's breeches out of his reach. "Stop fretting and let them do their job. Everything is going to be all right. Now, lie back and relax," she whispered as a nurse came to take his blood.

Alec glared at Valerie but allowed the nurse to put a tourniquet around his arm and tap his vein with her finger to make it easier to see. He gasped as she injected the needle into his arm and watched in fascination as dark-red blood flowed into several test tubes, which the nurse switched with practiced efficiency. Alec wasn't afraid of blood; he'd been bled several times in the past, but the process intrigued him and distracted him from worrying about the surgery, which was just as well since it seemed inevitable.

It took another hour and a half to complete the tests, but the doctor's diagnosis had been correct, and surgery was necessary. A surgeon came in to talk to them, followed by the anesthesiologist, who fired off questions about Alec's weight and past allergic reactions to medicine, and then the ER doctor who'd examined him initially.

"Don't worry, he'll be all right," the young doctor said, softening his tone when he noticed Valerie's anxious look. "I assure you, we do this all the time, and we haven't lost one yet. It hasn't ruptured, which is good, but you should have brought him in sooner."

He didn't mean to sound accusing, but Valerie felt a pang of guilt as she looked at Alec, who clamped his lips shut as another wave of pain tore through him, making him forget the indignity of having his butt exposed in the ridiculous gown. He moaned and clutched his side as the orderlies wheeled him out of ER toward the operating rooms. Valerie followed behind with Alec's things in a plastic bag and sank into a chair in the waiting area, knowing it would be a while before she heard anything. She was terribly worried, tired, and hot, and a drink wouldn't come amiss, but she didn't have any money at all, not even a quarter, not that it would do her much good. A cup of coffee would have been wonderful, especially since she hadn't had one since their trip to twenty-first century London over a year ago.

"Are you all right?" An elderly nurse was standing over her, her round face full of sympathy. "Your husband is in surgery? Don't worry. Dr. Patel is one of our best. He's young, but he's a very competent surgeon. There was even an article about him in one of the medical periodicals last month." Valerie recognized her as the nurse who took Alec's blood pressure and temperature in the ER. "There's a cafeteria just down the hall if you want something," she added kindly.

"Thank you, but I left my purse in my locker at work," Valerie improvised. "We don't usually bring our personal possessions to work. They look out of place." The nurse nodded, reaching into her pocket.

"Here, let me get you a cup of coffee. You look like you could use one."

Valerie began to protest, but the nurse held up her hand, already turning to leave. "Want a donut?" she asked, sheepishly. "God, I'd kill for one, but they are not exactly allowed on Weight Watchers. Been doing it for two months and barely lost five pounds," she complained as she smiled down at Valerie. "Chocolate or glazed?"

"Thank you," Valerie mumbled, awed by the woman's kindness. "Chocolate, if it's not too much trouble." She hadn't had a donut in nearly twenty years, and whether it was on Weight Watchers or not, she'd happily wolf it down given the opportunity. The nurse reappeared a few minutes later with a steaming cup of coffee and a donut. She patted Valerie on the shoulder as she turned to leave. "He'll be all right. I'm just at the nurses' station if you need anything, or if you'd like to call someone."

She hurried off, leaving Valerie alone in the church-like hush of the waiting area. There had been a couple there earlier, but they rushed off once the doctor came out to speak to them and tell them that their daughter was already in the recovery room.

Valerie suddenly felt very alone and scared. There was no one to call, no one to turn to for support. She was completely alone in this now foreign world. She had no money, no clothes, and no place to go should the hospital forbid her to stay overnight in Alec's room. She'd given a lot of false information at the registration desk, but how long would it be before they caught on that it was all made up? What would they do?

Alec would be in no condition to travel for a few days at least. Since she had no way of alerting Louisa that they were back and needed to be picked up in the trap, they'd have to find their own way back home and walk from Jamestown to the plantation. The time-travel watch was quite precise, but Valerie didn't know the exact coordinates for Rosewood Manor and would have to use Jamestown as the closest point. She'd need to find a place to stay until Alec was well enough to go home, and try to avoid giving any more fraudulent information. She sighed and bit into the donut. No matter how awful and scared she felt, the fried dough and the chocolaty glaze made her smile and lifted her spirits a fraction.

THREE

Valerie woke to find the sun streaming through the blinds and striping the room with narrow bands of light. A breakfast cart was making its way down the hall, the smell of eggs and toast wafting into the room and making her mouth water. She hadn't eaten anything since the donut and coffee the kind nurse had bought for her yesterday and her stomach was growling with hunger, twisting itself into knots with worry, which wasn't a good combination. Alec had been totally incoherent last night after the surgery, but at the moment he was wide-awake, if still a little pale, and watching an episode of *Star Trek* on the Sci-fi channel with the volume off.

"Good morning," he said cheerfully. "How did you sleep?"

"Fine. The question is, how are you?" Valerie was grateful that the nurses allowed her to take the bed next to Alec since there was no other patient in the room. By the time they finally had him settled after he left the recovery unit, it had been close to midnight and she told them she was a long way from home, which was technically true. Valerie hadn't slept on a real mattress since she and Alec had visited London two years ago where they had stayed at a small bed and breakfast. She now felt very well-rested, having slept soundly after a day filled with such emotional turmoil.

"I feel surprisingly well," Alec replied. "I didn't feel any pain during the surgery." He was still amazed that one could sleep through a procedure and wake up after it was all over with no memory of what happened.

"Does it hurt?" Valerie asked, sitting down next to him and giving him a kiss on his stubbled cheek.

"Not overmuch," Alec replied, shrugging his shoulders. They must have given him some strong painkillers since he looked strangely happy and comfortable. Having never had any kind of medicine before, the effect would probably be more potent on his unsuspecting system. "I'm hungry."

"Me too." An orderly entered the room, bringing Alec a tray of food which he placed on a table in front of him. "I'll get you one too, ma'am," he promised with a big smile and ducked back out into the hall, returning with a tray laden with a covered hot breakfast, a container of orange juice, and a cup of steaming coffee.

"Everyone is so nice," Alec said, tucking into his eggs with relish, "even that Indian fellow. It's wonderful that they allow foreigners to practice medicine." Valerie chuckled.

"They're not foreigners, Alec; they are Americans. They come from all different backgrounds now. I can't even fathom how many different nationalities live in the United States, and they all have the same rights."

"Fascinating," Alec said through a mouthful of egg. "When can we go home?"

"Not for a few days yet. I'll have to go get myself some clothes and find a place to stay. They won't let me hang out here for several days. I brought a few little things to sell, so I'll go out after breakfast. Is there anything you'd like me to get you?"

"A magazine about cars, like the one I saw in London, and maybe some pizza."

"I'm not sure they'll let you have pizza, but I will get you a few magazines. You just rest and get better. I'm so glad you're all right," Valerie whispered, suddenly feeling very emotional. "I don't know what I'd do if anything happened to you."

"Nothing will happen to me. I will live for many years, just long enough to become a crotchety old man and drive you to distraction with my unreasonable demands."

"Promise?" Valerie asked with a smile.

Alec nodded, looking around the room. "I like it here," he informed her as he savored his orange juice, his gaze sliding to the TV where a new episode of *Star Trek* just started.

"I know you do."

FOUR
VIRGINIA JUNE 1626

Kit wiped his forehead with the back of his hand, cursing the infernal heat that made sweat run down his back and into his breeches. He'd been at the docks since dawn, supervising the unloading of the *Morning Star* as a favor to Charles, who had a touch of fever. Probably just wanted to sleep in for a change, not that the children would let him, Kit decided with a smile of satisfaction. They could raise the devil himself when they wanted their breakfast.

He'd woken early, getting out of bed as quietly as possible so as not to wake Louisa. She looked peaceful as the sun that filtered through the curtains drew a halo around her head, making her look like a saint in a church painting. Actually, not many saints were painted with their golden hair down and their breasts swelling above the low-cut shift, but that was just splitting hairs. She was a saint to him. He wished he could wake her and make love to her, but guilt made him leave the room and go outside to splash some cold water on his face and neck. His cock throbbed mercilessly, the remnants of the dream swirling before his eyes and making his guts burn with shame. He had the dreams less frequently now, but sometimes they still came, taking him by surprise and leaving him quaking with desire and cringing with self-loathing.

When awake, Kit never permitted himself to think of George. He'd firmly put Buckingham from his mind once they left England, refusing to succumb to the occasional desire to feel sorry for himself and wallow in self-pity. Nothing would change what had happened, and as long as Louisa was none the wiser, he would do everything in his power to make her happy and be a good husband and father. The episode with George was over, and if he had a say in the matter, they'd never see each other again, since Kit had no intention of returning to England anytime soon, and George Villiers, Duke of Buckingham, was not likely to turn up in Virginia without a damn good reason. He had plenty to occupy him at home, especially since the death of his beloved King James and the possible war with Spain. Kit had heard that Buckingham had been by James's side when he died last year and had taken the loss very badly.

Kit had never understood their relationship, but Buckingham had been truly in love with the king, feeling an emotional attachment to him that had gone beyond lust. They were kindred spirits, united by more than physical love. They were spouses of the heart. Kit felt a momentary pang of compassion for the bereaved queen and for Buckingham's wife. What was it like for these poor women to be married to men who preferred other men? They were bound to know after all these years, but maybe they had just convinced themselves that it was all vicious lies and that their husbands were the same as other men in their appetites, rather than dreaming of strong thighs and hard cocks.

But dreams were a different realm altogether, and sometimes Kit woke in the middle of the night dreaming that George was on his knees, his mouth hot and demanding as his black eyes gazed up at him, dancing with mirth. He throbbed with need, his body begging for release. Kit would turn his back to

Louisa and go at himself until he felt as if he would rip the damn thing off, his seed exploding all over his hand, the climax leaving him trembling, and as always, reeling with shame. Would he ever be able to forget? Just the other day Charles had leaned against him while reaching for a cup and Kit had nearly hit him, fury coursing through his veins as his body tensed like a wooden plank, his teeth clenched until his jaw nearly cracked. If Charles had been taken aback by this reaction, he didn't say anything, but hastily pulled away, clapping Kit on the shoulder by way of apology.

Kit found himself keeping his distance from all men, never allowing any physical contact for fear that he might feel something more than revulsion. At least Alec understood, and although he never brought George up, he made sure to keep his distance, allowing Kit to heal in his own way and preserve something of his dignity in the face of Alec's knowledge. Alec never asked, and Kit never told, but knowing that Alec knew didn't make things any easier.

Thankfully, the unloading was complete and he could stop at a nearby tavern for a tankard of cool ale before starting for home. He'd jump into the pond and have a quick bath before going back to the house and facing whatever needed to be done there. With Alec away, he was responsible for the workers and the livestock, especially while Charles was indisposed.

"Lord Sheridan! Yoo-hoo, Lord Sheridan!" Kit spun on his heel, looking to see who was calling him. He didn't recognize the voice or the man it belonged to. He was grossly fat, his head sitting on his massive shoulders as if he had no neck at all, the double chin straining against the stiff collar of his coat, which was made of a heavy velvet completely inappropriate to the climate, and his wig slightly askew as he hurried down the quay.

"Lord Sheridan, it *is* you," he announced, still panting as he finally came to a stop in front of Kit. His cheeks glistened with sweat and Kit was momentarily distracted by a barely perceptible movement inside his wig as something crawled among the powdered curls.

"I'm afraid you have me at a loss, sir," Kit said, desperately trying to place the man. He had seen him before, he was sure of that. He just couldn't recall where.

"Why, it's me, Aloysius Deverell. We met at court, before we all fled the city to save ourselves from the plague, don't you recall? Terrible business. So many taken. Thankfully, it's mostly the poor that sicken and not people of quality, although death doesn't discriminate, does it?" Deverell shook his head as if these philosophical questions were too heavy for his feeble brain.

"My nephew died of the plague. He was twenty," Kit replied, his voice flat and his eyes narrowed as he took the measure of the man in front of him. Yes, they had met, but Kit never wanted to pursue the acquaintance, unlike Deverell who was only too eager to ingratiate himself with powerful men. He was a younger son of a prominent family, wealthy, but not titled, and very ambitious. His girth made him appear older than he was, but in truth, he was no more than thirty-five. Kit briefly wondered what Deverell was doing in Virginia before dismissing him from his mind. It was time to bid his new *friend* a good day and take himself off to the tavern, Kit thought, but his escape was not to be.

"Is there anywhere we might have a drink and get out of his insufferable heat?" Deverell asked as he followed Kit down the quay. "It's like the last circle of Hell, isn't it?" Kit didn't care to find out how hot the last circle of Hell got, nor did he want to have a drink with this man, but it seemed churlish to refuse, especially since he was going to have one anyway, so he led the way to the tavern, hoping the man would just have one drink and leave him in peace.

"Ah, much better," Deverell uttered as he took a long pull of his ale, his face regaining something akin to normal color. "I've just arrived last night as it happens. I'm looking to buy a tobacco plantation. Most profitable, I hear, most profitable. And with indentured labor to rely on, it practically runs itself. You live on a plantation, do you not?" he asked, gulping down the last of his ale and signaling the serving wench for another one.

"Yes, but it hardly runs itself," Kit replied, not giving anything away. He didn't want to get into a lengthy discussion about life on a plantation, just have his drink and leave. In either case, even if Deverell bought a plantation, he would hardly be running it himself. All he had to do was hire an efficient overseer and never have to involve himself in anything other than the counting of the profits. Most plantation owners weren't like Alec and didn't take part in the day-to-day running of things. Alec knew every one of his men by name and made sure no one was mistreated or ill.

The overseer, Mr. Worthing, brought all problems and complaints directly to Alec, who personally resolved each situation. Kit had to admit that he'd never realized quite how much Alec actually did until he had to step into his shoes these past few weeks. Kit worried about Alec constantly but kept up a cheerful disposition for Louisa's sake. He could see the constant worry in her eyes and the way her eyes kept straying to the road a hundred times a day, praying that she would finally see Alec and Valerie returning home. Louisa wasn't quite whole without Valerie, and Kit admired the bond between the sisters. He still missed his own sister Caro every day, but they had never been as emotionally entwined as his wife and her sister.

"I say, how is your lovely wife? Louisa, is it not?" Deverell asked, watching Kit closely.

"Lady Sheridan is well, thank you," Kit replied, itching to escape. Something about the way the man looked at him made him feel defensive and he just wanted to part company and, hopefully, have as few dealings with the man as possible. Kit believed himself to be a good judge of character and Deverell's character was something he wanted no part of. He vaguely recalled some talk about him at court, but it had been a long time ago and he couldn't recollect the details. He did, however, remember that Deverell had an association with Thomas Gaines, Annabel's brother, who died under mysterious circumstances nearly two years ago.

"A most handsome woman, Lady Sheridan," Deverell opined, clearly annoyed by Kit's lack of attention. "You are a lucky man, a lucky man indeed. I wager she's happy to be away from court." Deverell gave Kit an innocent look, his piggy eyes glued to Kit's face, watching for a reaction.

"Why would you think she's happy away from court?" Kit put his musings aside and finally gave Deverell his full attention. Something in the way Deverell was watching him put him on guard and he resolved not to get caught in whatever trap the man was setting, if that's what he was about. Could be that Kit was just oversensitive about the past and was reading something that wasn't there into an innocent comment.

"Why, with the close relationship you shared with Buckingham, I would think she'd be glad to have you all to herself. Poor George was heartbroken when His Majesty died. He was so devoted to him. I fear he might never recover." Deverell scrunched his face in mock pity, still watching Kit and licking his lips like a hungry cat.

"My wife misses court, as it happens, and would like to go back in the near future." Louisa wanted no such thing, but Kit wasn't about to give this weasel the satisfaction of admitting to anything. The less he said, the better.

"Does she, indeed? Well, I'm certain that she would be welcomed back with open arms, as would you, Lord Sheridan. I think dear George would be overwhelmed with joy to see such a beloved friend, knowing what you meant to each other."

"What are you implying, sir?" Kit demanded, his patience coming to an end, and the look on Deverell's face belatedly alerting him to the fact that this was exactly the reaction he'd been hoping for.

"Why, nothing my dear man, nothing at all. What would I be implying other than the fact that you and Lord Buckingham were great friends? You spent much time in his rooms discussing state business, a very bonding experience, I imagine. I'm sure your wife was quite proud, knowing you helped shape the foreign policy of our great nation, working so *intimately* with one of our country's leaders." Deverell smiled, stressing the word intimately as he held Kit's gaze.

"I must go," Kit said tersely, rising from his seat, "I have business to attend to."

"It was a pleasure to see you, Lord Sheridan, a pleasure indeed. We'll see each other soon, I think. Very soon. As a matter of fact, I would relish the pleasure of having you and dear Lady Sheridan to supper once we've settled, my wife and I. I'll send a note, shall I?"

"I'll look forward to it," replied Kit, bowing stiffly and fleeing the tavern. Was he being overly suspicious, or was the man hinting at his knowledge of Kit's relationship with Buckingham? Was this spawn of the devil merely having a bit of fun with him or did he have something more practical in mind? Kit dug his heels into the flanks of his horse, harder than he should have perhaps, and the horse took off at a gallop toward Rosewood Manor. *Damn it all to hell*, Kit thought, *why can't the past ever stay in the past?*

FIVE
VIRGINIA JUNE 1779

"Come on, little man," Sam whispered as he lifted the solid little body of his son out of the cot and tiptoed toward the door. "Let's let mama sleep for a while longer."

He smiled at Susanna's face, relaxed in sleep and slightly more rounded now that she was in the last months of pregnancy. Her stomach looked like a mound under the covers, moving of its own accord as the baby kicked and frolicked in its cushy world.

"Want mama," Ben screamed, pushing at Sam with his hands and straining to catch a last look of Susanna. "Want mama," he repeated again.

"Why don't we go up to the big house and visit with everyone? I think they might just be sitting down to breakfast, and Grandma always has bacon on Sunday mornings. Hmm, what do you think?" Sam asked, taking advantage of his son's legendary love of bacon. Ben only started eating table food two months ago, and bacon had been the one thing that seemed to appeal to his finicky palate. He was indifferent to everything else. Ben nodded happily and stopped fighting as Sam deftly changed his clout, washed his face and hands with water from the barrel outside the door, and ran a hand through Ben's hair in an effort to get it to actually lie down for a change. It always stood on end when he woke up, making him look slightly wild, but oh-so-adorable.

Sam covered the distance to the house in record time, eager for some bacon, porridge, and a cup of real tea, not the swill he made over a campfire. He'd just come back from his latest mission last night, climbing into bed just as Susanna was falling asleep, Ben curled up at her side with his thumb in his mouth. Susanna mumbled words of love and welcome and was out before he even had a chance to give her a proper kiss. She was tired, which was natural in her condition, and he would give her a chance to rest while spending an agreeable hour with his family. He hadn't seen them since Ben's first birthday two weeks ago, and besides, he had information for his father.

Ben nearly fell out of Sam's arms as he let out a squeal of joy at seeing Diana. She was already being fed, porridge smeared over her little face, and her hands sticky with honey dripping from the piece of bread she was holding onto for dear life. She was equally excited to see Ben, so Sam sat them next to each other and let them feed each other bacon while he took a seat on the bench next to Finn and exchanged greetings with everyone. His mother placed a plate piled with porridge, bacon, bread, and butter in front of him and kissed the top of his head, as she had when he was little. It was nice to be home.

"How's Susanna?" John Mallory asked, pushing away his plate with a little burp of satisfaction. Sam knew his father was eager to hear the news, but he wasn't budging until after breakfast. Susanna hadn't left anything for him to eat last night, not expecting him home, and he was starving, having had nothing in his belly since the previous afternoon.

"She's well. Still sleeping," Sam replied as he popped a piece of grease-soaked bread into his mouth and sighed with satisfaction. "It can't be long now. She's huge."

"She's not due for two more months, son," Mrs. Mallory cut in, giving Sam an amused look. "I hope it's not twins."

"That wouldn't be so bad, would it?" Sam asked, winking at Finn, who rolled his eyes at the idea.

"Having three children under the age of two is not what most women aspire to," Hannah Mallory replied, shaking her head. "It's hard enough with two, especially since Ben seems intent on escaping every chance he gets. Your father caught him by the stream yesterday, trying to fish with a stick. He could have fallen in."

Sam threw a look at Ben, who was in seventh heaven as he shoved a piece of bacon in his mouth, his eyes closed in concentration. With only four teeth, it took him a while to chew, which was actually beneficial to them all since it kept him quiet for a few minutes at a time.

"I will try to stay at home until Susanna's delivered and look after Ben." Sam got quiet as he glanced at his father, who pursed his lips. Clearly, he had the next mission already lined up, needing Sam more than ever since Uncle Alfred was up north gathering valuable information to be passed on to the Continental Army.

"Pa, I need to be there for Sue. I know you all help her, especially the girls, but it's me she needs."

"All right son, maybe we can send Finn to Savannah instead."

Abbie's head snapped up at this, her own breakfast forgotten. "Not if I can help it," she cried, the memory of their last mission still fresh in her mind. Finn had made some local runs, but Abbie resolutely refused to let him go any further, especially behind enemy lines. Their experience in New York left her fearful and over-protective, and with good reason.

"Abs, it's all right," Finn said, laying a hand on her arm. "It won't be the same as New York. Will it, Mr. Mallory? I won't be in any danger."

"There's always danger," Abbie protested, her face pale. "People die every single day, and not only in battle. I won't let you go. I won't." With that, she scooped Diana off the bench and stepped outside, Ben's howl clearly audible through the open window.

"I won't let him go," Abbie mumbled to herself and set off for the stream. Diana squirmed in her arms, but Abbie paid little attention as she stomped away from the house. She was angry with her father, furious that he wanted to expose Finn to danger after what happened in New York. She didn't think of it as often anymore, but it was still there, never far away, especially at night. She had come within an hour of her execution, and that was something she'd never forget. Abbie still had nightmares in which she was trapped in the airless little cell, afraid to close her eyes and miss even a minute of her last hours on earth.

She had never been as terrified, alone, or heartbroken. Her baby was going to die with her and they would spend an eternity in some unmarked grave, carelessly tossed on top of a pile of other corpses, people who'd met the same fate and were left to rot without so much as a funeral service or a marker of some sort.

And then they'd nearly lost Sam. Those weeks of watching and waiting, praying for some word of him, and coming to accept the reality had almost been as bad as waiting for death. Susanna didn't stop Sam from going on missions for the Committee, but then Susanna had never gone through what Abbie had. Susanna had been safe at the British fort, nursing an American rebel back to health under the assumption that he was a British corporal. She'd never experienced the agony Abbie had felt during those weeks.

It had taken Abbie months to finally stop waking in the night, convinced Sam was dead and that she hadn't really escaped at all; death waiting for her as soon as the sun came up.

And although she'd learned to live with the fear, she'd never feel entirely safe again, not as long as the war continued.

Her father had never again suggested that she undertake any kind of assignment, especially not since she was now a mother, but he still wanted to utilize Finn, and Abbie was terrified every time he left home, believing he would never come back. Her father told her that her fears were irrational, but Abbie knew several women who'd lost their husbands and she was sure many more would before this conflict with England was finally resolved.

Savannah was controlled by the British, so Finn would be walking into terrible danger. He wouldn't be in uniform and no one knew him, not even the contact he was to meet with, but that didn't mean that something couldn't go wrong—terribly wrong. The thought of losing Finn was even worse than the thought of her own death. At least if she were dead, she wouldn't be conscious of her situation and wouldn't have to live with the terrible aching loss every single day, her mind constantly replaying images of them together while he was alive.

How was it possible to love another person so much that you'd rather die than live without them? Abbie pondered as she washed Diana's face and hands with cool water from the spring. Diana managed to grab a stone and toss it into the water, splashing Abbie's face and bringing her to her senses. She pulled the little girl close and kissed the top of her dark, curly head, needing to feel that bond that tethered her with an invisible chain.

She had to let Finn go, had to have faith. If she kept him at home, he would grow to resent her and feel that she was taking away his manhood. He was a grown man, and he knew how to assess risk. If he felt this was something he could do, then she had to trust his judgment. They were fighting a war for freedom and she couldn't prevent Finn from taking part. At least he'd been true to his word and hadn't joined the army, where he would be right there in the thick of it, like Jonah. Thankfully, Jonah was still alive, but the man who'd come back wasn't the boy who left. He'd seen horrors beyond his worst imaginings, and nothing would ever bring his idealism back or erase the images that now permanently lived in his mind.

Abbie sighed and picked up Diana. She hated to do it, but she would go back and give Finn her blessing. However, she still wasn't ready to forgive her father, no matter how patriotic he was. He put the Cause before the welfare of his children. Abbie supposed she respected him for that, but she still felt the pain of that choice.

SIX
WILLIAMSBURG, VIRGINIA JUNE 2010

Valerie walked out of the hospital into a hazy and stiflingly hot morning. She stood still for a few moments, taking in the deafening noise of modern life. She'd forgotten how loud things could be, especially on a weekday morning. It was still early enough that people were rushing to work and the streets were congested with rush-hour traffic, cars and buses fighting for space on the narrow street and blaring their horns at a garbage truck that had the audacity to block half the street as the garbage men tossed bags into the back, oblivious to the frenzy they were creating. A yellow school bus inched into view, the laughter and shrieks of kids erupting through the open windows. They still had a few weeks of school left until summer vacation, but mentally, they were already on break, just barely sitting through these last days, eager to finally put away their books and enjoy all that summer had to offer.

Valerie looked up and down the street, deciding which way to go. Her plan was to go find a store where she could sell her coins. Seventeenth-century coins could fetch a lot of money, but she only had two left and needed to use them wisely. They rarely used coins at home, most transactions being paid for in tobacco, so the ones she had were still from England and worth their weight in gold. Louisa had pressed a ring into her hand as they were leaving, but Valerie was reluctant to sell it. Kit had given it to her and would be upset to find it gone, even if it'd been used to help Alec in his hour of need. She would leave the ring for now and hope she could get enough for the coins to last several days. Even once Alec was released from the hospital, they would have to wait a few days to make sure there was no infection and that the stitches were ready to come out.

Valerie walked down the street slowly, her eyes scanning the still-shuttered storefronts when she suddenly stopped, astounded by an idea. When she set the device to the future, she chose 2010, not because it had any significance, but because it really didn't matter what year they went to as long as Alec got help, and 2010 had been the last year that she had lived in the twenty-first century. It was now the second week of June, and technically, she was still in 2010, preparing to go to England with Louisa. She would be gone from the twenty-first century by the end of the month, but as of now she was still very much in the here and now.

There were now two of her: one in her twenties, living in New York, and one in her forties, wandering around Williamsburg. This revelation presented a whole new world of possibilities. If she were still in the here and now, she still had a bank account and credit cards in her name. She didn't have a bank card, but she remembered her account and PIN number since she always used her birthday, so if she filled out a withdrawal slip and went to a teller, she should have no trouble taking money out. Of course, this might present some problems later on as the search for her led the authorities to check her bank activity, but everyone would just assume that it was a case of identity theft since she was still very much in New York this week in 2010.

Valerie did a quick estimate in her mind. They would have

to stay at least until the end of the week, which would mean they'd need to find a B&B that wouldn't ask for ID, buy clothes, toiletries, and food, and possibly do something fun since they were here anyway. Alec might enjoy a tour of Colonial Williamsburg since he could compare it to the real thing, and maybe go to a movie and have a few nice dinners. Two thousand dollars should cover it she decided as she proceeded down the street at a quicker pace. Now that she had a plan, all she had to do was put it into action.

Valerie looked around, spotting the familiar Citibank logo just a block away. Bingo! She walked into the cool lobby of the bank, conscious of her weird getup, but no one paid her any attention. They were close enough to Colonial Williamsburg to assume she was merely on her way to work and took her job so seriously that she got into character before punching her timecard. The bank had just opened and there were only two tellers behind the counter, both looking sluggish and sleepy as they prepared to start their day. Valerie filled out a slip and walked over to the teller's window, her heart pounding in her chest. What if they called the police? She held her breath as the teller punched in the numbers and looked up at her. She was a young girl who looked as if she'd rather be anywhere rather than at work.

"I'll just need some ID," she said, yawning behind her hand.

"I forgot my purse," Valerie lied, shrugging her shoulders and smiling guiltily at her own absentmindedness.

"Okay," the teller replied without even looking up. "Just verify some information for me, and I'll get your money. I need your social security number, date of birth, and mother's maiden name."

The social took a moment to recall, but Valerie answered the questions and nearly jumped for joy when the teller handed her two thousand dollars in crisp, new notes. Too bad she had no pocket or purse to put them into. Valerie slipped into the ladies' room and distributed the bills inside her bodice, leaving a few out to go buy herself a bag of some sort. It would look strange if she started groping inside her dress for money as she came up to pay for her purchases. She stepped back into the street feeling guilty, as if she'd just gotten away with something. After all, it was her own money, she reasoned with herself, but it still felt strange.

Valerie walked around until she came upon a TJ Maxx. That would serve her purposes very well. She could get a few nice things at a reasonable price. There was no point spending a lot of money on clothes since she'd be throwing them in the trash as soon as they were ready to return home. She secretly wished she could take the modern clothes with her and put them on from time to time, but that was just a fantasy. Being caught with anything like that could lead to all kinds of questions that she didn't want to answer, and when living in such close proximity to so many people, it was virtually impossible to hide anything.

Well, she would enjoy them while she could. She couldn't wait to shed the cumbersome skirt and bodice and rip off the stockings that made her sweat behind the knees beneath all the layers of fabric. Valerie pulled her cap off and shoved it into the pocket of the skirt. She no longer had to pretend she was working at Colonial Williamsburg and the feel of her hair around her shoulders made her smile. It'd been years since she walked around in public with her hair down, and she felt wanton.

Valerie took a shopping cart and made her way down the first aisle, enjoying the cool air- conditioning and the familiar song playing over the loudspeakers. God, how she missed music. At home, the only time there was music was when players were invited for a special occasion, which wasn't often. Seventeenth-century colonists were not a joyful lot and didn't put much stock in *degenerate* amusements such as dancing and theater.

Unless a member of the family played a musical instrument, which none of them did, they went for months without hearing a tune.

Valerie hummed along as she cruised from aisle to aisle, loving the feeling of being surrounded by goods. There were so few things to buy in Jamestown. Valerie chose a pair of jeans, a summer dress, a few tops and a pair of sandals, along with two bras and several pairs of underwear. That should last her for a few days while she waited for Alec to be released. He'd need some clothes as well, so Valerie detoured to the men's department and found some loose summer slacks, underwear, polo shirts, and a pair of loafers. He'd need loose clothes that wouldn't chafe against the incision.

Valerie threw a colorful canvas purse into the cart and made her way to the cash registers. She would stop at a pharmacy and pick up a few toiletries and magazines for Alec, as well as some Coke and some chocolate bars, and then her shopping would be complete. Sometimes she missed chocolate even more than music. Their diet at home was very basic, the food prepared mostly from whatever they could grow or kill. Cook occasionally made a pie or some stewed fruit. Eating fruit raw was paramount to insanity in Cook's opinion, but there was never any type of dessert that really satisfied Valerie's sweet tooth. Valerie gleefully paid for her purchases and left the store, eager to get back to Alec. God, it felt good to shop.

SEVEN

Alec flipped through the pages of the magazine between taking bites of chocolate. The painkiller had worn off somewhat and he was cranky and in pain, grumbling about the indignity of wearing a flimsy gown that left most of his backside exposed. According to him, no man should be so humiliated, especially in a place of learning and medicine. Valerie just smiled at him and agreed, knowing that it wasn't really the gown he had an issue with, but the feeling of helplessness. He was used to being in charge of a situation, but right now he probably felt like a guinea pig, with doctors and nurses coming in to check his vitals, take his temperature, and examine the incision to make sure it showed no signs of infection.

The glossy pictures of race cars and the bittersweet chocolate melting on his tongue soothed him a bit, as did the sight of Valerie in a flirty summer dress that bared her shoulders and stopped just above the knees. She looked twenty years younger with her hair loose and her long legs bare beneath the hem of the dress. It reminded him of how she had looked when he first laid eyes on her, thinking her some deranged maiden who was wandering about the countryside in her undergarments. Alec finished off the chocolate and glanced up at Valerie, who seemed very agitated as she rummaged through her bag and turned out the pockets of the homespun skirt that she'd removed only a few minutes ago.

"What's wrong, Val?" he asked, taken aback by her stricken expression. She was holding the coins and Louisa's ring in her hand, but her face was white, her eyes brimming with tears.

"Alec, it's gone. Oh, God, it's gone," she whimpered as she sank into a chair, her legs buckling beneath her.

"What's gone?"

"The watch—the time-travel watch. It's gone. I must have dropped it while I was trying on clothes. I have to go back to the store."

With that, she ran from the room, leaving Alec feeling sick to his stomach. She had to find it. It was probably in the room where she tried on clothes, on the floor, just waiting to be found, unless someone else found it already. Maybe they'd turned it in, but maybe they simply smiled at their good fortune and shoved it in their pocket before leaving the store and destroying their only chance of returning home. Alec took a deep breath, trying to calm himself. She'd find it; she had to.

Alec put aside the magazine and the candy, unable to concentrate. In a crisis, he normally assessed his options and tried not to assume the worst until he had reason to, but this time it wasn't working. The only option was to find the watch. The alternative was unthinkable. Alec tried to remain calm, but he wanted nothing more than to rip out the tube hooked up to his arm, tear off the offending gown, and go find Valerie. He knew it was out of the question but sitting by idly while their lives hung in the balance was intolerable. Every minute felt like an hour as he waited for Valerie to return, his thoughts spinning out of control and his blood pressure spiking enough to alarm the nurse.

Valerie finally returned three hours later. Alec didn't need to ask if she'd found the watch. Her face was ashen, and the look in her eyes was that of someone who'd just lost all hope for the future. Valerie's hands were shaking, and she threw herself into a chair and burst into tears, her hands over her face as she sobbed, her body convulsing with grief. "It's gone," she wailed. "We're trapped. We're trapped forever. We'll never see our family again, and they won't know what happened to us. Oh, Alec, what have I done? How could I have been so careless?"

Alec opened his mouth to comfort her, but the enormity of the situation crashed over him, making him feel hollow inside. As much as he liked it in the future he wanted to go back where he belonged. He wanted to see his home, hear the children laughing and playing, and have a game of dice with Kit as they stayed up late, talking and enjoying their brandy. And Louisa! She would go mad not knowing what happened to them. Oh, God—Finn and Abbie. What would they think if they never showed up again? Alec took a deep breath and forced himself to focus on Valerie.

"Val, it will be all right. We will find a way back; I promise you." He had no idea what he was talking about, but it seemed like the right thing to say, and his first priority was to calm her and make her realize that she wasn't to blame. He could have lost the watch just as easily.

"How? How will we find a way back? And what of the person who found the watch? What if they transport themselves to God knows when?" Valerie moaned.

"We can't worry about some unknown person who found a watch and didn't turn it in. We have to worry about us." And worry he did.

"Alec, how on earth will we get back? It's not as if we can walk into a store and buy a replacement. People don't travel through time, at least not normal people."

Valerie walked over to Alec and climbed onto the bed next to him, desperately in need of comfort. Alec wrapped his arms around her and stroked her hair in an effort to soothe her, but he felt the erratic beating of her heart and her ragged breath against his chest.

"I think I have an idea," he finally said to the top of her head. "And it just might work."

EIGHT

VIRGINIA JUNE 1626

"Where are you going, Jenny?" Evie whispered, her white nightdress looking ghostly in the moonlight, her face lost in the shadows of the corridor. "Can you tell me a story? I can't sleep. Millicent would like one too. Wouldn't you, Millie?" she called out to her cousin, who was fast asleep on her trundle, snoring softly, a smile of contentment on her face.

"Of course, Evie, but a very short one. I just wanted to step outside for some air. It's so very hot tonight."

Genevieve obediently stepped into the nursery, smiling at the sleeping forms of the children. There wasn't enough room to separate the boys and girls, so they all slept in the same room, their trundle beds lined up on opposite ends of the wall. Robbie, Harry, and Millie were all asleep, but little Tom lay quietly in his bed, his eyes huge in the moonlight. "I want story too," he mouthed, holding out his arms to Genevieve. She allowed the children to climb into her lap as she told them an old French fairy tale that Madame Collot had told her many times when she was a toddler and living with her foster parents.

She had been a kind woman, much kinder than most of the nuns who had the care of her after she was taken away from the

Collots. Genevieve still remembered some of the stories and songs that Madame Collot sang to her as she rocked her to sleep, giving her the love that she would so sorely miss in her later years.

Genevieve's melodious voice finally lulled the children to sleep and she scooted carefully off the bed, leaving Evie asleep with Tom, her arm possessively around his belly and her dark curls intertwined with his blond ones. Aunt Valerie wouldn't mind as long as they were quiet. She wondered when Aunt Valerie and Uncle Alec would return. They'd been gone for close to a week now, and Lady Sheridan was starting to look worried, her eyes scanning the horizon a dozen times a day as she shielded her eyes from the merciless summer sun.

She said Aunt Valerie took her uncle to a physician in another settlement who had some renown in treating stomach ailments, but Genevieve wasn't convinced. She seemed furtive when she said that, her eyes sliding away from Genevieve's and focusing on the wall behind her as if she weren't telling the whole truth. Perhaps they went to visit Finn's grave again. They went from time to time and stayed away for several weeks, a strange sense of peace emanating from them when they finally returned. Although, Uncle Alec had been ill the past few weeks, so maybe Lady Sheridan was telling a partial truth, and concealing the seriousness of his condition from the rest of them.

Genevieve couldn't quite blame Louisa for lying, when she herself hadn't been truthful with Uncle Alec. She'd meant what she said about marrying a Catholic, but she hadn't been entirely honest when Uncle Alec asked if anyone had caught her eye. There was someone, but she was too afraid to tell her uncle since she couldn't imagine that his reaction would be a favorable one.

She'd met Cameron a few months back while helping Cook serve meals to the indentured servants who worked on the plantation. Normally, the task fell to Minnie, but with more people in the house, she had a lot more housework and Genevieve would much rather dole out stew than do the laundry or knead dough for bread. For some reason, Minnie dreaded being among the men, so she happily traded with Genevieve and took on the extra laundry in exchange for not having to go down to the barracks several times a day.

Most plantation owners treated their indentures and slaves appallingly, with men lasting no more than a year or two before succumbing to illness or dying from being overworked and underfed, but Uncle Alec was known for being kind and fair. The men worked only ten hours a day with several breaks, had three square meals a day. They also had Sundays off to spend as they pleased after the church service conducted outside just for them. They didn't attend church in town, not being free men. Still, they were blessed to have a master like Mr. Whitfield, and they knew it. He'd even freed one of the indentures a few years ago, allowed him to marry one of the maids, and gave him some money to start his own carpentry business. Richard was quite the gentleman now, living in Jamestown with his wife and children.

It had taken Cameron weeks to finally speak to Genevieve, but she often caught him gazing at her with an expression in his sky-blue eyes that made her feel warm all over as she handed out the chunks of bread and poured ale for the men. He kept to himself and rarely spoke, but when he did, he had a deep, melodious voice and a broad Scottish brogue that she had difficulty understanding at first. She liked the way he called her lass and smiled his appreciation when she gave him an extra helping of stew or piece of bread. He was one of the youngest workers at the plantation, and one of the most recent arrivals. Genevieve had been curious to know his story but was too shy to ask.

It was one hot evening at the end of May when Genevieve had come upon him sitting by the pond. Uncle Alec allowed the men to take a walk after their evening meal or wash in the pond, as long as it was after dark and no women were there to see them strip down to nothing. Most of the men bathed rarely, but Cameron was always clean, his auburn hair brushed and neatly clubbed, more to keep out the lice than to appease his vanity. On this particular night, he'd sat on the bench, his hair dripping wet and his shirt next to him, drying. He washed his clothes regularly, allowing them to dry overnight. Cameron quickly pulled on his wet shirt, brushed the hair out of his face, and sprang to his feet, ready to flee.

"I'm sorry, Mistress. I thought nae one was about." It sounded like *aboot* when he said it, but Genevieve liked it. "I'll be going now." There it was again. It sounded like *noo* instead of now, but it rolled off his tongue so naturally.

"No, please, you don't have to leave because of me. I was just taking a walk. It's too warm in the house, and I enjoy a bit of quiet after the children go to sleep."

"Aye, the bairns are a handful, they are," he said, smiling, "but I do love seeing them running about. They remind me of home."

"Where is your home?" Genevieve asked, sitting down on the opposite side of the bench and looking at Cameron from beneath her lashes. He was in his mid-twenties, tall and broad, with a strong muscled body that spoke of years of hard work. Most of the men wore a beard, because they were too tired and lazy to shave, but Cameron was clean-shaven, his face lean and tanned to a golden brown from hours in the sun.

"My home is near Glasgow, on the West Coast o' Scotland." He seemed sad as he answered, his eyes full of nostalgia for his homeland. Genevieve didn't mean to pry, but she just had to ask. "How did you come to be here?"

"Oh, tis a long story, lass, one for another night. I must find my bed if I'm to do an honest day's work tomorrow. Good night to ye, Mistress Genevieve."

He gave her a warm smile before heading toward the barracks, his wet shirt stuck to his back and his damp hair framing his face. Genevieve sat for a little while longer, curious about this man who seemed so different from all the rest. Most of the men either sold themselves into servitude or were sent down as punishment for a crime, but Genevieve couldn't imagine that Cameron fitted into either category, unless he just wanted to come to the New World and start a new life, but had no means of doing it. He probably hadn't realized that the men were worked to the bone, their spirit broken, and their health destroyed before they could finally work off their contract and strike out on their own. She hoped to find out in time, eager to learn anything she could about the reticent man who drew her eye every time he was in the vicinity.

She wasn't sure if they met by accident or if Cameron timed his baths with her walks, but they ran into each other a few more times before he became more forthcoming. He told her of his home, of how the sky was so vast and blue, blending with the sea in the distance, so that it was impossible to tell where one ended and the other began. He spoke of great mountains rising out of fertile valleys where the land was green as far as the eye could see, except when heather bloomed, and then it was like a carpet of purple, rippling in the wind and beckoning the young girls to abandon their chores and go wading through that endless sea, running their fingers over the little flowers and putting sprigs in their hair. Cameron never spoke of what happened to make him leave his home and become an indentured servant, and Genevieve didn't ask. He'd tell her in time. For now, he seemed happy just to have someone to talk to.

It seemed very natural when he cupped her cheek with his work-roughened hand and kissed her softly on the lips, sending shivers up her spine. His kisses were chaste, but the warmth that pooled between Genevieve's thighs was anything but, her body craving what it had been denied for so many years. He must have sensed it, for he pulled away, rising to his feet abruptly and bidding her good night. He was an honorable man, despite his status, and he would do nothing to cause her any distress or compromise her reputation.

Genevieve ran down to the pond, hoping she wasn't too late. If only Evie hadn't heard her coming out of her room, but if Cameron wanted to see her, he would wait. He was bound to be there after the kiss they'd shared last night. He might have bolted, but he must have thought about it during the day, as eager to see her as she was to see him. She imagined his face, alight with yearning, his eyes smiling in that special way that was reserved only for her, and blushed in the darkness, ashamed to be so eager for more kisses.

But the bench was empty when she finally got there, and the lane to the barracks deserted. Genevieve sat for an hour, her ears straining for any change in the nighttime sounds around her in the hope that some of them were human. Was that the sound of a footstep? A twig breaking under the foot of a large man? But it wasn't. The leaves rustled above her head, the frogs croaked by the pond, and light bugs floated above the ground like fallen stars, but there was no man. The sky went from indigo blue to an inky black, and even the frogs got tired of croaking, and the owls took up where the birds left off, but no one came.

Genevieve reluctantly stood and went back to the house and her lonely bed, suddenly worried that she'd scared Cameron off by returning the kiss. What if he never came back? She fell asleep at last, tired of worrying and hoping that she'd misread the situation and Cameron had been unable to come this evening. Maybe he was particularly tired after a day in the fields and wanted that extra hour of rest that he gave up when he came to see her by the pond. He'd be there tomorrow; she was sure of it. Kiss or no kiss, she knew he liked her. It was there in the way he looked at her, in how he said her name, and in the way he moved a little closer without even realizing it. He was as drawn to her as she was to him, of that she was sure.

But Cameron didn't come the next night or the night after that. Genevieve had seen him during the day, tried to catch his eye as she doled out the food, but he wouldn't look at her, and made sure to get his portion from Cook. When their eyes finally met, he gave her an imperceptible bow and turned away, leaving her confused and embarrassed. What had she done? Had it been so wrong to return his kiss? Had he been testing her and found her wanting? She didn't understand, and he didn't seem willing to explain himself. She knew he wouldn't come, but still she sat by herself in the dark, staring at the still, black waters of the pond. She longed to hear his footsteps, but all she heard were the usual sounds of nature as the day gave way to night, and creatures large and small settled in their nests and burrows, needing their rest for the day to come.

It took a week for Cameron to finally come back, and when he did, he kept his distance, sitting at the other end of the bench and keeping the conversation neutral. Genevieve could sense the need in him, the desire for intimacy, but his back was rigid, and his eyes never strayed past her face despite the relatively low-cut bodice she was wearing, a hand-me-down from Lady Sheridan. He didn't offer any explanation, but he had taken her hand after a while, and held it in his big, warm one until he rose to his feet and kissed her palm before disappearing into the darkness.

NINE

WILLIAMSBURG, VIRGINIA JUNE 2010

"It won't work," Valerie said for the tenth time, pacing the small room of a B&B located on the outskirts of Williamsburg. She'd been grateful to find it, since most accommodations were booked for months ahead in anticipation of hordes of tourists descending on Williamsburg in the summer months, eager for a bit of history. The house was old and smelled a little musty, but at least the room was clean, the sheets fresh, and they had their own bathroom. The innkeeper provided a hearty breakfast and didn't ask too many questions, which was just as well since they had no answers.

Alec had been released from the hospital with a clean bill of health and told to return in a week to remove the stitches. They had no plan beyond that. An invoice for thousands of dollars lay folded neatly in Valerie's purse, but that was the least of her problems. They'd gone over their predicament time and time again but were no closer to a solution than the day Valerie lost the watch. Alec's idea might have worked had they not had to deal with modern laws and security measures.

"I think it can work," Alec replied stubbornly, gazing at her from the bed. "Technically, Mr. Taylor is still in Newton

Ferrers, running his antique shop and watching football. He has the clock, and we just have to get to him. It's not as wild of a plan as you think," he said defensively.

"Alec, you don't understand," Valerie began to explain yet again, "people don't just go from place to place the way they did in the seventeenth century. You can't just buy passage on a ship and sail to another country. There are border patrols, and we need to have a passport in order to leave this country and enter another one. Even if we manage to get out of the United States, we would not be permitted to enter the United Kingdom. It won't work."

"You are right; I don't understand," grumbled Alec. "Why should anyone care if we leave this country or enter another one for that matter? We are not criminals, and we are not hurting anyone. Why does the government need to know my every move, especially if I don't exist?" Valerie softened when she saw the confusion in his eyes. They were running out of ideas. If they couldn't get to Mr. Taylor, how would they go back?

Alec suddenly brightened. "What if we call him? We can just explain the situation and ask him to come here with the clock. He has a passport and can travel, can he not?"

Valerie thought about that for a moment. Technically, they could call Fred Taylor, but would he even believe them? He hadn't met any of them yet at this point so their story would sound completely insane, ridiculous even. Why would he get on a plane and come to Williamsburg to help some people he'd never heard of? And even if he were willing, he had to remain in England at present because this was the week that Valerie came into his shop and vanished, and the investigation into her disappearance began. Valerie shook her head in response to Alec's idea, and his face fell in disappointment.

"I just thought of something," Valerie said miserably, sitting down on the bed next to Alec, her shoulders drooping in defeat.

"What?

"If we had come to Mr. Taylor for help in 2010, he would have told us that when he came to the seventeenth century because it would have happened before, but he never mentioned it, so we never came."

"I'm very confused," Alec said, taking Valerie's hand in his. "If he came to us after this happened and we were there, then we somehow got back, right?"

"Wrong. Very wrong," answered Valerie and burst into tears. She'd been crying non-stop for the past few days. This was all her fault, and now they would never see Louisa, Kit, or Finn ever again and have to somehow make a life for themselves in the twenty-first century. She supposed it would be easier for her since she could just go back to her old life and somehow explain away her disappearance, but then, oh dear God, Louisa was still there in New York and her whole life would be undone because she would never go back to look for Valerie and meet Kit.

And what to do about Alec? All she could think of to make Alec legitimate was identity theft, and she nearly laughed out loud at the ludicrous thought. The giggle turned into a sob, and Valerie allowed Alec to pull her into his arms and stroke her hair as she finally quieted down and allowed herself to listen to the beating of his heart, strong and rhythmic, full of love and devotion. At least they were together; the rest would somehow have to take care of itself.

TEN

VIRGINIA JULY 1626

Louisa subtly pulled up her bodice as Aloysius Bloody Deverell's eyes traveled over her breasts again, his rubbery lips moist with longing. The man's wife seemed not to notice as her odious husband ogled Louisa, his thinly disguised lust repulsive and inappropriate. Kit, who was normally social and animated, sat quietly, answering questions like an automaton, and became more vocal only when addressed by the governor, who didn't seem too inclined to talk to Deverell either. The dinner party was larger than Louisa had expected, boasting some of the most affluent members of Jamestown society, who were curious to meet the new arrivals and take their measure.

Louisa wasn't surprised they were invited but was astounded that it was hosted by the Deverells, who had so recently arrived from England. She remembered them from court, having avoided them like the proverbial plague there. The husband was a sleazy, power-hungry opportunist, and the wife was a quiet, almost invisible woman, who nodded in agreement whenever Aloysius uttered another ignorant statement. She seemed to have no opinions of her own, or if she did, kept them well-hidden, probably to avoid being browbeaten by her husband. *Poor woman*, Louisa thought as she took a sip of wine, *what must it be like to spend her days with a man who clearly didn't love or respect her enough to disguise his lust for others?*

At least the food was good. She hadn't eaten such delicacies in a long time and wondered where Deverell had managed to obtain oysters on the half shell and goose liver. This certainly wasn't the normal fare of Virginia residents, not even on special occasions. Deverell obviously thought he was still at court. Louisa might have enjoyed the oysters more had her stomach not been twisted in knots over Valerie and Alec. Where were they? It'd been over two weeks since they left and twinges of panic were beginning to come more frequently, taking Louisa by surprise as she realized that another day had gone by with no word, not that they could send one.

Louisa was distracted from her thoughts by Aloysius, who was speaking directly to her. "Lady Sheridan, I apologize most profusely, but I nearly forgot to pass on His Grace's, the Duke of Buckingham's regards. He asked after you most specifically, given his close friendship with your husband." Louisa glanced at Kit, whose eyes seemed glazed with either boredom or too much wine.

"He was most envious when I mentioned that I would be travelling to Virginia. He particularly wished me to convey his love to Lord Sheridan, whom he holds in such very high esteem, very high, indeed. Why, one would almost think he was pining for him." Aloysius smiled, revealing small, crooked teeth. "Such a handsome man, dear George. Why, if I were a woman..." He let out a girlish giggle, startling Sir George Yeardley out of his reverie, and making him scowl.

Louisa gave Deverell a sly smile and matched his sugary tone. "Why, if you were a woman, you would be most handsome yourself, my dear Master Deverell, no doubt the jewel of the court and the envy of every woman there. George Buckingham would be at your feet, burning with desire and dreaming of you alone, no doubt in a very compromising position."

Louisa nearly laughed out loud at the stunned expression on Deverell's face and Kit's look of amusement. Sir George nearly choked on his meat, throwing Louisa a warning look. As far as he was concerned, she was still a blasphemer and a criminal, one who should keep her mouth shut unless spoken to directly. He was a stern man, not blessed with a sense of humor or a whit of fun. Louisa lowered her eyes, acknowledging that she had spoken out of turn, but the damage was done. Everyone was looking at Deverell and sniggering, no doubt picturing him in drag. He would make a hideous woman, on that everyone was sure to agree.

Louisa was only too happy when the meal finally ended and they could decently leave without being rude to their hosts. She practically skipped to the waiting trap, eager to return to Rosewood and her bed. The air was velvety and fragrant, the whiffs of fish from the James River overpowered by the smell of sun-warmed earth, grass, and wildflowers perfuming the air.

The moon was high in the sky, casting a silvery glow over the wooden houses and muddy streets, and making Jamestown appear almost beautiful; something it would certainly have no claim to during the daylight hours. Louisa was tired, worn out by worry and uncertainty, her imagination putting forth every horrible scenario it could think of just to torment her further. Kit was silent next to her as he took up the reins, urging the horse into a dignified trot until they left the confines of Jamestown.

"What an awful man," Louisa said, leaning against Kit's shoulder. "I would be happy never to see him, or his boring wife, again. Why is he here?"

"To buy a plantation, or so I gather. He might become a permanent fixture in the colony," replied Kit with a look of such disgust on his face it nearly made Louisa laugh. "He's an absolute snake. I wager he isn't even acquainted with Buckingham. George Villiers wouldn't bother with a maggot like Deverell. He doesn't suffer fools gladly."

"Oh, but my dear Christopher," Louisa intoned, mimicking Deverell, "George and I are on most intimate of terms. Why, he barely takes a shit without inviting me to wipe his handsome arse. Indeed he does, because there's no greater ass wipe at court than Aloysius Deverell." Kit burst out laughing, his arm relaxing beneath her cheek.

"You had better tread carefully, Lady Sheridan. Sir George was very displeased with you tonight, being the blasphemous besom that you are, so keep a civil tongue in your head, or I will be ordered to exercise my husbandly duty and give you a sound beating on that lovely, round behind of yours. Oh, it gets me going just thinking about it," he said, giving her a meaningful glance.

Louisa giggled and smacked Kit playfully. "Behave, Lord Sheridan, or you might find yourself on the receiving end of a stick." Kit laughed, all tension gone from his body. Aloysius Deverell was forgotten for the moment as they enjoyed the beauty of the summer night and the feeling of being all alone and unencumbered, which didn't happen often.

Kit suddenly stopped the trap and turned to face his wife, the gleam in his eyes unmistakable as he reached for an old blanket tossed carelessly into the back of the trap. She returned his gaze as he helped her from the trap and spread the blanket in a shadowy spot beneath the trees. There was no reason to rush home, and they hadn't made love beneath the stars in a very long time. In fact, the last time was a few years ago at their country estate in England, when they snuck out one beautiful night and spent a few delicious hours by the lake under the droopy cover of the weeping willow. She still smiled when she remembered that night since it had been one of the few times she actually forgot about the children, her forced separation from Valerie, and the death of her parents. She'd felt like a teenager, making out in the back of a car with her boyfriend, consumed with desire and oblivious of everything but the moment.

Louisa gasped with pleasure as she felt Kit's hand sliding up her thigh and between her legs, the moonlight making his face look strangely pale and unfamiliar. The smile had been replaced by naked desire, making her shiver in anticipation. She could tell by the look on his face that he wasn't interested in a quick romp, but rather had every intention of teasing her mercilessly and bringing her to heights of passion that erased all thought from her mind as her body took over in a primal need that went back to the beginning of time. She reached out a hand to unlace his breeches, but he gently pushed it away, not ready to take any pleasure for himself. This was going to be all about her, and she willingly surrendered all control and gave herself up to him, knowing she was safe in his keeping.

For a good while, all worry was purged from Louisa's mind as she stared up at the moon, not wanting to tear her gaze away from its mystical power. Her body felt weightless and untethered, the tension building inside her until she shuddered beneath Kit, closing her eyes at last and floating on a cloud of contentment.

ELEVEN
VIRGINIA JULY 1779

Finn stretched luxuriously, reluctant to get out of bed. Abbie was already up, changing Diana's clout before bringing her into their bed for her morning feeding and cuddle. Diana was already eating solid food, but Abbie still nursed her in the mornings and before bed to make sure she got enough nourishment. Diana usually wore more of her food than she ate, and Abbie worried, as any new mother would, that her baby would starve. Finn kissed the rounded cheek, thinking that the cherubic Diana looked far from starvation with everyone constantly offering her freshly baked bread with butter and honey, apple sauce, or biscuits.

Finn tried to kiss Abbie, but she moved away, still annoyed with him for accepting the assignment. Deep down, she knew he had to go; he couldn't just sit there by his wife's side while men died fighting for freedom. He'd promised his parents that he wouldn't join the army, but he had never promised that he wouldn't work behind the scenes, bringing and receiving important messages and trying to sabotage the enemy in any way he could. Finn cuddled Diana while Abbie readjusted her shift and got out of bed. "Why don't you hand Diana to your mother and come back for a cuddle yourself?" he suggested, patting the space next to him. He was never sure of what her reaction was going to be these days.

They'd resumed marital relations two months after the birth and Finn naively expected things to go back to normal, but although he couldn't get enough of Abbie, she didn't seem to share his ardor. She was always tired, and her body tensed every time he touched her, her hips swiveling away from him almost of their own accord as he tried to make love to her. Abbie's face expressed anything but joy, making Finn feel guilty for pressuring her to do something she didn't want to do. He wished he could talk to someone about this, but he could hardly ask his father-in-law if Hannah Mallory had the same aversion to sex after the birth of their children, so all he could do was bide his time and hope that Abbie's body would finally return to normal.

He had finally broken down and confided in his father during one of their visits shortly after the baby was born, relieved to see his father's smile of understanding.

"Just give her a little time, Finn," Alec had said, patting him on the shoulder. "Her body has just gone through her first pregnancy and birth, and now it's working to produce enough milk to nurse a child. She's overwhelmed, tired, and anxious about the baby, as all new mothers are. The first year is crucial, since so many things can go wrong. She still loves you and wants you, but you are no longer her first priority. Get used to it, my boy," Alec said with a grin, "you won't be for quite some time, especially once you have more children."

Finn felt a little better after the talk, doing his best to be understanding and giving Abbie time. His father had been right, and Abbie finally began to come around once Diana stopped nursing every few hours and slept longer during the night. Her full sexual appetite returned a few months ago and she was eager to make love, especially in the mornings when she was still full of energy and drive.

Abbie smiled seductively as she dove back into bed. "Hurry. I left Diana with Annie and Sarah, so we only have a few minutes until she starts wailing from them smothering her with attention." Abbie yanked her shift over her head, and straddled Finn with a look of determination on her face that nearly made him laugh. He was about to be ridden like an Arabian stallion, and he meant to enjoy it.

Throwing her head back, her full breasts bouncing above Finn's face as she moved her hips, Abbie went slowly at first and then faster and faster, panting and moaning as she dug her fingers into his shoulders. Finn was glad she was in a hurry, since there was no way he could have made this last any longer even if he had been reciting the latest sermon by Reverend Greene in his head. It wouldn't have helped. He wrapped his arms around Abbie as she collapsed on top of him, a smile of pure bliss on her face.

Their bodies were still joined, their hearts beating in unison as Diana let out a cry of outrage, followed by the pounding of feet that announced Abbie's younger sisters coming upstairs to bring the baby. Abbie and Finn barely had enough time to cover themselves before the girls erupted into the loft, holding a wailing Diana and talking over each other as they tried to explain themselves. Abbie reached out and took the baby, pressing her against her naked breasts in an effort to hide her nudity, but Sarah noticed. She poked Annie in the ribs and whispered something before they both giggled and headed back downstairs.

"Think they know?" asked Finn as he got out of bed and began to pull on his breeches.

"Of course they do," Abbie replied as she set Diana down on the bed and began to dress for the day. "I wish we had our own house like Sam and Susanna. At least they have privacy."

"And look where it got them," retorted Finn, referring to Sue's second pregnancy. "She must have gotten with child the first time they lay together after Ben was born. If that's what you want, come back to bed and I'll see what I can do."

Abbie swatted Finn with her mobcap before picking up Diana, who was trying to climb off the bed, and turning to go downstairs. "Don't even think about it, Finlay Whitfield. I'm not ready for another child, and neither are you."

"You are right there," Finn mumbled as Abbie disappeared down the stairs.

Finn wished he could spend another hour in bed, but he finished getting dressed and headed downstairs to wash and eat. He had to finish his preparations before leaving for Georgia tomorrow. The Winter Campaign waged by Lieutenant-Colonel Campbell had been successful and had resulted in the entire colony of Georgia falling under British rule once again. Except for a disastrous skirmish at Briar Creek in March, which ended in the decimation of the Rebels, and a loss of a quarter of General Ashe's army, either to British guns or drowning in the swamps or the Savannah River as they tried to flee, no successful effort to reclaim Georgia had been made. The Continental Army needed intelligence to plan their offensive, and men like Finn and Sam were their best bet at getting the information they needed.

The sun was already hot, a humid haze coating everything in sight, the air shimmering and shifting as a slight but welcome breeze stirred the trees. Finn was just coming out of the barn when the sight of a wagon caught his attention and he waved to Mr. Tunstall, who was sitting next to some woman who wasn't his wife. Mrs. Tunstall was roughly as big as Susanna, but she wasn't with child. The woman next to Tunstall was young and thin, the broad brim of her hat covering her face, and her hands holding onto the bench as the wagon swayed from side to side. The wagon seemed to be heading straight for the farm, so Finn waited politely, eager to hear what Mr. Tunstall wanted.

Finn's mouth opened in surprise as the wagon drew closer,

the face of the woman on the bench now clearly visible. He'd know her anywhere. He smiled and waved, glad to see her recognize him as well. She looked just as he remembered her, big blue eyes that danced with mischief, red curls, and buxom breasts that swelled above the bodice of her dress. He tore his eyes away from the breasts and concentrated on the woman's face. She did look a little older and noticeably more tired, probably from the long journey. But why was she here, and how had she found them? Sam never gave her his real name, calling himself Patrick Johnson, and she knew Finn only as John. He supposed she put two and two together after the escape, Abbie's name on everyone's lips as the search for her and her rescuers, one of them being her husband, got under way.

Finn gave her his hand as she descended from the wagon, smiling at him with genuine pleasure. "Diana, what are you doing here?" he asked once they were face to face. "It's such a surprise to see you. Abbie and Sam will be thrilled."

"Oh, I do hope so, Finn. I was so worried I wouldn't get a warm welcome, but I simply had to come," Diana replied, smoothing down her skirts and adjusting her hat before taking her valise from Mr. Tunstall and handing it to Finn.

"Were you in the area?" Finn asked carefully, trying to understand the purpose of Diana's visit.

"Not exactly. I made the journey specially," she answered coyly, looking up at Finn with a playful smile that made him uneasy. She was up to something, and for the life of him, he couldn't imagine what that might be.

Finn was just about to invite Diana into the house when a child's sleepy face appeared above the side of the wagon, his thin arms reaching out to Diana.

"Here mama?" he asked, scrambling to his feet and nearly falling over the side and into Diana's arms.

"Yes, lovey, we're here," she said softly into his hair as she set him on the ground.

It was hard to tell exactly how old the child was since he was small and thin, his narrow face devoid of baby fat. Finn would have placed him at about one, but he walked and talked, which made him older, at least in his estimation. However, he was still wearing a gown, which meant he wasn't toilet trained and likely younger than three. Besides, as far as he knew, Diana didn't have a child when they had known her in New York.

"Finn, this is Nathaniel, my son," Diana announced dramatically, picking up the boy and handing him to Finn. As he looked into the child's face, he finally saw exactly what Diana wanted him to see. The wide gray eyes fringed by thick dark lashes were very familiar. The Mallory eyes, as his mother called them. Diana watched from beneath her lashes, her mouth drawn into a tense line as the realization of Nathaniel's paternity dawned on Finn, making him subconsciously suck in his breath. So, that's why she was here.

"Diana, wait. You can't do this," Finn pleaded, handing the child back to Diana and picking up her case. "Sam is married and has a child, and his wife is pregnant again. This will shock her." Diana turned to Finn, her face full of innocent surprise.

"Do what, Finn? I'm simply visiting dear friends. I thought you and Abbie would be happy to see me, and Sam too. Didn't you just say so?"

"I'm not blind, you know," Finn hissed, so as not to alert Mr. Tunstall to the problem. The last thing they needed was unwelcome speculation about the surprise visitor to the Mallory farm and the child that looked just like the eldest son. "He's the spitting image of Sam, and you've come here to make him claim responsibility, not that he shouldn't. Just please, talk to him in private. Don't spring this on the whole family. Sam's wife will be devastated."

Diana ran a hand through her son's curls as she kissed his temple and smiled up at Finn. "You have nothing to fear, Finn. Now, take me to the house."

TWELVE

Finn threw Mrs. Mallory an apologetic look as he led Diana into the kitchen, introducing her all around. Abbie jumped from her seat, sweeping Diana into a huge hug before noticing the boy, but she wasn't really seeing him as she focused all her attention on his mother.

"Oh, Diana, I can't begin to express my gratitude. You helped save my life. If it weren't for you, Finn and Sam would have never been able to rescue me," she gushed, still holding on to Diana's hand. "We even named our daughter after you. There she is," Abbie announced proudly, drawing Diana's attention to her namesake. Diana smiled at the child, her face alight with pleasure at being so warmly received.

"Please, sit down and let me get you something to eat," Mrs. Mallory offered, setting out a plate for Diana. "Finn, maybe you can run along and fetch Sam. He'll be so glad to see Diana and her son." Finn nodded, unsure of how to proceed. Nathaniel was staring at the floor and hiding behind his mother's voluminous skirt. He was clearly scared, but remained quiet, which was unusual for a child. Had it been Diana or Ben, they would have been screaming for attention and begging to be picked up, but Nathaniel inched behind his mother in an effort to make himself invisible.

"Would you like something to eat?" Mrs. Mallory asked Nathaniel, bending down to meet his gaze. Finn heard the sharp intake of breath as their eyes met, but Mrs. Mallory smiled at the boy and held out her hand. "Come, dear, let me get you some bread with honey and a cup of milk. Would you like that? I bet you're hungry after your long journey." Nathaniel permitted himself to be led to the table where he climbed into a chair and folded his hands in his lap. He was either a very well-behaved child or one who was used to being ignored.

There was a collective gasp as Nathaniel looked around, his eyes round with fear. Mr. Mallory's lips virtually disappeared into his beard, and Sarah and Annie exchanged glances, their faces full of shock and incomprehension. Abbie stared at the boy as Annie finally blurted out what everyone was thinking.

"He looks just like Sam."

"Go do your chores," Mrs. Mallory ordered, her tone brooking no argument. "You too, Sarah."

The girls reluctantly filed out, knowing they were about to miss out on something really good. Annie was still too young to comprehend the truth of what happened, but Sarah was old enough to grasp the meaning behind the uncanny resemblance.

"Diana, first of all, I would very much like to thank you for the part you played in our daughter's rescue. If not for you, we might have lost not only Abbie, but Finn and Sam as well. You are always welcome in our home and can stay for as long as you wish," Mr. Mallory said, watching Diana warily. "Now, if you would be so kind as to answer the question that's uppermost in our minds. Is Sam Nathaniel's father? And if so, does he know?"

Diana took a deep breath before facing Mr. Mallory and replying. "Mr. Mallory, I'm very proud to have helped Abbie, Finn, and Sam. Knowing that I saved a life, possibly more than one, makes everything I've been through in my life worthwhile. Now, to answer your question. No, Sam is not Nat's father – Jonah is."

"What?" Mr. and Mrs. Mallory asked simultaneously. Their faces were almost comical, relief mixed with wonder and disbelief as they took in what Diana just said.

"It's true. It was, in fact, Jonah who introduced me to Sam. He was in New York just before Washington's troops were driven out, and we became... eh, close. I would never have come here, had I not been desperate. You see, once my pregnancy became obvious, I lost my place at the bro—, my place of employment, and with it my source of income," Diana explained.

"I stayed with a friend, a Mrs. Morse, whom Sam is familiar with, but I couldn't impose on her for much longer once Nat was born. She took care of him while I took jobs cleaning and doing laundry, but that doesn't pay much as compared to whoring, if you'll pardon me saying so. We never had enough to eat and I couldn't put anything by for the future. Both Sam and Jonah always spoke of what kind people you are, so I thought that you might find it in your heart to help us. I would be most grateful."

"Of course, we will," Mr. Mallory said, finally smiling. "You will stay with us, and once Jonah is back, you two can work things out between yourselves. I can't speak for him, but I have no doubt that my son will do what's right."

Mrs. Mallory let out a pitiful squeak, but Diana just smiled at her. "Mrs. Mallory, I didn't come here to ensnare your son. I understand how you feel, and I wouldn't want my boy to marry beneath him either. I just need a little help until I can get on my feet again."

"Of course, dear," Mrs. Mallory said, focusing on practical matters. "You and Nathaniel can share the girls' room. It'll be crowded, but we'll manage. And how old is Nathaniel?" she asked carefully.

"He's nearly one and a half. I know, he's small for his age," Diana said, giving them all a sad smile, "but things have been difficult for us both. If you'll excuse me for a moment." Diana disappeared through the door, going in search of the privy while Nat happily munched on his bread, his face tense with concentration as he tried to chew the crust.

Everyone watched him, a palpable tension passing between Mr. and Mrs. Mallory as they exchanged looks of shock and disbelief. Finn looked on until Mrs. Mallory physically turned him around and pushed him out the door. "Get Sam."

THIRTEEN

"Oh, thank you, thank you, thank you," Sam intoned as he leaned against the stile and gazed at the purpling sky, scattered with the first twinkling stars of the evening. "Thank you, Lord, for not making Nathaniel mine."

Seeing Diana had been a shock, but seeing her son left him nearly mute. The boy looked so much like him when he was a child that it unnerved him. Thank God Sue hadn't come with him. He'd left his parents' house nearly half an hour ago but couldn't bring himself to go straight home. Sam leaned against the stile and watched the sun slowly sink below the horizon, the puffy clouds that were white only a little while ago now tinged blood red as the sun finally disappeared, plunging the world into semi-darkness. Another quarter of an hour and the tree line in the distance would become just a jagged black line against the darkening sky, and the moon would rise, bathing the meadow in a silvery glow that would light his way home.

Diana looked much the same at first glance, but on closer inspection, she had aged, fine lines appearing around her eyes and a deeper groove running from nose to chin around her supple mouth. She'd suffered in the past year; he could see it in her eyes. Why hadn't she come sooner? Sam wondered. Jonah would have seen right by her. Of course, their parents would not have been very happy with his choice of wife, but in view of the child, there's not much even they could say against the union. Jonah, you dog! Sam chuckled. Who would have thought?

He turned as Abbie climbed onto the stile next to him and looked at the stars. "I guess we were all wrong about Jonah. He's more like you than we thought," she said, nudging Sam in the ribs with her elbow. "At least you were always careful."

"It does seem out of character, but war does strange things to people. Jonah has been away from home for years. He's lonely and battle sick. He probably just needed some comfort, and Diana was there to provide it. She's beautiful and spirited with a quick wit and a sense of humor. She would have made him feel at ease and happy. I can't blame him. Can you?"

"No, of course not. I really like Diana. I'm glad she's decided to stay. Doesn't seem as if life has been very good to her," Abbie speculated, still gazing at the darkening sky.

"No, the past year must have been very trying," Sam replied, feeling guilty for never writing to her after returning home.

"I wasn't just referring to the past year, Sam. No woman goes into prostitution because she has a happy life, or because she really wants to service countless, random men. She's had it rough for much longer than you think, brother," she said quietly. "Men! How blind you can be."

"I suppose you're right. Diana was always so vivacious and fun; it was hard to imagine that she might be unhappy."

"I hope she can be happy here," Abbie replied, "not sure how happy Jonah will be, though. I can't think what she'll do here."

"How do you mean?" Sam asked, turning to gaze at Abbie. She always made astute observations, especially where women were concerned. If Abbie said something about Sue, Sam was sure to listen and follow her advice, since she was usually right, and he was thick as a brick, according to her. He knew a thing or two about women, but mostly in the physical sense. Their emotions were a mystery to him, now more than ever.

"I mean that Diana is used to a certain kind of life. Just look at her clothes. She's wearing silk stockings and a lace tucker, for God's sake," Abbie said, partly in disgust and partly in envy. "She's likely never felt homespun next to her skin or dyed her old garments to give them new life and make them last a little longer. How will she adjust to life on a farm? She was too polite to say anything, but I think she expected us to have servants."

Sam shrugged. Abbie was right as usual. Mabel's brothel was a thriving concern, catering mostly to officers of whichever army happened to be in New York. Mabel employed young, healthy girls, who were good at putting on airs. She dressed them in fine clothes, and even provided perfume to mask the smell of sweat or other men still clinging to the girls. There were several servants belowstairs, cleaning, washing, mending, and cooking for the girls. Diana worked late into the night, but she slept half the day away in preparation for the next evening. She woke up to a cooked meal, a drawn bath, and a clean gown laid out for her by a maid. Her hands were soft as velvet and her skin creamy and white, unused to being exposed to the elements or to hard work. There would be no maids at the farm, and if Diana chose to stay, she would have to pull her weight and do her share of the work.

Sam said goodnight to Abbie as she slid off the stile and headed back toward the house. It was time to get Ben ready for bed, and for Abbie to enjoy an hour of quiet time with Finn before retiring. She looked tired, but happy, Sam thought as he headed for home. The next few days would certainly be interesting.

FOURTEEN

Susanna sighed with relief once Ben's fussing finally stopped, signaling that he was down for the night. It took him forever to fall asleep and he rarely slept for more than a few hours at a time, always waking just as she was in her deepest sleep and asking for a drink or a hug because something had frightened him. He usually went to sleep after taking a sip of water or a pat on the back, but Susanna had a hard time falling back asleep or even finding a comfortable position. If only she could get a few nights of uninterrupted sleep. She couldn't wait for this baby to be born.

Susanna folded her arms over her bulging stomach and rested her head against the wooden headboard, waiting for the evening performance to begin. It took only a few minutes and then her belly began to move and roll, small bulges appearing here and there as a head, or maybe a butt, pushed against the womb, the baby frolicking inside as if it were doing somersaults. She yelped with surprise as an elbow, or possibly a foot, smashed against her ribs and retreated just as quickly to strike lower down. The baby's head suddenly pushed down lower against her bladder, forcing her to get off the bed and head for the privy behind the house.

So far, this pregnancy was completely different from the first. When pregnant with Ben, Susanna felt energetic and happy, her body changing gradually and beautifully, and her soul serene and full of joy. She still felt like herself and very much wanted Sam to make love to her, which he did, nearly until the day Ben finally made his appearance into the world. The birth itself was easy as well. Ben was born with the minimum of fuss, his head already crowning as the midwife burst through the door prepared for a long night of labor, but actually working for only a few minutes until the newborn was washed, swaddled, and placed in his mother's arms.

This time was completely different. She had become pregnant again before even getting her monthly flow, and the babe made itself known from the first. She felt ill from the time she woke in the morning to the time she stumbled to bed at night. Her stomach twisted and lurched, she was ambushed by dizzy spells, and the persistent vomiting left her weak and sweating, even when the weather was cool. The thought of Sam touching her was unbearable, so he stayed away, fearful of making things worse. Of course, Susanna still had Ben to care for and those first few months were a terrible trial. Negative thoughts swirled in her head, no doubt brought about by her physical state and she nearly drowned in feelings of guilt as she realized that she wasn't enjoying Ben at all, but barely going through the motions, desperate for a few moments of rest.

Susanna climbed back into bed and blew out the candle, eager to get to sleep. Things were finally turning around, and she smiled into the darkness as she heard Ben's even breathing. The baby would be born soon, and this time she wouldn't let Sam anywhere near her without taking precautions. Only a few years ago, she would have given anything for a family of her own, and now she had it, and she would love her husband and enjoy her children every single day. She would also not lose hope that someday her estranged father would come and see her and give her his blessing, and that her sister would answer at least one letter, opening the door to an eventual reconciliation.

FIFTEEN

The house sighed and breathed like a living thing as it settled for the night around the sleeping family. Finn heard Mr. Mallory coming to bed about a half hour ago, his heavy footsteps finally dying away, replaced by gentle snoring and the occasional creaking of the bed frame as he shifted his bulk. He hardly ever came to bed before midnight, so it was probably going on one o'clock. Finn was physically tired, but his mind refused to settle as he once again went over the details of his upcoming journey. Nothing was ever put in writing, so he had to make sure to remember everything, including the contingency plan that was put in place before every mission.

He would leave tomorrow after breakfast and make his way to Georgia on foot. It would be faster to go on horseback, but the Mallorys didn't have a horse to spare and a man on foot wasn't as noticeable to others, which was always an advantage. It was much easier to lose himself in a crowd or hitch a ride with some unsuspecting farmer, who was only too happy to talk and divulge important information without even realizing it.

Finn's contact would meet him at the *Pig and Rooster Tavern* near the Savannah harbor. Finn knew him only as John, but that probably wasn't even his real name. It was always best to know as little as possible so as not to unwittingly betray a compatriot. John would have a copy of Shakespeare's sonnets in his possession as a signal to Finn. Finn chuckled to himself. Not many men in the colonies devoted their time to reading Shakespeare, much less his sonnets, which is why it was the perfect choice.

Finn hoped he would get at least a few hours of sleep as he would spend most of the following day walking. He needed his rest. He was about to close his eyes and try breathing evenly, as his father-in-law suggested as a sure-fire method for battling nerves, but a strange, mewling sound had him sitting up in bed, fully alert. The sound came from Diana's cot, so Finn got out of bed and went to investigate. She was sitting up, her chubby arms reaching out to him in a silent plea to be picked up, which he gladly did. Finn held the child close to his heart and stroked her hair gently, but she continued to fuss, letting out a desperate squeal as he tried to lower her back into the cradle.

"All right, all right, I understand," he whispered to her, "you don't want to go back to bed. Let's go outside then, so you don't wake everyone up." Finn wrapped Diana in a blanket and made his way downstairs on silent feet, letting himself out of the house and settling on a bench beneath a leafy maple. Abbie often sat there during the afternoon, letting Diana play at her feet as she sewed in natural daylight.

Finn held Diana close as she peered at him in the darkness, her eyes full of wonder at being outside at night. She might have been frightened by something and woken up, but now she seemed perfectly content, leaning her head against Finn's heart and listening to the steady rhythm. Finn had to admit that he was kind of glad Diana had woken up. He rarely got to spend any time alone with her, not for lack of trying, but for lack of opportunity.

It seemed that someone was always plucking her from his

arms and taking her away. In a house full of women, it was difficult for a man to be with his daughter. Abbie was overly protective, as any new mother probably was, and Mrs. Mallory doted on her beautiful granddaughter and liked to carry Diana on her hip as she went about her chores. Sarah and Annie were at an age where they wanted to mother the child and play with her all the time, and Mr. Mallory liked to sit Diana on his lap in the evening and sing to her as she listened with rapt attention. Finn was glad his child was so loved and cared for, but sometimes he longed for a few quiet moments alone with her. He loved the feel of her small body against his own and the wonderful smell that only she had.

It was strange how this little girl was such a mixture of all the people around her, yet uniquely her own. She had his eyes, which Finn was secretly proud of, and Abbie's smile. Her hair was dark with some lighter chestnut strands, so much like his mother's, and she looked remarkably like Mrs. Mallory when she was displeased with something and wrinkled her nose in distaste. There was even something of his father in the way Diana cocked her head to the side and stilled when something caught her attention. It would be fascinating to see who their next child would resemble.

One naked foot came out of the blanket and Finn enveloped it in his hand, marveling at how well it fitted. Diana wiggled her toes and let out a little giggle, then settled back into the crook of Finn's arm. "Sing," she commanded, and he began to sing a mournful song he'd learned from Mr. Mallory. It was about lost love and fading hope, but Diana loved it. Her eyelids began to flutter as they grew heavier and her breathing became deep and measured. Finn continued to sing after she grew heavy in his arms, her mouth open in sleep, not wanting the moment to end, but it was time to take Diana back to her bed and try to get some sleep before setting off in a few hours.

SIXTEEN

Susanna threw a grateful smile at Sam as he cleared the table after breakfast and covered the leftover bread with a cloth to keep it from getting stale. They could have it for breakfast tomorrow, perhaps with some cheese, so she could get a few extra minutes of sleep instead of cooking porridge. Sam peered into the pot from last night's stew, the bottom badly burned with pieces of potato and meat gristle stuck to the metal like an impenetrable suit of armor.

"Sorry I burnt it," Susanna mumbled apologetically. "Ben was crying and I forgot to stir the pot." She'd also forgotten to let it soak, so the pot would need some vigorous scrubbing to get it clean again.

"Nothing to worry about. I'll just take it down to the creek and wash it out," Sam offered, eager to help.

"No, it needs to soak first. Just pour some hot water into it and then fill this basin for me. I need to wash Ben's clouts and gown. He goes through them so quickly." She was too tired to wash anything, not having slept well at all, but if she didn't do it, Ben wouldn't have enough clouts to last till noon. Susanna sighed and rolled up her sleeves, ready to attack the smelly pile.

"I'd offer to do it, but I promised Pa I would muck out the barn. I would have done it yesterday, but with all the excitement of Diana's arrival I never got to it. Best do it now." Sam reached for his boots, clearly reluctant to go. He looked as tired as Susanna felt.

Susanna leveled her gaze at Sam. He seemed awfully jumpy since coming back from his parents' house yesterday evening, and strangely upset about the arrival of their unexpected guest. Susanna heard of the part Diana had played in Abbie's rescue, so she was a little perplexed as to Sam's reaction. She supposed no one had expected Diana to arrive with a child, especially Jonah's child. The family owed Diana a debt of gratitude, which made the situation awkward to say the least.

Even if Jonah had slept with Diana, he certainly wasn't the first or the last. Diana's bold move implied that she expected Jonah to marry her, but as of yet, no one knew how Jonah felt about any of this, or if he even knew of the child's existence. The Mallorys, of course, were less than pleased to find that their son had sired a child with a prostitute and might now be obliged to make an honest woman out of her. No one seemed to entertain the idea that the boy might have fallen in love, but it was perfectly likely, Susanna mused.

Jonah held a soft spot in Susanna's heart, for he reminded her of herself. He was sensitive and shy, desperate to love and be loved, but not brave enough to put his heart at risk. Maybe loving Diana had been easy since she wasn't likely to reject him. She'd probably made him feel ten feet tall, and he, in turn, might have made promises he'd meant wholeheartedly at the time but didn't keep.

Susanna smiled as she thought of Sam's sister, Martha. She would have a mouthful regarding this situation. Martha always had a mouthful. Susanna had to admit that she admired her spirit. Martha wasn't afraid to speak her mind, and often voiced what everyone else was thinking, but were too afraid to say out loud. She'd have to make sure to be there when Martha came over with baby Joe. Her husband, Gil, was off with the Militia, so Martha liked to come over at least twice a week to visit her parents and siblings and give Joe a chance to play with his cousins.

"Sam, what will your parents do?" Susanna asked, the dirty clouts steaming in the basin and filling the house with an unpleasant aroma.

"About what?"

"This situation with Diana. Do you think Jonah was one of her clients, or they really had some sort of relationship?"

"I couldn't say. Jonah never gave any indication that he was interested. He introduced us in New York, but I'd never seen them together after that first time. I thought that to him Diana was simply a messenger, but then, you never know with Jonah. He holds his cards close to his chest when it comes to private matters. Funny, he used to be so chatty when he was a boy. You couldn't shut him up, but now he'd rather listen than talk."

Sam shrugged as he pulled on his right boot. "Of course, Jonah does tend to fear girls. Diana is so easygoing that it would have made it easier for him to approach her rather than risk rejection by some virginal maiden." Sam chuckled. "Poor Jonah finally lies with a woman and now he'll have to pay for it for the rest of his days."

"Don't joke about it, Sam. Jonah will be in for a shock when he returns."

"I know. Actually, what I find strange is that she kept the child at all," Sam mused as he pulled on his other boot and rose to leave.

"Why?"

"Women of Diana's profession know how to avoid pregnancy, and when the inevitable happens and they do get with child, they know ways to get rid of it. Having a child is not usually an option, unless they can marry the father and leave it all behind."

"Isn't that why she's here? To marry the father?" Susanna asked, suddenly apprehensive. "Sam, how well did you know her in New York?"

"She was good at ferreting out information and passing it on to the right people. I saw her from time to time," Sam replied, inching toward the door.

"Did you ever...?

Sam wrapped his arms around Susanna, kissing her softly to put a stop to her questions. "I love you, Sue. Now, I hear the barn calling." He disappeared into the balmy morning, leaving Susanna with more questions than answers.

SEVENTEEN

Sam was relieved to get out of the house and away from Susanna's questions. They'd never really discussed his past, and he felt no desire to share stories of his sexual conquests with his wife. It would only upset her and make her doubt his love for her. All those women had come long before he met her and had been nothing more than a pleasant diversion, as he had been for them. No words of love had been spoken or promises made. He'd liked Diana. She was witty and fun, and wonderfully adventurous in bed, but that was all it had been for him.

Had his little brother really fallen for her or had she tricked him into something? Jonah could be so gullible sometimes, but that was one of the traits that made him so dear. He was so earnest and devoted to the people he loved, and if he'd promised Diana anything, he would fulfill that promise, no matter what their parents thought, especially since now there was a child.

Nat was a sweet little mite, and so like Ben. He deserved better than a life at a brothel, but Sam had seen the look on his father's face and the way his mother avoided meeting Diana's challenging stare. They weren't pleased, and who could blame them? Bringing home a British bride had been shocking enough, but to marry a whore was another matter altogether. Poor Jonah better stay away until his parents got used to the idea of having Diana for a daughter-in-law, or there'd be hell to pay.

Sam had to admit that seeing Diana had been something of a shock after all this time, and he was glad that Susanna hadn't been there to witness his reaction. She would doubtless read something into it and assume that he had feelings for her, when in truth, what he'd felt was surprise tinged with pity. The pretty, vivacious girl looked drawn and weary, her face gaunt, the rosy blush replaced by a grayish pallor and smudges of fatigue under her eyes. No doubt she'd had a hard time of it this past year and coming to the Mallorys had been a last resort. It would have taken courage for any girl to show up on someone's doorstep with a baby, but for a girl who earned her living whoring it was downright brazen. Sam had tried not to stare at the child in Diana's arms, but his eyes kept straying to the shock of dark hair and the clear gray eyes that were so like his and Jonah's. There was no doubt the child was a Mallory, but which Mallory?

Sam was so caught up in his thoughts he only noticed her as he got closer to the barn. She was leaning against the stile, a light-colored shawl carelessly thrown across her thin shoulders. At first, he thought it might have been Abbie, since the spot was a favorite of hers, but he immediately realized it wasn't, since the woman's hair was hanging down her back, the auburn curls caressed by the gentle breeze as they framed her face, which was turned up to the heavens, watching the clouds scuttling across the summer sky and casting shadows on her face as they obscured the sun.

"I needed some air," Diana said by way of explanation, her gaze sliding over him and settling on his face.

"It's warm out this morning," Sam replied noncommittally.

"Yes, it's much balmier than in New York, but I like it. It smells different too. Where are you going, Sam?"

"I was just on my way to muck out the barn," he answered as he came nearer. "Should have done it yesterday."

"I'll come with you," Diana announced unexpectedly, throwing Sam for a loop.

"If you want, but it's hot and smelly in there, not the best place to get some fresh air."

"I'll gladly give up air in favor of your company," Diana replied with her usual coyness, slipping her arm through Sam's as she peeled herself away from the stile and joined him. Sam tried not to stiffen, but her presence made him nervous. This was all just too strange. He was glad when they finally reached the barn and he was able to disentangle himself from her. He picked up a pitchfork and went to work. The air was close with the smell of manure and soiled straw, but at least the stalls were empty, since the girls let the cows and goats out to pasture after milking them this morning. Sam tried not to breathe too deeply as he cleaned out the first stall and threw down some fresh straw, eager to finish as quickly as possible.

Diana made herself comfortable on a bale of hay, reclining on her elbows as she watched Sam work. He wasn't sure what to say to her, so he tried not to meet her gaze, which never left his face, her eyes demanding that he stop what he was doing and look back at her.

"Why did you keep him?" Sam blurted out. He hadn't meant to be so blunt, but the question kept coming back to him, making him wonder about Diana's intentions.

"Every woman wants a child by the man she loves," she replied quietly, making Sam feel ashamed of himself.

"So you love Jonah? How well do you even know him?"

"Well enough," she replied, still watching him intently.

"Well enough to truly love him?" Sam knew he was being mean, but he had to figure out what she was after.

"I love Nat's father," she replied defensively. "Do you not think me capable of love, Sam? I do have a heart, you know."

SHATTERED MOMENTS

Sam felt suddenly guilty. He had no idea what had driven Diana into prostitution, but she was a lovely girl, and he was being unnecessarily cruel. "I'm sorry. I didn't mean to imply anything. I just thought that because we also..." He didn't finish the sentence, knowing she understood.

Diana slid off the hay and walked over to him, standing close enough that he could smell her hair and see the sheen of perspiration on her creamy breasts. "Do you ever think about it?" she asked, her voice breathless as she inched just a little closer.

"At times." He hadn't thought of her in a long while, but he didn't want to hurt her feelings. She obviously wanted him to say that he did.

"I think about it too," she whispered, suddenly cupping his balls through the fabric of his breeches. He wanted to shove her hand away, but his treacherous body was already reacting to her, his cock straining against the fabric, begging for her body to envelop it like it used to. It'd been months since the last time he'd made love to Susanna and he was hungry and eager for release. That moment of hesitation cost him dearly as Diana pulled on the laces of her bodice, loosening it and baring her breasts to him as she arched her back, bringing the rosy tips closer to his mouth.

"Sam," she breathed, "how I missed you."

Sam tore his eyes from her breasts as he grabbed her wrist and pushed her hand away from his throbbing cock. "You came here with my brother's child, and now you're trying to get me to fuck you? Once a whore always a whore," he spat out and strode from the barn, angry and frustrated. He wished he could go home and slake his sexual frustration with Susanna, but she wasn't receptive just now and his sudden ardor would only alarm her and make her wonder what he'd been up to while he should have been mucking out the barn.

Sam strode into the woods, where he leaned against a stout

tree and gazed up at the sky. He closed his eyes and tried to focus on Bible verses and boring chores, but all he could think of was the desire coursing through his veins and the sight of Diana with her bare breasts just begging to be kissed. Images of her as she had been in New York raced through his fevered brain as he slid his hand down his breeches and went to work.

He was panting by the time he finally came, sliding down the length of the tree, his heart pounding wildly. He'd wanted her; he couldn't deny it, and he felt like the lowest form of scum for nearly betraying Susanna. If only Diana would leave. He couldn't allow her to ensnare Jonah; she'd never be true to him, and Sam would never be at peace if she were nearby.

EIGHTEEN
SAVANNAH JULY 1779

Finn pulled his hat lower to keep the blazing sun out of his eyes and walked down the street at a brisk pace. He'd never been this far south before and hoped never to be again. The heat was unbearable, and he felt a trickle of sweat snake down his back and into the waistband of his breeches as he wiped his forehead with the back of his hand to keep the perspiration from running into his eyes. He wished he could take off his coat, but it seemed inappropriate, especially since all the passersby were properly attired and showed no signs of being uncomfortable. Maybe they were just used to the climate, having lived here all their lives. He was gratified to see that the British soldiers were sweltering in their wool tunics, their pasty English faces red and glistening with sweat.

Finn looked around in dismay. He'd been hoping to find some sort of haberdashery shop where he could buy a gift for Abbie, but so far, he'd seen nothing that fit the bill. Georgia was a relatively new colony compared to Virginia, and Savannah, its capital, wasn't nearly as cosmopolitan or prosperous as Williamsburg. Finn had learned during his short stay that most of the colonists' wealth came from either exporting deer hides or growing rice in the marshes outside the city that were tended by Black slaves, who'd been brought to Savannah expressly for that purpose.

He'd never tasted rice until two days ago, and the verdict was still out on whether he liked it or not. It had a strange texture that sort of reminded him of barley. The taste was kind of odd, too. By itself, it was tasteless, but when mixed into the gravy from the meat, it was quite delicious. Maybe he should buy a small bag of rice and take it home with him. Mrs. Mallory could cook it up with some venison stew. The rice, mixed with meat, carrots, onions, and wild garlic, would make a nice change from their usual fare and give them a taste of the south.

His stomach growled as he thought of food. He hadn't eaten since early that morning and the heel of bread and cup of milk he was given at the small boarding house did nothing to keep the hunger at bay. It was well past noon, and he was ready for something more substantial. He'd buy something for Abbie, then go get a hot meal somewhere before heading out of Savannah.

The information he'd come to collect was already hidden in a secret compartment sewn into his coat by Mrs. Mallory, detailing the number of British troops in the area, positions of cannon, and stores of ammunition. An invasion of Savannah was being carefully planned by the Continental Army, so the information he was carrying would be invaluable. The whole thing had been relatively uneventful, the Redcoats disinterested in a young man in civilian clothes who sauntered past them with secrets for the Rebels.

The soldiers were everywhere, but they seemed to move slower somehow, maybe from the heat, or maybe from the knowledge that there was no immediate threat. They called out greetings to each other as they passed, and snippets of laughter reached Finn's ears as someone told a bawdy joke. The bayonets and gorgets at the soldiers' throats gleamed in the sun, casting rays of light onto the faces of the already overheated men and blinding anyone who looked at them directly.

Finn grinned, happy in the knowledge that they wouldn't win the war. His mother didn't remember details, but she remembered the important things, like some decisive battles that led to the defeat of the British. Too bad she hadn't mentioned anything about Georgia. It would be nice to know that his reconnaissance wasn't in vain. Finn stopped in front of a shop displaying colorful ribbons and swathes of fabric. This was exactly what he needed. Maybe he'd buy a bit of lace for Abbie to make a new tucker or trim for her mobcap.

Abbie wasn't hugely impressed by luxurious things and would likely save the lace for a special occasion, but his motives for getting it were entirely selfish. He knew how she fretted, and who could blame her after what she'd been through in New York? Buying a gift was so much more than bringing something home with him. It was a non-verbal way of conveying to Abbie that he hadn't been in danger. He had time to stroll around town, go into shops, and pick out a present before leaving Savannah. It would put her mind at rest to know that he'd been safe the whole time.

Finn was about to enter the store when something caught his eye. Two six-pointed stars were on either side of the sign, quite small, but distinctive. His contact had mentioned that many Sephardic Jews had settled in Savannah, having come from Spain in search of a new homeland. Finn was curious about those people. Were they like Spaniards or were they like the few Jews he'd seen in New York, dressed all in black and wearing a little cap beneath their hats, their strange, curled forelocks swaying above their cheeks? He pushed open the door and entered, just as a bell chimed above his head.

The man behind the counter was about his age, tall and dark, with eyes that glinted like pieces of onyx in his swarthy face. He looked decidedly more Spanish than the men in New York, Finn concluded as he noted his uncovered head and lack of forelocks. A beautiful woman came into the store from the back, her lustrous black curls piled high on her head and covered with a lace cap, the rest of her hair framing her face. She had the same black eyes and an olive complexion and bore a strong resemblance to the man – probably his sister.

Finn wondered if their family had at some point escaped the Inquisition and fled Spain. Where had people like them gone, and had it been better? Probably not, if they wound up in Georgia. They were strangers in a strange land, but at least they were better off than the Negroes, who'd been plucked from their homes and brought to the New World in chains, aboard slavers' vessels, where they were treated worse than any animal and left to wallow in their own filth until finally being sold off at auction to people who saw them as animals. At least the Jews were free and able to own their own shop, if not to worship openly. They probably went to church with everyone else and then held their own services at home, much as his father did at Rosewood Manor. Funny that the more things changed, the more they stayed the same.

The woman smiled shyly at Finn and he smiled back, realizing that he'd been so caught up in his own musings he hadn't replied to her offer of help. The lace had been too expensive, so Finn chose a mauve ribbon, which would look lovely in Abbie's golden hair, and a little cloth dolly with yarn hair and button eyes.

"My sister makes them herself," the man said proudly. "All the little girls in Savannah want one, don't they, Leah? Every dolly is a little different." Leah blushed as she wrapped up Finn's purchases.

"I started making them as a little girl because I had no one to play with," Leah explained, her cheeks turning pink with embarrassment, "but I wanted to give each one her own personality, so I used different color yarn for the hair and unique buttons for each doll." She handed Finn his parcel tied with a piece of twine. "I hope your little girl likes it."

"I've no doubt she will," Finn replied, taking the package and bidding them farewell as he left the store. *How wonderful it would be to own a shop*, he thought, *but maybe one that sold books*. Maybe after the war was finally over, he and Abbie could move to town and open up a shop of their own. He hated farming. It was backbreaking work that never seemed to end. As soon as you finished one thing, there were twenty more tasks to see to.

He could almost see himself running a prosperous book shop, his name in gold letters on a green background over the door, the front window displaying the latest books from the Colonies and around the world. Maybe he could even get his mother to write and illustrate a picture book for children that he could then have printed and offered for sale. She was a fine artist and could duplicate something she'd seen in the twenty-first century. She said that books and toys for children were big business in the future, but in the eighteenth century people hardly bothered with entertainment for the kids. Only children of the wealthy had handmade toys, made by master craftsmen who created works of art rather than playthings. Working people couldn't afford to buy china dolls dressed in satin and silk for their little girls, or rocking horses that looked just like real horses, with flowing manes and strong flanks that were almost the size of a real pony. Maybe he could introduce some affordable toys into his bookshop as well, Finn thought, suddenly inspired.

Finn was so caught up in his fantasy, he barely noticed the older man walking toward him. The man was a high-ranking British officer, judging by his uniform, but his face was obscured by the black tricorn that threw a dark shadow over his features and was at odds with the whiteness of his wig. His rigid bearing bespoke of years in the military and his uniform was pristine despite the heat, his gold gorget gleaming in the sun and casting a golden glow over the lower part of his face. Finn was about to pass by when the man grabbed his arm roughly, startling him out of his reverie and forcing him to look more closely at the blazing eyes and clenched jaw of the officer who'd accosted him.

"You!" the man hissed. Finn found himself gazing into the enraged face of Major Horace Weland. The man was panting with fury, his lips stretched into a humorless grin of triumph as he brought his face closer to Finn's. "You're not getting away this time, you scoundrel. You will hang, as will your wife, once I find out where she's hiding."

Finn had scored a major victory against the Major when he managed to escape arrest in New York and free Abbie just before her execution for spying. The Major wasn't accustomed to being outwitted and the humiliation must have burned in him all this time, eating at him like a cancer and causing him to doubt himself. If the Major managed to get Finn to headquarters, he was as good as dead. He had one chance to get away, and it had to be now. Finn brought the heel of his boot down on the Major's foot as hard as he could and yanked his arm out of the vicious grip, taking off at a run down the dusty street. He had to get off the main thoroughfare as quickly as possible as there were British soldiers within shouting distance who could help the Major.

"Stop him!" the Major bellowed. Several soldiers immediately responded to the plea for help and joined the chase. Finn turned corner after corner, trying to lose his pursuers, but all he heard was the stomping of boots and the shouts of Major Weland. "Don't shoot. I want him alive."

Finn's heart pounded against his rib cage, more from fear

than from running so fast. He was in good physical shape and could run for miles, but so were the soldiers. They were hampered by muskets and tight uniforms, but they weren't far behind, and he was as trapped as a rat in a maze. Had this been New York or Philadelphia, there'd be more places to hide, but Savannah wasn't a sprawling metropolis, more a growing town where he was bound to get caught very quickly if he continued to run. The next group of British soldiers who spotted him would apprehend him, correctly assuming that he was running from the law. He needed a place to hide while he still had the advantage. Finn vaulted over a low wall of someone's back garden and erupted into a kitchen, where a stunned girl screamed in terror.

"Help me, please, the soldiers are after me," Finn begged. She just pointed to the stairs leading to the cellar.

"Go and stay there till I tell you to come out," she whispered urgently, regaining her composure surprisingly fast. Finn ran down the stairs and hid in the darkest corner behind some sacks of flour. His lungs were burning, and his breath came fast and hard, breathing made more difficult by the dust in the cellar. Finn looked around. There was no other way out of the cellar, so he was effectively trapped, with no way out and no place to hide. If the girl decided to betray him, he was finished. Finn looked around for a weapon, but there was nothing to hand, not even a shovel or a rake.

The best he could do was throw some flour into the eyes of the soldiers, which would buy him about ten seconds, he thought bitterly. His chances of fighting his way out were nonexistent. Forcing himself to breathe evenly, Finn considered his options, which were few. If taken, he would be brought to headquarters, where he would be sentenced and locked up until execution. His only chance of escape would be once they hauled him outside, assuming he was still conscious. Once they locked him up, he would be guarded and fettered, which would make escape impossible, especially since there was no one to help him.

Finn put his head into his hands and muttered an urgent prayer. He suddenly wondered if God got angry with people who didn't much believe in him until they needed help and then came begging, as he just had. He didn't have time to ponder this. The thudding of boots on the wooden floor above and the infuriated tones of Major Weland as he questioned the girl put his musings to an end. Finn inched closer to the door so that he could hear what was being said.

"Yes, sir, he did come this way. Scared me something awful, he did." The girl's voice rang clear, a note of defiance creeping in as she answered the Major. "A thief, is he?"

"Worse—a rebel," Major Weland barked. "Where did he go?"

"He ran right through the house, sir, and came out the other side into the street, and after I just swept the floors." The girl sounded irritated, the cleanliness of the floors clearly very important to her.

"Which way did he go?" the Major demanded.

"I think to the left, sir... or maybe to the right. I couldn't be certain, being scared as I was," the girl said, her voice shaking. "Thanks be to the Almighty that he didn't hurt me. In a hurry, he was, and now I can see why."

"Thank you. Please pardon the intrusion, but we must search the premises before we leave," Major Weland said, his voice gruff with anger. "You and you, go after him and search the street in both directions. You, search the house. If we lost him, I want every patrol in the city looking for him, you hear? Stop anyone who might even vaguely resemble him. We'll get him. There aren't that many roads leading out of Savannah. We'll man every single one until he's caught."

Finn heard the door slam as someone left the house. He listened intently. It grew much quieter, and he could hear only one set of boots on the floor above. The Major and the other soldiers must have gone to search for him outside, so that left one, or at most two, soldiers in the house. He could take them if he had to.

"Don't you dare go into my bedroom," the girl shrieked. "Do you think I'm in the habit of hiding young men in there? I'm a God-fearing woman of high morals, sir." She sounded outraged, and Finn heard the mumbled apology of the poor sod who had the misfortune of crossing her.

"If I might check the cellar, ma'am?"

"Get out of my house, you hear? There's no one here, and if your Major, or whoever he is, doesn't believe me, well then he can just come back with a warrant. I'm a private citizen and a loyal subject of His Majesty; I will not be harassed in this manner."

"Yes, ma'am. My apologies. There's clearly no one here, and I will tell the Major that there's no need to return."

Finn heard the footsteps die away and the slamming of the door as the last soldier departed, leaving Finn shaking with relief. It was another quarter of an hour before the girl finally opened the cellar door and came down the stairs.

"I think you can come out now, Mr. Rebel. They've gone." She was dimpling at him in the dimness of the cellar, her eyes dancing with glee. "I don't know what you've done to get the whole army after you, but if it's something to annoy the British, I'm happy to have been of help. Mayhap you should stay here for a bit. They're not likely to come back. You can leave after dark."

"Thank you. You saved my life," Finn said, knowing he was speaking the honest truth. "I'm Finlay, what's your name?" he asked, dusting off his coat and breeches.

"I'm Dora, short for Dorothy. I live here with my father. He's a rebel too, but the armchair kind. He talks a lot, but doesn't actually do much," she supplied, making sure the coast was clear before allowing Finn to step through the door. "With the British in full control of Georgia, it's not wise to proclaim your loyalty to the opposition." Dora looked out the window to make sure the soldiers were gone and beckoned Finn to come to the kitchen. "Let me get you a cool drink. You look like you can use one." She poured him a cup of beer and offered him a slice of meat pie that sat cooling on the windowsill. "I made it for our supper, but father won't mind. He'll be home in an hour."

Finn wolfed down the pie and drank his beer, his mind working overtime as Dora silently gave him a second slice. The girl was right; it was probably best to leave after dark, but that would also give Weland more time to mobilize the patrols and hand out his description. They would be monitoring every road leading out of Savannah.

"I don't think I can afford to wait," Finn said thoughtfully. "They'll be searching for me. If I know Major Weland, he won't give up till he has me. That man is as dogged as they come, and he has a score to settle with me."

"What have you done?" Dora breathed, her mouth a perfect little circle as she looked at him in admiration.

"I kidnapped a prisoner bound for the gallows and killed two soldiers in the process."

"You must be very brave." Dora pushed another slice of pie toward him, assuming that brave men required more food.

"Thank you, but leave some for your father," Finn replied with a smile.

"Would you like more beer?" she asked, eager to do something for him.

"I better keep a clear head if I'm to get out of this mess."

Suddenly, she clapped her hands together like a child, her eyes lighting up. "I have an idea, a wonderful idea. Father and I will get you out of the city once he gets home. I know just the way to do it."

Finn was almost afraid to ask, but the girl had helped him

once already, and he had to have faith. She was clever and her theatrical streak didn't hurt. She seemed to have enjoyed her run-in with the soldiers and was bursting with pride at having saved him from being arrested.

"My life is in your hands," Finn replied, making her beam.

"I won't let you down."

NINETEEN

"I don't know, Dora," Mr. Powell said as he listened to her idea. "I passed at least three patrols on the way home, and I've seen them stop several young men and take them in for questioning. I can't imagine how we can get Finlay out of Savannah without being stopped. I know they are not looking for a family, but they might still stop us on account of him being the right age and coloring." He shook his head, smiling indulgently at his daughter. "Perhaps we should let him take his chances after it gets dark."

Mr. Powell had been surprised to find a strange young man at his kitchen table when he finally returned home from his job at the Customs House. He was a burly man with a shock of white hair and kindly brown eyes that lit up as he listened to his daughter tell the tale of how Finn came to be in their house. He was clearly proud of her desire to help, but Finn could see what Dora meant about him being an armchair rebel. Mr. Powell didn't seem like the type of person to take risks; he was a talker, not a doer. Another man might have put forth some ideas and tried to be of help, but Mr. Powell was reluctant to participate, shooting down Dora's ideas with doubts. He likely wouldn't betray Finn to the British, but he would be grateful if Finn just departed quietly and left them to their supper.

"Thank you, Dora, but your father is right. I'll just leave by the back door and keep to the shadows. I'll be all right." He probably wouldn't be, but he didn't want to burden the Powells with his troubles. Dora had helped him enough, and he had no desire to put her or her father in any danger. Mr. Powell might be a patriot at heart, but that didn't mean he was ready to be taken into custody, questioned, and possibly thrown into prison for aiding Finn.

Dora turned to her father, all fury. "How can you say that? You know they will arrest him, and possibly hang him. Can you live with that, Father? You are always saying how you wish you were twenty years younger so that you could join the Continental Army. Well, this is your chance. We are not sending him out there to be captured."

Her eyes were full of accusation as she faced down her father, who had the decency to look shamefaced at her outburst. Finn had no doubt that he genuinely wanted to help, as long as it didn't put him in any danger. He was about to protest yet again that he would be all right and find his way out of town when Dora stilled, pulled back the curtain and threw open the window, hanging out nearly to her waist.

"Oh, God," she moaned. "They are going door to door. We don't have much time. Father, stall them for as long as you can if they come here. Finn, let's go." Dora grabbed Finn by the wrist and dragged him along to a room down the hall. Finn followed her obediently. She didn't lack for spirit or courage, so he hoped whatever idea she had up her sleeve would work. He didn't have too many options other than going back down to the cellar where he was sure to be found this time.

Dora led him into a feminine-looking bedroom, decorated with frilly muslin curtains and lace doilies. Finn assumed that this was Dora's room, but there was something about the room that looked forlorn and uninhabited. There was nothing out of place, and everything appeared to be preserved just so, as if to honor someone's memory. The embroidered coverlet was yellowed with age, and the curtains at the window were faded from years of facing the sun. Finn found it odd that he would notice such trivial details when faced with possible death, but it was as if time had stopped, and there was no urgency or loud British voices coming from just down the street.

"This was my mother's room," Dora remarked, noting Finn's confusion as she opened a large, carved chest at the foot of the bed and looked at the contents with a gimlet eye, her hands on her hips. She finally made a decision and pulled out some garments.

"Get undressed," she ordered, "get this on, and I will be right back." Dora tossed him a shift, petticoat, a gown in primrose yellow, a lace-edged tucker, and a pair of cotton stockings. Finn unbuttoned his coat with trembling fingers. He could hear the soldiers getting closer, banging on people's doors and demanding admittance, which was readily given. No one wanted to stand up to the occupiers and draw attention to themselves. Most of them had nothing to hide, so it was easier just to let the patrol search their house than protest their innocence and demand to see a warrant of some sort authorizing the soldiers to be there.

Finn had to admit that the girl was a genius. No one was looking for a woman, so the disguise should work, at least long enough to fool the soldiers who would be there any minute. He pulled on the stockings and shift but fumbled with the laces which were at the back of the bodice. It felt odd to have nothing on below the waist. The stockings came up mid-thigh, and the soft cotton of the shift brushed against his skin as he finally managed to secure the bodice.

Dora erupted into the room carrying a valise, cap, and a wide-brimmed straw hat. "My mother's," she explained, setting the hat on the bed and reaching for a hairbrush. "Need help?" she asked sheepishly as she watched him struggle with the tucker. She didn't wait for an answer as she deftly inserted the tucker to cover the hair on his chest and smoothed down the skirt, brushing her hand lightly over his manhood.

"There now. You're a picture," she said with satisfaction as she reached for a hairbrush.

"You are a clever girl, Dora Powell," Finn said as she wound his hair into a bun at the nape of his neck, pulled a linen cap over his head, and jammed the hat over it. Dora produced a pair of round spectacles, which must have belonged to her mother as well, and handed them to Finn. The lenses blurred his vision a little, but they did alter his appearance, enlarging his eyes and making him look like a rather bookish female.

"I think that will do. I'll put your clothes into a satchel and take it with us."

"You're somewhat lacking in the bosom department," Mr. Powell commented, "but other than that, you make a fairly handsome woman. "I have a sister who lives an hour north of Savannah. Her husband owns a rice plantation and hates King George with a passion few of us dare to show. We'll just go there. You will be able to change and spend the night before setting off for home," he said, jamming his hat onto his head and beckoning for Finn and Dora to follow him.

They were just walking out the door when the patrol finally reached the house. There were three of them, led by an officer with a ruddy complexion whose ginger hair protruded from beneath his dusty wig. He gave them a stiff bow before stating his purpose. Dora opened her mouth to protest, but Mr. Powell silenced her with a hand gesture before turning to the captain.

"You're welcome to search the house. Dora, why don't you show the soldiers around while your sister and I get the trap? We're just heading out to visit my sister, Captain," Mr. Powell explained as he took Finn by the elbow and guided him toward the stables where the horse and buggy were kept. "Do hurry. We'd like to get there before the sun goes down."

"Yes, sir. It shouldn't take more than a few minutes," the officer replied already barreling his way into the house, followed by Dora and the rest of his men. Mr. Powell moved surprisingly quickly for a man of his girth as he hitched the horse to the buggy, checked the straps, and led the horse out of the stable, closing the door firmly behind him.

Finn climbed onto the bench next to Mr. Powell, feeling very conscious of his pant-less state. He was awfully warm too. There were too many layers of fabric between him and the cooling breeze of the late afternoon, or maybe it was just nerves, but his forehead was covered with a sheen of sweat under the wide brim of the hat. The wait was agonizing, but the patrol finally moved next door and Dora climbed into the back, holding the satchel with his clothes. She put a few of her own things on top, just in case the bag was searched. If anyone asked, the men's clothes were her father's despite being a few sizes too small. Mr. Powell was a rotund man, wider in the middle than in the shoulders.

The streets were swarming with soldiers, stopping any man between the ages of fifteen and twenty-five and checking him against the description provided by Major Weland. Finn looked with interest as one man was hauled off for questioning, while another two were released. He couldn't believe this manhunt was all for him. He supposed the Major had the manpower to pull off this search since there was nothing currently going on in Savannah that required military attention. He tensed when he spotted the tall figure of Major Weland himself, sitting atop his horse, and barking orders to two corporals who were noticeably nervous. The search wasn't yielding results, and Major Weland was angry.

"I'll skin you alive if he slips through your fingers, do you hear me?" he bellowed, his cheeks a mottled red and spittle flying out of his mouth. "He's one, stupid, uneducated farmer boy with no military training. You find him, and you bring him to me. Is that clear, you nincompoops? He couldn't have left the city, so it stands to reason that he's still here and looking for a way out—like a rat. Find him!"

"I take great offense at that description," Finn mumbled, making Dora giggle.

Major Weland stopped yelling as the buggy pulled closer, his eyes fixated on the occupants. He bowed stiffly, raising his hand to his hat. "Ladies." Dora looked at her lap for fear that Major Weland would recognize her from that afternoon, but Finn smiled demurely, giving the Major a ladylike wave as the buggy rolled past him. Mr. Powell was sweating profusely as he greeted the Major, eager to be on his way.

"You look awfully nervous, sir," the Major called out to Mr. Powell. "Do stop a moment." Mr. Powell reined in the horses, his breathing ragged with fear.

"My good man, you have no reason to fear for your safety, or that of your daughters. This man is dangerous, but he means no harm to civilians, I assure you, and he will be dealt with the utmost severity once he's caught, which I promise you he will be. He will not escape me a second time. He will hang, and soon."

Dora gasped, fanning herself with her hand, her eyes growing round and frightened and Mr. Powell turned to comfort her. "You've frightened my daughter, sir," Mr. Powell growled, suddenly enjoying himself. "What type of gentleman says such things in front of an innocent young girl? Why, I should report you to your superior officer. I think we'll be on our way now, if you don't mind."

Mr. Powell stared down a shamefaced Major Weland, the look on his face one of pure disgust. Finn might have found all of this immensely entertaining had his heart not been beating wildly, his stomach cramping, and a telltale tickle doing its level best to close his throat, making him feel as if he would choke if he didn't cough. He covered his mouth with a gloved hand and coughed into his fist, effectively averting his eyes from the Major as they drove past.

"My sincere apologies, ladies," Major Weland called after them, his tricorn in his hand.

"I certainly hope so," Mr. Powell tossed back over his shoulder, urging the horse into a trot as they headed to the outskirts of the city.

"Well done, Mr. Powell," Finn said, clapping the older man on the shoulder. "Well done."

"I must admit, I rather enjoyed that," the older man said, grinning from ear to ear. "Did you see the look on his face?" Mr. Powell giggled like a girl, making Finn and Dora smile as they exchanged glances.

"You were very brave, Pa," Dora said with a small smile as her father squared his shoulders and puffed out his chest with her praise. Finn let out a long breath and squeezed Dora's hand in gratitude. She'd pulled it off. They could use more people like Dora working for the cause.

TWENTY

The drive to Mr. Powell's sister's plantation was uneventful and Finn allowed himself to relax a little as he leaned against the back of the bench and closed his eyes. He was getting a headache from the unfamiliar glasses that distorted his vision, and the tight bodice was squeezing the life out of him. It would be nice to finally change back into his own clothes. Mr. Powell had been talkative before, but now he settled into silence, a dreamy look on his face. Finn turned to look at Dora. She was sitting in the back of the trap, her knees drawn up to her chest and a look of such profound sadness on her face that Finn sucked in his breath in surprise.

"Are you all right?" he asked, but Dora just nodded and turned away, unwilling to talk. Had he done something to upset her? Finn sighed and looked around. The countryside was bathed in the last rays of the southern sunset. Blood-red arrows of the setting sun painted the clouds in bold shades of crimson, while the sky turned a deep lavender as the encroaching evening slowly leached the remaining daylight in preparation for night. The road was flanked by live oaks, moss draping the branches and making them appear ghostly in the gathering darkness. The moss swayed in the gentle evening breeze, giving the impression that the trees were indeed alive and moving.

Finn sat up straighter when he heard something on the wind. It was guttural and mournful and accompanied by something like the beating of a distant drum.

"What's that?" he asked Mr. Powell, who looked toward the sound as well.

"Oh, that's just the slaves singing as they sit around their cooking fires," Mr. Powell replied, shifting uncomfortably in his seat. Finn couldn't make out the words, but in his heart, he knew what the song was about. It was a lament for a different life, a longing for home, and a prayer for loved ones left behind, never to be seen again. He suddenly understood why Mr. Mallory refused to own slaves. No human being should own another, even if the law sanctioned it, Finn thought in disgust. His mother told him that slavery had been long abolished in her time and he wished he could see the future with his own eyes and live in a time when people were free and unafraid.

His thoughts were interrupted by the appearance of the manor house at the end of the lane. It was grand by colonial standards, the white columns gleaming in the light of the rising moon and the tall windows alight with the warm glow of candles. Finn suddenly wished he could say his goodbyes and head home, but it would be rude to desert the Powells after they'd saved his life. Besides, he was awfully tired. He'd spend the night and leave tomorrow.

TWENTY-ONE

Finn tried not to gape like a country dolt as he was ushered into the foyer by Mr. Powell and Dora. He'd never seen such grandeur in his life, much less in a colony that was relatively young. His slippered feet sank into the soft carpet and a chandelier with at least thirty candles glowed overhead, the candlelight casting eerie shadows onto the walls upholstered in pastels. Elegant furniture carved with whimsical patterns graced the spacious rooms, and the woman who came out to greet them looked more like a confection of some sort than a plantation owner's wife. Finn could hear snippets of conversation and laughter coming from what he presumed to be the dining room, and several Negro slaves came and went on their way to the kitchen.

"Edgar, what a surprise!" the woman exclaimed, smiling with delight. "Jeb and I were just entertaining two of his associates and their wives, but you are most welcome to join us. You must be hungry." She tore her eyes away from her brother and snuck at peak at Finn. "And who is this charming young lady? I don't believe we've met. I'm Amy Talbot."

"Finlay Whitfield," Finn stammered, feeling like a complete fool.

"A pleasure to meet you, Miss Whitfield," Mrs. Talbot answered, despite the confusion in her eyes.

"Amy dear, Mr. Whitfield needs a place to change his clothes before he can join your little party," Mr. Powell stated, his face shining with glee. "We've quite a story to tell, don't we, Dora?" Dora nodded and smiled at her aunt. "Where are the children?"

"They're in bed where they should be, the little rascals. Ran me ragged today," Amy Talbot said, still glancing at Finn from beneath her lashes. "Ah, Mr. Whitfield, if you'll follow me," she suggested, leading Finn to a room off the main corridor. "I'll have Mamie bring you some hot water, shall I?"

"Thank you, ma'am," Finn mumbled as he snatched the valise with his clothes from Dora's hand and entered the room. He'd never felt so humiliated in his life, but he was alive and far from the clutches of Major Weland, which was all that mattered at the moment. The embarrassment would pass, but not if Mr. Powell had anything to say about it. Finn could tell he was bursting to tell the story, eager to be praised for his bravery and quick thinking.

A young Negro woman shyly entered the room, setting a pitcher of hot water and an ewer on the little table with spindly legs that stood in the corner. It was a sitting room of some sort, furnished with an upholstered settee and several chairs that stood clustered around a round table. Finn wished he could just lie down and sleep till morning, but that was not to be. He was about to be the source of entertainment at a supper party. Well, at least he'd eat. He was starving, and very thirsty.

* * *

The dining room was ablaze with light, an even larger chandelier hanging just over the center of the table laden with real porcelain, crystal, and silverware. Finn's mouth watered as he took in the roast beef, in pride of place on a large platter, surrounded by small potatoes and other vegetables. There was a bowl of greens, some kind of creamed corn, and squares of cornbread, which filled the room with their sweet aroma. Finn was introduced all around and shown to his seat, where the same young woman who brought the water instantly piled his plate with a little of everything and poured him a glass of wine from a crystal carafe. The blood-red liquid reflected the light of the candles and cast a mauve shadow onto the snowy tablecloth.

Finn gave Mamie a grateful smile before tucking into the food. They never ate like this at home. Mrs. Mallory made mostly stews, which was the easiest way to feed such a large family. A stew could be made with anything that was to hand, in addition to some sort of meat. She threw in barley, parsnips, carrots and onions, leftover bacon, and sometimes even pieces of stale bread to increase the quantity and make it last longer. Roast beef was a luxury the Mallorys could seldom afford. Finn took a bite. The meat was so tender it melted in his mouth, especially when washed down with the wine, which had a delicate flavor Finn wasn't used to.

Mr. Powell was already telling the story of how Finn came to be at his house, the other guests making appropriate noises of shock and sympathy. Dora seemed awfully quiet as she picked at her food, her large eyes never leaving Finn's face. She'd been terribly sad since they left the outskirts of Savannah, unlike her father, who was relishing the adventure and embellishing the story shamelessly.

"You are so brave, Dora," one of the women remarked. "I would have swooned had someone just burst into my house followed by armed soldiers. How did you know he wouldn't hurt you?" she asked, glancing at Finn.

"Oh, I knew," Dora replied, smiling at last. "I knew I had to help him as soon as I set eyes on him."

"Why is it that Major Weland holds such a grudge against you, son?" Jeb Talbot asked as he raised his wine glass to his lips, but didn't drink, waiting for Finn's answer.

Finn finished chewing and took a sip of wine to buy time. He couldn't tell these people the truth. His work for the Committee was strictly confidential and they were not to know that even now information that could change the outcome of the war was hidden in his coat. He'd told Dora before that he helped rescue someone from the gallows, so that was the story he had to stick with.

"I interfered with the Major's plans to execute a suspected spy and killed two soldiers in the process," Finn finally replied, knowing this would only raise more questions.

"A spy?" Mrs. Talbot exclaimed. "How exciting! Was he truly a spy?"

"She, and no she wasn't. She was just a girl who happened to be in the wrong place at the wrong time, but Major Weland never forgave the interference." Finn sighed, knowing these people weren't about to let it go. They were prosperous landowners, who would make peace with whoever happened to be in control of Georgia. Their loyalty was to their profit, and not to any cause, so he had to be very careful.

"Oh, my," Mrs. Talbot said, fanning herself. "A girl? They would execute a young girl for spying without proof? How beastly these British are. Was she able to get away?"

"Yes, ma'am, the young lady in question is safe," Finn said, his voice flat. He wasn't going to answer any more questions about the incident for fear of giving himself away. "Please, tell me about your plantation," he urged, to change the subject. "Do you own many slaves?" Finn hated to ask, but he knew that no other question would shift the focus of the conversation as this one would. Jeb Talbot put down his wine glass, his chest swelling with pride as he launched into a description of his assets and operations. Finn learned more about rice than he ever hoped to know, but he'd accomplished exactly what he meant to. His escapade was forgotten for the moment as attention shifted to other things.

The kitchen slaves silently cleared the table and brought out pots of coffee and dessert. Finn was stuffed, but he couldn't pass up on the lovely concoction made with stewed peaches and sprinkled with slivered almonds. The combination of sweet peaches and buttery crust paired with crunchy nuts was the most delicious thing Finn had ever tasted, and he gratefully accepted a second helping, glad that the men were still talking about growing rice and keeping slaves in line and thus distracted from questioning him.

TWENTY-TWO

Finn threw open the window, letting in the fragrant southern air perfumed with flowers and the scent of freshly cut grass. The night was alive with the sound of crickets and other insects and he fancied he could hear singing from the slave quarters, but it was probably just his imagination. It was well past midnight, and everyone was asleep, the house silent and still. He needed to get some rest, for he had a long journey ahead of him tomorrow, but although he was physically tired, his mind refused to settle. Thoughts tumbled over each other, colliding and spinning in his tired brain, refusing to let him be. Had Dora Powell not chosen to help him, this could have been his last night on earth as the British preferred to execute people the morning after their arrest.

At this very moment, he could have been locked up in some cell, awaiting death and praying that his family would at least find out what happened to him and not think that he simply vanished. They wouldn't even have a body to bury, or a grave to visit. The thought of never seeing Abbie and their daughter nearly made Finn cry as he tossed and turned, unable to find a comfortable position.

He hated to admit it, but Abbie had been right to worry. An unexpected twist of fate was all it took to make him realize that. He was just a puppet whose strings were being manipulated as he went about his business, never knowing if this day or the next could be his last. What were the chances of Major Weland being in Savannah and actually walking down the street where Finn happened to be? And what was the likelihood of him bursting into the house of a girl who was willing to risk everything to help him? God had spared him and Abbie in New York, and now he had spared him once again, but eventually his luck would run out. He wanted to survive this war. He wanted to live in peace and plan a future for himself and his girls without the constant shadow of war hanging over them. Two more years, he thought, two more years.

Finn's feverish thoughts were interrupted by the turning of the door handle. The door opened slowly and the ghostly shape of Dora in a flowing white nightdress appeared on the threshold. She closed the door softly behind her and tiptoed to the bed on silent feet, her breathing ragged in the silence of the room. Finn closed his eyes pretending to be asleep in the hope that Dora would leave, but she reached out and gently touched his face, her finger lingering on his bottom lip. She sat down on the side of the bed and laid her head on his chest, listening to his heartbeat as Abbie sometimes did after they made love.

Finn wasn't sure what to say, so he remained quiet, letting Dora stay where she was. He owed her his life, so the least he could do was be mindful of her feelings. She seemed to be crying, so he wrapped his arms around her and let her cry in peace until the little storm of emotion passed.

"I don't want you to go," Dora whispered as she finally raised her face to his, her lips only a few inches from his own.

"I have to go home. I have a family waiting for me."

"Who was the girl you rescued?" Dora suddenly asked.

"She was my wife."

"My mother always said that when the time was right, my intended would walk into my life," Dora whispered. Her voice was shaky as she tried to hold back the tears.

"And he will, you'll see, but I'm not your intended. I'm married already."

"Do you love her?" Dora was watching him in the darkness, her eyes reflecting the feeble light of the moon and making her look slightly possessed.

"Yes," Finn said simply.

"Then she's the luckiest woman on earth," Dora said.

"I think she knows that," Finn replied with an impish grin.

"And you will be lucky too. I just know it." Dora nodded.

"I'm sorry. I didn't mean to embarrass you," she said as she made to rise from the bed.

"You didn't. What man isn't flattered by the attentions of a beautiful girl, especially one as brave and selfless as you are?" He wanted to make her feel better, but he meant every word. Dora suddenly leaned forward and kissed him full on the mouth. Her lips were warm and soft and tasted of the peach dessert.

"Just something to remember you by," she giggled as she stood up and moved toward the door. "Goodbye, Finn. I will remember you always."

"And I you," said Finn, and meant it.

TWENTY-THREE
WILLIAMSBURG, VIRGINIA JULY 2010

Valerie glanced up at the gathering clouds, eager for rain. It had been sunny only a half hour ago, but now the gunmetal sky seemed to hang lower, the clouds turning a threatening shade of aubergine as a flash of lightning split the sky, warning the swarms of tourists of an imminent downpour. The vendors selling tricorns, mob caps, and rolled-up Declarations of Independence began to cover their wares just in case the heavens opened up, and the throngs of tourists began to thin as they headed toward the parking areas eager to get to their cars before the rain came down.

The past few days had been stifling, Valerie's newly bought summer clothes doing little to keep her cool. She was wearing fewer layers, but she was somehow hotter and more irritable, and felt strangely exposed despite the fact that most people were dressed in a similar fashion. Years of living in the seventeenth century left her more aware of modesty and propriety, something she'd paid very little attention to when she lived in the twenty-first century.

Alec seemed oblivious to the weather as he strolled down the street, looking at the replicas of storefronts and inns lining the Duke of Gloucester Street, his gaze searching for the inn where they'd stayed while looking for Finn several years ago. So much had happened to them in Williamsburg, but this display, although accurate, did little justice to the real thing. It all appeared so forced, so staged.

Alec shook his head as they neared the Capitol building. It had seemed so grand in the seventeenth century, but now it appeared quaint rather than imposing, the sentry standing guard looking bored and tired. Alec turned on his heel and took Valerie by the arm, leading her back toward Merchant's Square. Fat drops of rain began to come down, mixing with the dry dirt of the road and quickly turning into mud. Parents grabbed their children and ran for cover just as thunder boomed loudly over their heads and a little boy screamed in terror as lightning flashed again, much closer this time.

Valerie scampered after Alec as she tried to keep up, but she didn't care if she got wet. She was hot and frustrated, her guts twisting with misery as she looked around Colonial Williamsburg and felt a tearing pain in her heart at the knowledge that this might be the closest they could get to the past. They'd spent countless hours going over every option, every idea, no matter how far-fetched, but had come up with nothing of value, nothing that got them closer to a plan.

Alec kept his emotions under tight control, but Valerie cried herself to sleep, her heart breaking at the thought of being torn from the people she loved. How long could they stay here? What could they do? Eventually, the money would run out, and they would have to decide how to proceed and where to make a home for themselves. Alec would be no better than an illegal immigrant, with no status, identification, or chance at any decent employment. They'd gone over it a million times, but still hadn't come up with anything useful. They were trapped, existing on two different planes, their life torn to shreds by her carelessness.

* * *

Valerie used a napkin to wipe the rainwater off her face as she watched the rain run in rivulets down the not-so-clean window of a small pizzeria they'd found on a side street. She was huddled in a booth, her legs sticking to the plastic bench and her skin covered with goose bumps as the arctic blast of the air conditioner hit her wet T-shirt and damp hair. Alec slid in opposite her, pushing a slice of pizza and a can of Coke in her direction, his expression strangely serene despite their visit to Colonial Williamsburg.

Valerie expected him to be as torn up as she was, but he just happily bit into his pizza, a faraway look in his eyes as he gazed out the window. She knew she should probably make some attempt at conversation, but she couldn't bring herself to make small talk when she felt as if her whole life was falling apart, everything dear to her getting further and further away with every passing day. Every time she thought of home, she wanted to howl with misery, especially when she imagined little Tom, who was probably missing them and crying for Grandma and Grandpa. Louisa was probably frantic as well, imagining all kinds of horrible scenarios in which Alec was on his deathbed, diagnosed with stomach cancer or something equally terminal.

Alec had stopped chewing and was looking intently at the two old men playing a game of chess in the corner. They were staring at the board as if the pieces would come to life and start planning their strategy, moving and battling like real men, not pieces of plastic moved around the board by players. One of the men exclaimed in disgust as the other took his queen, then took a long pull of his beer to take some of the sting out of his loss.

"Where is Princeton?" Alec suddenly asked, his eyes alight with something Valerie couldn't understand.

"It's in New Jersey. Why do you ask?" Alec asked her random questions all the time. Despite their predicament, he was fascinated with everything he saw and wanted to learn as much as possible, even if the information had no bearing on anything relevant.

"No reason," Alec answered cryptically. "Would you like to come with me to the library? There's something I'd like to check." He had that look on his face, the kind he got when he tried to plan some kind of surprise for her but couldn't keep the glee out of his eyes. What had he seen that suddenly gave him hope? He was already halfway out of his seat, eager to get going.

"Alec, I'm not going anywhere until you tell me what this is all about." Valerie crossed her arms and stared him down, willing him to sit back down and explain.

"Val, I don't want to give you false hope," he said quietly, but took a seat and clasped his hands in front of him as if he were trying to contain his excitement.

"At this point, false hope is better than no hope, so please tell me what's on your mind."

"Mr. Taylor loves to play chess," Alex announced out of the blue, a gleeful smile playing about his lips.

"So?"

"So, he's very competitive and loves to distract his opponent by chatting about this and that. It usually works too, because he wins most of the time."

"So?"

"So, we've had lots of conversations about his time at university and how he first came to be interested in time travel. He tried to explain to me how it all works." Alec looked very pleased with himself, but Valerie just moaned with disappointment.

"Are you going to build a time travel-device? Alec, this isn't *Star Trek*; this is real life. You know nothing about physics."

"Oh, ye of little faith," Alec retorted with a smile, "I have no intention of building anything. I've just figured out how to use the TV remote, I'm hardly qualified to build a time-travel device. However, Mr. Taylor did not work alone. He had a partner, a man named Isaac Bloom."

"Who is either dead by now or living in England where we can't get to him," Valerie grumbled as she looked at her ever-optimistic husband.

"Mr. Bloom may be dead, but he isn't in England. He immigrated to the United States in the 1970s and took a teaching post at Princeton University. Now, let's go to the library and Google our Mr. Bloom. If he's still alive, he might be able to help us."

"Oh, Alec, that's genius," Valerie exclaimed, "pure genius. I hope the man is in very fine health and still living in New Jersey. Come, let's go."

The library was pleasantly cool and quiet, most computers unoccupied as it was lunchtime. A few people read quietly, while the librarian peered over her glasses at the tall man with the British accent and the woman who looked like a drowned rat with her wet hair sticking to her forehead and her damp shirt clinging to her breasts. Alec carefully lowered himself into a chair, conscious of his incision which still pained him, especially when he sat down or got out of bed.

Valerie couldn't bear to watch, so she flipped through a magazine as Alec laboriously typed with one finger, scribbling something on a notepad from time to time. They couldn't get too optimistic. Anything could have happened to the man since the '70s, and even if he were still alive and well, he might not want to help. According to Alec, Mr. Taylor and Isaac Bloom fell out and hadn't spoken in decades. Valerie lowered the magazine and looked at Alec. He didn't seem too upset, so maybe he found something worthwhile. He finally rose and came to get her, notepad in his hand.

"Mr. Isaac Bloom still teaches at Princeton University, and as it happens, just had an article published on something I don't pretend to understand, but it proves that he's still in full control of his faculties, which is very good news. How do we get to Princeton?"

"It's probably cheaper to take the bus. I don't think there's one that goes directly there, but we can take a bus to a central location, such as New York, and then take a local bus to Princeton. There must be one that goes from Port Authority. Let's check the bus schedules. We need to conserve our money, Alec. I don't want the bank to alert the authorities that I've accessed my account since I would have gone missing by now. It would give my parents something to hold on to, and I don't want them hurt any more than they already are."

"I understand. Will you be all right being in New York and not seeking them out?" Alec asked carefully.

"I can't promise anything. Now, let's check those bus timetables."

TWENTY-FOUR
MARYLAND JULY 2010

The Greyhound bus cruised down the highway, stores and gas stations whizzing by as they passed town after town on their way north. Alec sat by the window, gazing out like a little kid on his first car trip. They were somewhere near Washington D.C., the city skyline visible in the distance. Alec would have loved to stop and spend a day, but Valerie was desperate to get to New Jersey, her whole body vibrating with anxiety at what they would find once they got there.

"Why are there so many of the same stores and restaurants?" Alec asked, turning to Valerie who was trying in vain to take a nap. "I see signs for the same places every few miles."

"It's called brand recognition. People like knowing what to expect, so they go to the same places."

"That sounds rather dull," Alec mused. "Why would anyone want to do that?"

"I suppose it is dull, but it has its advantages. You see, say you want to buy a flat-screen TV or an iPad. Why would you go to some small local store that you have no knowledge of when you can go to Best Buy? You know that you will get a good product, great service, and a reasonable price, especially if there's a sale. If there's anything wrong with your purchase, Best Buy will take it back, no questions asked, and either give you a refund or a new product, whereas a different store might sell you something refurbished or refuse to exchange or refund."

Alec nodded his approval of this reasoning. "Yes, that makes perfect sense. What about restaurants?"

"It's the same principle, really. People like to know what they're getting, and when they go to a place they're familiar with, there are few surprises such as terrible food or bad service. It's all about expectations. Marketing is a science unto itself. People spend millions on advertising campaigns, building brand recognition and a favorable reputation."

"How marvelous," Alec replied. "Maybe Charlie and I can work on brand recognition for the cane liquor we import. We should give it a name and convince the tavern owners that our rum is better than someone else's."

Valerie burst out laughing. Alec was such an optimist. Not only did he think he was going back, but he wanted to start a rum competition between the only two taverns in Jamestown. "I love you, Alec Whitfield," she said between giggles. "You are truly a Renaissance man."

"I'm not sure what you mean by that, but I will take it as a compliment." He turned back to the window, gaping as a Maserati flew past the bus, its gleaming red body sleek and beautiful. Alec exhaled, his face full of longing. Valerie patted him on the arm in understanding. If they were stuck in the twenty-first century, maybe he would eventually learn how to drive. Getting a driver's license might be a problem, but at this point, that was the least of their worries.

She had to admit that looking for Mr. Bloom was a long shot, but at this point, they had nothing left to lose. There were no other avenues to explore. If they failed to find him, or if he refused to help, they would be back to square one, except they would now be that much closer to her family. It was the beginning of July and Louisa would likely be back from England by now, the bearer of terrible news. She supposed, at this point, her parents would still harbor hopes that Valerie would be found and returned to them, but Valerie knew better, and her heart squeezed as she thought of what they were about to go through.

To lose a child was bad enough, but to lose a child without any explanation was that much worse. There would be no clues, no body to bury, and no grief to come to terms with. Louisa said that her mom and dad lived with the hope that someday something would come to light and they would find out what happened to their beloved girl. If only she could see them and tell them the truth, but that was out of the question; she knew that. Valerie had to live with the knowledge that her parents would die in just over a year, never knowing what happened to her or finding peace in the knowledge that she was alive and well, living four hundred years before her time.

Valerie sighed and closed her eyes again. *One day at a time, she told herself. One day at a time.*

TWENTY-FIVE
VIRGINIA JULY 1626

Genevieve threw off the bedclothes in frustration, wishing she could take off her shift and lie naked on her narrow cot, but that was out of the question. She was hot and unable to settle down. The window was open and a cool evening breeze stirred the curtains and filled the small attic bedroom with a smell of grass, earth, and a slightly stagnant odor coming from the pond, but she felt as if she were on fire, either with shame or desire, she couldn't quite figure out which.

At twenty-five, she was ripe for marriage, as Uncle Alec liked to point out, but she'd never known anything that resembled attraction. She'd met plenty of men, especially since crossing the Atlantic and settling in Virginia, but none of them ever stirred any deep feelings. She had an eye for beauty and could appreciate an attractive man, but that was as far as it went. None of them ever touched her heart or made her long for a brush of the hand or a sweet kiss.

Cameron was the first man she'd ever encountered who stoked these feelings in her, making her yearn for physical contact. *Is that what married people felt for each other?* she wondered. She frequently saw signs of affection between Uncle

Alec and Aunt Valerie, and Lord and Lady Sheridan. A warm hug, a kiss, or a look of such naked intimacy that it made her blush more than any physical gesture. They loved each other, and the rest came naturally, or so she assumed. She'd always thought that married people had relations only in order to procreate, but she'd since learned that wasn't the case, as the thin walls of the house could attest. Genevieve had been embarrassed by what she heard, but Minnie just giggled, fanning herself with her hand as she rolled her eyes in mock ecstasy. "Oh, I do hope I find me a man who can make me sound like THAT!" she said on occasion, making Genevieve smile at her lack of inhibition.

Genevieve had to admit that she had been very naive before coming to live with her newfound family. She knew the basic facts, but her life had been sheltered and secure, undisturbed by anything untoward until she met her cousin Louisa. She still thought of her often, wishing that she had lived despite her many sins. Louisa couldn't help who she was any more than most people could help their own flaws. Watching her had been an education in itself. Seeing one so young so aware of her sexual attractiveness and using her feminine wiles to get what she wanted was almost a talent, one not to be discounted, especially in a time when women obeyed the men in their lives and did as they were bid, whether it be fathers or husbands. Louisa might have gotten away with her plotting had she managed to survive Tom's birth and the subsequent plague that claimed the life of the man who loved her so blindly.

Genevieve often wondered if Theo had ever realized Tom wasn't his, or had he gone to his grave believing that his wife loved him and had presented him with a son and heir, a sacrifice that cost her life? *Poor Theo*, Genevieve thought, *he didn't deserve the cruel fate that befell him*. She could rationalize God punishing Louisa for her transgressions, but why Theo? What had he done other than be loyal and loving, making a desperate attempt to save his son before succumbing to the plague and dying at twenty-one? He'd be happy to know that Tom was alive and well, as was Elsie, who'd come running to Uncle Alec with baby Tom when Theo first sickened with the plague.

Genevieve and Elsie had shared a cabin on the crossing with nothing to do but talk for hours on end during the endless days at sea and the dark nights when the ship was tossed on the waves like a toy, just barely managing not to get engulfed by the monstrous waves that pounded the hull and threatened to tear it to bits, sending them all to a watery grave. Genevieve had never been so scared, but Elsie was very matter of fact about the whole thing, her upbeat attitude a wonder considering the life she'd led. She looked younger than her years, her bouncy blonde curls and wide blue eyes at odds with the experiences that had led her into service.

Elsie made Genevieve realize that although she'd known terrible loneliness and uncertainty, she'd never known true hardship, the kind that comes of extreme poverty and hunger that gnaws at your insides day and night making you wish you were dead. Elsie had known that kind of poverty growing up in Southwark, and she told Genevieve of winter days when she'd huddled in her threadbare shawl, her teeth rattling with cold as she begged on the streets in order to feed herself and her siblings.

"But what of your parents?" Genevieve asked, shocked that children would not be cared for by their elders.

"Oh, Mam died years ago, and Da went to sea, working on a merchant vessel. It came into port from time to time, but by the time he came home, he'd spent most of his wages on drink. There wasn't enough to last for more than a few weeks. I'd take in sewing, do some cleaning, and help out at the pub to earn money, but poor people don't pay other poor people to do their dirty work, do they?" Elsie shrugged her thin shoulders as if that bit of wisdom should be obvious.

"I could have made some money whoring. There were plenty of men at the local taverns who were only too eager to pay, but I just couldn't bring myself to do it, not yet. Once you go down that road, there ain't no coming back," she announced, rolling onto her belly on her narrow berth. "I wanted the first time to be for love."

"And was it?" Genevieve asked, eager to hear the story.

"I'm not all that sure that it was love, but it felt good all the same. So handsome he was, my Bill. He was a sailor like the rest of them, and he turned my head with words of love and the money he spent on me. Other girls yearn for ribbons and trinkets, but all I wanted was food. He bought me hot pies and even got me some sweeties. Oh, they were so good I can still taste them now, melting on my tongue, sweetness filling my mouth until I thought I must be in heaven," she whispered, a smile on her face. "I meant to share some with the others, but somehow there were never any left," she confided with a guilty giggle.

"What happened to him?"

"Oh, the same thing that happens to all sailors. He got me full in the belly and left me with nothing but promises. I never saw him again. He might have tired of me, or drowned off some foreign shores, but all I know is that he never came back. I thought that'd be the end of me. I finally did some whoring then. Not like I had much to lose. I was already with child, so not like I could get pregnant twice, and I needed the money. I only took one or two a night, just enough to survive. My sister was barely eleven, and I didn't want her doing it, did I?"

Elsie sat up as Tom began fussing in his hammock, ready for a feeding. She unlaced her bodice and put Tom to her breast, holding her breath as he latched on, sucking furiously as if he hadn't eaten in days.

"What happened to your baby, Elsie?"

"Thank God he was stillborn. I couldn't manage to support another child, not without a husband. But the good Lord in his infinite wisdom gave me a way to support myself. I could now hire myself out as a wet nurse. I managed to save a little money before the babe came, so I bought a secondhand gown and shoes and went across the river to look for employment. I'd heard that fine ladies don't suckle their babies but hire other women to do it. I found a job and was able to support my brother and sister while living in the lap of luxury." She switched breasts and leaned back against the wall closing her eyes with fatigue.

"Do you know what the best thing is about being a wet nurse?" she asked, her eyes still closed as Tom continued to drain her breast. "The absolute best thing is that you always get enough to eat. You're feeding their baby, so they want you well-nourished. I got to eat hot food every day, and even got a pudding from time to time, or even a piece of fruit. It was bliss. I got to share a room with the baby, so I had my very own bed with clean sheets and a chamber pot that I didn't have to share with no one, or go out to the privy on those frigid nights when it felt like your arse might freeze as you're doing your business.

Once the baby was weaned, I got the job with Lord Carew. He was a nice man, he was, and so kind to me. He just wanted his little mite to be happy and healthy. I still say a prayer for his soul every night before I go to sleep. To lose your wife, and then die yourself within a few months—such a tragedy." Tom finally fell asleep, his mouth releasing Elsie's nipple with a pop as his eyes rolled into the back of his head, sated and drowsy. He'd need another feeding in a few hours, but for now, Elsie could get her rest.

"How long will you keep doing this?" Genevieve asked, trying not to stare at Elsie's swollen breasts, the white skin lined with blue veins that looked like rivers on a map, her nipples sore and cracked from so much nursing.

"Oh, I'll do it as long as the milk keeps coming. It's a small price to pay for living in comfort and security and knowing that my brother and sister are fed and warm. They'll be old enough to fend for themselves soon, and I must see to my own future. I hear there are lots of men in the colonies who are looking for wives. Maybe I can find a good man and suckle my own babies for a change, but until then, I hope the milk flows like a river," she mumbled as she drifted off to sleep, her bodice still open and her full breasts already starting to leak milk again.

Genevieve's mind turned back to Cameron. She wished she'd been able to talk to Elsie about him, but she'd left the plantation after Tom was weaned, taking a position with a family in Jamestown. They still saw each other from time to time, but not on a daily basis as they used to, and Genevieve missed Elsie's counsel. What would she make of her rendezvous with Cameron?

The meetings had been completely platonic until that last one when he leaned in and kissed her, turning her world upside down. She'd often envisioned being kissed by a man, but she always thought that she would pull back in revulsion. She felt anything but disgust when Cameron's lips brushed her own. She wanted more. She wanted him to pull her close, to wrap his strong arms around her, and keep kissing her until all thought fled from her mind and she felt as if she were drowning in sensation, desperate for him to continue.

Genevieve thought he shared her feelings, but his rejection had been unexpected and hurtful. She could understand his explanation, but logic wasn't strong enough to overpower her feelings. They had met two hours ago, just as darkness was settling over the plantation, and everyone was indoors finishing their supper and getting the children ready for bed. She left by the back door, heading to the pond in the hope that he'd be there. Genevieve's heart thundered in her chest when she saw a flash of white on the opposite side of the pond. Cameron was there, waiting. He smiled cautiously as she approached, his head cocked to the side and his eyes full of something that didn't look like joy. She sat down, sliding a little closer than usual and hoping for a kiss, but Cameron moved a few inches away, his face suddenly serious.

"Mistress Genevieve, I was hoping to see ye tonight, but I feel I must apologize for my behavior." He looked contrite, watching her face with apprehension.

"What do you mean?" she asked, her insides suddenly quivering with fear. He was sorry, and he'd come to tell her as much.

"I had nae right to behave as I did, and I hope I dinna offend ye." Genevieve reached out for his hand, but he drew it back, clasping his large hands in his lap. "I had nae right," he repeated.

"But I wanted you to," she whispered, shamed by her brazen admission.

"I wanted it also, but it was wrong."

"It can't be wrong if we both wanted it," Genevieve protested, trying to understand.

"I'm a slave, Mistress Genevieve. Your uncle is a kind and generous man, but I'm still his slave. I belong to him, and he can do with me as he pleases until my contract is up. And even then, I will be nothing. I will have nothing but the clothes on my back. I have naught to offer ye, and I have nae right to even speak to ye, much less dare to touch ye as a man might." He sounded angry, his breath coming fast and hard. "I have nae right," he repeated again, as if trying to convince himself.

"You are not a slave," Genevieve protested. But he was. She knew the way other plantation owners treated their men. They beat them and starved them and few of them reached the end of their indenture without their body or spirit unbroken. Uncle Alec was a good master, but in the eyes of Cameron, he was still his master.

"Why do you come and meet me then?" she asked, the hurt obvious in her voice.

"I meet ye because when I'm with ye I feel like myself again. I forget for a short time that my life is no' my own and fool myself into thinking I have a choice. Then I go back to my pallet and remember the reality of my situation, and I want to die. Master Whitfield is a saint among men, but I've been treated worse than an animal in Scotland and on the crossing, reminding me that I'm nothing and my life means nothing. My only value being the price I would fetch on the market. I'll work hard and work off my purchase price so that I can be a free man in six years."

"What will you do once you are free?" Genevieve asked, fearing the answer.

"I will work until I can earn enough money to return home."

"I thought as much," she said, rising to her feet, her heart aching with a sense of loss. "We won't be meeting again, will we?"

"I'm sorry, lass. It's no' for lack of wanting to, I can tell ye that. I'm sorry."

Genevieve nodded, not trusting herself to speak, and walked away.

TWENTY-SIX

Cameron walked back to the barracks, his pace unhurried, his mind whirling with unbidden thoughts. The lass clearly wanted him, and in his current situation, any affection or human contact was the only thing that stood between him and total withdrawal from life. Most of the men shared a camaraderie born of loneliness and a need for comfort, but he kept himself to himself, not only because of his faith, but also because friendship led to sharing, and that was about the last thing he wanted. How could he tell the other men that he'd been accused of murder and sentenced to hang, when most of them were there out of financial need, selling themselves into slavery to feed their families back home?

He would have been a dead man long ago had his father not sold everything he could get his hands on, nearly bankrupting the family, to get the sentence commuted to transport to the Colonies rather than hanging. Cameron's guts burned with fury every time he thought of that time, nearly two years ago, when his life was torn to shreds in a single moment, a moment that was burned into his heart forever, never to be forgotten or forgiven. How was it possible for a man to have so little say in his own destiny just because he was born a peasant rather than a gentleman? And Mary... his poor Mary.

Cameron suddenly stopped, sliding to the ground until he was leaning against a stout tree, and glancing up at the heavens sprinkled with stars above his head. Even the sky was different here. It was smaller somehow, a little patch of blue compared to the vast and all-encompassing sky of Scotland, where the air bracing and fresh, unlike the humid embrace of the Virginia summer. Cameron closed his eyes trying to picture the green valleys and majestic mountains rising in the distance, all under that endless sky that was reflected in every river and loch, mirroring its grandeur and making a man feel small against the awesome power of nature and a God who was supposed to be loving and kind and treat men the same whether they were farmers or lords.

Every night before he fell asleep, he tried to picture home, letting his mind roam over the fields and forests, getting a bird's-eye view of the house and outbuildings as his parents and siblings went about the daily tasks of running the farm. He could almost hear the cows lowing in the barn, and the horses neighing softly as they settled in for the night. He pictured the field of wheat, the stalks heavy with grain, ready to be harvested and ground into flour to be stored for the winter or taken to town and sold at a handsome profit. He loved the harvest and the feeling of accomplishment and completion after the last of the grain was finally harvested and golden haystacks dotted the fields looking like giant beehives, fragrant with the smell of drying grass and sun. How often had he fallen asleep in one of those stacks as a lad after a day of helping his father?

Most nights, Cameron managed to fall asleep with the smell of home in his nostrils, and not the noxious odors of men who rarely bathed and shared a small space with only a tiny window for ventilation, but some nights, Mary's face would swim before him, her cornflower-blue eyes gazing into his own, her dimples deepening as she smiled at the sight of him, happy to have him all to herself at last. He remembered pulling off her cap and wrapping a silky curl around his finger, yanking gently so that her face came closer to his, her eyes closing in expectation of a kiss.

How sweet those moments had been, and how much sweeter still had he known what was about to happen. She had so nearly been his bride, but instead, she'd been buried in her wedding finery since her shroud hadn't been ready. Most women started working on their shroud once they got married, but Mary never got the chance. She was still a maid, eager for life to begin with her beloved Cameron and her body to swell with new life, which would combine the best of them and make them into a family.

The priest had called Mary gregarious at the funeral, which Cameron thought a bit of an insult, but now that he thought of it, he supposed she had been. Mary had always been quick to talk and to laugh, to give a needed hug or a word of comfort. She'd been his exact opposite, laughing at his taciturn nature and teasing him mercilessly. He hadn't minded; he liked her teasing. It meant she loved him. He supposed he was taciturn when he had no reason to be.

Life had been grand, but now it was nothing but a game of survival, the putting of one foot in front of the other until night finally came and he sank into fevered dreams, fragmented images of home and Mary often shattered by the memory of her face as it stilled in death. Her blue eyes had reflected the clouds floating overhead, but no longer seeing them, her neck broken and bloodied, her small hand on her breast as if she were protecting her heart. Cameron would wake up with a start, tears of anger and loss sliding down his cheeks until he got hold of himself and lay quietly until dawn finally came and it was time to leave his bed and go get his breakfast before going out into the fields for another day's work. He didn't mind the work. At least it kept him busy and left him tired enough to fall asleep quickly and get some rest before the dreams came again.

TWENTY-SEVEN

The sun was beating down mercilessly, the earth parched and desperate for rain after several weeks of hot, dry weather. Louisa walked slowly from the springhouse where she'd gone to fetch a can of buttermilk for the children's midday meal, sparing Minnie the trip. Minnie had her hands full with helping Cook prepare lunch for the adults while shepherding the children into the kitchen for their own meal and keeping the peace.

Louisa didn't mind having the kids eat at their table, but the men thought it was the height of impropriety to have children under a certain age eating with the adults and chattering incessantly the way they did all through the meal. They were used to different ways, but she had to concede since this was their time and not hers. In truth, it was nice to have some peace while they ate since the children ran amok for most of the day, being too young for schooling or chores. The house was always filled with the sound of running feet and laughter, which was a blessing on some days and a headache on others, like today when she was suffering from a terrible migraine brought on by her worry for Alec and Valerie. What she wouldn't give for an Aspirin right about now, or even a pair of sunglasses to keep the blazing sun out of her eyes.

Louisa put a hand to her eyes to shield them from the sun as a cloud of dust appeared on the horizon signaling a visitor. The tubby figure of Aloysius Deverell swayed dangerously astride a horse as it galloped at breakneck speed toward Rosewood Manor. *What does he want?* she thought irritably, subconsciously pulling up her bodice to cover more of her bosom. Perhaps he wanted to see Kit, so she would just make herself scarce. She'd bring the buttermilk to the kitchen and then go lie down for a few minutes before lunch. It would be bliss to close the shutters and lie undisturbed in the dim coolness of the room. But, as lady of the house, it was rude to walk away from a visitor she'd clearly seen. Deverell had seen her as well, his pudgy hand raised in greeting as he slowed down to a trot and cantered into the yard, sliding off the horse with all the grace of a sack of potatoes. He bowed to Louisa before wiping the perspiration off his face with his gloved hand and asking after her health, his eyes gliding over her breasts and hips. *Insolent bastard*, Louisa spat out mentally, before forcing her lips into a smile of welcome and inviting him into the house.

"Do make yourself comfortable, Mr. Deverell. Would you care for some refreshment?" she asked through clenched teeth.

"You are very gracious, Lady Sheridan. I wouldn't say no to a cool drink," he replied as he settled into a chair, fanning himself with his hat. "Hot as hell out there," he puffed, smiling at his own wit. "Is Lord Sheridan about, my dear lady? I'd like a quick word."

"Was he expecting you?" Louisa asked, hoping the man realized he wasn't welcome to drop in whenever he felt the urge. There was something about him that made her flesh crawl, and it wasn't the lascivious look in his eyes. It was something else, something she couldn't put her finger on.

Louisa was rescued from any further dealings with Deverell

when Kit strode in, surprised to see their uninvited guest. He plastered a smile on his face and bowed to Deverell but remained standing to indicate that the visit would be brief and businesslike. Deverell threw back a cup of ale provided by Minnie and rose laboriously to his feet.

"My dear Lord Sheridan, what a pleasure it is to see you again. I was hoping for a private word. A stroll outside perhaps?"

A stroll outside was the last thing Deverell needed, considering that his face was already beet-red and his coat was stained with sweat stains, but he obviously wanted to speak to Kit in private, which was just as well since it gave Louisa a chance to escape. She bid Deverell a good day and fled to her bedroom, her head beating like an Indian drum calling the braves to war. Louisa didn't even bother to speak to Annabel as she came down the stairs with her sewing basket, heading for her favorite spot by the parlor window.

* * *

Kit nodded and led the way outside. He tried hard to conceal his irritation at finding Deverell in the parlor, but he could hardly ask the man to leave. After all, he couldn't help being an arse any more than Kit could stop being civil. His courtly manners prevailed, and he smiled at Deverell, inviting him to speak. "What can I do for you, Aloysius?"

Deverell didn't answer right away but kept walking away from the house toward the pond, glancing back from time to time to make sure they were far enough away, before finally broaching the subject that brought him all the way to Rosewood Manor.

"I wanted to speak to you regarding a property I found yesterday." Deverell was watching Kit as if expecting him to say something, but Kit remained silent, waiting to see exactly what it was Deverell wanted with him.

"Christopher... May I call you Christopher?" he asked, not waiting for a reply. "I found a suitable property not an hour from here, with a manor house and barracks for the workers already in place. It's a thriving concern, but the owner wishes to return to England and wants to sell up quickly. I think I'd rather like to buy it." Aloysius wet his lips and glanced at Kit, his eyes twinkling.

"If you think the man is naming a fair price, then you should seize the opportunity and make an offer," Kit replied, wondering what Deverell expected him to say. Maybe he simply wanted some advice from someone who knew something of growing tobacco and supervising a large number of workers. Kit suddenly felt ashamed of himself for being uncharitable. The man simply wanted counsel, being new to Virginia and the ways of tobacco growing, and here he was acting like a total cad and wanting to get rid of him.

"Well, I'd like to, but that rather depends on you," Deverell stated, his piggy eyes never leaving Kit's face.

"In what way?" Kit felt a sinking feeling in the pit of his stomach, all thoughts of contrition forgotten. This didn't bode well, and he was just waiting for this nasty little man to spring his trap.

"I seem to be somewhat short of funds, dear boy, and I thought you might make up the difference, about seventy-five percent of the purchase price, I'd say." Deverell stepped back slightly, probably afraid Kit would strike him, but Kit remained calm, watching him intently.

"And how did you arrive at this conclusion?" he asked, smiling pleasantly.

"It seems to me that there are a few people in this colony who would be very interested to learn about the nature of your relationship with Buckingham, including your dear wife, and I would be happy to enlighten them should you fail to meet my demands."

"Blackmail is a dangerous game, Deverell," Kit stated, his voice flat and expressionless.

"Are you threatening me?" Deverell squeaked. He was even redder in the face than before, his mouth slack with shock.

"You are threatening me, are you not? Why shouldn't I do the same? Two can play this game."

"I have prepared a document which is in the keeping of my wife, stating that if anything should happen to me, you are responsible. You will hang. So, either you help me buy the plantation and we keep this business between us, or everyone finds out what I know." He was sweating profusely, his cheeks glistening in the hot sun, sweat stains clearly visible under his arms and down his back.

"What is it that you claim to know?" Kit asked, keeping his voice calm and mentally forbidding himself from beating this heap of dung to a pulp.

"I know that Buckingham is a sodomite, and so are you. You welcomed his advances and willingly went to his bed, where he buggered you, and you most likely buggered him. Should I continue?" When Kit didn't say anything, Deverell went on, strolling back toward the house and his horse should he need to make a hasty exit.

"Buckingham's manservant is related to one of my own, and he saw you two together, you disgusting degenerate. Does your wife know about that? I wager she'd be interested to find out about her husband, the father of her children, as would Sir George Yeardley and the rest of Jamestown society. Do they hang people for sodomy, I wonder?" he asked pleasantly as if asking if they'd have fine weather tomorrow.

They were now closer to the house, the sound of shrieking children spilling from the windows, and Cook's shrill voice ordering them to be quiet. Kit had to raise his voice to be heard over the ruckus, "You have two minutes to walk back to your horse and get off my property. If I still find you here at that time, I will horsewhip you until you are one big, bloody, pulpy mess that no one will recognize, and then I will throw you into the harbor and let the fish have a feast the likes of which they've never known. Is that clear?"

Deverell was already running for his horse, his curses flying through the air to land on deaf ears. Kit couldn't hear him over the blood roaring in his ears and the fear coursing through his veins. The man had the power to destroy everything he held dear, but he would not, WOULD NOT, give in to blackmail. He would just have to hope that people wouldn't believe Deverell and weigh Kit's character against that of the odious little man who chose to spread such vicious gossip, true though it may be. Although, if people loved anything as much as a good hanging, it was juicy gossip, be it true or not.

Kit trotted back to the pond where he tore off his clothes and jumped in, needing to cool off, both mentally and physically.

TWENTY-EIGHT

Louisa opened her eyes and looked around in confusion. The room was nearly dark, the house strangely quiet, and her headache finally at bay. She walked to the window and threw open the shutters, surprised to see the slanted shadows of late afternoon painting the meadow and the outbuildings in a golden haze that would soon give way to twilight. She must have fallen asleep and missed lunch, a fact that her stomach attested to as it growled in protest. She'd just go down to the kitchen and grab something before going to find Kit and the children. She wondered briefly what Deverell wanted, but it probably wasn't important.

"Where's everyone?" Louisa asked Cook as she sauntered into the kitchen and reached for a fresh roll. Cook was busy shelling peas, her face red from the heat and her cap pushed back from her face to reveal her graying hair. She smiled at Louisa and pushed a crock of butter toward her. Louisa slid onto the bench across from Cook, buttered her roll, poured herself a glass of buttermilk, and took a grateful sip. She wasn't a big fan of buttermilk, but it was cool and fresh, and her throat was parched from the heat and lack of hydration.

"Master Charles and Mistress Annabel went into Jamestown, and Miss Jenny took the kids to the woods for a walk. Lord Sheridan left just after luncheon. He didn't appear to be in good spirits, if I may say so."

"Where did he go?" Louisa asked, her roll forgotten.

"He didn't say, but he promised to be back in time for supper." Cook smiled warmly at Louisa. "You look flushed, my dear. Perhaps a walk would do you good."

Louisa crammed the rest of the roll into her mouth and rose to leave. Barbara was the closest thing she and Valerie had to a mother and she felt great affection for the woman. She was quiet and unassuming, but her devotion to them was unmistakable. "Why don't you go visit Fred? I know he'd relish a game of chess."

"That sounds like a very good idea," Louisa replied. She was in no mood to play games, but she wanted a chat with Mr. Taylor. Something had been gnawing at her and she hoped that he would put her mind at ease. Of course, he had no way of knowing for sure, but maybe he could soothe her. He was in truth a very comforting man when he wasn't sending people hurtling through time.

Mr. Taylor was puttering in the small herb garden situated beneath the front window of the cottage. The house itself consisted of one room that was divided into a sort of parlor and separated by a curtain that led to the sleeping quarters, but it was enough for him and his wife. Barbara spent most of her time at the big house, and Fred found ways to keep himself occupied, mostly outdoors. He loved taking long walks and foraging in the forest for useful plants and edibles. Strings of mushrooms hung beneath the ceiling. They would be dried and used in the winter to make soups and stews. And several jars of jam stood on the shelf, ready to provide much-needed vitamins in the winter months.

Fred washed his hands and poured a cup of cider for

himself and Louisa before taking a seat and reaching for the chessboard. "Would you care for a game?" He was already arranging pieces on the board, but Louisa shook her head.

"I'm sorry, Fred, but my mind is not on games right now. I want to talk to you about Valerie and Alec. They've been gone for an awfully long time now, and I'm worried. What could be keeping them?" She watched in silence as Mr. Taylor put away the board and sat down across from her, his brow creased in thought. She knew he wouldn't want to feed into her fears, but Fred Taylor wasn't the sort of man who would tell you what you wanted to hear simply to make you feel better. He believed in being honest and facing a problem head on, rather than indulging in denial and speculation.

He sighed and faced Louisa across the table, his eyes full of compassion. "The obvious answer would be that Alec was more ill than we realized. Maybe he needed to stay at the hospital longer, or perhaps there were some complications or a devastating diagnosis." Louisa knew he was referring to cancer and the thought brought tears to her eyes. Fred took her hand in his and made her look at him.

"The other explanation is that something is wrong with the device, but that's unlikely. Unless they stepped on it, or got their wrist caught in a door, the watch should work. It has a lithium battery that's good for years." Mr. Taylor gave Louisa his most reassuring look, but she dissolved into tears, days of worry and his suggestion that Alec might be dying finally taking their toll.

"What if they decided to stay?" she whispered, voicing her worst fear. Fred Taylor drew Louisa into a fatherly hug, stroking her head and shushing her. "Louisa, Valerie would never, ever leave you behind. You know that, and so do I. They will come back; you'll see. Nothing short of some unimaginable disaster would keep them away. Now stop your crying and give me a game of chess. I need a worthy opponent and you need something to take your mind off things. Barbara won't be home for some time yet, so we have a few hours of peace in which to battle each other."

Louisa gave Mr. Taylor a weak smile, nodding in agreement. "All right. I suppose I needed to hear it from a rational person who has knowledge of time travel and my sister. Oh, I do hope you are right, Fred. Life without Alec and Valerie is too empty to contemplate. Besides, they would never leave Tom behind. They dote on him. And even if Alec is gravely ill, he'd still want to come home."

"Precisely. Now, stop fretting and let's play. White or black?"

TWENTY-NINE

After a few days had gone by with no further threats from Deverell, Kit allowed himself to relax a little. Maybe the pathetic little maggot had merely been testing him in the hope that he'd bite and pay him for his silence. Perhaps he'd lost his nerve after Kit's threat, knowing that Kit was a man of his word. Kit had no intention of causing Deverell bodily harm, but if need be, he'd find a way to shut him up. Everyone had secrets and Deverell was no exception. He just had to wheedle something out of his wife. The woman was mousy and prim, but Kit had seen a glimmer of hatred when she looked at her husband, so maybe if handled properly, she could become an ally.

Kit hated even thinking along those lines, but he had to be ready in case something happened. Of course, it didn't make sense for Deverell to simply divulge what he knew. He would hurt Kit and his family, but he wouldn't profit from it, which was the whole point of the initial threat. He'd most likely try some other tactic before either giving up altogether or doing something underhanded to show Kit that he wasn't in the business of making idle threats.

Funny how you could be thousands of miles away from

court and still find yourself embroiled in blackmail and intrigue, as if the lavish chambers and shadowy passages of the palace were right here in Jamestown, the courtiers buzzing with the latest gossip and gleefully orchestrating someone's downfall. How he hated the whole thing. Life in Virginia had been so much simpler, until now.

Deverell be damned, Kit thought bitterly as he slapped the shaft of his boot with his riding crop without even realizing he was doing it, until he missed the shaft and hit his thigh instead, the sudden pain bringing him to his senses. He wouldn't give Deverell the satisfaction of working himself into a lather over his threats, especially when there were other things to worry about, like Alec and Valerie. He kept telling Louisa they would turn up any day now, but his anxiety was escalating. Something must have gone terribly wrong to keep them away this long.

What if Alec was gravely ill and there was no one there to comfort Valerie or help her care for him? He wished Louisa had gone with them. He'd hate to be away from her, but at least Valerie wouldn't be alone. Genevieve and Annabel would see to the children, and he knew Louisa would never think of staying in the future when her children were in the past. He would have suggested it, had he been there when the decision was made. Kit sighed as he stabled the horse, making sure it had water and fresh hay before heading toward the house. Maybe Louisa would be up for an afternoon nap, or more accurately an afternoon romp. The thought of spending a quiet hour with his wife made him happy and Kit forced all negative thoughts from his head and strolled to the house whistling a merry tune.

Louisa was perched on a settee in the parlor, a crumpled letter in her lap. Her face was the color of whey, her eyes red-rimmed from crying. She didn't bother to look up at Kit as he entered, just handed him the letter, averting her eyes when he tried to look at her. "Is it Alec?" he asked quietly. She shook her head, fresh tears running down her face. Kit squinted at the letter, trying to make out the words. The ink was smudged by tears in some places, but he could still make out the gist of it. His heart nearly stopped when the words finally sank in. The letter was from Deverell, detailing Kit's assignations with Buckingham and threatening to expose him to all of Jamestown, not only to his wife, should he fail to meet the demands set forth by Deverell by the end of the week.

"You actually believe this?" he demanded, deciding to go on the offensive. It was his only hope of salvaging his marriage and retaining whatever shred of dignity he had left. He had to talk his way out of it, then deal with Deverell. Louisa finally looked up at him, her eyes strangely blank.

"Yes, I do. It all makes sense now: the gifts, the letters signed with the letter G, the urgent meetings with Buckingham. No wonder you were so tense, so angry. You were vicious in bed, as if exorcising some demons. Now I know the demon had been Buckingham, I just don't understand how it could have happened. I can't begin to wrap my mind around this; I just can't." Louisa rose from the settee, turning to flee the room. Kit grabbed her by the arm, but she tore out of his grasp, her face contorted with anger.

"Let go of me!"

"Louisa, please, let me explain. Buckingham blackmailed me." Kit sounded desperate even to himself, but his plea didn't help. Louisa turned to look at him, her eyes full of the type of pain he'd never seen in her before, not even when she thought Evie might die on the crossing to England.

"Kit, I'm sure there was a good reason for what you did, but whatever it was, I don't want to know. I can't bear to live with this knowledge. I keep trying to force images of you with Buckingham from my mind, but I can't. Now, please leave me alone; I can't bear to look at you just now. I need to be alone."

"Louisa, please, listen," Kit begged, but she covered her mouth with her hand as her face turned even whiter.

"I feel sick to my stomach," she blurted out as she ran from the room and out the front door.

Kit stood there, in the middle of the room, shocked and helpless. He'd imagined this type of scene hundreds of times, terrified Louisa would find out and never forgive him, and now it had happened. He'd managed to keep his shameful secret for a long time and would have taken it to his grave if not for that vicious blackguard who was willing to destroy a man and his family for money. What was he to do if Louisa wouldn't let him explain? Would she ever be able forgive him? What woman would be willing to forget that her husband had betrayed her, especially with a man?

Women were taught to overlook men's appetites and turn a blind eye to an occasional indiscretion, but this was completely different. This was beyond the pale, and even though Louisa had come from a time when homosexuality was accepted and practiced in the open, she would not understand it in her own husband. He wasn't even homosexual, just a victim of circumstance, but how could he erase those images from her mind now that they had been planted there by that malicious bastard?

Kit wanted to ride to Jamestown and confront Deverell, but he simply couldn't find the strength. His knees buckled under as he plopped down on the settee, unable to stand any longer. His hands were shaking, and his insides turned to water as the realization of what just happened finally sank in. Louisa would never get over this. She might learn to live with it in time, but she would never forget and never forgive, images of him and Buckingham always in her mind, especially when he touched her. Deverell had proven stronger than Kit had expected, and had struck where it hurt most, destroying the one thing in Kit's life that meant everything. He finally got to his feet and stumbled from the house. He had no idea where he was going or what he would do once he got there, but he had to get away.

THIRTY

Louisa tripped over a root and nearly fell as she ran from the house, her vision so blurred by tears she couldn't even see where she was going. She felt like a wounded animal that needed to find a quiet place to lick its wounds. Her stomach heaved, and she was sick into a bush before wiping her mouth with the back of her hand and continuing to run toward the forest. The brilliance of the sun mocked her cruelly, the birds singing and the brook bubbling as if everything was as it should be and life went on as before. Only this morning she was wearing herself out with worry over Alec and Valerie, and now they were the furthest thing from her mind, her brain afire with the terrible knowledge that now ate its way through her like a cancer, devouring every good thing in its path.

She hadn't really believed it when she'd read the letter, thinking it a vicious lie, but it was Kit's face that alerted her to the truth. She'd seen the tightening of the mouth and the pallor that suddenly appeared beneath the tan, making him look ashen. It wasn't merely fury at being unjustly accused – it was the look of a man whose worst nightmare had just come true.

He had challenged her, but she saw the fear in his eyes, the pleading look when he tried to explain. God, she'd known there was something going on, but this?

Louisa sank to her knees next to a little brook, not caring that her gown was muddy or her shoes soaked as she leaned forward and gulped some water from her cupped hand, needing to wash away the taste of vomit that was burning her mouth and stinging her nostrils. The water was cold and fresh, but the taste wouldn't leave. It was now in her mind, tainting everything just like the knowledge of Kit's betrayal. What was she to do now? Was she supposed to go back home and pretend like nothing happened? Lie in bed with him and give him her love and understanding as if the episode with Buckingham never happened? How could she? But how could she not? What could she do?

Under the law of the colony, she was Kit's property, as were the children. As a woman, she had no rights, no assets, and basically no say in her own life, unless she was a widow. Kit held all the cards, and even if she chose to punish him at home, he was still her master and keeper. He could do anything he chose, such as leave her in Virginia and take the children back to England.

Louisa leaned against the trunk of a gnarled old tree, oblivious to the discomfort in her back. She closed her eyes and forced herself to breathe deeply while counting to one hundred, something she'd done sometimes when she tried to meditate back in the future. She needed to calm down and think rationally, if not for herself, but for the sake of her children. They couldn't know that something was wrong between their parents; it would devastate them and affect the rest of the household as well. No one could know, and before any decisions were made, something had to be done to stop Deverell from spreading this evil gossip all over the colony. He would wait a day or two before making another move, in order to give Kit time to come to his senses and pay the price, so now was the time to act. She would deal with Kit later, but for now, they had to put on a united front and save their life and their family.

THIRTY-ONE
VIRGINIA AUGUST 1779

Keeping away from Diana proved much harder than had Sam anticipated. She always seemed to be there, now dressed in a more modest gown and with a frilly cap covering her auburn curls, but no amount of cloth could cover up the look in her eyes. They followed him around wherever he went, caressing him and taunting him, adoring him and tantalizing him, especially when she dropped her gaze to his breeches and innocently licked her lips. Thankfully, no one seemed to notice as Diana picked her moments carefully, playing the role of the reformed whore to the hilt. She went out of her way to help Hannah Mallory, make an ally of the girls, and to bond with Abbie and Martha over the joys of motherhood. Sam did his level best to keep Susanna away from the main house and oblivious to Diana's intentions, but it was proving harder and harder.

He hadn't been alone with Diana since that time in the barn, and he planned to keep it that way, despite the fact that she was invading his dreams and leaving him panting with desire. He wished his wife would notice his desperate state, but she was too tired and preoccupied with Ben, her body bursting with new life, and her belly growing larger by the day. Sam didn't dare trouble her at a time like this, taking his father's advice and leaving her alone. Diana, on the other hand, bloomed brighter with every passing day. Plenty of good food and fresh air put the color back into her cheeks and some flesh onto her thin frame, making her look radiant and full of life.

Only yesterday, when Sam had come by to bring some cream from the springhouse, she was sitting on the bench by the house, somnolent in the afternoon sun, Nat dozing in her lap. Diana's eyes opened wider, her lips curling into a coy smile as she unlaced her bodice slowly, her gaze never leaving Sam's face. She exposed her full breast, giving him an eyeful of the rosy nipple before putting Nat to her breast, his cheeks puffing out as he sucked greedily, his little hands holding on to the luscious breast for dear life. He hadn't realized she was still nursing him, but then some women nursed longer than others. Sam nearly moaned with misery as he tore his gaze away and strode into the house, hoping that his mother and sisters wouldn't notice the very obvious bulge in his breeches.

Dear God, why was she tormenting him this way? Something had to be done to rectify this situation, and it had to be soon, before he either lost all control, or Diana did something to ruin his life permanently. She obviously meant either to have him or hurt him, and he wouldn't let her have her way. *He'd kill her if she did anything to hurt Sue*, he thought viciously as he slammed the can onto the table and strode from the house without saying a word. He had sinned and deserved whatever punishment was coming to him, but Sue's only sin had been to love him and trust him, and he would do nothing, NOTHING, to betray her trust. Sam walked past Diana without acknowledging her presence and felt her eyes burn a hole in his back. *Damn her*, he thought.

* * *

It was the following evening when Sam came in from the fields to find Diana seated across the table from Susanna, daintily sipping a cup of tea and picking at a piece of crust left over from her pie. She smiled a warm welcome as Sam came in, the reaction not lost on his wife.

"Diana, what a surprise to see you here," he said, taking off his hat and kissing Susanna on the cheek. "Where's Nat?"

"Oh, he's with Sarah and Annie. They're like two mother hens, clucking over him day and night. It's so nice to have some help. I hardly see him at all, except for feedings," she added meaningfully, her eyes meeting Sam's in an open challenge. "Does Sam like to watch you nurse Ben, Susanna? I hear some men find that to be quite arousing." She giggled prettily at Susanna's look of surprise, but quickly dropped her eyes in mock embarrassment, her hand flying to cover her mouth. "I'm sorry, I shouldn't have said that. Sometimes I forget myself."

"More often than not," Sam mumbled, taking a seat at the table as Susanna put a plate of mutton and boiled potatoes in front of him.

"Well, I best be going and leave you to your domestic bliss," Diana purred, lazily rising from the table. "Thank you so much for the tea and the chat, Sue. Let's be sure to do it again soon. I don't see nearly enough of you, with you tucked away here in your cozy little house." Diana looked out the window, a look of concern creasing her brow. "It's quite dark outside. I'm afraid I still get a bit disoriented when walking at night. It's not like New York where there are proper streets and light spilling from the windows to light the way. It does get pitch dark here, doesn't it?"

"Sam, would you please walk Diana back to the house?" Susanna asked, throwing him an apologetic look. She didn't look too pleased with the idea of Sam being alone with her in the dark, but manners prevailed, and she smiled warmly at Diana, thanking her for the visit and inviting her to come again soon.

Sam gulped down the last of his meal before getting to his feet and following Diana into the inky darkness of the summer night. The air was fragrant with the smell of warm earth, summer flowers and pine from the forest. It was warm and balmy with not a trace of a breeze to dispel the heat of the day. The night was alive around them, with the sound of chirping crickets and frogs croaking their hearts out by the stream, the rustling of leaves overhead a soothing whisper despite the lack of wind. They walked in silence for a few moments, Diana waiting for Sam to say something, and Sam striving for control as he tried to keep a tight rein on his anger.

"What do you want?" he finally asked, his voice low and menacing, even to his own ears.

"I want you," she answered simply, her hand reaching for his before he had a chance to snatch it away. Sam carefully removed her hand, coming to a stop and turning to face her, his eyes blazing in the darkness.

"I'm not there for the taking, am I? I have a wife and a son, and another child on the way."

"You have two sons," Diana replied without any sarcasm or accusation. She was simply stating a fact, a fact that she needed him to acknowledge.

"So, he's mine?"

"Of course he is. If that brother of yours has a prick, he still hasn't figured out what to do with it, poor lad. He looks so like you, but he lacks the fire that burns in your belly, Sam Mallory, and I like your fire."

Sam felt a fire in his belly, but it wasn't the kind she was hoping for. He was furious, his hands curling into fists and uncurling again as he realized what he was doing. He could hardly hit the woman, tempted though he might be.

"Diana, I might be many things, but liar isn't one of them. I paid you for sex, like the rest of your clients. I made no promises or spoke any words of affection. You have no claim on me."

Diana cocked her head to the side, openly studying him and smiling as if she alone knew some great secret. "Well, *Patrick*, I wouldn't say you're not a practiced liar. You'd have to be, wouldn't you, to do what you do. You deceive people without thinking twice and squeeze them for information, which is all for a good cause, of course," she added with a sly grin. "As far as promises and words of love go, those are still to come if you let me make you happy, and I *can* make you happy. Look at you standing there, all tense with fury coursing through your veins. Wouldn't you rather put all that fire to good use? I won't tell her, I promise. All I want is for you to take me, right here, right now. I'll make you forget why you were so angry in the first place," she purred, inching closer to him, her hand reaching out toward his face. Sam grabbed her wrist, making her cry out in pain.

"I won't let you manipulate me this way. I'm a man, not an animal; I can control my urges. I want you gone from here," he snapped, turning his back on her.

"And what about your son?"

"My son is sleeping in his cot next to my wife." Sam's shoulders slumped a little as he realized the cruelty of his words. It wasn't the boy's fault, was it? Whether he wanted it or not, he had sired that child, and now he had to take some responsibility for him.

"Diana, you are a beautiful, clever girl. Find yourself a good man who will marry you and take good care of you and Nat," he said, turning to face her again. Sam was surprised to see the venom in her face at his suggestion.

"Marriage is just another form of prostitution," she spat out, "I won't be a slave to any man."

"I wouldn't think my wife thinks of herself as a whore or a slave to me," Sam replied, confused by her reaction.

"Well, she's a lucky one, isn't she, to have such a kind and devoted husband. Not all women are wed to men who care for them or remain faithful. Do you know how many loving husbands frequent brothels, husbands who often return to their wives riddled with the pox? I'd rather take their money and keep my freedom if it's all the same to you and be mistress of my own destiny."

"Is being alone, penniless, and hungry, with a small child the destiny you were hoping for?" Sam fired back, angry again.

"I won't be penniless for long, and we're not finished, you and I." Diana stormed off into the darkness, her shape swallowed by the shadows after a few minutes as Sam just looked after her, baffled and frustrated. What in holy hell was he supposed to do?

Sam stomped across the meadow, anger coursing through him like poison. Diana's last comment to him sounded like a threat, and he had to admit that he was nervous. He'd made it clear that she wouldn't get his love, but now maybe she wanted something other than affection; she wanted revenge, although he couldn't imagine what he'd done to her to cause such fury. Yes, he'd rejected her, but he never promised her anything. It had been a simple business transaction—money for sex. He hadn't been in the habit of frequenting brothels, but he'd been alone in New York for months, and he'd been lonely. He'd been in no position to start any kind of romantic entanglement, and Diana had been placed in his path by people from the Committee. They'd had a few romps, nothing more. To think that she'd carried a torch for him all this time and had his child was baffling. Had she allowed herself to get pregnant in the hope that he would be guilt-tripped into marrying her?

Sam suddenly stopped, the realization hitting him like a brick. She'd said that any woman wanted to have a child with the man she loved. She'd fallen in love with him and nursed her feelings for months, allowing hope to blossom in her chest, especially during the months of pregnancy in the hope that he returned her feelings. He'd been kind and respectful to her, always bringing her flowers or a bag of sweets he bought along the way. He hadn't meant to give her any notions, but few men treated whores with kindness, and she had mistaken his attention for love. What a fool he'd been. And now she'd come here in the hope of a future, only to find him married with a child of his own. "Hell hath no fury like a woman scorned," Sam whispered into the night, quoting a line from William Congreve's play *Love for Love*. He sighed and walked on, eager for his bed.

The door to the bedroom was firmly shut, Susanna already in bed. She didn't respond when he called out to her but turned her back as soon as he got into bed, pretending to be asleep.

"Sue, are you angry with me?" he asked, puzzled.

Susanna flipped over, her eyes blazing in the darkness as she stared him down, her nostrils narrowing as she sucked in air in an effort to regain control over her feelings. "Am I angry? Oh, yes, I'm angry. That woman, if you could call her that, came to my house, sat at my table, and oohed and aahed over my child, all the while sneaking peeks at the door every few minutes in the hope that you would walk through it. I see the way she looks at you, the knowing smile playing about her lips."

"Sue," Sam implored, but she pushed his hand away.

"I might not have had much experience before I met you, but I'm not a fool, Sam. You've been with her before, and it's quite possible that you've been with her again. Now, get out of this bed before I kick you out and go sleep in the other room."

"Sue, I..." Sam began, but she cut him off, her voice shaking with emotion.

"I don't want to hear it, Sam, not now. I need time to calm myself before I can deal with this, but if I find out that you've so much as laid a finger on her, there'll be hell to pay. Is that clear?"

"Crystal," Sam retorted, grabbing his pillow and striding from the room. "Good night," he called over his shoulder, his tone dripping sarcasm.

THIRTY-TWO
VIRGINIA AUGUST 1626

The sun was fiercer than ever, the smell of manure and hay strong in his nostrils when Kit woke up, his head pounding and his stomach heaving mercilessly as bright lights exploded before his eyes, blinding him and making him dizzy. He was covered in straw, and for one brief moment, he couldn't remember why he was in the barn or why he got blind drunk the night before. The memory came flooding back as he stumbled outside and threw up, more from misery than from a hangover.

He'd have to go back to the house eventually, but the thought of facing Louisa was more than he could handle. The look on her face when she found out about his liaison with Buckingham was something he couldn't erase from his mind. It had been a combination of shock, disgust, fear, and worst of all, betrayal. And he deserved it, every bit of it. He would have to face her eventually, but not in the state he was in. He needed to clear his head, come up with a plan, and somehow find a way to regain control of the situation, even if only superficially. Crawling back home with his tail between his legs would only make things worse, and she would despise him for his weakness and lack of self-control.

But he couldn't hide out in the barn forever, so Kit washed his face and hands, ran his fingers through his tangled hair, and brushed the straw from his clothes. He would go into town and meet Charles at the docks. At least he wouldn't be here where he could run into Louisa at any moment. She needed time to think, and he needed time to regain whatever dignity he could muster, what little of it he had left. He saddled his horse and vaulted into the saddle, his head nearly exploding as the horse galloped over dry, packed earth, each hoof beat echoing in his brain.

Kit was surprised to see all the frenetic activity in Jamestown. It was just going on noon, so most people would normally be at home, having their midday meal and taking a little rest before returning to their chores and working straight through the afternoon until they could return home for supper. Everyone seemed to be rushing toward the docks, children whizzing past him as he tried to make his way through the crowd without trampling anyone. Kit finally gave up, left his horse by the tavern, and continued on foot, finding it easier to weave through the growing crowds. Everyone was gawking at something laid out on the dock, ladies gasping and covering their mouths in shock. Kit could see Charles's tall figure at the front, his face white with shock. Kit was finally able to elbow his way to the front, his eyes falling on the object of everyone's attention.

He was lying on his back, his clothes soaked and covered with bits of seaweed and muck, a pool of water forming beneath him as it dripped from his soggy coat and breeches. His round head was pink and nearly bald without its elaborate wig, which was lying next to the body and resembling a drowned animal. The face was badly disfigured, beaten to a pulp and nibbled by fish, but Kit knew without doubt that it was Deverell. He was bloated, so he must have been in the water for some time before someone finally fished him out, probably this morning. Kit's eyes met Charles's in mute inquiry. Charles shrugged in response and shook his head in dismay.

"Who would do such a thing?" Charles asked. "His purse is still there, so he wasn't robbed."

"Perhaps he was drunk and fell in," Kit suggested. He tried to arrange his features into some semblance of shock or grief, but all he felt was overwhelming relief that flooded through him like water through desert sands. Deverell was dead, and Kit's secret just died with him. Charles shook his head at Kit's suggestion. "He was savagely beaten. His skull is bashed in on the other side. This was no accident, Kit."

Kit opened his mouth to reply when a terrible shriek tore through the crowd, causing them to part. Mistress Deverell stood at the end of the human tunnel, her face frozen with terror and disbelief. "Oh, dear God," she murmured. "He's dead. He's really dead."

Kit wasn't sure if she was lamenting her husband's passing or trying to convince herself that he was really gone for good, but he remained quiet, keeping his distance from the body. Thank God no one had heard him threaten Deverell the other day or they would think he was responsible. Kit nearly keeled over, suddenly realizing that Louisa might think just that. He had motive and could have found the opportunity, especially since he hadn't slept at home last night, and as far as he knew, no one had seen him.

Sir George Yeardley was already pushing through the crowd, offering his deepest condolences to Mistress Deverell and calling for anyone who might have seen or heard something. Kit stumbled from the quay, eager to get away. This was all too much to take in. He suddenly, desperately, wished for Alec, knowing that he would give him good counsel and help, if necessary. Not only was he his brother, Alec was his closest friend in the world, and suddenly Kit's vision was blurred, his guts on fire with acute misery. Why did this terrible thing have to happen? He thought he'd been free and clear, but now it was all coming to haunt him and there was no place to run or hide. Sir George would launch an investigation into Deverell's death and Kit's dealings with Deverell might become public knowledge, especially since Deverell had mentioned some document that he'd left in the possession of his wife. What if this was far from over and only just beginning?

THIRTY-THREE
VIRGINIA AUGUST 1779

Abbie tiptoed away from the crib as Diana snored softly, her mouth slightly open in sleep. She'd be out for at least two hours, giving Abbie a much-needed break. She had Finn's shirts to mend and a torn hem to repair, followed by dyeing some old garments that still had some wear left in them but needed to be spruced up. She'd boil up some madder root to dye them a dark red, which would cover all manner of sins, such as stains and discoloration of the fabric from being washed and dried in the sun so often, but first, she had to attend to the shirts.

Annie and Sarah were in the kitchen, helping their mother with dinner, so they'd listen out for Diana in case she woke up. Abbie stepped outside, heading for the bench beneath the maple tree. She loved this spot. It was private and quiet, the perfect place to think and dream. In this instance, it was a place to worry. Finn still hadn't returned, and she was beginning to fret, doing mental arithmetic in her mind of how long it would take him to get to Savannah and back. He should have been back at least a day ago, but she had to be patient. Maybe he had to wait to make contact or needed time to rest.

She smiled as Diana the Elder appeared around the corner

of the house, Nathaniel trailing her like a puppy. He hardly ever let her out of his sight, his eyes anxious and round in his pale face. He was wearing old breeches left over from when Jonah was a child, which made him suddenly look like a little man. Diana normally kept him in gowns, but Mrs. Mallory felt that a boy going on two should be potty-trained, and she took over the task with zeal, making poor Nat use the pot every half hour until he learned how to ask for it himself when he needed to go. He seemed to like wearing breeches and a shirt and smiled happily as he sat down on the grass beneath the tree with a carved pony that his grandpa made for him over the last few days.

"May I join you?" Diana asked, sitting down on the bench before Abbie had a chance to respond.

"It's so quiet here, so very quiet," Diana said. "I'm not used to that. It was always noisy in New York—soldiers cantering down the street, vendors selling their wares, and ships being unloaded at the docks. I miss it. It's better for Nat though. He loves it here."

"Did he live with you at the brothel?" Abbie asked, pulling the needle through the fabric, her eyes on her work.

"He did for a short time. I used to take him down to the kitchen as the clients started to come in the evening. No man wants to deal with a mewling baby when he's feeling amorous," Diana said with a rueful smile. "Sometimes he cried and cried because he was hungry, but I couldn't see to him. Madam Mabel was furious because he disturbed the clientele. She threw me out when Nat was two months old."

"So, what did you do?"

"I went to Deborah. She's a friend who hid Sam for a while. She has a child of her own, so she was able to watch Nat while I got whatever business I could at the docks. It was different than working at the brothel. They took me against the wall, or sometimes just wanted me to... Never mind; I shouldn't be telling you this. I'm sorry." Diana looked contrite, her cheeks stained pink by shame. Nat seemed immune to what his mother was saying, his eyes fixed on the clouds floating overhead, the pony forgotten for the moment.

"Nat, come have a bun fresh out of the oven," Sarah called, waving to him from the house. Nat looked up at Diana, who smiled and told him to run along. "Never pass up a fresh bun, my boy," she said, giving him a quick kiss before he toddled off.

"Diana, I know it's none of my business, but how did you get into prostitution? What of your family?" Abbie asked, thinking that her parents would do anything in the world to protect her and their other children from that kind of life. Diana's parents must be dead, or she wouldn't be in such a predicament.

"It's not a pretty story," she said, sighing. "I try not to think on it too much, but sometimes I still dream of those days, and I wake up crying."

"You don't have to tell me. I didn't mean to upset you," Abbie mumbled, ashamed of herself for being so insensitive.

"You have a right to know. After all, I'm almost a part of your family now." Diana began to talk, her gaze on the clouds floating overhead. Maybe she was too embarrassed to look at Abbie, or maybe she was seeing her old life floating before her eyes instead.

"I was born into a happy family, a family where parents loved each other, and I was cherished and cosseted. There was me and my brother. My father worked at the docks, and my mother took in sewing to supplement his income. She nearly went blind sitting up night after night, sewing by candlelight. She didn't mind though because it was for us. I was thirteen when she died and my brother six. My father was heartbroken. He'd loved her since he was a boy. There was never anyone else for him. It was his grief that made him careless. He got in the way when a heavy crate was being lowered from one of the ships and it crushed his chest. He died in agony, calling for his dead wife.

Sid and I were left on our own, and the money my mother stowed so carefully in a little tin ran out within two months. I took in sewing from her clients, but it wasn't enough to pay rent, buy food, and keep us warm in the winter, and it was a cold winter that year. The icy wind off the East River was enough to freeze you in your tracks."

A single tear ran down her cheek, making Abbie reach out and take her hand. "Sid was always crying that he was hungry and kept asking when our parents would come back. He was so sad. One day, I went to buy some bread, but I didn't have enough money because I already bought some milk for Sid. The baker said I could pay him in other ways. I didn't understand what he meant, but he gave me the bread and told me to come back at closing time. His wife was upstairs cooking supper, so he was alone in the shop.

He took me to the back and told me to get on my knees and make him happy. I had no idea what he wanted, but he explained, and I bolted. I didn't go back for days, but eventually the bread ran out, and so had the money. There was nothing to eat. The money I made was barely enough to pay the rent, and if we got thrown out, we'd freeze to death on the streets. I went back to the shop. I did what he wanted and continued to do it once a week. In return, he gave me bread and even a spice cake for Sid."

"I'm so sorry, Diana," Abbie whispered. She'd been loved and cared for all her life. Both her parents were alive and well, and she'd never known cold or hunger. And here was this poor orphaned girl, who'd been forced to choose between selling her favors and starving.

"Don't be. We survived. A lot of others didn't. I quickly discovered that I could get just about anything I wanted as long as I was discreet. All these men had wives and children, some even had daughters my age. They thought that as long as they didn't actually stick their prick in me, they weren't being unfaithful to their wives or sinning in the eyes of God. I wasn't interested in the logic, just the money. Sid and I managed to live that way for three years. We had enough money for rent and food, and I even managed to put something by in my mother's tin. I still took the sewing in and did some cleaning so no one would start to question how we managed on our own."

"What happened then?" Abbie asked, curious why things changed.

"I met a girl who worked in a brothel. She said that she had a roof over her head, hot food, and that the soldiers and sailors were usually kind and paid well. They even gave her presents, and occasionally brought her treats like sweetmeats and candy. I wouldn't have to worry about rent or keeping warm anymore. So, I apprenticed Sid to a gunsmith, thinking it was a good trade to have with all the warmongering going on, and went to Madam Mabel's. She took me in and taught me how to protect myself and keep myself clean from the pox, gave me room and board, and a cut of what I made. By that point, my maidenhead didn't mean much to me anymore. I knew I couldn't afford to wait for a husband to save me from a life of woe."

"And you never got with child except with Nat?" Abbie asked, trying to keep the incredulity out of her voice.

"Oh, I did. Twice before. Once, I miscarried, and the other time Mabel helped me get rid of it. See, I couldn't get rid of Nat. It's hard to abort a child when you love the father."

"So, you truly love Jonah?" Abbie asked.

"I truly love Nat's father," Diana said quietly. "I best go now. I promised to help your mother with the laundry." Diana got up, turning to face Abbie, her face suddenly serious. "You are very lucky, Abbie. So many people love you. Don't ever take it for granted."

"I won't."

THIRTY-FOUR

Diana's eyes never left the pulpit as she irritably adjusted the frilly tucker modestly covering her bosom and tried to ignore her overwhelming desire to tear it off and run right out of the stifling church. She hadn't worn one of those things in ages, probably not since she'd been to church. The last time had been when one of the girls at Madam Mabel's died of a botched abortion and Mabel herded them all to the local Protestant church for the funeral. Diana had been baptized a Catholic, having been born into an Irish family, but she didn't advertise the fact, knowing that the British soldiers who patronized Mabel's establishment would somehow feel diminished if they discovered they were sticking their pricks into a Catholic whore.

It didn't matter really, since she'd given up on God long ago, probably not long after he'd given up on her. The story she told Abbie had been embellished to elicit sympathy and make herself look like a victim of her circumstances, but she supposed she was no different from the legions of poor Irish girls who knew hardship from an early age and had to fend for themselves since they were scarcely older than children. It was true that her parents loved each other at one time, but her father hadn't been made careless by grief or crushed by a crate.

He drank himself to death and used up all the money her mother so carefully put by for a rainy day, leaving his children orphaned and penniless. Diana always knew she wouldn't spend her days stooped over her sewing as her eyesight failed or scrubbing pots until her hands bled. No, that life wasn't for her. The first few punters had been difficult, she'd readily admit that, but then it got easier. There were a few right bastards, but most of the men were nice enough, their loneliness as easy to spot as the red tunics they so proudly wore.

The soldiers were mostly young, if not all good-looking, but servicing them was much easier than having to deal with older men. Diana couldn't abide the wrinkled skin or the sagging flesh as they dropped their woolen underwear and went to work, grunting and panting with effort for the few minutes it took them to finish. It wasn't even worth pretending for those men; they didn't expect it. The young soldiers did, though. They wanted to know that she was enjoying herself and not just lying there counting the moments until they would pay her and leave.

Sometimes she did enjoy herself, as she had with Sam. She'd been drawn to him from the moment Jonah introduced them. He was so handsome and charming, with none of that British reserve that made the soldiers appear as if they had a rod stuck up their arse. Sam was funny and playful, making her laugh despite her impenetrable guard and taking the time to pleasure her before satisfying himself. She hadn't been used to that, hadn't expected it from a customer, but then he wasn't just a client; he was a contact, and a rebel like herself. Jonah was one too, but despite his good looks, she never gave him a moment's thought. He wasn't the type of man she found attractive. He lacked the confidence and arrogance so abundant in his lovely brother.

Poor Jonah. She'd never meant to use him this way but

naming him as the father bought her some time to rethink her strategy and approach the situation with some subtlety rather than go in guns blazing. That would never work with Sam, and she'd been a fool to try, although getting the family to accept her had been easier than she'd expected. Abbie and Finn named their daughter after her—*what a hoot*, she thought with a wicked smile, before noticing the displeasure of the minister and wiping the smirk off her face.

Diana still had no idea what had possessed her to allow Sam to touch her without protection. She'd always stuffed a vinegar-soaked rag deep inside herself to block the man's seed and hopefully kill it on contact. Mabel had taught all the girls how to look after themselves and expected them to be diligent in their efforts. Unwanted babies weren't welcome at the brothel, and Mabel had little sympathy for girls who'd been negligent and managed to get with child despite the weekly lecture they got from their Madam on the importance of protection and douching after each client. She'd used the rag with Sam the first few times, but then she *forgot* to put it in, enjoying the feel of him inside her rather than the uncomfortable feeling of the rag being pushed up against her womb.

Of course she'd gotten pregnant, as she knew she would, and she wouldn't hear of getting rid of it. Sam had been nice and kind, had come from a good, well-to-do family. He'd take care of her and his son and give her the life she secretly yearned for. She'd whored long enough, and she was more than ready to turn respectable and leave the old days behind, but she hadn't bargained on him being married; he wasn't the type. The sight of his uptight British wife nearly made her laugh out loud, but she'd been weeping on the inside. What was she to do now? Sam was clearly in love with his wife and their little sprat, who was only a little younger than Nat.

Diana fidgeted in her seat, wishing the sermon would finally end and they could all go back and have their Sunday dinner.

She was always hungry since coming to Virginia. She supposed it was all this fresh air, or maybe the fact that there was very little of interest to do but eat. She tried not to think too much on it, but she had to admit that this life simply wasn't for her. Getting up at the crack of dawn to start the chores and then working through most of the day with only breaks for meals and for tending to the children wasn't what she'd expected.

She thought the Mallorys would have a few Negro slaves to do the hard work, or at least an indentured servant or two, but she'd been mistaken. They weren't nearly as well-to-do as she had expected, and a life of hard work wasn't what she'd come for. She was used to sleeping late, having a leisurely breakfast with the other girls, and then having a few hours to herself before the first client of the day presented himself at the brothel.

Oh, the bliss of having her own room. She was sharing with Sarah and Annie, who asked her endless questions and fawned over Nat as if they'd never seen a child before. Of course, it was nice to have a bit of help. They were only too happy to take him outside to sit in the sunshine, point out clouds and various birds, and tell him stories. Nat soaked up the attention, thrilled to be in the care of someone who actually enjoyed being with him.

Diana had never realized how much work a child could be. Between the feedings, night wakings, and a mountain of soiled nappies, she barely had time to work. Mabel had taken pity on her and allowed her to stay on almost until she gave birth. Some men enjoyed that sort of thing, but she'd asked her to leave once the baby was born. Diana wouldn't be able to service customers for at least a month and no man wanted to have a screaming baby in the room while he did his business.

She went back when Nat was a month old but was promptly dismissed again after a few weeks, Mabel's irritation with the screaming child mounting daily until she gave vent to her anger and threw Diana out for good. She'd always planned to travel to Virginia to find Sam, but it had proved harder than she'd thought. She'd only known him as Patrick Johnson, and now she had to discover his real name and address. That took some doing, but finally, she had what she needed and started her journey—another surprise. Traveling with a baby was hard enough but finding ways to get to where she was going was even more difficult. There was no direct route, so she had to take coach after coach, get lifts from farmers, and once from a willing British colonel, until she finally made it to Williamsburg. It had taken weeks, and she was exhausted and nearly broke.

And now she needed a new plan, for the old one just blew up in her face like a puff of smoke from a smelly cigar. How long would it be before Sam confessed to his parents that Nat was really his and Diana had used Jonah as a scapegoat just to wheedle her way into the family and use her proximity to Sam to try and destroy his marriage? Abbie didn't seem to know anything, but she had a few days at best before her secret became common knowledge.

Diana rose from her seat and walked down the nave of the church, her head held high and her heels clicking on the dusty wooden floor. She ignored the whispered comments or the curious stares as she opened the door and slammed it shut behind her. She was done with God, and to hell with them all.

THIRTY-FIVE
VIRGINIA AUGUST 1626

Kit fortified himself with a cupful of brandy before getting ready to head upstairs. He'd spent several hours riding around aimlessly to get his thoughts in order after leaving Jamestown in a fruitless attempt to formulate a plan, but all he came up with was that he was, for lack of a better word, fucked. It wasn't bad enough that now his wife knew about the trysts with Buckingham, but now Deverell had died violently, most likely making Kit the prime suspect in her eyes. Charles had come back to the plantation several hours ago, so Louisa had heard the news and would have had time to form an opinion, so the only thing he could do was confront her and force her to listen. He had to explain. She might not be ready to forgive, but she needed to know the facts. Kit nodded to Charles who was still finishing his drink and rose to his feet, ready to face his wife. He was just about to climb the stairs when the sound of galloping horses distracted him.

"Who could that be?" Charles asked as he glanced out the window. It wasn't fully dark yet, but the light was fading fast, the purple shadows of a July twilight quickly darkening into all-encompassing blackness of a summer night. The crescent moon that hung at a jaunty angle in the starlit sky paled in comparison to the flickering light of the torches advancing at breakneck speed toward the manor house.

"There are at least five men," Charles announced. "What could they want?" He opened the door, smiling as he recognized Sir George Yeardley. "Sir George, what brings you here at this time of night?" Charles asked, opening the door wider to invite the governor in. The rest of the men remained outside, but they looked grim, their muskets slung across their shoulders and the light from the torches throwing strange shadows across their faces and making them look demonic.

"Good evening, Master Whitfield. As it happens, I'm here to see Lord Sheridan. My Lord." Yardley bowed to Kit, who was standing behind Charles, but was hesitant to speak. "Is Mistress Whitfield here?" he suddenly asked Charles.

"Annabel is upstairs with the children." A look of concern appeared on Charles's face, but the governor held up his hand, indicating that he had no reason to worry.

"And Lady Sheridan?"

"I'm here, Sir George," Louisa replied as she came down the stairs, her gaze fixed on the governor. "Is something wrong?"

Sir George stood by the door, stepping from foot to foot, his hands clasped behind his back and his expression unusually dour, even for him. He looked at Louisa for a moment before finally speaking, his voice low and even. "Christopher Sheridan, I'm arresting you for the murder of Aloysius Deverell. You will be taken into custody and remain incarcerated until the trial. Will you please come with me?"

Kit whipped around to see the look of incomprehension on Louisa's face as she processed the governor's words. She was pale and scared, but she remained silent as her eyes finally found Kit's. He thought he saw understanding and tenderness in them, but he was probably mistaken. They hadn't spoken since she showed him the letter, and things were far from resolved between them. And now this.

"On what grounds am I being arrested?" Kit asked quietly. He hadn't moved from his spot and the men outside inched closer to the open door, ready to move in. Annabel appeared at the top of the stairs behind Louisa, but no one paid her any mind, all eyes on Sir George.

"You threatened Master Deverell on your property three days ago and promised to beat him to a pulp and throw him in the river, which is exactly how he died. Now, please come with us peacefully, or we will have to exude force."

"Who told you this?" Kit asked, the shock probably evident in his face.

"A witness came forward this afternoon after the discovery of the body and signed a written statement describing the incident. Now, please come with us, Lord Sheridan."

"I'm not going anywhere until you tell me who this witness is. Who could have heard me threatening Master Deverell on my property?" Kit looked at Charles, but he just shrugged his shoulders, as shocked as the rest of them.

Sir George briefly glanced at Charles before facing Kit squarely and replying to his question. "The person who made the accusation is Annabel Whitfield. It seems she overheard you speaking to Master Deverell. I'm afraid the evidence is rather damning. I will do all I can to help you, but the law is the law, and murder is a hanging offense. Now, please come."

Kit glanced at Louisa, who stood frozen on the lower step, her face slack with shock, her eyes full of incomprehension as she stared at Kit. He could see Annabel at the top of the stairs, a look of intense satisfaction on her beautiful face. She'd never looked as ugly to him as she did at that moment.

"I didn't do it, Lou," Kit said. "I swear. I didn't do it," Kit called out as Sir George took him by the arm and steered him toward the door.

"I know you didn't," she replied, her fingers digging into the banister as she swayed and slumped to sit on the step, resting her head against the wall.

Kit didn't bother to look at Charles as he was led away. Charles had nothing to do with what Annabel had done, he was sure of that. Charles could be self-serving at times, but he was a good man who would never betray a friend. His one weakness was his wife, and what a venomous besom she could be at times. Why would she accuse him of murder? Suddenly, a chilling thought entered his mind. What if he had killed Deverell? He'd been so drunk he couldn't remember.

THIRTY-SIX

"How could you?" Louisa roared, advancing on a cowering Annabel, who was attempting to hide behind Charles. "How could you do such a thing? What would possess you to speak out against Kit? What has he ever done to you, you vicious shrew?"

Louisa took a gulp of air in an effort to calm herself. She felt as if the walls were closing in on her, the warm evening air not enough to fill her aching lungs. The children were crying upstairs, woken by her outburst as Genevieve tried to calm them, and Minnie's curious face appeared for a moment at the top of the stairs, her eyes round with curiosity. Louisa noticed everything through a haze of disbelief, her mind still trying to deny what just happened and to find a logical explanation for why her husband was hauled away by the governor to be confined in the local prison until the trial. The murder trial. The thought made her turn on Annabel again as she hissed, "You bitch," under her breath.

"Now, look here, Louisa, there's no need for name calling. I'm sure Annabel has a perfectly reasonable explanation, don't you?" Charles asked, turning to his wife and glaring at her from beneath his eyebrows. "Please tell me there's a good reason for what you did, Annabel, because at this moment, I'm ready to wring your neck."

Annabel was panting like a steam engine, her face red to the roots of her hair as she finally stepped out of her hiding place and faced Louisa. "I heard. I heard it all, Louisa. Your darling husband threatened to kill Deverell and toss him in the river. In my opinion, he deserves to hang."

"Well, no one is asking you, are they?" Louisa bellowed, ready to scratch Annabel's eyes out.

"Why would he want to kill Deverell?" Charles asked, skillfully inserting himself between the two women. "They hardly know each other."

"Ask her," Annabel spat out, "or maybe she doesn't know. Seems our Kit likes to keep secrets that are worth killing for." Charles visibly paled, but Annabel was on a roll now. "I might stay quiet about a lot of things, but I will not condone murder, you hear?"

"Murder?" Louisa yelled. "You just condemned my husband to hang. You are the murderer. And what secrets are you blathering about?"

"Do you think I don't know that Tom is my brother's son? Do you think I'm ignorant of the fact that your whore of a niece spread her legs for everyone and anyone with a stiff cock and got herself pregnant? Lucky for her that dolt Theo married her or she would have been disgraced and ostracized. Well, Tom belongs to me, you hear? He is my flesh and blood. He's the only family I have left besides Charles and the children and my father's estate is lost to us because Tom is not legally my brother's son. I know that little whore had something to do with Tom's death, and it was Kit who allowed it to happen. It was Kit who failed to see the signs and rein her in before it was too late."

Louisa sank down on the settee, her legs shaking so badly she couldn't manage to stand for another second. So this is what this was about. With both Little Louisa and Theo gone, there was no one to blame besides Alec and Valerie, and they had been away when Tom died, with Kit acting as guardian to Louisa. So Annabel decided that this was a fitting punishment for the wrong done to her family.

"Charles, I think you need to take your wife and leave this house. Tomorrow morning will do. I will not stay under the same roof with this woman, nor will I ever speak to her again, and I cannot guarantee her safety once I regain the strength to get up."

"Come away, Annabel. We'll go stay with Cousin Wesley in Jamestown. I'm sure he won't mind. He was just complaining about how lonesome it is to be in that house all by himself. Pack a few things for yourself and the children. Now go!" he roared as Annabel stood rooted to the spot.

"Louisa, I'm deeply sorry for what Annabel has done, and I will do everything in my power to help Kit, but you don't have the authority to throw us out. Only Alec can do that, and I will have a word with him when he finally shows up. And I would dearly like to know where he is. All these unexplained absences are rather suspicious. Where are they, Louisa?"

Louisa looked up at Charles, her eyes swimming with tears. "I have no idea where they are, and that's the truth." She buried her face in her hands, her shoulders quaking as she sobbed quietly, her face averted from Charles.

"Louisa," he said, coming closer, but she waved him away. "Just go, Charles. There's nothing you can do."

THIRTY-SEVEN
PRINCETON, NEW JERSEY AUGUST 2010

Alec looked around in wonder as they passed through FitzRandolph Gate and walked across the campus of Princeton University to the physics department located in Jadwin Hall. Valerie hadn't been to Princeton since she was in college herself and had attended a football game with a few of her friends, crashing a wild party afterwards, much of which she still couldn't remember, but everything looked much the same. The main part of the campus boasted a cluster of stately, ivy-covered buildings built in the Collegiate Gothic style, so popular at one time for building places of learning.

Princeton was meant to remind one of Oxford and Cambridge, lending one to feel the weight of influence and power as soon as one passed through the gate onto this impressive campus. There were few students around as it was summer break, but some were seen here and there, lazing around on the lawn or reading under a leafy tree. Valerie supposed that summer classes were in session for those who wished to take them.

They walked past the imposing cathedral and made their way toward the newer part of campus, built in the twentieth century and cleverly hidden behind the older buildings. Alec stared in disgust at the ultra-modern building that housed the physics department, its angular shape so at odds with the beautiful architecture they'd just seen. A row of potted trees formed a path to the entrance, and a modern metal sculpture graced the open space in front of the building, looking like some alien creature dropped from outer space and about to go on a rampage of destruction.

"What in the world is that meant to be?" Alec asked as they passed the sculpture. He gave it a wide berth, but his eyes never left the metal panels that reflected the sunlight and glinted menacingly.

"I've no idea," Valerie replied, her voice tight with anxiety. Her stomach was twisted into knots and her hands ice-cold and shaking. This was their only chance, and it was a long shot at best. Alec put his arm around her as they approached the entrance and kissed the top of her head. "I know you're terrified but have faith."

"Oh, Alec, I just want to go home," Valerie moaned as her eyes filled with tears. "I want to go home."

"I know, sweetheart, so do I, but it's out of our hands now. We have to put one foot in front of the other and see where it takes us. If you think too far ahead, you'll never get through today."

"I can't help thinking ahead. The thought of never seeing any of them again just breaks my heart, again and again. I wake up every morning and look around to find myself not at home in our bed, but in this waking nightmare. I want to go home," she whispered.

Alec steered her through the door. She knew he felt the same, but he was more stoic. Men weren't supposed to fall apart at the first sign of trouble. He had to be strong for her, and he had been calm and supportive as he always was in times of crisis.

The secretary was a young, perky woman who seemed to respond to Alec's cultured British accent a lot quicker than she responded to Valerie. She practically purred when Alec asked for her help, batting her eyelashes and smiling provocatively, her face drooping when she realized she couldn't help.

"I'm sure you understand, Mr. Whitfield, that we are unable to divulge personal information about the staff, but I can confirm that Professor Bloom is still employed by the department and will be back to teach a class in September." She smiled pleasantly at Alec in the hope that he didn't blame her for the regulations that forbade her from helping him. Her smile indicated that she would have jumped through flaming hoops if he so much as offered to take her for a drink.

"I can't wait till September," Alec replied pleasantly. "Is there anything at all you can tell us, Amber?" He gave the woman a dazzling smile, which made her blush prettily.

"Well, I suppose it wouldn't be against the rules to tell you that although I can't provide you with Professor Bloom's address, you just might be able to find it in the phone book under Nancy Bloom. There's a phone book right over there." Alec practically beamed at her as Valerie leafed through the book, searching for Nancy Bloom. "Got it," she announced triumphantly as she found an address on Mercer Road. "Let's go."

"You've been a very great help," Alec said, smiling as the young woman purred, "Not at all, Mr. Whitfield, not at all."

"Oh, stop smirking," Valerie said as they left the office. "You're old enough to be her father."

Alec laughed and planted a sweet kiss on Valerie's lips. "I believe you're jealous, my sweet, and that makes it all the more enjoyable. Come, let's go find the professor."

THIRTY-EIGHT

The professor's house was a sweet cottage on a leafy street located not too far from the center of town, its white façade smothered by roses and hydrangeas, their shaggy heads a stunning purple and blue that contrasted wildly with the reds and yellows of the roses. The effect was dazzling. The garden looked well-tended, as did the man responsible, who was sitting on the porch, reading the paper and sipping a glass of something cold that looked like lemonade.

"Professor Bloom?" Valerie called out, hoping he couldn't see her nervousness. Her hands were shaking, her heart racing in her chest. This was it.

"Yes, how can I help?" He still had a slight trace of a British accent, even after all these years in America, and his well-pressed khakis, butter-yellow polo shirt, and polished loafers made him look as if he'd just stepped off the pages of some catalogue catering to older gentlemen. Valerie was relieved to see that he wasn't annoyed by the intrusion, quite the opposite. He seemed eager for company.

"We are friends of Frederick Taylor," she announced, carefully gauging his reaction, which was instantaneous and very positive. Professor Bloom's face broke into a warm smile, his eyes twinkling with pleasure.

"Is that so? What a wonderful surprise. How is dear old Fred? I haven't seen him in three decades at least, not since the last time I went for a visit when my auntie died. Do come in. Lemonade? Tea?"

"Actually, dear old Fred is living in the seventeenth century with his wife," Valerie supplied as she followed the old man into the house. She wasn't sure what she expected, but it wasn't the burst of laughter as Mr. Bloom smacked his knee with mirth.

"So he's finally gone and done it, has he? Do sit down. I want to hear all about it, but first things first." He disappeared into the kitchen and Valerie smiled at Alec and gave him the thumbs up. So far so good.

Mr. Bloom reappeared a few minutes later with a pitcher of lemonade, glasses, a plate of butter cookies, and a bowl of berries, all arranged on an old-fashioned tray. He set it down on the coffee table and sat across from Alec and Valerie, openly studying them as if they were interesting specimens and not two people who just appeared on his doorstep.

"You were born in the twentieth century," he observed as he looked at Valerie, "but you are far from home, aren't you?" He gave Alec a sympathetic look as he reached for a cookie. "I recognize the look of a man who feels utterly out of place. Please, tell me why you've come to see me."

Mr. Bloom listened carefully as Valerie told him their story, his eyes occasionally growing large behind his glasses and his eyebrows disappearing almost entirely beneath his bushy white hair. He completely forgot about his drink, the glass left untouched on a little end table by his elbow. "Is that so?" he asked several times as Valerie told him of her journey through time and their subsequent trip to the present to get Alec to a hospital.

"Women are always right," he said when Valerie finished. "It's their most annoying quality."

He gazed sadly at the portrait of a smiling middle-aged woman in a large sun hat. "That's my Nancy. She passed away two years ago. Breast cancer. It was Nancy that came between Fred and me." Mr. Bloom chuckled at the memory. "When she found out what we were up to, she gave me the mother of all ultimatums. Said it was either Fred or her and the boys. She would have left me, too. Nancy was always a woman of her word. She said it was only a matter of time until some poor, unsuspecting soul found himself God only knew when and where."

He looked at Alec, studying his features. "When that Hungarian student disappeared from Fred's village, Nancy had the right of it. She said, "Mark my words, Isaac, that girl didn't run away; she fell through time thanks to your friend. So, she was your grandmother, eh? Yes, I can see something Magyar in your face. Hungarians have some very distinctive facial features, don't you think?"

"I actually haven't met any, except for my grandmother, but she was very beautiful," Alec replied, smiling at the eccentric little man.

"Was she angry about what happened to her? I was always curious about that."

"She might have been at the beginning, but by the time I came along, she was very much a woman of her time. She did miss some things though, and she told me about them in secret. I think she just needed to feel that it had all been real and not a figment of her imagination."

"Yes, I can see how after a while it would seem like a dream. I'm glad to know she found a place for herself. I thought of her often and wondered how Fred was coping with the knowledge that he sent the poor girl to the past. I thought he might have gone back for her, but he obviously didn't."

"Would you have gone back for her?" Valerie asked. Mr. Bloom's answer meant a lot since it showed what kind of person he was beneath the charming exterior. Fred Taylor took the easy way out and let the girl fend for herself in the sixteenth century. He chose to protect himself and his secret rather than save Erzebet or save Valerie when the same thing happened to her.

"Yes, I would have gone back. It's one thing to want to time travel; it's quite another to wind up somewhere and have no recourse." He cleared his throat, suddenly realizing that he'd just described their present situation.

"Anyway, we had some good times, Fred and I," Mr. Bloom went on. "Fred was always interested in WWI and the Russian Revolution, but I was more of an Egyptologist myself. I went back a dozen times, saw them building the pyramids, my dears, and feasted my eyes on the beauty of Cleopatra," he confided, his eyes misted with memory. "She was actually quite plain beneath the paint, but no one dared to notice. She was a queen through and through, highly skilled in self-promotion and political maneuvering, a major accomplishment for a woman of her time."

Valerie couldn't help chuckling. He was so happy to talk to someone of his adventures. "One day, Nancy just happened to be in the room when I popped back in. She saw the white tunic and my kohl-lined eyes and nearly died of apoplexy. She guessed right away..."

"And put a kibosh on the whole thing, ha?" Valerie asked, smiling at Mr. Bloom.

"A kibosh doesn't begin to describe it, dear girl. It was a dressing down of epic proportions, with me cowering like an errant schoolboy as my wife read me the riot act. God, I loved that woman."

"Mr. Bloom," Alec interjected smoothly, "Can you help us?"

"Oh, of course, of course. Now, I haven't dabbled in time travel in decades. Promised Nancy and kept my word, even after her death. It will take time for me to build a device, and then it must be thoroughly tested before you can attempt to return. In the meantime, you kids should have some fun. Think of it as a vacation."

"It's actually rather difficult as we have no legal documents or ready funds," Alec replied softly.

"Not to worry. You can stay with me. I have plenty of room, and all the neighbors need to know is that my nephew from England is visiting with his wife. You can even borrow my car. I know you don't have a license, but even if you get a ticket, it's not as if you'll be around to pay it. Go to the shore, visit New York and see a show, go to the Metropolitan Museum. They have an excellent Egyptian display. Did I say something wrong?" he asked as Valerie's face visibly paled.

"My sister works at the Met. She's an art restorer."

"Better stay away then. Could royally mess things up, considering where she is now. Oh, sweet Jesus, can you imagine her reaction if you told her what you just told me?" Mr. Bloom was rubbing his hands and practically cackling. The old guy obviously had a good sense of humor.

"Now, there's a guest room at the top of the stairs. Fresh linens and towels in the cupboard, and a private bath. How does that suit? Valerie, my dear, do you perchance know how to make lasagna? Nancy always made it for me, but I haven't had it since she passed. I like it homemade."

"It will be my pleasure to make you lasagna, and anything else you might like as long as you send me home, Mr. Bloom."

"Deal." Isaac Bloom catapulted out of his armchair, looking around for his keys. "We're off then. I need to get some things for my device, and you, my dear, need to get ingredients at the supermarket. Alec, how are you with mowing the lawn? It could use a trim. I have one of those lawnmowers you can drive. Bet you'd like that," he beamed at Alec. "Not a sports car, but a start, eh? Try not to run anyone over." With that, he practically sprinted from the house with Valerie on his heels and a bemused Alec looking after them.

THIRTY-NINE
VIRGINIA AUGUST 1626

Genevieve paced in front of the bench, her heart beating wildly at the thought of Cameron refusing her. She'd asked Minnie to deliver a note to him asking him to meet tonight, but they hadn't seen each other in days, and she thought he might decide to stay away, simply to send her the message once again that their association was over. She whirled around at the sound of a breaking twig, letting out a breath of relief at the sight of Cameron's tall figure heading toward her from the direction of the barracks. He looked tired, and his hair hung down to his shoulders, not confined to the usual queue he wore while working. She tried to ignore the wary expression on his face as she invited him to sit down, her cheeks hot with embarrassment.

"Cameron, I didn't ask you here to... you know," she stammered. "I just really needed someone to talk to, and I suddenly realized that with both my uncles gone, I have no one to turn to."

Cameron's face softened, his eyes gazing at her with more affection than he probably wanted to show. "What is it, lass? What's troubling ye?" He didn't mean to, but his hand reached out for her, enveloping it in his calloused palms and instantly making her feel better.

"I just don't understand what's happening, and I'm scared," Genevieve whispered, looking into his eyes. "First, my aunt and uncle left, supposedly to see a physician. They've been gone for some time now, and no one knows where they are or when they'll be back. Lady Sheridan nearly jumps out of her skin anytime anyone asks. Then, Uncle Charles, Annabel, and the children left for Jamestown. I know there was a terrible confrontation the night before, but I don't know what about. And the worst is that Lord Sheridan has been arrested for the murder of Aloysius Deverell. Lady Sheridan is beside herself with anxiety. Everything seems to be unraveling like a ball of yarn."

Genevieve didn't mean to cry, but hot tears spilled down her cheeks, her hands pleating the fabric of her skirt as they always did when she was scared or nervous. It had taken her a long time to convince herself that she really had a family now and that she would be safe and cared for, and all of a sudden, everything was falling apart. Uncle Alec and Aunt Valerie disappeared, and Lord Sheridan could swing for murder. Just the thought of that made Genevieve cry harder. Kit was one of the nicest men she'd ever met and the notion of him dying such a horrible death was more than she could bear. No matter what anyone said, he couldn't have killed that man. He didn't have it in him.

"Lord Sheridan has been accused of murder?" Cameron asked, his face slack with shock. "Why?"

"It seems someone came forth with information about his involvement. I'm not sure exactly what. Lady Sheridan is keeping us in the dark, for the children's sake, I think. She still hopes Lord Sheridan will be exonerated." She looked up at Cameron, but he seemed to be staring off into the distance, his mouth a grim line across his face.

"What is it, Cameron? Did you see something that night?" she asked.

"Nae, but Lord Sheridan is a good man. I'd hate to see him hang for a crime he dinna commit. I ken well enough what it feels like to be accused of something ye had no' done."

That was the first time he'd mentioned anything of his past, and Genevieve remained quiet, hoping he would continue to talk, but he turned back to her, the moment gone. Genevieve leaned in as Cameron caressed her cheek with his knuckles, his face soft in the gathering darkness.

"I ken ye're scared, but try to be brave, aye? Yer aunt and uncle will be back soon; I'm sure of it. And Lady Sheridan will find a way to help her husband. She's a very clever woman; she'll think of something. Ye just do yer best to help her and mind the children. Everything will work itself out, aye?" He pulled away his hand, realizing what he'd done. "I best be going now, but I'll come back in two days to see how ye are. When's the trial?"

"Friday after next, so they can hang him on Saturday, and pray for their eternal souls on Sunday," Genevieve answered bitterly, angry with herself for feeling so frightened.

"Promise me ye'll be strong," Cameron demanded.

"I promise," she murmured, wishing she was promising to love and obey him till death did them part.

FORTY

Louisa jumped to her feet as Sir George Yeardley walked through the door, giving her a curt nod. "Good afternoon, Lady Sheridan. What can I do for you?"

He was normally very courteous, but Louisa could see the irritation in his eyes and the brisk manner in which he shifted papers on his desk before finally giving her his undivided attention. It had taken her a full two days to get an audience with him, his clerk constantly fobbing her off and telling her that Sir George was unavailable, but Louisa wouldn't take no for an answer. Time was of the essence, and she needed to plead Kit's case in person. It was always much harder to deny a person to their face than by letter. She'd waited in the governor's anteroom for hours both days, refusing to leave until he finally agreed to see her.

"Sir George, I implore you to release Kit. You've known him for years, and you know he couldn't have done such a thing. Besides, what possible reason would he have to kill Mr. Deverell? As a matter of fact, you just saw them both at the Deverells' supper party, and there wasn't a hint of animosity between them." Louisa smiled at Sir George in a futile effort to win him over.

"Lady Sheridan, I hold your husband in very high regard, and I personally don't believe that he would have killed Mr. Deverell, but as governor of this colony, I can't go about freeing people purely because I happen to like them. There's a credible witness who heard your husband threaten Mr. Deverell, and I can't simply dismiss her statement. Mistress Whitfield is also of high standing in the community, and I see absolutely no reason why she should fabricate such a scenario."

Sir George held his hands aloft, demonstrating his impotence to do anything about the situation. "Now, if you could vouch for your husband's movements on that evening, then we'd have grounds for doubting Mistress Whitfield's claim. Can you account for his whereabouts?"

"I went to bed with a headache, so I didn't see him, which is not to say that he wasn't there," Louisa answered defensively.

"Lady Sheridan, Mr. Deverell was killed either in the evening or during the night. Unless you can assure me that your husband was with you the entire night, I can't dismiss the testimony against him. Now, I would advise you to seek legal representation. There's Master Brooks, who is a man of the law and has assisted me in drafting several legal documents. He's an honest and learned man; you should go and see him."

"I would like to represent my husband," Louisa blurted out, staring down Sir George. Louisa knew little of the law, but she knew that a seventeenth-century lawyer who lived in Jamestown most likely had absolutely no courtroom experience. He drafted wills and deeds of sale, which was the only type of skill needed in the colony. In all her time in Virginia, there'd never been a murder trial that she could recall. There'd been hangings, but the accused had confessed in the hopes of getting a diminished sentence, which didn't happen.

"Out of the question. You are a woman and the wife of the

defendant. By law, you are his property, so it stands to reason that a servant cannot defend the master in court. Get help." With that, he rose to his feet, signaling that the interview was over.

Louisa would have liked to express her feelings on the subject, but bit her tongue and sank into a curtsy, her upper lip curling with sarcasm. "As you say, Sir George, a feebleminded woman should never take on the task suitable only for a man."

"Rightly so, Lady Sheridan, rightly so. I'm glad you see sense. Good day to you, ma'am."

"May I see my husband?" Louisa asked, smiling despite an overwhelming desire to kick him in the balls.

"You may not. You are overwrought and no good can come from a hysterical outburst. Your husband is accused of murder and is not permitted any visitors besides his counsel until the trial. I feel that's a wise course of action." Sir George had the decency to look contrite.

"Now, if you would like to bring something for him, the guard will make sure he gets it. Otherwise, stay away. The trial is set for Friday of next week. I suggest you consult Master Brooks with the utmost expediency. Now, good day, Lady Sheridan."

Sir George strode out of the office, leaving Louisa stunned and afraid. If he wouldn't even let her see Kit, things were worse than she thought. They were close acquaintances and had spent many an evening dining, talking, and playing at cards and dice. The governor didn't want his reputation tainted by an association with a possible murderer and might be that much more severe in his judgment of Kit just to avoid any implication that he was being lenient due to their personal relationship.

Oh, Kit, Louisa thought, stumbling from the governor's office, *how am I to help you?*

FORTY-ONE

Kit paced the tiny space, unable to settle down. The cell was airless, stinking of piss, feces, and fear. Not so long ago, Louisa had been locked up in here, and now it was his turn. All he could do was take three steps in either direction, but it didn't stop him from walking, desperate for something to do other than sit on the hard bench. He'd tried to sleep, but every time he closed his eyes, he saw the bloated and bloody face of Deverell. Now it was probably midmorning, judging by the position of the sun and the increasing heat inside the cell. A guard had brought him some bread and ale for breakfast but shrugged in ignorance when Kit asked him about the trial.

Would Sir George even bother to try and discover what happened or was he going to persecute Kit to the full extent of the law based on Annabel's testimony? He had to admit that he never particularly cared for Annabel. She was vain and foolish, always deferring to Charles, especially when it suited her own interests. What could she possibly gain by having Kit executed? Kit turned on his heel and began pacing again, three steps forward and three steps back. The guard brought his midday meal and then his supper, but still Kit paced, unable to stop thinking. His head ached, and his shoulders and neck were stiff with tension, but still he couldn't rest.

He had exhausted himself by the time he heard the key in the lock and Louisa stepped into the cell, her nose wrinkling in disgust at the smell, or maybe at the sight of him. The guard shut the door behind her, leaving them alone. The sun had set some time ago, allowing the cell to cool marginally and plunging it into darkness. Louisa's features were swallowed by the shadows as she stepped forward, holding out a basket containing food and a clean shirt.

"I've been to see Sir George," Louisa said as she watched him warily. "He forbade me to see you."

"So, how did you…?"

"I bribed the guard. He's a nice boy, and his mother is ill. A sack of tobacco can go a long way to make things easier for them." Her voice was flat and emotionless. Had she given up on him already?

"Lou, I didn't do it; I swear I didn't. I can't remember much of that night, but I was so drunk I could barely stand, much less walk to Jamestown, beat a man to death, and drag him to the docks. You've got to believe me," he pleaded with her, his stomach twisting into knots at the look on her face. Did she despise him for what he'd done?

"Kit, I know you didn't do it," she said quietly, "but we need to prove that to Sir George. Can you think of anyone who might have seen you that evening? Is there any proof that you never came into Jamestown?"

Kit shook his head. "I was in the barn, so unless they can get the cows to testify, I'm doomed," he said with a sad smile. "Lou, do you despise me?" he blurted out.

"I could never despise you. Kit, I can't begin to understand the way I feel right now, and that will all have to wait until after the trial, but right now we need to prove your innocence, and I need all the help I can get. What do you know of Deverell? Did he have any particular enemies at court? Is there anyone here who might wish him harm?"

"I don't know. I barely knew the man, but I know Buckingham didn't like him." Kit nearly bit his tongue when he saw the look of revulsion on Louisa's face. Mentioning Buckingham had been a mistake.

"Buckingham is a shrewd man. If he didn't like Deverell, he must have had his reasons. Maybe he was trying to blackmail him as well," Louisa speculated as she looked at Kit with some hope.

Kit let out a bitter laugh. "If Deverell tried to blackmail Buckingham, he would have been swimming in the Thames long before he ever made it to Virginia. Buckingham didn't play games with his enemies; he destroyed them." In more ways than one, Kit thought bitterly, watching his wife.

"What did he want from you, Kit?"

"Money, of course. He wanted me to buy him a plantation, and I'm sure he wouldn't have stopped there. He thought he had me over a barrel."

Louisa chose not to point out that he had. Deverell had the power to destroy Kit, and Kit knew it. Had he told anyone else what he knew or had the secret died with him? She would go see Mistress Deverell under the pretense of a condolence visit. Maybe she could learn something from her. Louisa felt a surge of hope as she thought of doing something to help Kit. She'd conduct her own investigation.

"Lou, how much did Annabel actually overhear?"

"Just the threat, I think. Had she heard more, she'd be cawing about it from every rooftop in Jamestown. It would be too good to keep to herself." Kit nodded. At least that was a blessing.

"Lou, will you come back to see me before the trial?" he asked, his voice breaking.

"I'll try. I think it's best if I don't incense Sir George right before the trial. Kit, I won't let them hang you. I won't," she said fiercely, finally leaving her spot by the door and pulling him into a hug. Kit's arms went around her, his head dropping to her shoulder as she stroked his hair and kissed his forehead. "I won't let them hang you," she whispered again.

FORTY-TWO
NORTH CAROLINA AUGUST 1779

Finn made his way through the clearing, weaving between canvas tents that reminded him of Indian wigwams. The night was lit by dozens of campfires, dark silhouettes of men moving about as the firelight illuminated the faces of those who sat near. Some were talking softly, some laughing at a bawdy joke, and others just staring into the flames, their faces creased with fatigue and loneliness. Finn could hear the restless neighing of horses and the occasional click of metal as someone unbuckled a belt or cleaned their musket, but otherwise the camp was unusually quiet, the atmosphere strangely subdued.

He hadn't planned on coming this way, but he wanted to see Jonah and bring word home that he was all right. Jonah had written only one letter in the past few months, asking after everyone and assuring his parents that he was well, but Mrs. Mallory was sick with worry, certain that her son wasn't telling the truth. Finn missed Jonah more than he cared to admit. Sam and Jonah were the closest thing he had to brothers, and whereas Sam seemed to have the proverbial nine lives, Jonah wasn't as lucky or as resourceful. If Mrs. Mallory was worried, she likely had good reason to be and would welcome any news he could bring her.

It took Finn the better part of an hour to finally locate Jonah's tent since it was situated on the outskirts of the camp, closer to the woods. Finn almost didn't recognize him at first. Jonah had always been lean, but now he was whippet-thin, his lean cheeks covered by a thick beard that made him look ten years older, his skin waxy in the light of the fire that was burning low, its flames reflecting in Jonah's fixed gaze.

"Finn! What a surprise!" Jonah exclaimed, as he invited Finn to sit down and held out a cup of strong tea that was bitter and lukewarm. Finn took a sip, grimaced and set the cup down. "I'm so happy to see you, Finn. How's everyone? Did Susanna have the baby?"

"Not as far as I know. Everyone is well, and they miss you. Your mother is frantic, since she hasn't had a letter from you in months." Finn didn't mean to sound accusing, but Jonah seemed well able to write, and months without word was torture for people back home.

"I miss them too," Jonah sighed and took a sip of tea, seemingly oblivious to the bitterness. "I'm so sick of this war, Finn. I just want to go home. Sometimes I dream of being at home and I'm so happy, then I wake up and I'm in some godforsaken place: cold, hungry, and dirty. It seems as if it will never end."

"You couldn't wait to join up, remember?" Finn asked, smiling at Jonah. He had been so young and idealistic then, so eager to fight for his beliefs. The illusions had been stripped away, replaced by the grim reality of war and the senseless carnage that never seemed to end.

"Yes, I remember. I didn't think it would go on for years though, did I? There's no end in sight, and no guarantee of victory."

Finn desperately wanted to tell Jonah that the rebels would

win the war and that it would end in 1781, but he couldn't, not without having a lot of explaining to do. The final battle would be fought mere miles from the Mallory farm, at Yorktown, finally forcing the British to admit defeat and return home in disgrace.

"It will end, Jonah. You'll see. It won't be long now."

"I don't know, Finn. We seem to have reached a stalemate. We win one, they win one, and nothing really changes except that more people die on both sides," Jonah replied with disgust.

"You just stay safe and don't do anything foolish," Finn admonished as he watched Jonah over the fire.

"Speaking of foolish, where have you been?" Jonah asked, setting his cup down and gazing into the flames.

"I was in Savannah. All was going smoothly until I ran into Weland."

"No kidding!" Jonah exclaimed, gaping at Finn. "Did he recognize you?

"He sure did. He gave chase and called for reinforcements that had me cornered in a cellar."

"How did you get away?" Jonah perked up a bit, eager to hear the story.

"You wouldn't believe me if I told you, so I won't. A lovely girl helped me."

"Ah, what I wouldn't do for a lovely girl," Jonah replied, clapping Finn on the shoulder.

"You have one waiting for you at home."

"Oh?"

"Remember Diana Littleton? Well, she showed up out of the blue—with her son. He's yours, or so she claims." Finn watched a series of emotions play out over Jonah's face, the most obvious being disbelief.

"How old is he?" Jonah finally asked.

"About a year and a half. Sweet lad with those gray Mallory

eyes. He looks just like Sam. So, are you going to make an honest woman of her?"

Jonah shook his head, staring into the flames again, his shoulders slumped. This was obviously unwelcome news and Finn was almost sorry he'd said anything. Jonah looked as if he were about to cry.

"What it is?" Finn asked, sensing some inner battle raging inside of Jonah. "What's wrong?"

Jonah scratched his bearded jaw, his eyes clouded by indecision, but then he turned to Finn, ready to tell the truth. "Finn, I met Diana while I was stationed in New York, but I never slept with her, not once. I was supposed to put her in touch with Sam since she was willing to pass on information she'd learned from her clients, but I was never one of them. Whores are not really my thing, you know? Her son can't possibly be mine."

Finn's mouth opened in astonishment, the meaning of Jonah's words sinking in. If Jonah hadn't fathered Nathaniel, he could only be Sam's. So, why would Diana say that the child was Jonah's? And then Finn understood. He'd been the first one to see Diana, to tell her of Sam's marriage and coming child. Diana didn't want to ruin Sam's life, but it was too late to turn back, so she'd improvised, telling a lie that would take care of her immediate problem, but knowing that eventually the truth would come out anyway.

"Susanna will be devastated if she ever finds out," Jonah said. "It was before her, but no woman wants to come face to face with her predecessor, especially one with a child. What is Diana going to do, do you think?" Jonah asked.

"I think she hopes you might see her dilemma and keep silent, but your parents will expect you to marry her for the sake of Nathaniel. You're in a real bind, my friend."

"I can't marry her, Finn. Sam's going to have to clean up his own mess this time. I won't say a word to Susanna, but I will have a conversation with Sam once I get back. I won't be roped into this." Jonah spoke softly, but there was a stubborn set to his jaw, and his shoulders were tense as he rested his elbows on his knees.

"I'll talk to Sam once I get back. You look like hell, by the way," Finn observed as he studied Jonah. Jonah tossed another log on the fire and poked it with a stick until the flames rose higher, filling the night with a shower of sparks.

"I'm lucky to be alive, Finn," Jonah said quietly. "I didn't write because I couldn't. I was at the battle of Brier Creek."

Finn looked up in surprise. Everyone had heard of the disaster at Brier Creek, and it was said that the defeat was a major setback that could cost Americans the war. Some blamed General Ashe for poor strategy and lack of foresight, but Finn thought that was unfair. Battles were won and lost all the time, and Brier Creek came on the heels of a major victory at Kettle Creek which raised morale for a short time, but that was months ago. The battle had been fought at the beginning of March, and now it was July.

"Jonah, what happened?"

Jonah shrugged and looked away for a moment before finally turning to meet Finn's eyes. "It was a massacre, Finn, pure and simple. The British suffered hardly any losses, while the Americans were slaughtered. It wasn't even the battle itself, it was the aftermath. We had our backs to the creek and swampland and surrounded by the British. The patriot forces consisted mainly of North Carolina and Georgia militias, and several Continental Army units under Samuel Elbert. Some of the militiamen ran without even firing a shot, and many took to the Savannah River and the swamps once they sensed defeat. There's no saying how many people drowned that day."

"And you?" Finn asked softly, sensing Jonah's need to talk.

"It was complete chaos, so a few of us tried to flee through the swamps and regroup on the other side. That was the plan at least, but it didn't work out that way. Two men drowned in the swamp within the first several minutes. I watched them get swallowed up by the mire, screaming for help until the last second, still hoping to be saved."

Jonah's voice cracked as he remembered those awful moments. "They were just boys, Finn, no older than seventeen. I wanted to go back, but someone held me back. Those men were lost, and we had to help ourselves. I don't remember how many hours we spent wading through the swamps; it felt like days, and maybe it was. Only two of us made it to the other side. We were soaked, exhausted, and chilled to the bone. There was nothing to start a fire with, so we covered ourselves with old leaves while we slept, hoping we wouldn't freeze to death. I'd never been so cold and hungry in my whole life." Jonah's voice was flat as he spoke, a faraway look in his eyes.

"Were you able to rejoin the Continental Army?" Finn asked, already guessing at the answer.

"No. We started walking after we rested, but we were hungry and fevered; we had no strength to walk all that way. Captain Lee, whom I was with, could barely stand, so we had to rest every few minutes. It was so cold, Finn, and our uniforms were still wet and clinging to our skin. My teeth were chattering so bad I thought my jaw would break."

"What happened then?"

"I don't know. I must have lost consciousness because when I woke, I was in a farmhouse, stripped to nothing, and sitting in front of a roaring fire wrapped in a blanket. A woman found us by the side of the road and brought us home. I was so delirious I didn't even ask after Captain Lee for several days. I kept slipping in and out of consciousness, and she tended to me day and night, feeding me beef tea and putting cold compresses on my forehead." Jonah poured another cup of tea and took a sip. The night around them was warm, but he shivered, cradling the cup as if he were still freezing in that swamp.

"Captain Lee died two days after Augusta found us, but I managed to survive. It took nearly a month until I was finally feeling better and ready to leave. That's when I wrote the letter to my parents. It was a few days later that the malaria set in. Augusta said it took weeks to manifest itself and that I must have contracted it in the swamp. I thought I was going to die, Finn. I had fever and chills, my head hurt like it was going to split open, and there were periods of time when I couldn't see. I couldn't keep anything down, not even broth."

"She nursed you?" Finn asked.

"She did. She made decoctions of basil leaves, and something with honey and pepper, which tasted awful, but seemed to help. It took me several months to recover fully, and then I stayed for a while and helped her tend the farm. The army thought me dead, so I decided not to rush back." Jonah smiled for the first time since beginning his story, the boy Finn had known suddenly there again beneath the shaggy beard and the pallor.

"And Augusta?"

"Augusta was a godsend. I would have died had it not been for her. Helping her on the farm was the least I could do. Her husband died a few years back, leaving her with two small children," Jonah added by way of explanation. "I'm going back there as soon as I can."

"You love her, don't you?" Finn asked, smiling at Jonah. He'd never met Augusta, but he wished he could express his gratitude to her for saving Jonah.

"I do," said Jonah with a huge grin. "She's a few years older than I am, but it doesn't matter."

"I'd love to meet her."

"Oh, you will," Jonah supplied. "I married her before I left, so I'll be bringing her and the children to meet the family after the baby is born." He seemed a little defiant for a moment, but Finn clapped him on the shoulder.

"Congratulations. I'm happy for you." Finn rose to his feet and looked down at Jonah. "I need to get some sleep. I have a long walk tomorrow. Should I tell them back home that you're married and a father of two, soon to be three?"

Jonah chuckled. "No, just tell them I'm well. I'll tell them the rest myself."

FORTY-THREE
VIRGINIA AUGUST 1626

Cameron had gone back to check on Genevieve, as promised, but then managed to stay away for a week. He swore he wouldn't seek her out, but loneliness won, as always, his feet turning in the direction of the pond as his mind furiously made excuses, telling his heart he was only wanting a bath and not searching for Genevieve's silhouette in the gathering darkness, nor hoping that she would be there waiting for him despite his unkind rejection. She was so different from his Mary--reticent and unassuming, but his soul reached out to her, felt her isolation. Genevieve was part of the Whitfield and Sheridan household, but in the dark recesses of her heart she was still the unwanted orphan, the child conceived in shame.

Master Alec had tactfully brought up the subject of marriage, but Genevieve secretly believed that he simply wanted to be rid of the burden of her upkeep. It would take time for her to finally acknowledge that she was loved and cherished, especially by her uncle, whose face lit up whenever he caught sight of her. Genevieve was a broken person, just like Cameron himself, and her soul subconsciously reached out to his, sensing a kindred spirit who would give her a home that she still longed for, a home where she would be an equal partner and not a poor relation.

Cameron sucked in his breath as he saw her strolling across the lawn toward the pond. She walked slowly, her face turned up to the dramatic colors of the summer sunset, her cheeks flushed with the damp heat of the evening. Genevieve normally covered her hair with a simple linen cap, like the other women of the plantation, but tonight she was wearing it loose, the tendrils snaking down her shoulders and breasts and framing her lovely face. His Mary had been plump and buxom, but Genevieve was slight, her body appearing almost childlike from a distance. She hadn't seen him yet, so Cameron drank in the sight of her, the unselfconscious way in which she twirled and dipped, dancing to the music she heard in her head.

He smiled with pleasure as he saw her lift her arms and take a turn, happy to see her innocent abandon. She was so rarely uninhibited. It's as if she watched her every step and censored her every word, for fear that she would somehow disappoint her aunt and uncle, causing them to doubt the wisdom of bringing her to live with them. Why was she so reluctant to believe that she was loved and wanted when any fool could see that her new family cared for her?

Suddenly, Genevieve stilled, sensing that she was being watched, but smiled as she recognized Cameron's hulking shape in the gathering darkness. She didn't walk any faster, but she was no longer twirling. Instead, her eyes remained glued to his as she closed the distance between them, her lips stretched into the slightest smile of surprise.

"You came," she said, stopping a few feet away from him, her head cocked to the side as she looked up into his face. "I hoped you would, if only for the pleasure of having a cool bath on a warm evening."

"I came to see ye." He hadn't meant to speak the words out loud, but they slipped out of their own accord, defying his best intentions and making his purpose plain. He knew he was being contrary and hated himself for it, but despite his best intentions, he simply couldn't stay away, and she likely knew that, That's why she kept coming back, safe in the knowledge that sooner or later he would return like a faithful puppy.

"I've looked for you every night. I knew you'd come," she replied shyly, taking a step closer to him. "I missed our talks."

Cameron suddenly felt panicked. He wanted to be with her, and she was openly saying that she wanted to be with him. There was no denying the attraction between them, or the fact that this was the deciding moment in their relationship. He either had to walk away and mean it or allow her to love him and return her love with an open heart. He knew the impediments, but so did she, and was willing to live with them. Maybe God was smiling upon him at last and giving him something beautiful to make up for the suffering he'd endured in the past. Cameron glanced away for a moment in indecision, but in his heart, the choice had been made long ago. He turned back to Genevieve's anxious face and gave her a brilliant smile.

"I'd like to bathe first if ye dinna mind, lass. I'm nae fit to be in the company of a lady after a week in the fields with nae proper bath. Will ye turn around for a moment?" he asked as he pulled his shirt over his head slowly, so as not to offend her and give her a chance to turn her back to him. But she didn't budge. She just stood there, staring at him, her face tense and frightened, but her eyes burned with determination to see this through, whatever it was she meant to do.

"Mistress Genevieve, please turn around," he repeated, wondering what she was about. She didn't reply but began to unlace her bodice and push her skirt over her hips until it pooled at her feet, leaving her in just a linen chemise. She took a step closer, her eyes never leaving his as she stepped into the cool water, sighing with pleasure.

"Are you coming?" she asked as the water reached the top of

her breasts. Cameron had two choices: he could bathe in his breeches, which would probably be best under the circumstances, or wade into the water completely naked. Had it been Mary, he wouldn't have thought twice and would have undressed in front of her with no shame or apprehension, but this was Genevieve, his master's niece, and he wasn't sure what the protocol was under the circumstances despite their mutual attraction.

Genevieve watched him hesitate, her face full of disappointment. Had she thought this through or was this a spur-of-the-moment decision on her part? If she felt like being reckless, he had to be the one to keep a cool head. Cameron took a deep breath, decided to keep his breeches on, and stepped closer to the pond, but Genevieve suddenly pulled her shift over her head, tossing it to the shore at his feet. Her eyes daring him to refuse her. Cameron sighed and dropped his breeches against his better judgment. The girl clearly wanted this, and it would be an insult to her if he bolted back to the barracks and rejected her advances. Oh God, what was he to do? Was it just a bath she was after, or did she want more?

Cameron saw her eyes widen in shock as she stared at him. He tried to think of Bible verses and Hail Mary's, but his cock refused to obey, rising to attention at the sight of the beautiful naked sprite in the water. He closed his eyes in shame, his face flaming as she continued to look at him, her mouth opening of its own accord. She'd likely never seen a naked man before, much less a man as aroused as he was. It had been nearly two years since he'd last been with Mary. They never actually made love, but she allowed him to kiss her, sometimes pulling down her bodice to release her ample breasts for him to fondle and suckle. She'd pleasured him too, promising him more delights once they were truly married and their union was sanctioned by God.

Mary would leave him burning with desire, giggling as she

slipped out of the barn and into the night, and him finishing himself off with a few urgent strokes before he exploded with frustration. He dreamed of their wedding night, counting the minutes until she would finally submit to him, allowing him to do all the things that nearly drove him mad in the stillness of the night when the house was asleep around him and he was free to dream and plan.

Cameron waded into the water, not daring to get too close to Genevieve. If she wanted this, she had to come to him, had to make it clear that this was her wish, and she did. She came closer to him, pressing her body against his in the water, the tops of her breasts just visible in the darkness, her mouth parted with desire. She reached for his hand and cupped it around her breast, her other hand closing over his cock in the space between them.

"Genevieve, please..." he whispered, "We canna do this. Ye canna do this."

"Cameron, I'm twenty-five years old, and I've never even been properly kissed. Please don't reject me or I will die of shame. I'm not the kind of woman who begs a man for love, but I can't take this yearning anymore without finding out what it is I'm yearning for. Please, Cameron."

He opened his mouth to protest, but she pulled his head down and kissed him shyly, her body even closer to his than it had been before. Cameron grabbed her buttocks, pulling her to him as he kissed her back, all reserve forgotten, his tongue sliding into her warm mouth and shocking her into momentarily pulling back. He froze, ready to let her go, but she came back into his arms, kissing him with all the abandon of her innocence. Cameron bent his head and kissed her wet breast, cupping it with his hand and bringing it just above the water so that he could get her nipple in his mouth. Genevieve threw her head back, arching her back and closing her eyes as his warm lips tugged at her nipple, and his tongue swirled around until it was hard in his mouth.

This was completely out of character for this shy girl, and his mind was yelling at Cameron to stop and come to his senses for nothing good could come out of this for either of them, but he was already lifting her and wrapping her legs around him as he fitted himself inside her, not surprised by the resistance he encountered. She was still a maid, and it must have taken her all her courage to come to him like this and give up her maidenhead to a slave, one who hadn't spoken any words of love or made any promises.

"Ye're so bonny," he whispered as he moved inside her, stifling her cry with his mouth. She was tense in his arms, clearly surprised by the feelings that were coursing through her. He hoped she wasn't in pain, but what he saw in her face was surprise and desire, not a grimace of suffering. He began to move a little faster, panting with pleasure as he momentarily forgot about her and allowed himself to feel, something he hadn't done in a long time. Suddenly, all the feelings he'd been suppressing came crashing over him, his heart and soul crying out in need as he loosened his hold on his emotions and buried himself deeper in Genevieve. She cried out, but this time it was with pleasure, her hips closing around him like a vise as she moved against him until he exploded inside her, his teeth gently biting her shoulder as he shuddered with release.

He lowered her gently, searching her face for signs of remorse, but saw none. Genevieve opened her eyes, looking up at him with a mixture of wonder and fear. She was probably looking for signs of remorse as well, but she wouldn't find any, not anymore. He pulled her to him, kissing her hair and whispering words of love. They came naturally, suddenly making him feel human again, like a man who was capable of love, even if he was in no position to make any promises. They walked out of the water together and dressed in silence, their eyes finding each other every few seconds and glancing away in sudden awkwardness. What were they to do now?

Genevieve was the one who addressed the question as she stepped into her shoes and sat down on the grass, patting the space next to her. "Please don't say anything," she mumbled. "Let's just enjoy this moment and not think about tomorrow. It will come soon enough, and so will the need to face up to what we've done, but for now, I just want to be with you a little bit longer."

Cameron settled on the grass next to her and kissed her temple. He wanted to tell her all manner of things, but she was right; now wasn't the time. They were floating on a bubble of emotion and lust, and eventually the bubble would burst, allowing in all the impediments that stood in their way.

"Cameron, how did you come to be here?" Genevieve asked.

He knew it was time to tell, but although he'd thought of nothing else since that day, he'd never actually spoken the words aloud, not since the day he was sent down, his life stolen from him. Cameron took a shaky breath as his arm tightened around Genevieve. She wouldn't like his story, and possibly wouldn't like him after he told it, but he owed her the truth, and it was time he forgave himself and took some comfort from a woman who was willing to give it.

FORTY-FOUR

Cameron's voice was soft when he finally spoke, but Genevieve could hear the emotion he tried to hold in check as he recounted the events of that day and what followed. He didn't look at her but at the clouds floating above their heads, as if he could float away too and leave everything behind.

"It happened in early September, nearly two years past, at harvest time. I was in the fields by myself since Da had taken poorly, and Mam bid him to stay abed. He grumbled, but he was relieved. It was hard work, and he was getting on in years, ready to hand over the running o' the farm to me." Cameron was silent for a moment, no doubt picturing that day in his mind. Genevieve didn't push him; he'd speak in his own good time.

"I'd been there since early morning, cutting the wheat with even, rhythmic strokes, the stalks falling to the ground, their heads heavy with grain, and leaving a wide path through the uncut bit. I remember stopping to wipe my brow and looking around me, thinking what a glorious day it was to be alive and how happy I was. I was to be married in a week, ye see, to a lass

I'd loved since I were a wee lad. It'd always been Mary for me—my Mary."

Cameron felt Genevieve tense against him as he spoke the words, but if she wanted the truth, it had to start with Mary and his love for her. He drew Genevieve closer to let her know that it was her he wanted now, but the story had to be told, and it would bring her pain.

"It was just around noon, the sun riding high in a sky that was just a vast expanse o' blue, so brilliant, it hurt the eyes to look at it, but look at it I did, and let it caress my face and warm my shoulders. I smiled, thinking that Mary would be coming soon with my dinner, and that she'd stay and we'd share a few peaceful moments together before she went back to her chores and I finished that section of the field. She always stayed, prattling on about this and that as I ate, and filling my head full o' village gossip. I loved listening to her. She took such an interest in everything and everyone, and always told me I was too much of a loner for my own good. She was all the company I ever needed, her and the bairns we were going to have."

Cameron let out a quivering sigh at the mention of children, but forced himself to go on with the story, eager to have it done with. "I saw her walking down the lane, her hips swaying in time with the basket on her arm. She wasna in a rush, enjoying the little time she got away from the farm and all the chores that were just waiting to be done. Mary stopped in the middle o' the lane and shielded her eyes from the sun, smiling at me. I waved to her, and she waved back. Had I no' waved, she might o' kept walking, but she just stood there for a moment, watching me, and then glanced down to adjust something inside the basket."

Cameron grew silent and looked as if he would choke on his next words, but he finally managed to get them out, his voice flat and emotionless as he tried for dear life not to fall apart.

"They came 'round the bend in the lane at breakneck speed, the dirt churning beneath the hooves o' the horses as the driver cracked the whip, urging them to go faster. The other man cried out in alarm, screaming for the driver to slow down, but he dinnae. He mowed Mary down where she stood and never even stopped. Ye see, she was naught to him, just a peasant girl who happened to be in his way. He was an English gentleman from a neighboring estate, and although I'd never met him, I'd heard o' him, and it was naught to his credit."

Genevieve put her hand over Cameron's, but he hardly noticed, his eyes glazed with the memory of that horrible day.

"I ran through the field, calling her name, but I kent she was gone before I even got there. She was sprawled across the lane, her body broken, but her face miraculously untouched, her wide blue eyes staring up at the sky as if she were just watching the clouds racing past on a windy day. Her expression was no' one o' pain or fear, but rather surprise, unable to believe that this happened to her. What kind of animal would just run over a young girl and keep going as if she were nothing more than a carcass of sheep? I picked her up and carried her back to the farm. I must have got there, for I remember my mam screaming and crying, and my da stepping into the yard still wearing his nightshirt. I remember my sisters weeping, but I canna remember the walk back or what I did until the funeral."

Cameron wiped his eyes with the back of his hand, his gesture almost angry. Genevieve wasn't sure if he was angry with himself for crying, angry with Mary for dying, or still angry with the men who ran her down. Or maybe he was still grieving.

"Mary had lived with us since her own mam died, so it was my mam who laid her out and dressed her in what would have been her wedding finery. Most lasses start working on their shrouds once they're wed, but Mary never got the chance. My mam got the best banshees from the surrounding villages to come and keen at Mary's funeral."

"What's a banshee?" Genevieve asked, unfamiliar with the

term. Cameron answered matter-of-factly, his mind still on the events that changed his life forever.

"That's what they call women who keen at a funeral. They're paid mourners who wail and lament, but it's a sign of love and respect to have a good banshee, even more so to have more than one, aye?"

"I see," Genevieve mumbled, unsure what the point of paid wailing was, but wise enough not to question Cameron in the middle of his account. "Please, continue."

"My Mary had a fine funeral; we made sure of that. She would have liked that. After the funeral, I just couldna settle down to anything. I was burning with rage, and I was naive enough to think that the law would be on my side. My da warned me to let it be, but I wouldna listen. I went to Glasgow to see the local magistrate, since there was nae form of legal representation in the villages. I accused the man who ran Mary down o' murder, and a hearing was set."

"It didn't go as you imagined it would, did it?" asked Genevieve softly, feeling the tension coursing through Cameron's body. A Scottish peasant didn't stand a chance against an English gentleman, even if he were in the right.

"Nay. The man testified that I killed Mary in a fit o' jealousy and threw her body into the lane. His friend, who had been there that day, confirmed the account, and even said that my Mary had lain with him on more than one occasion, making me a laughingstock and a cuckold." Genevieve noticed that Cameron's hands had balled into fists and laid a hand over his, silently asking him to relax. He took a deep breath to steady himself and went on.

"They dinna just kill her; they sullied her good name and accused me o' murder. The magistrate sentenced me to hang in three days' time. My da sold what he could to bribe the magistrate to commute the sentence to deportation to the Colonies for indentured labor, which he did."

"The magistrate openly took a bribe?" Genevieve gasped, astonished.

"Oh, aye, as I'm sure he took a bribe from the other two as well to provide them with a desirable outcome. He made out very nicely that day, the magistrate did. He profited, and the culprits went free. I was the only one who paid the price, and will continue to pay for the rest o' my life, as will my family."

"Was there no way to prove your innocence?"

"Nae. Who would listen? Who would care?" Cameron sighed with the futility of it, his hand no longer in a fist, but covering Genevieve's with his own.

"They kept me locked up until there was a ship bound for the Colonies, and then just sent me to the docks at a moment's notice. I never even got to say goodbye to my parents or sisters. There were about ten o' us being transported, all men of varying ages, all sentenced for some crime. They dinna even bother to protest their innocence; it nae longer mattered."

Cameron sighed. "The captain had us locked below decks and fettered the whole time for fear of a mutiny. No' that any o' us had the strength to rebel. After the first few days, we were so weak, we could barely stand. They gave us just enough food and water to stay alive, but nae much more than that. We were nae allowed on deck, no' even for a few minutes a day, and the stench in the hold was enough to make yer nose burn and yer eyes water. Two men died during the crossing, and they left them there for several days before finally tossing them overboard, without so much as a prayer for their departed souls." Cameron raged, the memories still fresh and painful.

"All the way across the Atlantic I burned with the injustice o' what was done to me, and to Mary. I spent every waking moment thinking o' revenge, and how to carry it out. I became delirious with it, rambling incoherently until one o' the other prisoners intervened. He was an older man who'd been sent down for thieving. He sat with me and kept talking to me, telling me that I needed to get a grip on myself if I wanted to live. He kept telling me I needed to survive to get my revenge. That got my attention. So, I did my best to live through that awful crossing. I ate what was given to me, tried to walk around the hold as much as I could to get some exercise, and kept myself to myself. I'd forbidden myself to think of home, concentrating only on survival. And then I came here."

"And met me," Genevieve added as she rolled on top of Cameron and kissed his lips softly. He wrapped his arms around her and held her tight, their hearts beating together as they lay quietly in the dusk of a summer evening.

FORTY-FIVE

The world seemed to still around them, the evening breeze wrapping them in a gentle caress as it dried their damp skin. Distant stars were just appearing in the darkening sky, winking at Genevieve as if they knew her little secret, and possibly approved. Somewhere at the back of her mind, she knew she might be missed and it was only a matter of time before someone thought to look for her, but she couldn't force herself to stir from the reassuring comfort of Cameron's arms. His wet hair was spread on the grass, the blades mingling with the strands of deep red, the color of a fox's pelt in the waning light of the evening.

His eyes were open wide, staring at the heavens as if the answers to all his questions would just be handed down like a judgment from a benevolent God, *but God wasn't benevolent, was he?* thought Genevieve, feeling the surge of resentment that had become a constant companion since she found out what happened to her mother all those years ago at the convent of Loudon. Her poor mother, whose only desire had been to dedicate her life to God, had been raped, left pregnant, and then murdered, her death made to look like a suicide, so even the comfort of Heaven and a burial in consecrated ground had been denied her for over twenty years. No, God wasn't benevolent; he was cruel, and at times probably very bored, for what other reason would there be to cause such suffering and grief if not for entertainment? A verse from Exodus sprang to mind,

You shall not make for yourself an idol, or any likeness of what is in Heaven above or on the earth beneath or in the water under the earth. You shall not worship them or serve them; for I, the LORD your God, am a jealous God, visiting the iniquity of the fathers on the children, on the third and the fourth generations of those who hate Me, but showing loving-kindness to thousands, to those who love Me and keep My commandments...

It wasn't just other gods God was jealous of, but happiness and joy, Genevieve thought. Well, she would snatch her happiness and hold onto it for dear life, and he wouldn't take it away from her—not ever.

A few years ago, she might have been shocked by such blasphemous thoughts, but that was before she went out into the world and learned something of life. She still believed in God with all her heart, but in her mind, he was no longer the benevolent, loving entity, who rewarded piety, honesty, and hard work. He was someone to be feared, for sometimes he punished even those who'd been his faithful servants and tore them apart for no reason, as he had Cameron and the poor girl he'd loved. And her own mother.

Genevieve forced herself to concentrate on the steady beating of Cameron's heart to soothe herself. She was allowing her fears and anger to get the best of her, and she wouldn't go down that path; she would just take it day by day and hope that her love and determination would set things right, and that she and Cameron could find a way to be together. Maybe she could talk to Uncle Alec when he came back and find a way to get justice for Cameron. Uncle Alec would listen; he had to.

FORTY-SIX

Louisa hurried to the window, happy to see Master Brooks cantering down the lane toward Rosewood Manor. He'd promised to come as soon as he had anything to report and she was hoping and praying that he'd been able to find something out. Sir George had been right in recommending him. The man clearly knew the law, and his intelligent brown eyes held a hint of reassurance as he promised to take the case and do his utmost to help Kit. Her intention to represent Kit herself had been a moment of madness, one she was ashamed of.

What had she been thinking, that watching a few legal dramas on TV qualified her to defend a man accused of murder? She supposed she was being too hard on herself considering all that had happened over the past few weeks. She was normally a calm and rational person, but with Valerie and Alec missing, revelations about Kit and Buckingham coming to light, and Kit now accused of murder, she was allowed a little insanity.

Louisa threw a grateful look at Genevieve as she herded the children out the door and into the morning sunshine, knowing that Louisa would need to have a private meeting with the solicitor. What a lovely girl Genevieve was, Louisa thought as she watched her scoop up Tom and carry him to the stables, where he would get a much-anticipated pony ride. The rest of the children clustered around Genevieve, laughing and talking all at once.

Normally, Genevieve was reserved and quiet, but today she was practically sparkling, her cheeks flushed, and her face wreathed in a smile that spread from ear to ear as she twirled with Tom in her arms and made him giggle. Louisa was glad to see her happy. Her own problems had nothing to do with Genevieve. The girl had suffered enough and deserved whatever happiness she could carve out for herself in this wretched world.

Louisa was distracted from her morbid thoughts by the arrival of Minnie, who sank into a curtsy, making Louisa smile. She'd asked everyone repeatedly to call her Louisa and not stand on ceremony, but this was a class-conscious society, where her title was like a stone wall that separated her from the rest of the women in the household, except for Valerie. Genevieve, Minnie, and Cook all called her, Lady Sheridan, and practically fell over themselves curtsying, which was just ridiculous given their living situation, which was pretty much devoid of privacy.

"Minnie, please bring some refreshments into the parlor," Louisa asked, eager to make a good impression on Master Brooks. She knew it'd make no difference if she offered him oat cakes and a cup of cider, but somehow it made her feel as if she had a modicum of control over the situation.

Louisa paced the room until Master Brooks finally appeared on the threshold. He looked hot and dusty, his forehead glistening with sweat. Louisa motioned him to a chair, her hand trembling with nerves as she poured him a cup of cider and wordlessly handed it to him. Master Brooks nodded gratefully and drained the cup before taking a seat across from her, his hat on his knees.

"What have you been able to find out?" Louisa asked eagerly.

"Lady Sheridan, I must be honest with you in order not to raise your hopes. I have spent the last two days questioning everyone I could think of who might have any connection to the case. I spoke with Mistress Deverell, the crew of the *Charlotte*, which the victim made the crossing on, dock workers, and shopkeepers. No one could shed any light on what happened. According to Mistress Deverell, her husband didn't have any enemies to speak of, and no one could recall any disagreements or quarrels involving Master Deverell. The crew of the *Charlotte* swear that he was perfectly agreeable during the crossing."

Master Brooks took a deep breath and looked up at Louisa. "I've also spoken to your husband. He says he spent the night drunk in the barn. There are no witnesses to this claim, and he refuses to tell me why he never came home that night, or what prompted the heated exchange with Master Deverell. Can you shed any light on the subject, your ladyship?"

Louisa sighed, wondering if she should tell the truth, but quickly dismissed the idea. If she told Master Brooks of Deverell's threats, the case against Kit would be watertight. The less he knew of that particular problem, the better. She smiled at the lawyer sadly. "Master Brooks, I'm very embarrassed, but my husband and I had a marital spat. It was entirely my fault, but Kit took it very much to heart and wound up having too much to drink, out of self-pity no doubt. It's happened once or twice before." Louisa averted her eyes in an effort to look ashamed and hoped that Master Brooks was buying the performance.

"I see, but that doesn't explain what the two men argued about."

"I don't know that they did. Annabel Whitfield seems to be the only one who'd heard them arguing. Perhaps she's mistaken." Louisa gave the man an imploring look. "How can they accuse a man based on one instance of circumstantial evidence?" Brook's eyebrows nearly disappeared into his hairline as he stared at Louisa.

"Do you know something of the law, Lady Sheridan?" he asked, curiosity overtaking his businesslike manner. *No*, Louisa thought, *but I watched a lot of courtroom dramas in the twenty-first century*.

"Ah, no, Master Brooks. I must have heard the term somewhere." She pushed the plate of cakes toward him to smooth over the awkward silence that fell between them. Master Brooks shook his head in refusal and rose to his feet.

"Lady Sheridan, I will do everything in my power to prove that Lord Sheridan didn't do this terrible thing, but until I find someone who saw or heard something, the task proves to be very difficult. Good day to you. I will call back if I have any news."

Louisa slumped back onto the settee, her arms around her middle as she doubled over with misery. This wasn't twenty-first century law; this was Jamestown, and if there was no proof of guilt, suspicion was enough to convict. She wiped away a tear with the back of her hand as Fred Taylor poked his head into the room, his face sympathetic.

"Louisa, dear, may I have a word?" he asked, inching further into the room and closing the door behind him.

"I couldn't help but overhear the last bit of the conversation with Master Brooks. Now, I know this is not the legal system we are used to, but I believe I might be able to help."

Louisa's head shot up, her eyes fixed on Fred Taylor. He was a surprising man, full of useful knowledge and shrewd ideas. If he had a plan, she would definitely listen.

FORTY-SEVEN

Jane Deverell stared listlessly out the window, her black gown making her appear even more sallow and thin than before. Her skin looked waxy in the gentle sunshine illuminating her face, and her graying hair strayed from the confines of her cap, giving her the appearance of a wasted hag. She turned at the sound of Louisa's footsteps, her eyes taking a moment to focus before she reached out her hand and stretched her lips in something meant to be a smile of welcome.

Louisa was relieved that she hadn't refused to see her, considering the circumstances. Master Brooks had mentioned that he got nowhere with Mistress Deverell, but Louisa felt it was imperative to speak with her all the same. No one knew a husband's secrets like a wife, she thought, before reminding herself that she'd known nothing of her own husband's darkest sins. Louisa forced herself to put Kit's transgressions aside and concentrate on offering succor to the widow.

"Jane, I'm so very sorry for your loss. Is there anything at all I can do to help you during this difficult time?" *I sound so false*, Louisa thought to herself as she took a seat across from Jane Deverell, feeling uncomfortable under her intense gaze.

"Thank you, dear Louisa, but I'm afraid there's nothing anyone can do. Sir George has taken it upon himself to arrange the funeral, and I'm most grateful." She turned her head to the window again, her eyes half-closed against the brilliance of the sun.

"Jane, Kit didn't kill your husband; he couldn't have. I know he never left the plantation that night, although I can't prove it. Is there anyone you can think of who might have wanted to harm Aloysius?" Louisa asked gently, hoping that Jane might find it in her heart to feel some sympathy for her.

Jane Deverell turned to Louisa, her eyes burning with something akin to hatred, spots of crimson appearing in her cheeks and making her look fevered.

"Louisa, I don't care who killed him. I'm just happy he's dead. I've prayed to the good Lord to rid me of that monster for nearly two decades, and he's finally seen fit to answer my prayer."

She suddenly stilled, ashamed of her outburst, her hands clasped in her lap and her eyes averted from Louisa. She was silent for a few moments before her head snapped up defiantly, daring Louisa to judge her. "It's wrong to speak ill of the dead, I know, but Aloysius was a terrible man, a cruel and heartless man, who's finally got his comeuppance. I know you must think I'm a wicked woman, but as God is my witness, I'm telling the truth."

"I don't think you're wicked, Jane. Your husband must have treated you most cruelly for you to feel this way, so you have my condolences for that as well. What has he done?" Louisa asked carefully. Jane was in a hysterical state, and although Louisa hated to take advantage of that, Jane was ripe for the picking, eager to get her grievances off her chest.

"I can't speak of it," Jane moaned, a tear sliding down her cheek. "I just can't speak of it. But he did have enemies, more enemies than you might imagine."

"Who?"

"I don't know specific names; he never told me, but we had to leave England, you see. He was afraid for his life." Jane was staring at her hands as if seeing them for the first time, her rings sparkling against the pale skin.

"Why did he have so many enemies?" Louisa thought she already knew, but she wanted to hear it from Jane.

"Aloysius had a few cronies at court who fed him tidbits of useful information. Thomas Gaines was one of them. I believe you were acquainted with him," she said flatly before resuming her narrative. "Once Aloysius had suspicions about a particular person, he made it his business to ferret out the rest. He'd send out our stable boy to spy on them, making sure he had some proof before approaching his victim and demanding payment for his continued silence. He made quite a good living from his hobby. He kept us in style, that I can tell you."

Jane looked up at Louisa, her gaze full of shame. "Oh, I hated him, Louisa. He was a wicked man. Once he found out someone's secret, he bleed them dry, and then he'd bleed them some more. He didn't need the money; he enjoyed the power, you see. It made him feel God-like, he said. Does your husband have a secret?" she suddenly asked, her eyes boring into Louisa.

"Not that I know of, Jane, but even if he does, he's not a murderer. He didn't kill your husband, but someone did, and we need to find out who did."

"I don't care who killed him," Jane spat out, her eyes blazing again. "To the world I must appear as the grieving widow of a good man. I will not speak ill of him in public or testify on your husband's behalf." Jane suddenly jumped to her feet and pulled a rolled-up document from an intricately carved wooden box sitting atop the mantel. "Here, I will give you this, and you can do with it as you see fit. It states that if anything should happen to Aloysius, Lord Sheridan is to be held responsible. That's all I can do for you."

Louisa snatched the document and unrolled it, scanning the contents. She had no idea there even was a document, but Jane just laughed without mirth, amused by her naiveté. "Oh, there are several like it, naming various people, but I won't surrender any of them to the law. No one deserves to be blamed for trying to save their skin, so I will just consign these to the flames, as I am sure you will as soon as you get home."

Jane's face fell as if she realized how bitter she sounded. She reached out and put her cold hand over Louisa's, her eyes pleading for understanding. "I'm sorry, Louisa, but my dignity is all I have left, and I intend to preserve it. I will complete my year of mourning, then take my well-deserved freedom, go back to England where I belong and try to enjoy what's left of my life. I wish you much luck in proving your husband's innocence, but it won't be with my help. Now, I must wish you good day, dear. I'm suddenly rather tired."

Jane rose to her feet and floated out of the room, leaving a stunned Louisa to seethe with frustrated fury. She could try pleading with Jane Deverell, but she could sense that her mind was made up, and truthfully, she didn't blame her. If what she said was true, she'd suffered enough, and Aloysius Deverell left her well-enough provided for that she could enjoy the rest of her life without needing to involve herself in anything she didn't wish to. After all, she had absolutely no incentive to testify on Kit's behalf, and every reason to remain silent. Louisa needed a new angle.

FORTY-EIGHT

"She has the power to help Kit, but she won't," Louisa exclaimed as she paced the tiny sitting area of the Taylor cottage, her tirade fueled by rage. "She flat out refused." Louisa had already burned the offensive document proclaiming Kit's guilt, but she was still angry with Jane's refusal to testify on Kit's behalf. She could understand her reasons, but Kit could die to save Jane's dignity.

Fred Taylor's eyes followed Louisa for a few moments before he finally spoke, his voice soft and soothing. "Louisa, come sit down and we'll talk this through. You're wearing yourself out with anxiety and that won't do anyone any good, least of all Kit. Now, come dear girl, not all is lost." His eyes looked large behind his glasses, the sympathy in them nearly making her cry.

"How can you say that?" Louisa asked, turning on him. "Someone was willing to kill Deverell to keep their secret safe, so chances are they are not coming forward to confess, are they, especially when someone else is poised to swing for the crime. The only way to free Kit is to find out who killed Deverell, and I have no idea where to even begin. Master Brooks questioned everyone and came up with a big, fat, nothing. So we are right back where we started, before we knew that Deverell was a blackmailer and an extortionist."

Fred shook his head and pointed to a chair across from him, inviting Louisa to sit and calm down. He never got worked up or overly emotional, and his calm demeanor and rational nature appealed to Louisa, especially in a time of crisis. She sat down and fixed her attention on Fred. He looked as if he had something to say.

"Louisa, the law is not always about right and wrong, and black and white. There are many shades of gray, even in this century. Mr. Brooks doesn't have to prove that Kit is innocent, all he has to prove is that there's reasonable doubt of his guilt."

"But he is innocent," Louisa stated, stamping her foot for punctuation.

"I'm sure he is, but there's no way to prove that, especially since he didn't sleep with you that night. No one saw Kit from late afternoon until the following morning when he stumbled from that barn with a raging hangover. Had Deverell been blackmailing him, then he had both opportunity and motive," Fred pointed out reasonably.

"You're not helping!" Louisa retorted, angry.

"Oh, but I am. No one saw him, which means no one can place him at the scene of the crime. No one can say with any certainty that Kit did it. So, if we can discredit Annabel's testimony, there's no case against him whatsoever," announced Mr. Taylor triumphantly.

"Do you think there's a way to discredit Annabel?" Louisa's heart swelled with hope as she considered this new tactic.

"Absolutely, and I know precisely the way to do it. We just need Mr. Brooks to comply, which I'm sure he will. He should be ashamed for not coming up with this idea himself."

"I don't think Mr. Brooks has ever done more than draw up

a will or a deed to a house. He's not a trial lawyer, if there is such a thing these days."

"No, but we'll turn him into one," Fred replied with a grin, reaching for the chessboard. "Come, let's have a game. It always focuses the mind and I have a few details to iron out before I present my plan to our esteemed attorney."

"I only hope it works," Louisa said, giving Mr. Taylor a small smile. She was feeling slightly more hopeful, and he knew it, which in turn made him happy. Sometimes Louisa thought that he regarded her and Valerie as the daughters he never had, and it gave her some comfort to have a father-figure, especially since her own parents were gone, or more accurately, hadn't been born yet.

FORTY-NINE
PRINCETON, NEW JERSEY SEPTEMBER 2010

Alec switched off the TV but made no move to rise from the couch. The house was peaceful and silent, the night outside filled with the buzzing of insects and the occasional sound of a passing car. He heard loud, drunken voices of young people as they made their way home from some bar, intoxicated and happy to be alive, their only concern in the world that of avoiding a blinding hangover tomorrow. His own life had been vastly different when he was their age, and he was glad of it. These young people seemed to act much younger than their age, carrying on like children and refusing to take responsibility for their actions. In his time, men of twenty were mostly already married and fulfilling their duties as husbands, fathers, and providers.

Alec suddenly remembered his brother at that age. Finn had been carousing, drinking, and wenching with the best of them, marriage the furthest thing from his mind. It wasn't until Valerie showed up on their doorstep that he finally began to consider a future in which he was loyal to only one woman, and even that might have been caused by Alec's own interest in their strange guest. Would Finn have fallen in love with Valerie if he hadn't wanted to snatch her from under Alec's nose? He always had been competitive when it came to women, and that had been the first time they'd both wanted the same woman.

How long ago it all seemed. Well, as of now it was about four hundred years ago, but really, it'd been just over twenty. How he missed Finn and wished he could talk to him and tell him what was happening in his life. Of course, had Finn lived, Valerie would still be his wife, and they'd most likely still be in England, living in their ancestral home and tending to the family business, not growing tobacco and importing cane liquor to Colonial Virginia.

Alec finally stood, took a Coke out of the fridge, and stepped through the sliding doors into the moonlit back garden, where he folded himself into an Adirondack chair and opened his drink. Sleep didn't come easily these days and he spent many an hour watching late-night TV or just walking the streets of Princeton. Valerie said it was due to his newfound love of coffee and Coca-Cola, but he knew it wasn't that. He had to admit that he did love the bitter richness of a good cup of coffee and the fizzy sweetness of Coke, but what was keeping him up at night had nothing to do with caffeine.

He tried hard to find something to keep him occupied during the day, his anxiety mounting as the days flew by with them being no closer to returning home. He loved the modern conveniences that others took for granted and never got into a hot shower without smiling at the ingenious contraption that allowed an unlimited amount of hot water to cascade over his body, warming and soothing at the same time, made even better when followed by a cool drink from the refrigerator. And he still marveled every time he flipped a switch and the room was flooded with light. But no amount of TV, driving around town in the professor's car, or tasting new and exotic foods could make up for the sense of displacement he felt, made worse by the countless clocks that he was exposed to every day.

There were clocks everywhere—on the car dashboard, on the cable box, on the computer, and even on the billboard in front of the bank. Never before had he been so aware of time, or the passage of it. All his life he'd lived by the dictates of nature. He rose in the morning, went to bed at night, and worked during daylight hours. There was no loud alarm clock to wake him up or constant reminders of what time it was on any given day. It made him feel anxious and rushed, despite the fact that he didn't actually have to be anywhere. How could anyone be comfortable with living such a regimented existence, always being reminded of exactly what time it was and how much time they had left until the end of the workday, the next class, or some appointment? Days seemed to fly by in the blink of an eye in this modern world, the pace of life so hectic compared to the more harmonious rhythm of the seventeenth, or even the eighteenth centuries.

No, he didn't belong in this world. He was a non-entity, a man without a name, a history, or a bank account. He was no one. No one besides Valerie and Isaac would even know if he'd gone missing. No one would care, for he didn't exist in this world, had no resume to list his accomplishments or even a credit card to document his spending. He was a speck of dust in the wind, here today, gone tomorrow—hopefully.

However, no amount of anguish Alec felt could compare to what Valerie was going through. She tried to remain cheerful, cleaning the house, cooking exotic dishes, and running errands for the professor, mostly in a desperate effort to get out of the house and put her time to good use. She hadn't said a word, but Alec hadn't been married to her for nearly twenty years not to understand the turmoil that was tearing her apart. At this very moment, Valerie existed in two places and had the power to change everything that had happened, erase their entire life together. All she had to do was show up and make up some story about where she'd been since she disappeared from the antique shop in a small, nondescript town in Devon, England.

Louisa was sure to be back from England by now, devastated by her sister's disappearance, but still hopeful that she would somehow turn up and explain everything away. Her parents were still very much alive and praying for the safe return of their daughter. Alec knew how desperately Valerie wanted to see them, to catch a glimpse even from a distance, to feel for that one fleeting moment that a reunion was possible and she could fly into her mother's arms and tell her that everything was all right and she wasn't really gone forever. Maybe she could even prevent the accident that would claim their lives only a year from now, although Alec wasn't sure about that. Fate had its own way of making things happen, and if something interfered with destiny, the universe auto corrected itself and simply found another way of reaching the same outcome.

They had to watch their money now since Valerie was officially missing and any activity on her account would be reported to the police. They had plenty of cash left from when Valerie visited the bank in Williamsburg, but what would they do if Isaac couldn't send them home? The mere thought of being stuck in this time and place made Alec feel hollow inside, not only for himself, but for Valerie. Regardless of how much she wanted to reveal herself to her family, her other family waited in the past. Little Tom was the only living, breathing reminder of their willful daughter, who wouldn't have died in childbirth had she been living in the future. All it would have taken was a cesarean section and their girl would still be alive, as would her poor husband, who died of the plague. It hurt Alec to think of all the horrible things that could have been avoided had their children been born in the future, but to dwell on that was totally pointless.

Valerie would never be whole, even if she managed to somehow find a reasonable way to see her family again. Finn and Abbie, their granddaughter Diana, and everyone at Rosewood Manor would be forever lost to them. Louisa would never go back in time, meet and marry Kit, or have her children, and Alec would likely never know the love he'd known since Valerie stumbled into his study all those years ago and promptly fell in love with his reckless brother. So much water under the bridge, so much love, loss, and pain. But it had to happen. It had happened.

The sooner they went home the better for everyone involved, but Alec was beginning to have doubts in Isaac's ability to send them back. He was kind and generous, eager to help, but he was also an old man, one who hadn't done this kind of work in decades. He loved having them there, for they relieved some of the terrible loneliness he felt since the death of his wife, but they had to get back, and soon. They had to pick up the threads of their life and let go of the future once and for all.

Valerie had to come to terms with never seeing her parents again, and the further away from them she was, the easier it would be. Louisa, on the other hand, must be going mad in both centuries, looking for her sister in the here and now, and overcome with anxiety in the seventeenth century, not knowing what happened to them or if they would ever come back. Alec hoped everything was running smoothly back at home, his mind conjuring images of ripening fields of tobacco, their overflowing house, and all the dear people in it. He longed to hold Tom as he fell asleep on his shoulder, or have a game of chess with Genevieve or Kit while sipping French brandy in the parlor and trying to drown out the never-ending noise that was always the backdrop for everything that went on at Rosewood Manor.

He even missed Charles and Annabel, although relations had been somewhat strained since Annabel realized that Tom was actually the spawn of her ill-begotten brother, who seemed to ruin their lives every time he showed up anywhere near their daughter. Now they were both dead, so there was no point going over all the what-if's, but Alec couldn't help wishing that he had made his peace with Louisa before she died, had told her he loved her one more time, and had enveloped her in a hug as he often did when she was a little girl and came to him for comfort after she'd fallen or had a fight with her brother. Alec sighed and rose from the chair, his Coke empty and his heart full. It was time to go to bed, although he knew he'd lie awake for hours before sleep finally found him in the early hours of the morning and gave him a few hours of oblivion from his thoughts. And then it would be another day.

FIFTY
VIRGINIA SEPTEMBER 1779

"Sam. Sam. I think it's time." Susanna was shaking him by the shoulder, trying to wake him from a deep sleep. "Sam."

Sam finally opened his eyes and looked at his wife. Susanna was sitting up in bed, her hair neatly braided and her nightdress pristine, but her eyes were full of fear, her lips quivering as she looked at him. "It's time," she said again as Sam pulled her into his arms, the tension of the past week forgotten.

They had made up after the argument, but Sue's suspicion was still there, hovering behind the eyes every time she looked at Sam. And who could blame her? She had the right of it, and no matter how vehemently he tried to deny it, they both knew the truth. Sue probably suspected the truth about Nat as well, but she hadn't brought it up, not ready to deal with such a weighty issue just before the birth of their own child. They would have to talk about it sooner or later, but now wasn't the time, and Sam hoped that Diana would just stay away from his wife and leave her in peace. She hadn't come back since her last visit, but if Sam knew anything of Diana Littleton by now, it was that she wasn't a quitter, and she had nothing to lose by perpetuating her charade until the bitter end.

Susanna clutched Sam's hand in a death grip as another contraction began, forcing her to cry out. The baby wasn't due for another few weeks, so she was worried. Annie had come two months early, he remembered that, and she turned out all right, although she had been very small and fragile, and his mother watched over her day and night, feeding her every hour until she began to gain weight and look more like a baby and less like a skinned rabbit. *Probably best not to bring that up right now*, Sam thought.

"Don't be afraid. I'll just go get Ma, and Pa will go for the midwife. Everything will be all right." Sam jumped out of bed, pulling on his breeches and shirt, and reaching for his boots. Susanna was panting, her eyes round with disbelief as pain ripped through her, making her moan.

"It's too soon," she squeaked, reclining back on the pillows as the contraction finally passed. Sam barely had time to put his boots on before the next contraction came on, leaving Susanna breathless.

"How long have you been feeling the pains?" he asked, looking down at her.

"About two hours now."

"Why didn't you wake me?" he asked, incredulous that she'd waited that long.

"I thought they'd stop. It's not unusual to have pains toward the end. I had them with Ben." Susanna suddenly looked like a frightened child, her expression matching Ben's as he lifted his head off the cot, staring at them with huge eyes.

"Mama?" he whispered.

"It's all right, darling, go back to sleep." But Ben wasn't deceived. He looked as if he were about to cry, so Sam scooped him up out of bed and wrapped him in his arms.

"How'd you like to go visit grandma?" Sam asked, making it sound like any ordinary visit.

Ben looked toward the window where the sky was pitch

black and the stars dotted the heavens, pinpricks of light that made everything look magical to a little boy.

"All right," he said. "Can mama come too?"

"No, mama is tired. We'll just let her rest." Sam grabbed Ben's blanket and wrapped him up into a tidy cocoon before heading for the door.

"Sam, hurry," Susanna called after him, her voice tight with pain.

Sam opened his mouth to reply, but Susanna let out a desperate moan, spurring him on to get help. "I'll be back in half a tick, you hear?" She nodded, breathing like a grampus, her eyes bugging out as another contraction rolled over her.

Sam held on to a gleeful Ben as he sprinted toward his parent's house. In the feeble light of the moon, it was hard to see where he was going, the ground around him dark and his perception of depth distorted, making him stumble as his foot landed in a depression in the earth, and throwing him off balance. He managed to remain upright but slowed his pace for fear that he would fall and crush Ben beneath his weight.

The windows of the farmhouse were dark square shapes, like eyes that were closed in slumber against the pale skin of the face. The white walls gleamed in the darkness, and the dim shape of the chimney poked at the sky like the barrel of a cannon. Sam knocked on the door, hoping they would hear him right away. His father opened the door, fully dressed, with his pipe dangling from between his lips. He silently took Ben from Sam's arms as Hannah Mallory appeared in the doorway, ghostly in her white nightdress.

"Is it Sue?" she asked, her face full of fear.

Sam nodded. "You must hurry, Ma. We don't have much time." Hannah nodded and disappeared back into the bedroom to get dressed.

A sleepy Sarah appeared next, obediently taking Ben from her father as he left to fetch the midwife. Everyone was awake now; Annie asking endless questions, Abbie coming down from the loft to find out what was happening, and Diana standing in the doorway, her hair cascading over her breasts, her lips partly open as she watched Sam with undisguised amusement. Sam barely noticed her as followed his mother out the door and into the night.

FIFTY-ONE

Sam had been gone only half an hour, but by the time he came running back with his mother, Susanna was screaming, her hands clawing at the sheets and her nightgown soaked with perspiration. She seemed oblivious to their presence as she braced for another contraction.

"Right," Hannah Mallory said, taking in the scene. "I hope your father gets here soon with Mrs. Baker. I don't think we have much time."

She removed her bonnet, tied an apron around her waist, and washed her hands in the basin before coming to sit next to Susanna. "Sam, put some water on to boil, get me some towels, and prepare a blanket for the baby. Do you know where it is?"

Sam nodded, sprinting to the hearth to light the fire. Hannah smiled, thinking that her son looked like a little boy again, his eyes full of trepidation. It seemed as if he'd been born not all that long ago, a perfect little boy after nearly three days of labor and John sick with worry and pacing outside their bedroom until the midwife finally called him in and placed Sam in his arms. He'd been so happy and proud, thanking her for giving him such a wonderful son, and now her boy was about to become a father again. Hannah wiped Susanna's brow, whispering words of comfort as she timed the contractions, noting that they were very close together. Mrs. Baker might not get there in time. Hannah closed her eyes for a brief moment and prayed that the baby was coming as it should and there were no complications.

Susanna let out another wail, her stomach heaving beneath the nightdress as her hands grabbed onto Hannah's in a death grip. Her eyes were full of panic. "This isn't like the first time," she moaned. "This is so much worse."

"No two births are the same. It doesn't mean there's anything wrong. You just breathe now, Susanna. In and out. In and out. It won't be long now."

Sam came in with a basin of hot water, clean towels, and a little woolen blanket for the baby. He looked scared out of his wits, his eyes fixated on Susanna's belly.

"Go wait outside. This is no place for a man. I'll call you if I need you," Hannah said, giving him a reassuring smile before waving him out of the room. Sam opened his mouth to protest, but Susanna opened her eyes, staring him down.

"Go. I don't want you to see me like this. Please, Sam." He gave her a quick kiss and left the room. Hannah heard him go outside to sit on the bench in front of the house. He'd be able to hear everything, but not actually see it, which was a blessing.

Sam stared up at the sky, the stars bright in the heavens, and the gibbous moon peeking from behind wispy clouds that floated lazily across the night sky. A light wind moved through the trees, the leaves rustling overhead in a soothing lullaby. Everything was quiet except for the screams of his wife, who labored to bring their child into the world.

"Please, dear God, let her and the babe be safe," Sam whispered, suddenly scared. He'd been terrified when Ben was born, his knees sagging with relief when he finally heard the baby's cry and Susanna's voice asking to hold him. So many women and children died during childbirth, why should his family be spared? Sue had been spared the first time, but it was no guarantee that she'd be as lucky the second time around. What if the baby was coming the wrong way or had the cord around its neck? Sam jumped off the bench, unable to remain seated. He paced back and forth, Susanna's screams tearing through him like a sharp knife. Let it be over quickly, he prayed. He wished Finn or Jonah were there to keep him company, to distract him from being so scared, but he was all alone.

Sam suddenly wondered who'd been there for Diana when she gave birth. Who was there to comfort her and reassure her that everything would be all right? He hoped Deborah Morse had been by her side. She was a kind soul, always eager to help, and knowledgeable about such things. A wave of guilt washed over him as he thought of Nat. Poor mite, he'd never known a real family, and likely never would. Eventually Diana's secret would come out and she would be forced to leave Virginia and return to her life in New York. Sam couldn't imagine that she would seek some kind of respectable employment, so Nat would be raised in a whorehouse, keeping out of sight while his mother entertained her clients.

It was clear that Diana didn't really want Nat, so how long would it be until he struck out on his own, leaving that life behind? With the port being so near, it was possible that Nat would sign on to some ship's crew and leave, possibly forever. Sam would never know what happened to his boy, his guilt at having failed Nat eating away at his conscience year after year, but what was he to do? Was he to tell his wife that the boy was his and risk losing her as well? She was in a delicate condition, and he had to be mindful of her emotional state, especially after the birth. He heard that some women's milk went sour and dried up when they were in a state of anxiety, so he had to be extra careful not to upset Susanna as she nursed the new baby and recovered from the birth.

Sam sat back down again as the sky above the tree line turned a slightly lighter shade of dark. Dawn wasn't far away. Where was his father with Mrs. Baker? Sam scanned the horizon but saw nothing moving in the distance. All was still and quiet, almost eerily so. He closed his eyes and leaned his head against the rough wood of the cabin, his head spinning with fatigue. He must have fallen asleep for a few minutes because when he woke with a start, a sliver of pale peach was spreading across the sky in the east, the stars giving him a last wink before disappearing from view. How long had it been since Sue went into labor? Sam strained to hear something, but all he heard was his mother murmuring something inside the house. Sue was no longer screaming or panting, and his heart seized with panic at the realization that it was all over.

Sam got to his feet and stumbled toward the door but stopped just before entering. All was strangely quiet, and that didn't bode well at all. He nearly jumped out of his skin when a baby's thin wail pierced the silence, his mother's voice full of joy as she called for Sam. Susanna lay back on the pillows, her face sweaty and flushed, and her nightdress stained with blood, but the smile that spread across her face was full of joy. She held Sam's eyes as he came closer, gazing at the tiny bundle in her arms.

"A girl," she said. "A beautiful girl." Hannah wiped her eyes as she looked at them. She suddenly felt very old, and tired. They were just starting out on their journey together, but her journey was already more than half over. Her children were practically grown, and her grandchildren were multiplying. She and John would grow old before long, their day done. Hannah kissed Sam and quietly left the room, giving the new parents a moment of privacy before everyone got wind of the birth and came running.

Sam took the baby from Susanna, looking at its tiny face. It was so small and round, the eyes firmly closed against the milky light streaming through the window and dispelling the gloom of the night. The baby yawned as a tiny fist escaped from the wrappings to touch Sam's face. "She's perfect," Sam breathed. "Just perfect. What shall we name her?"

"I don't know," Sue giggled. "I was convinced it was another boy, so I hadn't picked a girl's name. Is there any name you like?"

"How about Rachel?" he asked, glancing at Sue, who was lost in thought.

"Rachel Hannah," Sue finally replied. "I'd never have gotten through this without your mother, and she has been so kind to me since you brought me here unannounced," Sue said, grinning at Sam. "What do you think?"

"I think my mother will be honored."

"I'm so tired. I suppose I should try to feed her before I go to sleep, although she doesn't seem hungry."

The baby was fast asleep in Sam's arms, completely indifferent to her parents. She'd had a tough night as well.

"I think Rachel would like to rest for a while," Sam said, placing her next to Susanna. "I'll just get her basket and then you can sleep. I'll watch over her," he said, his face full of wonder. "I'll watch Rachel."

FIFTY-TWO
VIRGINIA SEPTEMBER 1626

Louisa stared at Sir George resentfully as he took his place at the little table placed next to the pulpit. For lack of a courthouse, the trial was to be held at the church, in full view of God and man. Members of the governor's council would sit in the front pew, and act as both judge and jury in the case of the Colony of Virginia against Lord Christopher Sheridan. The council consisted of about a dozen wealthy and influential members of Virginia society, most of them friends and acquaintances of several years, which could either serve to gain Kit favor, or work against him as they meted out a harsher judgment in their effort not to show favor to one of their own. Sir George avoided Louisa's piercing gaze, choosing instead to rearrange some papers and make sure that he had enough wine in his cup should his throat run dry during the proceedings.

Women were expected to sit toward the back, but Louisa took a seat in the third pew next to Frederick Taylor, who was alone, since Barbara had stayed back to look after the children. She'd chosen her most somber gown and a simple bonnet for the trial in the hope that she would appear God-fearing and deserving of the council's sympathy, but she knew it made no difference. They all knew her and their opinion of her had been formed a long time ago. Although some members of the council were kind, forgiving men, the rest still remembered her transgression from a few years ago, their disapproval at her lack of appropriate punishment still as fresh as it had been when she and Kit first returned to the colony. Well, there was nothing she could do about any of that now. It was water under the bridge, and hopefully, would have no bearing upon the outcome of Kit's trial. All she could do was hope and pray that these men didn't allow past incidents to cloud their judgment as they decided her husband's fate.

Louisa barely acknowledged Charles as he stopped by to offer his support, his face tight and full of contrition as he stood over her, desperate for forgiveness. Annabel didn't bother to greet Louisa but took a seat at the back of the church, only there to testify against Kit. Annabel normally dressed as fashionably as she could, favoring pastels and lace, but today she was wearing a gown of charcoal-gray, relieved only by a little white lace at the sleeves and throat. Her golden hair was tucked into a matching bonnet, making her look like a good little Quaker.

Louisa felt an overwhelming wave of rage as she studied Annabel's complacent face. She held Kit's life in her hands, but she didn't seem to care, ready to give her venomous testimony and send him to the gallows, based on a snippet of conversation she just happened to conveniently overhear. Louisa turned her back on Annabel and resumed her relentless study of Sir George. She hoped that the goddamned coward would have enough guts to do the right thing, but Sir George was a political animal, interested only in his own standing in the community and advancement. Sacrificing Kit to appear to uphold the law of the colony would be a small price to pay if it made him look good in the eyes of the king, who might or might not hear of his good deeds.

The church filled up quickly, the high society of the colony starved for entertainment and unwilling to miss the social event of the season. The trial would be discussed for months to come, especially if the verdict was death. Louisa nearly gagged with disgust when she realized that most women were wearing their finery, eager to see and be seen by the rest of Virginia society. They nodded to each other as they scanned the pews, searching for a place closest to the front.

Louisa was surprised to see that Jane Deverell was not among the spectators, either out of guilt or out of desire to gain pity by playing the grieving widow. However, Sir George's wife swept into the church in an ill-concealed attempt to make an entrance and wearing a gown of an alarming shade of chartreuse that made her look greenish and sallow. Her bonnet sported matching feathers that shook with indignation when she couldn't find a seat appropriate to her station. Most women of the colony wore clothes made of homespun, dyed in muted colors derived from colorants found in nature, but Lady Yeardley had all her gowns shipped from England and dressed as if she were still at court.

Once the church was full and all the members of the council seated, along with the lieutenant governor, Kit was finally brought in and made to stand facing the spectators, his wrists shackled, more in an effort to humiliate rather than restrain. Kit had donned a clean shirt and shaved for the trial, but his face was pale and gaunt, the resentment clearly visible in his gaze as he scanned the crowd, looking for Louisa. His face seemed to relax a fraction when he found her and gave her an imperceptible nod to reassure her that he was all right and ready to face whatever came.

She gave him a reassuring smile as her stomach heaved with fear, the muscles clenching and the bile rising in her throat. Louisa averted her eyes before Kit could see the unbidden tears that blurred her vision and made her nose run. Louisa concentrated on extracting her handkerchief out of her skirt pocket, unwilling to allow Kit to see her fears. She blew her nose and looked around for Master Brooks, who was consulting with Sir George. The lawyer was wearing an elaborate wig, which would have made Louisa giggle had she not been so terrified.

Louisa sucked in her breath as the court was called to order, the charge read against her husband as a pregnant hush fell over the crowd that was eager for the trial to begin. Kit's face remained bland, but she could see his lips compress and his hands ball into fists beneath the iron shackles. If Master Brooks failed to prove his innocence, he would hang as soon as tomorrow. Of course, Master Brooks could hardly prove that Lord Sheridan was innocent without presenting the court with some evidence of who had actually killed Aloysius Deverell, but they'd worked out a plan, which would hopefully be enough to get Kit off.

Sir George called Annabel to come up and testify, referring to her as a respected member of the community and a woman of faith and virtue. *That bastard*, Louisa thought, fuming inwardly, *he's practically saying that her testimony is indisputable.* Annabel rose from her seat and made her way to the front, walking as if she were performing a complicated balancing act on a rope suspended over a precipice. She didn't look at anyone, especially Charles, whose eyes were still begging her to reconsider. Louisa knew he'd tried to forbid her to testify, but Annabel was adamant. She'd have her say, no matter what. She wanted someone to pay for her brother's death, and if that someone happened to be Kit, then so be it. She'd have her pound of flesh, regardless of whose flesh it was.

Annabel recounted the conversation she'd overheard that afternoon, her voice low and shaking with emotion as if she had personally suffered through Deverell's death. Her face was chalky, her eyes glazed with memory, and her hands clasped in front of her. Louisa had to admit that it was quite a performance, if that's what she'd been aiming for. Thankfully, there were no other witnesses against Kit, so Annabel's story would have to be iron-clad in order to produce a sentence of death by hanging. Louisa reminded herself to breathe as Master Brooks approached Annabel and bid her a good morning.

His appearance was so mild and unthreatening that Annabel relaxed slightly, nodding in greeting and even smiling a little. Her hands unclasped, smoothing the fabric of her skirt as she looked at the lawyer expectantly, ready to flee to her seat and watch justice in action. What could this little man do to dispute her testimony? After all, she'd heard Kit threatening to kill Deverell loud and clear. What could the lawyer say to dispute that? A barely noticeable sneer appeared on Annabel's face as she raised her chin defiantly, daring Master Brooks to question her. He gave a small bow to the council before proceeding.

"Mistress Whitfield, it's so good of you to come and testify before this court. As a person of impeccable moral character, it's surely your duty to see justice done, especially since the crime is so heinous and unexpected. It must have taken a great deal of courage to speak up against your brother-in-law with whom you've been residing at Rosewood Manor for some years."

Louisa watched with satisfaction as Annabel's pride at being called courageous and virtuous was tinged by embarrassment at Master Brooks' implication that she was a snake in the grass.

"Mistress Whitfield, would you be so kind as to tell us exactly where Lord Sheridan and Master Deverell were situated during the course of this heated exchange?"

"They were halfway to the pond, sir," Annabel stated, clearly confused by why he would ask such a question.

"Halfway to the pond, you say? Well, that's actually a very interesting point. You see, I've measured the distance from the house to the pond, and it's over a hundred feet. Their voices must have been quite loud for you to hear every word of their conversation from fifty feet away."

Annabel's mouth opened with indignation, her eyes firing daggers of resentment at the little lawyer. "I was sewing by the window, and their voices carried on the wind. I heard them as clearly as I hear you," she spat out, looking over the assembly and daring them to contradict her.

"I see. I don't recall that we've had any particularly breezy days these past two weeks, but I will certainly take your word for it. After all, you are only doing your civic duty by reporting what you've heard, and I don't doubt for a second that you are confident in your recollection of the events. I applaud your self-sacrifice in coming here today, Mistress Whitfield, and thank you for your candor. I only have one question before I release you. What time did you say you overheard this exchange between Lord Sheridan and Aloysius Deverell?"

"It was at noon. The sun was riding high in the sky, and Cook was preparing luncheon," Annabel answered defensively.

"Thank you, dear lady," Master Brooks intoned, bowing to Annabel. "You are free to go."

He waited until Annabel floated back to her seat, her face now less tense and a sly smile of satisfaction playing about her lips. There were no other witnesses, so the outcome was certain. Sir George was about to say something when Master Brooks held up his hand, asking for patience.

"Sir George, as it happens, I have three more witnesses that I would like to call to testify today. If you would just indulge me, please. After all, we're talking about the life of a man, a pillar of the community, and a good friend to us all, someone who could always be counted on in times of need to rise to the occasion and help in whatever way necessary." Sir George glanced away in shame, but Kit just smirked into his goatee, strangely amused by Mr. Brooks' tactics.

"By all means, Master Brooks. You must call as many

witnesses as you can muster. We'll be here all day if we must to see justice done. We would never pass such a grim sentence lightly, and all avenues must be explored."

"I respectfully agree, sir." Master Brooks turned to face the congregation as if searching for someone. He smiled benevolently as he spotted his next witness, calling Minerva Pike to the front.

"Good morning, Mistress Pike," he said, smiling his most reassuring smile. "Would you be so kind as to tell us what your role at Rosewood Manor is?"

"Yes, sir. I work as a maid at Rosewood Manor, assisting in all household duties. Everyone calls me Minnie, though. Minerva is so lofty." Minnie giggled nervously, making a few people smile at her lack of guile.

"Minnie, can you tell us what tasks you normally perform at noon? Are you in the house at that time?"

"Oh, yes, sir. Noon is a very busy time. Cook usually prepares dinner for the family while I see to dinner for the children. They eat in the kitchen at noon before the rest of the family dines at one o'clock."

"Really? The children eat separately?" Master Brooks looked over the assembly as if shocked by this bit of news.

"Why, yes, sir. They are still little, they are, and they need help eating. Besides, they don't eat the same food as the grown-ups."

"And how many children are there, Minnie?"

Minnie gazed up at the ceiling as she took a mental roster. "There are five, sir. Mr. Charles's children are no longer there, but before they left, there were five. They're aged one to four."

"They must be quite a handful," Master Brooks remarked as he gave Minnie an exaggerated look of sympathy.

"Oh, yes. They cause such a ruckus I can barely hear myself think. We all breathe a sigh of relief when they go down for their nap after luncheon. It's the only quiet time we have until they go to bed at night."

"Minnie, do you see to the children all by yourself?"

"No, sir. Genevieve also helps since Tom, Millie, and Robbie still need feeding."

"Minnie, you've been most helpful. If you would just answer one more thing for me. How close is the kitchen to the parlor?"

"Oh, it's just down the hall, sir. There's also an outdoor kitchen that's used for roasting meat and making food for the field workers but Cook uses mostly the indoor kitchen for making meals for the family."

Minnie curtsied and scurried away, blushing furiously as Master Brooks praised her once again for having the courage to take the stand. Sir George fiddled with a ring on his finger, his brow creased with annoyance as Master Brooks called his next witness to the stand.

"I call Genevieve Whitfield." Genevieve took her place, her cheeks stained with patches of red as she shyly looked around the full church. She looked as if she'd rather be anywhere else, but she would do anything to help Lord Sheridan.

"Mistress Whitfield, can you recall the afternoon in question?" The lawyer asked, smiling in an effort to put her more at ease.

"Yes," she whispered.

"Was there anything unusual about that day?"

"Robbie and Harry were chasing each other around the kitchen table, bringing Cook to the edge of reason, especially when they knocked a bowl over, spilling peas all over the floor. Cook berated them most severely, and they began to cry, which in turn, led to Millie and Tom crying. Evie considers herself to be too old for such childish behavior, so she just laughed at them, but it took Minnie and me a good quarter of an hour to restore the peace. They were still sniveling as they ate their meal, and I finally shepherded them off to the nursery."

Master Brooks nodded, allowing a moment for Genevieve's account to sink in. "So, it was unusually noisy, was it?"

"Oh, yes. It's normally very noisy as is, with so many small children, but that day was particularly chaotic. I could barely hear my own voice over all that wailing."

"I see. Thank you, Mistress Whitfield. You may step down."

Master Brooks looked around the assembly, his gaze showing nothing more than mild curiosity at all the people gathered to watch the proceedings. His eyes briefly met Louisa's, who was perched on the edge of the bench, her hands gripping the worn wood like that of a drowning man hanging on to a bit of flotsam in a roiling sea. She was waiting for the next witness, hoping and praying that her gamble would pay off. Master Brooks had been stunned when she had suggested it. He'd never heard of such a thing before, especially from a woman, but he had to admit that the idea had merit.

Proving that Annabel might have misheard the conversation was certainly very useful in creating doubt, but the council could still go either way. With no other suspects and no witnesses to vouch for the whereabouts of Lord Sheridan on the night of the murder, discrediting Annabel would only go so far. The elders of the colony were eager for justice, no matter what form it took, and sending an innocent man to his death went a long way to keeping order and instilling fear in the population. A murder couldn't go unpunished, and some of the members of the council, as well as Sir George, could happily convince themselves that Lord Sheridan was guilty, simply to put the matter to rest and move forward.

The sentence would hinge on this last witness, so the lawyer had to make the testimony as dramatic as possible, although it would be shocking enough in itself. Calling a physician to testify in a murder hearing was certainly radical, and as far as he knew, had never been done by any other lawyer before. He would either be lauded as introducing a groundbreaking new aspect of the law or laughed at by his contemporaries for turning a respectable hearing into a spectacle and making a mockery of the trial.

The room finally quieted down, countless pairs of eyes watching Master Brooks to see what he would do next.

"Will you be making your closing argument now, Master Brooks?" Sir George inquired, clearly bored with the proceedings. It was nearly time for luncheon, and Sir George was very fond of his cook, in more ways than one, if the gossip happened to be true.

"Ah, no, Sir George. I have one more witness that I would like to call to testify. Dr. Jacobson, would you kindly step forward please?" He speared Jacobson with his gaze, daring him to refuse.

The physician, or "the Butcher", as he was known in Jamestown, due to his propensity for killing rather than healing, had been appalled by the suggestion that he take the stand in the murder hearing, but Master Brooks had hinted that testifying might improve the good doctor's reputation in Jamestown, especially if his controversial testimony helped save the life of a good man, a man who was wealthy and would show his appreciation should he be cleared of all charges. Jacobson got the hint and reluctantly agreed, but now that the time had come, he looked nervous and ready to refuse. He was just about to say something when Master Brooks cut him off, addressing the assembly.

"Dr. Jacobson has some very important information that will shed new light on this puzzling case, and it's only his vast expertise and knowledge of the human body that has made these new discoveries possible. Dr. Jacobson..."

The physician reluctantly rose from his seat, beaming at all the faces that were now watching him with undisguised curiosity. Maybe Brooks was right and these people would finally recognize him for the great physician he was, especially Lord Sheridan, who might indeed be feeling very grateful after his testimony. The man pulled back his shoulders, raised his chin and marched forward as if going into battle. His demeanor would make all the difference to how his answers were received, according to Brooks that is, and he was about to put on the best show he could.

The lawyer smiled with more confidence seeing the change in Jacobson. The man was a vain, pompous imbecile, but he would play his part nicely, especially since he could almost taste the reward. Brooks glanced again at Lady Sheridan. *An admirable woman*, he thought yet again, *simply admirable. Who knew she had such a keen legal mind?*

"Ladies and gentlemen, I've taken it upon myself, with the express permission of Mistress Deverell, of course, to have our esteemed physician Dr. Jacobson examine the body of the late Aloysius Deverell. Dr. Jacobson, do you believe that the victim died by drowning?"

"I couldn't swear to it without performing a postmortem, but I don't believe there was any water in the lungs of the deceased. No liquid came out when his chest was pumped, so he was likely already dead by the time he was tossed into the James."

"So, how would you say he died?"

"Upon examining the body, I found many bruises consistent with a beating, and marks upon the neck that suggest he was strangled." Dr. Jacobson looked around the courtroom, clearly enjoying the attention he now commanded.

"I see," uttered the lawyer, turning to face the council. Now came the tricky part, the part he'd argued with Lady Sheridan about, but had to concede made sense. He hoped the members of the council would see it the same way. "Dr. Jacobson, would you say that Master Deverell was killed by a strong man?" This was speculation, but it could save Lord Sheridan's life.

"Yes, I would. The marks on the neck were very wide."

"And what would that tell us, sir?"

"It would indicate that the man who strangled him had large, powerful hands." Dr. Jacobson looked around as if he just explained something very profound, and indeed the spectators were all looking at Lord Sheridan's hands, which is exactly what Brooks had intended.

"Lord Sheridan, would you please raise your hands?" Kit threw him a look of pure resentment as he held up his fettered hands, but the point had been made. Lord Sheridan, although tall, was lean and aristocratic, with elegant, long-fingered hands that probably wouldn't even fit around the neck of the squat, corpulent Aloysius Deverell.

"Dr. Jacobson, do you think Lord Sheridan's hands are big enough to have strangled the victim?"

"No. As a matter of fact, I don't think Lord Sheridan could have beaten or overpowered Master Deverell, who was at least eight stone heavier than Lord Sheridan, possibly more. Master Deverell would have had the advantage in that fight. At a guess, Master Deverell was attacked by a much larger man, a man who was not only bigger, but much fitter and stronger." Master Brooks nearly smiled to himself as several people gasped, shocked by this new testimony.

"And do you believe that Master Deverell was thrown into the water near Rosewood Manor?"

"If he had, he'd probably been carried by the current and not wound up right in the harbor. Most likely, he was dumped into the river from the dock, where his clothing got tangled with a wooden pole and kept him from drifting away, thus allowing the body to be discovered."

"So, if Lord Sheridan had killed Master Deverell near Rosewood Manor, he would have had to transport the body to

Jamestown, where at least one person would have seen him. As it happens, no one saw Lord Sheridan that night, no one at all. He was nowhere near the scene of the crime, or so it would appear. Thank you, Dr. Jacobson. You may step down."

Master Brooks waited until the doctor took his seat at the back before diving into his closing argument. The church was so quiet, you could hear a pin drop as all eyes followed the lawyer around as he paced in front of the council, taking a moment to lock eyes with every member before finally speaking.

"Gentlemen, today we heard the testimony of four people, three of whom reside at Rosewood Manor, and who were on the premises on the day in question. Mistress Whitfield claims to have heard Lord Sheridan threatening to kill Master Deverell, a fact that she's willing to swear to. Her resolve is very commendable, and I don't doubt that she truly believes that's what she heard, however, the two men were conversing fifty feet away from the house during a time when five children were crying and screaming just down the hall. According to Mistress Pike and Mistress Genevieve Whitfield, the children were in the kitchen during the time of the exchange and carried on for at least a quarter of an hour before they were subdued enough to eat their dinner." Master Brooks looks around, making sure he had everyone's undivided attention.

"Now, I ask you, is overhearing a snippet of conversation, heated though it might be, over the cacophony of screaming children from a distance of fifty feet solid enough evidence to convict a man of murder and sentence him to death?"

Master Brooks paused for a moment, giving the members of the council a moment to process what he just said. Then he continued, "And then we have the testimony of our physician, Dr. Jacobson. According to him, it would have taken a much stronger man than Lord Sheridan to overpower and strangle the victim, a man who would have to have done the deed right here in Jamestown in order for the body to still be in the harbor the following morning. Everyone here knows Lord Sheridan, but no one had seen him in Jamestown or anywhere near the harbor on the night in question.

Now, we may never know who committed this gruesome crime, but based on the evidence presented today, I say it isn't Lord Christopher Sheridan, who has neither the disposition nor the strength to murder a man of Master Deverell's girth in cold blood. Thank you."

Master Brooks swept to his seat and sat down, crossing his legs and brushing a speck of lint from his coat, as if preparing to watch a performance of some sort rather than to hear the outcome of the trial in which his client might be sentenced to death.

"Ladies and gentlemen, the members of the council and I would like some time to consider the evidence, so I propose that we reconvene after a break, at say two o'clock."

The spectators shuffled out of the church, talking loudly amongst themselves and debating what they'd just heard. Louisa remained seated, her eyes glued to Kit's. "You're amazing," he mouthed as the guard led him away to his cell to await the verdict. *But am I amazing enough to have saved the day?* Louisa thought as she squeezed Fred Taylor's hand.

It had taken them hours to convince Master Brooks to talk to the physician. He gaped at them as if they'd suggested whipping out a broom and using it to fly across town, doing a few summersaults over the church. Medical evidence had been used in a court of law to confirm the cause of death but speculating as to the type of man might have killed a victim was unheard of. No forensic evidence of any kind would be used for centuries to come, but this was as close as they could get in the seventeenth century, using their twenty-first century knowledge. As Fred Taylor repeatedly pointed out to Master Brooks, they didn't have to prove Lord Sheridan innocent. All they had to do was create a reasonable doubt of his guilt, a doubt that would prevent any man of conscience from sentencing him to hang based on such circumstantial evidence. *Damn Annabel*, Louisa thought for the hundredth time. *If it weren't for her blasted testimony, none of this would be happening.*

Louisa finally rose to her feet, suddenly eager for a breath of fresh air. She hadn't eaten since last night and her stomach was growling in protest as she swayed with lightheadedness. Genevieve was instantly at her side, taking her by the elbow and steering her toward the door.

"You must take some food, Lady Sheridan. Cook sent a hamper with Minnie, so why don't we find a place to sit and you can have something to eat while we wait." She squeezed Louisa's hand in mute support, and Louisa nearly burst into tears, feeling the lack of Valerie. She needed her sister there, and Alec.

"Thank you, Genevieve, you've been a great help. I will have something to eat, and so should you. You girls were splendid," she said as Minnie approached them by the door, her face tense with worry.

"Do you think it will help, your ladyship?" Minnie asked, her eyes filling with tears.

"It must."

FIFTY-THREE

Nearly an hour later Louisa walked back into the church, followed by Genevieve, Minnie, and Fred Taylor. The small space was already full, spectators eager to hear the verdict. Louisa could hear snippets of conversation and muted arguments, as people voiced their opinion of the evidence and the possible outcome. She wished she could put her hands over her ears to tune out the malicious tongues that still thought Kit should hang. At that moment, she didn't care what Kit had done with Buckingham, or even if he really killed that odious man; all she wanted was for him to be cleared of all charges so that he could come home with her.

Louisa realized that she'd forgiven him long ago, and always knew she would. Whatever he had done, it had been because he had no other choice, and he'd suffered enough not only while it lasted, but long after, knowing there was a chance she might find out. Louisa watched as the members of the council filed in, led by Sir George who looked as if he'd had time to enjoy his meal after all. He appeared well-pleased with himself, rubbing his hands in satisfaction as he took his seat and surveyed the members of the council.

Then, Kit was finally brought in. He appeared to be calm, but Louisa knew him well enough to notice the lines of tension around his eyes and the defiant set of his shoulders. He was scared, and he had every right to be. Come this time tomorrow, he might be dead, and she might be a widow, her children fatherless and disgraced. Louisa said a quick prayer, but she didn't really believe that God would hear her. When did he ever? She sucked in her breath as Sir George rose to his feet, surveying his audience with an air of a man who was about to deliver a riveting performance.

"Ladies and gentlemen, the members of the council and I have considered the evidence most carefully. I must admit that the testimony of Dr. Jacobson was rather unorthodox, but we unanimously believe that there isn't enough proof to convict Lord Sheridan of the murder of Aloysius Deverell. We will continue to search for the perpetrator of this heinous crime and will bring him to justice once he's apprehended. In the meantime, Lord Christopher Sheridan, you are free to go. Guard, please remove the shackles."

Louisa nearly fainted with relief, her heart pounding with joy. She wanted to fly into Kit's arms and tell him that she loved him and forgave him everything, but this wasn't the time nor the place. Despite his calm demeanor, Kit was overwrought and needed a little time to deal with his emotions. Louisa strode to the front and put her arm through his, leading him out of the church. "Let's go home, Kit," she said, drawing closer to him as he kissed the top of her head.

"Yes, let's. We have much to discuss," he added wearily, knowing his ordeal wasn't quite over.

"There's nothing to discuss. It's over." Louisa smiled at Kit as he gazed at her in confusion. "It's over," she repeated, "and we shall never speak of it again."

Kit nodded, relief showing in his eyes. "Let's go home. I miss the children."

Louisa smiled happily as she drove the trap away from Jamestown and toward Rosewood Manor. Kit was free, and at this moment, that was all that mattered to her. He was emotionally wrung out, exhausted from lack of sleep, and could use a bath, but otherwise he was unharmed and would be back to his old self in a few days. Of course, there was still much to discuss once the dust settled.

She had offered him love and forgiveness on impulse, but things were far from resolved between them. She had pushed thoughts of Kit and Buckingham away from her spinning brain for the past few days, but now that the trial was behind them, she would have to finally analyze her feelings and try to come to terms with what she'd learned. In her heart she knew Kit loved her and the children and would have never submitted to Buckingham unless he had a very good reason, but the unbidden images of the two of them together still ambushed her when she least expected, leaving her gutted and sick to her stomach with revulsion. She supposed any person could submit to unwelcome sexual advances under dire circumstances, but what if Kit had enjoyed their trysts? What if he got a taste for men?

Louisa's twenty-first century brain tried to assure her that people didn't just become homosexual. The attraction to the same sex and the desire to act on it would have been there, possibly buried, but still there from the start. Kit had never shown the slightest interest in men. He had been a man's man, the kind Louisa rarely met in her previous life in the future. Surrendering himself to Buckingham must have cost him dearly, and now he had to deal with the knowledge that his wife might never fully forgive him or love him as she had before. She wanted to believe with all her heart that things could go back to the way they were, but only time would tell if the tear in the fabric of their relationship could be repaired, or if the seam would always mar the surface, a constant reminder of something ugly and forbidden.

FIFTY-FOUR

Louisa came slowly awake but refused to open her eyes. She could feel the warm sun on her face, streaming through the unshuttered window, and hear the voices of children coming from downstairs, but she wanted to lie there just a little bit longer, floating on a cloud of contentment and joy. Whatever doubts she had about Kit's love and devotion were dispelled last night after they were finally able to close the door on their family and have some long-overdue privacy to finally talk things out and make up in a way that left her quivering like jelly.

Kit was still asleep, his dark lashes fanned across his lean cheeks and a small smile playing about his lips. Maybe he was dreaming of last night, or maybe he knew, even in sleep, that he was finally home and cleared of the terrible accusation against him. They would probably never know who killed Deverell, but it almost didn't matter. Judging from all they knew of the man, it was no great loss to society, least of all to his wife, who obviously hated and feared him.

Louisa's eyes flew open at that last thought. How hard she'd become living in the seventeenth century. Things were more black-and-white here, which, in a way, made things easier for people. Shades of gray led to unrest, rebellion, and ultimately submission. Here, people were guilty until proven innocent, not the other way around. Thank God, Fred Taylor had the wisdom and foresight not only to try to discredit Annabel's testimony, but also to cast doubt on Kit's ability to take down a man of Deverell's size. It had been a gamble, but it'd worked, and that's all that mattered.

Louisa practically purred as Kit pulled her on top of him, his eyes now wide open and full of mischief.

"We have to go downstairs. The children are up," she whispered urgently, but he pushed the nightdress past her shoulders and cupped her breasts in his warm hands.

"The children can wait, but I can't," he stated matter-of-factly as he slid inside her, his eyes never leaving her face. Louisa closed her eyes as waves of pleasure rippled through her body, making her forget the children and everything else besides. She wished they could stay this way forever, free of suspicion and joined in body and soul. All thoughts fled from her mind as she gave herself up to the moment and told him over and over again, without uttering a word, that she was his forever.

FIFTY-FIVE

The sun was warm on his back as Cameron bent down to take a few handfuls of water. It was cold and sweet, and tasted of something he hadn't known in a long time—freedom. He pulled off his clothes and waded into the cool water, needing to feel clean and reborn. Most religions used water as a symbol of rebirth, a baptism, and he needed to be baptized a new man. Today his life began anew, and no matter what happened, he would never take another moment for granted.

He swam toward the waterfall cascading down from a rock formation high above his head and allowed the water to fall on his head, washing away both sin and grime. He closed his eyes and turned up his face, enjoying the rush of the water as it caressed his face and fell onto his shoulders, making him feel reborn.

Cameron would have liked to stay and swim for a while, but he couldn't afford to remain exposed, so he reluctantly got out, pulled on his breeches, and quickly washed out his shirt before making his way to the narrow opening of the cave. He would be well concealed while he took some rest, ate his meager meal, and waited to see if this time God was on his side.

The stale breath of the cave enveloped Cameron as soon as he crawled through the narrow opening and made his way to the slightly wider tunnel in the center. It wasn't high enough to stand, or long enough to lie down flat, but if he sat with his back to the rough stone or curled up with his knees drawn to his chest, he would be just fine. The most important thing was that it was secluded, and not easily spotted by someone who wasn't looking for the crevice in the rock behind the waterfall. Cameron sat down with his long legs folded in front of him and unwrapped the oatcakes he'd managed to save from the day before. It wasn't much, but the cakes would last him for two meals, then he was on his own. He patted the knife tucked into his boot. Getting that had been much harder, but he felt better knowing that he had a weapon as well as a survival tool. He'd need to hunt for food if he were to survive, and he could hardly do that without a knife. What he wouldn't give for a gun, but now he was just dreaming.

Cameron finished his food, wrapped up the remaining portion for later, and curled onto his side. He was exhausted, more emotionally than physically, and he needed to a refuge from his thoughts, if only temporarily.

FIFTY-SIX

Louisa took a sip of chicory coffee and balanced out its bitterness with a piece of toast generously spread with strawberry jam. If she didn't focus on the flavor too much, it could almost pass for real coffee, something she'd loved dearly in her old life. She hated drinking ale or beer for breakfast, so Fred had vowed to make her some coffee. He loved a project. Louisa and Valerie always assured him that the coffee tasted great and made sure to have some every morning with their breakfast. Cook normally made the coffee, but refused to touch the stuff, saying the smell alone made her want to gag.

Thoughts of Valerie threatened to destroy Louisa's good mood, so she pushed them away for the moment, determined to enjoy this beautiful day that was a gift snatched from the jaws of destiny, and permit herself to be happy for a few hours before resuming her constant worry and vigil over the road for any sign of Valerie and Alec. She smiled at Kit, who was watching her from across the table.

"They will come back," he said, "I know they will. Just keep the faith. Today I'd like to believe that anything is possible. I have to go thank Fred for his help with the trial and then speak to Master Worthing about plantation business. After that, I will come back, and you and I are going to have a picnic in the woods—without the children." He gave her a meaningful look, and Louisa felt her cheeks grow warm.

"I'll be waiting," she replied, giving him a sweet smile. She liked him like this. She was about to tell him so when Minnie erupted into the room, her eyes round in her flushed face.

"Sorry to disturb, your lordship," she panted, "but there are some men coming toward the house with guns and dogs." Minnie looked frightened, her eyes round and full of worry.

"Minnie, take the children upstairs and stay out of sight," Kit said as he rose from the table and headed for the door. Louisa followed close behind, but he waved her back. "Stay with the children until I find out what's happening."

Louisa motioned for Minnie to go, but remained behind Kit, eager to see what was going on. If Sir George had sent men to rearrest Kit, she needed to be there to find out what had transpired in order to change his mind. Could they charge Kit with the same crime twice? She didn't think so, but this was colonial Virginia, and in truth, they could do anything they wanted.

As Kit stepped onto the porch, Louisa peeked past his shoulder toward the road. Two men on horseback were coming toward them, the dust churned by the hooves creating a cloud on the horizon and making it difficult to make out who they were. She had noticed, however, that both were armed, muskets slung across their shoulders with several dogs running alongside, barking like mad. What if these men were the ones who actually attacked Deverell and murdered him in cold blood? She sucked in a shuddering breath as Kit gently laid a hand on her arm.

"It's all right, sweetheart. It's only Worthing and Barnes."

Now that Kit said it, she recognized the overseer of the plantation and one of the senior men. Arthur Worthing had been with them for years, and Peter Barnes had been his right-hand man for the past year, his indenture contract nearly done. Barnes intended to stay at the plantation once he'd fulfilled his obligation to Alec, having no family to return to or a desire to start over back in England.

Kit watched warily as the approaching men drew closer. They looked anxious, their faces sheened with sweat and dust from the hard ride.

"Is something amiss, Master Worthing?" Kit called out. Arthur Worthing removed his hat as a sign of respect, and bowed stiffly from the neck, his face tense and his eyes failing to meet Kit's.

"Seems one of the indentures has escaped, your lordship. It was discovered this morning when the men were roused at dawn. We thought he might be on his way to Jamestown to try to get aboard a ship bound for England, but we checked every vessel in port, and there was no sign of him. We checked the hold of every ship for stowaways as well," he added desperately. Master Worthing seemed to be bracing himself for a verbal lashing, but Kit looked more stunned than angry.

"Really? Which one?" Not a single man had tried to run away from Rosewood Manor, most of the workers grateful to have wound up at a place where they were well cared for and treated with dignity and respect. Runaways had little chance of actually getting away, and even if they did, they'd have no money, no food, and no weapon, reducing their chances of survival to almost zero. If caught, they would be severely punished by the law of the colony before being returned to the plantation, where they would likely be punished again by their master. Very few indentured servants attempted to run away, and those who had rarely made it longer than a day without being caught and flogged half to death.

"Cameron Brody, your lordship, the Scotch fellow. Hasn't been seen since last night when he went to bed with the rest of the men." Arthur Worthing visibly cringed as Kit glanced at the sun. Judging by the position of the sun it was close to noon, the sun riding high in the sky, its blazing orb hard to look at without shielding one's eyes.

"We've been searching around the plantation as well, Lord Sheridan, in case he's hiding somewhere nearby. Seems illogical for the man to head to Jamestown where he's sure to be caught before he even makes it as far as the docks, if that's what he's after."

"I suppose that makes sense," Kit mused, still watching Worthing with his head cocked to the side. "What about searching in the other direction?"

"I can't see that he would run that way, your lordship. That there is Indian Territory, so his chances of survival are minimal should he run into the savages, although he's likely got a better chance than most, Scots being nearly as savage as the Indians." Worthing smiled nervously at his joke, but Kit wasn't amused.

"Go back to the plantation and organize a search party. He couldn't have gone far. I'll leave this in your capable hands, Master Worthing," Kit announced, turning to go back in the house. "Keep me updated, if you please."

Louisa peered at Arthur Worthing as he cantered out of the yard followed by Barnes. The dogs were no longer barking, but trotting alongside the horses, their tongues hanging out from thirst. She hoped Worthing would at least give them some water before embarking on the next leg of the search. Brody couldn't have gone far, so they'd most likely find him by nightfall. She hoped Kit wouldn't be too hard on the poor boy. He didn't like to punish, but this was the first time anyone had ever run away and he would be duty-bound to punish him publicly and show the rest of the workers that escape wouldn't be tolerated. The normal form of punishment was flogging, and Louisa shrank at the thought. It was barbaric, to say the least, and the victim took a long time to recover, sometimes dying instead. The wounds healed, but the scars lasted forever, branding the person as someone who'd been flogged, which was a sure sign that he was either a criminal or a slave.

Poor Genevieve would be terribly upset to learn of Brody's escape. The girl seemed fond of him for some reason, possibly because of their shared Catholicism. Louisa hoped it wasn't anything more than that. Cameron Brody was a handsome devil, and a young, innocent girl like Genevieve just might be seduced by his good looks and brooding manner, her heart full of romantic notions and dreams of rescuing him from his fate.

Louisa suddenly wondered how Brody came to be at the plantation. She was so opposed to the notion of someone being reduced to slavery that she had as little to do with the workers as possible. She was kind and helpful, but kept her opinions to herself, venting only to Valerie when they were alone. Valerie felt much the same, but she'd been in the past much longer and had reluctantly come to accept the often-brutal ways of seventeenth-century society. There was nothing they could do for the men other than to make sure they were treated humanely.

Brody was younger than most of the men, and obviously not there by choice. A lot of the workers had willingly sold themselves into indenture for the sake of their families, but Louisa didn't believe that had been the case with Cameron Brody. Many convicts were sent down to the Colonies and sold into indentured labor. Maybe Brody was one of those, but if that were the case, what had been his crime, and were they safe now that he was on the loose?

She would have to make sure everyone stayed inside until Brody was captured and brought back to the plantation, just in case. She didn't think him a violent man, but a desperate man was always unpredictable, and if Cameron Brody chose to risk everything to run away, then he was more desperate than most.

FIFTY-SEVEN

It was several hours before Genevieve could finally make her excuses and hole up in the tiny room she shared with Minnie. The house was unusually quiet after the news of Cameron's escape broke, the children ordered to stay indoors and out of the way of the search party. Lady Sheridan was downstairs, but Lord Sheridan had gone down to the barracks where men were gathering in the yard, arming themselves with torches and ropes before heading off in search of Cameron. According to Master Worthing, he hadn't turned up in Jamestown, so the search party was heading into the woods around the plantation and along the shore of the James, just in case Cameron was following the river.

The barracks were a long way from the house, but Genevieve could swear she heard the barking of dogs and the neighing of horses as the men prepared to leave, eager to hunt their prey. Even though most of the search party was made up of other indentured servants, they wanted to prove that they were loyal and deserved to be treated fairly, not punished for the actions of one man. Cameron's escape could affect all of them adversely, and they were scared. If he got away, the master might feel compelled to implement stricter rules and take away their little freedoms. The men were angry and determined, and it scared Genevieve, for God only knew what they would do to Cameron once they found him.

Genevieve huddled in a corner, her aching head resting against her knees, arms wrapped around her legs. She'd been so happy yesterday when Lord Sheridan had been freed, but now she felt as if her world was falling apart. Where was Cameron, and why had he suddenly run away? Or maybe it wasn't sudden, and he'd been planning this all along. He gave no indication that he was planning an escape, but he was a man who was in control of his feelings and could have easily fooled Genevieve into thinking that everything was as it should be when his mind was teeming with plans and possibilities. Of course, had he been planning his escape, he might have asked Genevieve to bring him some food or something he could trade, but he'd asked for nothing.

Had something happened to set him off? Had he been mistreated by Worthing or Barnes? The men were forbidden to beat the workers or deny them food, but if Cameron had done something they considered unforgivable they might try to punish him on the sly while her uncle was away and Lord Sheridan imprisoned. If caught, he could be punished to the full extent of the law, and although she couldn't imagine that Lord Sheridan would have him flogged, or worse, she was still scared to death.

Did he have a plan or was this something he'd done on the spur of the moment, suddenly unable to bear another day of servitude? And what about her? Had she meant absolutely nothing to him? Had he used her to assuage some of his loneliness and anger, never meaning for their relationship to be anything more than a quick roll in the hay, or in their case a dip in the lake? They'd made love a few more times since that first time, and Genevieve suddenly froze with terror, realizing that even at that very moment Cameron's baby could be growing in her womb.

Oh God, what would she tell her uncle? What would he do if she found herself with child? Deep down, she knew he wouldn't throw her out, but he would assume that Cameron had forced himself on her, and that simply wasn't the case. He'd be branded a rapist and sentenced to death if caught, and it would all be her fault.

Hot tears streamed down Genevieve's face as she angrily wiped them away. What a fool she had been to allow herself to love him. How well did she even know the man? Everything he told her could have been lies, made up for her benefit. Perhaps he was guilty of the crime he had been accused of, and worse. But even if that were true, she'd been the one who'd pursued him. He'd never initiated anything, so she couldn't blame him for misleading her. He never had.

Genevieve wiped the tears with her sleeve, suddenly ashamed of herself. If Cameron had run away, he must have had a good reason, and she should be worried about him rather than assuming the worst and accusing him of everything under the sun. She might not have much experience when it came to men, but she knew when someone was genuine. She'd seen enough falseness in her life to recognize that his soul was in torment and was confident that he'd been reaching out to her, rather than just looking for a possible advantage. Deep down, she knew Cameron Brody was an honorable man, no matter what he'd been accused of, and she would support him in her heart and pray for him.

Genevieve remained seated in the corner long after the sun went down and the last glimmer of light faded from the room, plunging it into inky darkness. The house quieted down as Lady Sheridan retired to her room, overwrought by the events of the day, and the children were shepherded to the nursery by Minnie, who recognized Genevieve's need to be alone and gave her silent support. They'd never spoken of Cameron, but Minnie was no fool; she knew that Genevieve wasn't indifferent to the big Scot and often met him after dark. Lord Sheridan still hadn't returned, which was either a reason to hope, or a reason to feel dread.

Genevieve raised her head in trepidation when she heard the calls of the men as they galloped into the yard, the night suddenly illuminated by a dozen torches and filled with the sound of angry men and neighing horses. Genevieve sprang to her feet, peering out the window to see if they might have Cameron with them. The men were talking loudly, speculating as to where Cameron might be, their shoulders slumped with fatigue and their voices laced with irritation. They'd been out there for hours, but they hadn't found him. Genevieve sighed with relief as she sank to her knees, clasping her hands before her in prayer. If Cameron didn't want to be found, then she hoped they'd never find him. She would be happy in the knowledge that he got away and possibly made it back to his homeland and his people.

Having finished praying, Genevieve got ready for bed. She was exhausted, mentally and physically, and needed to rest. She removed her bodice, skirt, and stockings and pulled the pins out of her hair, letting it fall to her shoulders. The fresh breeze from the window caressed her bare arms and legs as she climbed into bed wearing only her shift. She closed her eyes, images of her and Cameron swimming before her as hot tears slid down her cheeks and into her hair. She wished she could sleep, but she was wide awake, her misery so acute it made her heart hurt. Genevieve feigned sleep when she heard Minnie outside the door. She couldn't bear to talk to her or anyone else until she had a chance to compose herself and put on an indifferent face, so no one would suspect how much she was really hurting.

Minnie quietly let herself into the room and closed the door softly, her dark silhouette outlined against the lighter color of the wall. She hesitated for a moment, but then Genevieve felt the thin mattress give under Minnie's weight as she sat down and took Genevieve's hand. "Jenny, wake up," she whispered.

Genevieve forced herself to open her eyes. Minnie was quiet as a mouse when she wanted to be, so it was odd that she would wake Genevieve on purpose. "What is it, Minnie?"

"I found something when I was putting the children to bed," she whispered, her eyes gleaming in the darkness. "It was in the pocket of Evie's skirt. I asked Evie and she said a man gave it to her."

Genevieve sat bolt upright, no longer feeling lethargic. "Let me see." The square of paper was creased and dirty, but one word was written in what looked like mud. "Cave."

"Does that mean anything to you?" Minnie asked, her face alight with curiosity. "Is it from him?"

Genevieve stared down at the paper. Cameron might have a piece of paper, but he would have no access to ink or a quill. Writing with a muddy stick would be the closest he could get. Perhaps he saw Evie by the pond and gave her a message, knowing that, as a child, she'd think nothing of it. Evie didn't know how to write, so couldn't have written the message herself, so it stood to reason that it might be from Cameron. Genevieve took Minnie's hand and squeezed it in gratitude.

"I think it might be from Cameron. I told him about the cave with the waterfall where Cousin Finn used to go. I'd been there with Uncle Alec and had described to Cameron exactly where it was. I'll go there tomorrow." Genevieve was already planning what she would take with her, and how long it would take for her to walk if she left at dawn. Her heart contracted with fear that Cameron might be gone by the time she got there, but she had to wait till morning. Besides, the estate was swarming with men; she'd be stopped as soon as she left the house, and all kinds of questions would be asked about her relationship with the escaped man.

"You should wait a day or two," Minnie whispered. "They're searching for him all over, and it might look odd if you suddenly disappear. The cave is hours away, and it would take you the whole day to go there and back. It's not safe."

Genevieve considered what Minnie was saying, acknowledging the wisdom of her reasoning. "Minnie, you're right, but he might not wait more than a day. If I don't show up, he might leave, and I'll never see him again. This is my one chance. Will you cover for me? Just tell them I'm indisposed. I'll leave before the sun comes up, so by the time anyone might notice that I'm not in my bed, I'll be long gone. Please, Minnie, please."

Minnie nodded. "I'd rather not lie to her ladyship, but I suppose you owe it to yourself to find out. I'll tell them you're not feeling well as it's your time of the month. Lady Sheridan is always sympathetic. She'll leave you alone as long as I promise to bring you some food and a hot-water bottle. It might work. What will you do if you find him?" Minnie's eyes were large in the darkness of the room, the light of the moon reflected in her irises. She wasn't a very pretty girl, but in the moonlight, she looked beautiful, especially when she smiled.

"I don't know. I just want to talk to him and make sure he's safe. I'll bring him some food, and maybe give him my emerald ring. He can trade it for food or passage home. I don't have much else to give him."

"How will you explain the missing ring? Wasn't it your mam's? Your uncle will be upset. He'd kept it all those years as a reminder of his sister," Minnie whispered as she watched Genevieve's face.

"I'll just tell him that I lost it and bear the brunt of his anger. What else can I do? I want to help Cameron and that's the only way I can do that. Besides, I want to say goodbye." Minnie nodded, squeezing her hand as Genevieve began to cry again.

FIFTY-EIGHT
VIRGINIA SEPTEMBER 1779

Abbie cuddled closer to Finn, his body warm and solid next to hers. He'd finally returned last night, tired, but happy to be home, especially after his run-in with Major Weland. Everyone had a good laugh over Finn's account of getting out of Savannah dressed as a woman, but things could have turned out very differently and they were all acutely aware of that. Diana was strangely quiet as Finn recounted his journey, especially when Finn mentioned that he had gone to see Jonah. She fidgeted in her seat, stealing looks at Finn from beneath her lashes.

Abbie supposed it was natural for her to be worried about Jonah's reaction. After all, he had no idea he had a son until Finn showed up. Finn was strangely reluctant to go into any details of his conversation with Jonah, but he didn't say that Jonah had been shocked or displeased. It would likely take some time for her brother to absorb the fact that he was now a father.

Abbie closed her eyes, eager for a few more minutes of sleep when she heard fussing coming from the direction of Diana's cot. "Go back to sleep," Abbie moaned as she forced herself out of bed. Abbie brushed the hair out of her face and bent over the cot, ready to lift Diana out, only to find her still sound asleep.

Maybe she'd been fussing in her sleep. It seemed pointless to wake her, so Abbie turned back toward the bed. She could steal a few more peaceful moments, but she was stopped in her tracks by low mewling. She glanced back at Diana, but her face was relaxed in sleep, her little hands raised above her head as if she were surrendering. Strange.

Abbie suddenly noticed something out of the corner of her eye. A dark bundle was just visible behind the cot, the sounds coming from there. She walked over, squatting down to get a better look. A pair of eyes stared back at her, lips trembling as Nat considered whether he should cry now or hold off for a little while longer. He was tightly wrapped in the blanket, his arms forced against his sides and his legs straight out. The blanket was tied with a string to prevent him from unwrapping himself. Abbie supposed Diana was afraid that Nat would throw off the blanket and try to get down the ladder, which he wasn't yet able to navigate. If he managed to get to the ladder, he'd fall down to the ground floor and possibly kill himself.

Abbie huffed with outrage as she reached for the child and untied the string. A strong smell of urine came off his gown as Abbie undid the wrapping. He must have wet himself hours ago since his clout was soaked through. Poor child, he must be hungry as well as wet. Where was Diana? And what the hell had she been thinking leaving him like that on the floor, tied up like a parcel?

Abbie carefully made her way down the stairs in search of Diana. She normally slept with Annie and Sarah, but her bed was empty, the blanket carelessly shoved aside. *She might have gone to the privy*, Abbie thought before stopping in the middle of the room. *But why would Diana leave Nat upstairs when he normally slept with her?* Sarah and Annie were still asleep in their bed, so they'd be no help at all, and her parents were in the other room, their breathing clearly audible in the somnolent silence.

Nat began fussing again. His face was a pale oval in the darkness, and his mouth looked like a black hole when he opened it to cry. When was the last time he'd been fed? He was obviously hungry. Abbie quickly changed his nappy and took him into the main room, where she poured some milk from a pewter pitcher and crumbled a piece of bread into the milk until it was a soupy mush. Nat practically inhaled the food, opening his mouth before she even filled the spoon. He was starving.

"What are you doing?" Hannah asked as she shuffled into the front room, wearing a shawl over her nightdress and a linen cap over her unbound hair. She pulled the shawl closer, taking in the sight of Nat being fed by Abbie.

"I found him in the loft behind Diana's cot. He was bound and tied, as well as hungry and wet," Abbie explained angrily. "And I don't see Diana anywhere."

"She must have gone to the necessary," Hannah said, taking up a poker to stoke the smoldering ashes back into life, "but that certainly doesn't explain the rest of it. Here, let me have him. You go see to your own child. I think she's awake."

Abbie handed the boy to her mother and rose wearily to her feet. "Thanks, Ma. I'll be down in a bit to help you get breakfast started."

"Don't trouble yourself about breakfast. Bring Diana down and see to your husband," Hannah said with a wicked wink. "He looked awfully forlorn last night."

"Ma!" Abbie hissed, trying to hide her smile, but Hannah was already adding more bread to the milk and humming softly to Nat.

FIFTY-NINE

Abbie sighed with pleasure as Finn finally rolled off her, his face wreathed in a satisfied smile. It'd only been a few weeks, but she felt as if they hadn't seen each other in months, despite the fact that the days just flew by, especially with Diana and Nat here, and Sue's baby coming early. Abbie hadn't been parted from Finn for any length of time since her arrest in New York, and she needed him close to feel safe.

It was only now he was back that she realized how terrified she'd been, and his humorous account of his escape from Savannah only reminded her of how easily one could go from being safe to being executed by the British. He brought her a present as well as a funny little dolly for Diana, which she clutched to her chest dramatically, ecstatic to have a baby of her own. As if presents, although a lovely surprise, could make up for the gnawing worry she felt while he was gone. *Will this damn war never come to an end?* she thought angrily. It'd been going on for years with no end in sight. The armies moved around like pieces on a chessboard, but no one seemed any closer to checkmate.

She just wanted to live a normal, peaceful life, finally build a house of their own, and have another child. She didn't want there to be too big of an age difference between baby Diana and her future sibling, but she just wasn't emotionally ready and always reminded Finn to take precautions. Her mother often looked at her with concern, too polite to ask straight out, but looking at her flat belly with a trained eye. She'd already had Sam and Martha by the time she was Abbie's age.

"That bad?" Finn asked as he traced a finger from her collarbone to her bellybutton. Abbie looked at him, confused by the question.

"You're scowling rather fiercely," Finn replied, his finger making its way lower. "Did I fail to satisfy, my lady?"

"No, of course not. I was just thinking about this blasted war, and about having another baby."

"Oh?" Finn's eyebrows shot up, making Abbie giggle.

"You do want another child, don't you?" she asked playfully.

"Of course, I want a houseful of children, but for that I require a house. I love your family, but it would be nice to have a home of our own."

"My thoughts exactly," Abbie said, straddling him and pinning his wrists down on the bed. "I say we press the issue after the harvest and demand that Pa and Sam help us build our own cabin. What do you say, Finlay Whitfield?"

"I say that's a splendid idea. The house will be finished long before you have the baby," Finn replied, suddenly rolling over and pinning Abbie down with his weight.

"What baby?"

"The baby we are going to make right now," Finn whispered as he kissed her tenderly, his eyes asking a question. Abbie smiled into his eyes, the answer there for him to see. She took him into her body and he moved slowly, his eyes never leaving hers. There were times when they just made love, but this was one of those times when it was a true union of body and soul, an experience that left them both speechless with wonder and aglow with love. "I love you so much, Abs," he whispered. Abbie nodded into his chest, overcome with emotion. If she ever lost Finn, she'd lose a part of herself forever.

Abbie's thoughts were interrupted by the ruckus coming from downstairs. Everyone was up and about now, and it was time to rejoin the world and go down to start the morning chores. "By the way, Diana was nowhere to be found this morning," Abbie informed Finn as she began to dress for the day. "Nat was here this morning, sleeping on the floor, and he was hungry and wet. I wonder if she's turned up yet."

Finn gave Abbie a strange look as he threw off the blanket and got out of bed. "Somehow, I doubt it."

"What do you mean?" Abbie stopped in mid-stroke, the hairbrush forgotten in her hand. "What do you know, Finlay Whitfield?"

"I know that Nathaniel is no more Jonah's than he is mine, and Diana knows that I know. Sam is married, so unless she can manage to destroy his marriage, which I'm sure she's tried, she's out of alternatives. Going back to her old life with a child in tow is tantamount to suicide, so I suspect she weighed her options and left in the night."

"She wouldn't leave Nat, would she? I could never just leave our baby," Abbie added, horrified by what Finn was suggesting.

"You're not Diana."

"Well, I think you're wrong," Abbie retorted as she picked up the hairbrush again, yanking at her hair as if it were at fault somehow. "We'll just go downstairs and see what's what, shall we?"

She didn't wait for an answer as she pulled the cap over her now brushed and coiled hair and made her way down the stairs. Finn was in no rush to join her. He wasn't sure what he hoped to find. If Diana had truly decamped during the night, it would certainly be better for the Mallory family, but he felt sorry for poor Nat, and even more so for Susanna. She would find out the reason for Diana's abrupt departure sooner or later, and it was bound to affect her marriage to Sam.

Of course, Nat had been conceived before Sam even met Sue, but that knowledge would do little to take the sting out of the fact that her husband's bastard was now living a stone's throw away. Finn sighed and pulled on his breeches. He hoped he hadn't done wrong by telling everyone he'd seen Jonah, but that was the only way he could let Diana know that he knew her secret.

Finn came downstairs to find everyone strangely subdued. Mrs. Mallory was setting breakfast on the table while Sarah and Annie saw to Nat, who was gnawing on a piece of bread. Abbie was holding a crying Diana, and Mr. Mallory sat staring into space as if he were alone in the room.

"Finn, join me outside for a moment, would you?" Mr. Mallory suddenly asked, rising from the table and reaching for his hat. Finn followed him outside, shrugging noncommittally at Abbie's inquiring glance. Mr. Mallory walked for a few moments until they were clear of the house before finally turning to speak to Finn.

"She's gone," he announced as he fiddled with his pipe. It took him three tries to light it, during which time Finn remained silent, waiting to see where this conversation was going. "I gave her money," Mr. Mallory continued.

"I'm sorry, Mr. Mallory, but I don't follow," Finn replied, confused by what was expected of him in this situation. Was Mr. Mallory seeking his approval or advice, or did he simply need to unburden himself?

"I knew Nathaniel wasn't Jonah's as soon as Diana came here, but I couldn't say anything until I was absolutely sure. You confirmed my suspicions yesterday when you returned." Mr. Mallory finally seemed satisfied with the pipe and took a deep drag, letting out a cloud of pungent smoke and sighing with contentment.

"But I didn't say anything," Finn countered, suddenly feeling guilty for his part in Diana's departure.

"You didn't need to. Diana was here for Sam, not for Jonah; that much was clear. It was decent of her to lie to spare Susanna's feelings, but I wasn't sure how long the lie could go on. I saw her outside last night. She was in a vulnerable state, and I'm ashamed to admit that I took advantage of it."

"So, you paid her off to leave?" Finn asked, surprised by Mr. Mallory's cunning. The man never missed an opportunity when he saw one.

"I did. I promised her that Hannah and I will look after Nat and give him all the love and care a little boy needs in exchange for her leaving and never returning to claim him." Mr. Mallory threw Finn a defiant look. "What was I to do?" he asked. "As long as Susanna believes that Nat is Jonah's, she and Sam should be fine."

Finn clapped the older man on the back in a silent offer of support. What was there to say? Mr. Mallory did what he thought was right to protect his son, no, both his sons, and his grandchild. Diana could have refused if she wished, but she wanted to be away from here as much as the Mallorys wanted her gone. Nat would be better off growing up in a loving family rather than in some brothel where he might be ill-treated or ignored. Finn sighed and followed Mr. Mallory back inside, but he'd suddenly lost his appetite.

SIXTY
VIRGINIA SEPTEMBER 1626

The house was eerily still, the only sounds the creaking of the wooden bed frames and light snoring coming from down the hall. It was at least an hour before dawn, that dark hour when the night is still battling to maintain its dominion as the sun slowly but surely begins its ascent, chasing away shadows and eventually dispelling the darkness and plunging the world into brilliant light. Genevieve crept down the stairs and into the kitchen where she grabbed half a loaf of bread, a wedge of cheese, and filled a burlap pouch with raw oats.

Cook wouldn't be pleased to see things missing from her pantry, but she would just assume that Lord Sheridan was hungry during the night and helped himself to some bread and cheese. She hadn't taken enough oats for Cook to notice, or so she hoped. She tiptoed out the door and closed it quietly behind her, before racing across the yard and toward the line of trees in the distance. The hem of her dress was soaked with dew within moments, and her shoes were sliding on the damp grass nearly making her lose her balance, but she kept running, hoping to make it to cover before anyone woke up.

The darkness in the woods was still nearly impenetrable,

the clouds obscuring moon and stars, but Genevieve knew the way and inched carefully in the direction of the cave. It was several hours' walk and she hoped to be well away from the house by the time the sun came up. She gasped as something ran in front of her, but it was probably a chipmunk or a squirrel startled by her presence. Genevieve stopped for a moment to catch her breath and calm herself before continuing. Her thin-soled shoes weren't meant for this type of terrain, and she felt every pinecone and branch she stepped on, the discomfort slowing her down and forcing her to tread more carefully.

She was well away from the house by the time the sky finally faded from an inky black to charcoal, a sure sign that dawn wasn't far off. The woods around her were coming to life as creatures big and small began to stir and climb out of their holes and nests to begin the new day. Genevieve breathed a sigh of relief as the blood-red rays of the rising sun lit up the clouds and finally dispelled some of the darkness beneath the canopy of the trees. Birds erupted in song, and the tips of the trees turned a brilliant orange as the sun began to rise above the horizon at last.

Genevieve meant to bring all the food to Cameron, but she realized that she'd hardly eaten anything since midday of the previous day. She didn't bother to stop walking as she tore off a chunk of bread and broke off a piece of cheese, chewing slowly as she tried to avoid stepping on anything that might be painful. She wished she'd thought to bring some cider but carrying a stone bottle along with the other provisions would be heavy and cumbersome. She'd just have to do without or find a stream to drink from. Her mouth was unusually dry from the bread and the exertion of walking.

The sun was warm on her back and shoulders by the time she finally walked out of the woods and into the glade. The waterfall cascaded over the hidden face of the cave, the spray reflecting the rays of the sun, a dazzling rainbow just visible over the crystal-clear water that foamed as it met the calm waters of the lake below. The glade was quiet and still, no sign of life other than the animals that scurried from one hiding place to another and the birds that sang all around her. Genevieve sat down on a rock and lowered her bundle to the ground.

Had she misinterpreted the message? Maybe it had been something that Evie wrote with a muddy stick and had nothing to do with Cameron at all. She looked around again, but she was quite alone, the clearing deserted. Genevieve walked to the edge of the pool and took a drink, enjoying the cold, sweet water after hours of walking. She'd just rest for a little while and head back, she told herself as tears slid down her cheeks. She'd really believed Cameron would be there waiting for her, but she'd been wrong. He was long gone, and she'd never see him again, never feel his strong arms around her or hear that Scottish brogue that turned her knees to water.

Genevieve sank down to the grassy bank and took off her shoes, shaking out the tiny pebbles and giving her stockings a chance to dry in the warm sun. There was no reason to rush back to face the reality of her barren existence. The grass was soft and fragrant beneath her head as she reclined, closing her eyes and sighing with bitter disappointment before suddenly bolting upright. She was a white woman, alone, and very close to Indian Territory. This was no time to sit and sulk. She had to leave, and quickly, before anyone realized she was there. She'd heard of the atrocities the natives committed against white people and her skin prickled with fear, especially when she heard the sound of a breaking twig somewhere not too far away. She nearly screamed when she saw someone lurking in the shadows and moving closer with every step.

"Shh, 'tis only me, lass," Cameron said as he lowered himself to the ground next to her. "I saw ye come, but had to make sure ye weren't followed, aye?" He looked tired and pale, but the smile in his eyes was unmistakable. "So, little Lady Evangeline gave ye my message?"

"Not exactly," Genevieve replied, putting her hand over Cameron's. "What have you done, Cameron? They're searching for you."

"Aye, I ken that, Jenny, but I had to go," he stated, not going into further explanations.

"Why?"

Cameron didn't reply right away, just looked at her with a mixture of hope and apprehension, his eyes sliding away and gazing out over the shimmering pool of water and the waterfall. "We can't stay here in plain sight. Come with me." He pulled her to her feet and led her into a thicket of trees, the space within shady and cool. The grass in the middle was flattened, and the remnants of a small fire were still smoldering nearby. Cameron had spent the night there in the hope that she would come to him in the morning rather than getting away as fast as he could.

"Why did you run away?" Genevieve asked again, needing to hear his answer to understand what prompted this rebellion. Why had he left her? Were things so bad at the plantation?

Cameron refused to meet her gaze, his body tense and unyielding beside her. "Genevieve, there's something I want ye to do for me," he said quietly. "Will ye hear my confession?"

"I'm not a priest," she answered bitterly, angry with his avoidance of her question.

"I ken that well enough, but ye're the only Catholic within miles, and I need to confess. Will ye hear it?"

Genevieve nodded, feeling strangely uncomfortable with his request. She supposed in times of need a Catholic could confess to another Catholic, or maybe just directly to God, but she had no right to hear his confession or any means of offering forgiveness.

"I can't give you absolution."

"Nae, ye canna, but I'd like to confess all the same. Can I start then?" Genevieve just nodded, unsure whether she should be looking at him, or turn her back to give him a sense of anonymity that you'd get in a church. She started to turn, but he took her arm, gently turning her to face him.

Cameron took a deep breath as he clasped his hands in front of his chest, looking ridiculously pious in the middle of a forest. "Forgive me, Father, for I have sinned. It's been nearly two years since my last confession."

He grew silent then, his face tense with emotion. Cameron opened his mouth to speak but closed it again in an effort to compose his words. "I ken the Bible teaches us to forgive and love our fellow man, but I've been consumed by a terrible anger and an all-consuming need for vengeance, o' which I'm deeply ashamed. Day and night, I've dreamed of punishing the man who took my Mary from me and stole what was left of my life. Day and night, I've envisioned meting out justice I had nae right to mete. They wrongly called me a murderer, but now I truly am one, for I've finally righted the wrong that was done to me and punished the man responsible. A life for a life, except 'tis two lives for a life, since my life is now forfeit if I stay here." Cameron paused for a moment before continuing.

"Forgive me, Father, for my arrogance and lack o' faith, but most of all, forgive me for my lack o' remorse. Amen."

Cameron's eyes never left Genevieve's face as he finished his monologue, his expression contrite and nervous. Had he really been confessing to God or to her, Genevieve wondered as she broke eye contact and looked away. What was she to do now? What was she to say?

"Jenny," he began, but she turned away, shocked by what she'd heard.

"So, you killed Deverell?" she asked, wishing that he would deny it and say he'd been referring to someone else, but he nodded slowly.

"Aye, I killed him."

"And you would have allowed Lord Sheridan to take the blame for his death?" Genevieve asked in disgust, stunned that Cameron was capable of such deception.

"Nae, lass, I wouldna have. That's why I waited till the trial was over. Had Lord Sheridan been sentenced to hang, I'd have come forward. I swear on the memory of Mary that I'd have done the honorable thing."

"Running away isn't honorable," Genevieve countered, feeling angry more with herself than with him.

"Nae, it isna, but I had to do it – for ye, for us."

"I don't understand you, Cameron. What are you talking about?"

"Genevieve, when Mary died and I was sent to the Colonies, I thought my life was over. My desire for vengeance was the only thing that kept me alive on that crossing, and the only thing that put a fire in my belly. I had to live to see justice done. I had to live, for dying would have been exactly what those men wanted of me. I tried to direct my anger into my work, and it helped for a time. I was alive, I was putting one foot in front of the other, but then I met you, and suddenly it wasna just hatred that kept me going. I love ye, Jenny, and I want to live my life with ye, honorably, no' like a dog, coupling behind bushes with his bitch. I kept trying to think of a way to buy my freedom back, to start a new life for myself when fate intervened."

"You saw Deverell?"

"One o' the men had stepped on a scythe while out in the field and cut his foot. Master Worthing sent me to Master Taylor's cottage to get some o' that ointment he makes, ye know the one."

"Yes," Genevieve replied. Mr. Taylor had become their resident physician, making poultices and tisanes with the help of Genevieve who knew something of herbs and plants as well.

"I wasna even meant to be there, but there I was, coming out o' the cottage when I saw Deverell talking to Lord Sheridan. I couldna hear what they said, but it seemed heated, and Deverell stormed off, leaving Lord Sheridan fuming in his wake."

"So what did you do?" Genevieve asked, strangely curious as to how Deverell's death had actually come about.

"I delivered the bandages and ointment to Master Worthing and went back out into the field to work, but my mind was afire. I couldna believe that the very man who'd ruined my life was right here in Virginia. I had to get to him."

"But he was killed a few days later," Genevieve said, needing to understand exactly what happened.

"Aye. I was trying to think o' a way to find him when he crossed my path again. I saw him leaving the plantation a few days later. He seemed very pleased with himself when he left, riding back to Jamestown and whistling a tune as he passed the section o' field where I was working. I told one o' the men I had stomach gripes and ran into the woods. There's a stretch of road that runs through the woods, and I waited for him there, bloodlust pounding through my veins, hatred burning up my gut. I dragged him off his horse and threw him to the ground. He did no' even remember who I was or what he'd done to Mary. We were nothing more than maggots to him, not even worth remembering."

"How did he end up in the river?" Genevieve asked.

"I left him in the woods to be devoured by animals and went back to the field. The men made crude jokes about my loose bowels, but I dinna care; I was too busy trying to hide my bloodied knuckles. My heart was pounding with the knowledge of what I'd done. I wasna sorry I killed him, but I felt no joy or sense of completion. I felt numb."

Cameron looked away for a moment, a look of bitterness on his handsome face. "As the day wore on, I began to think more rationally and it seemed wrong to leave his wife to wonder what happened to her husband and deny him a Christian burial, so I came back during the night and took his body to Jamestown. If anyone saw us, they might have thought I was supporting a drunken friend on his way home from the tavern. I couldna just dump him on the quay, so I pushed him into the river, knowing the body wouldna get far with all the boats moored there. He was sure to be found. I just never expected Lord Sheridan to get accused o' the murder. I had no idea what transpired between them, or that he'd threatened to kill Deverell."

Genevieve just shook her head. She wanted to rage at Cameron, to accuse him of murder, to report him to the authorities, but she knew she wouldn't. Deverell had killed an innocent girl and nearly sent Cameron to the gallows for a crime he didn't commit. He deserved his fate. It might have been unchristian to think so, but it was the truth. She couldn't fault Cameron for doing what he'd done. The law had failed him, so he meted out his own justice, a justice that was long overdue. But why had he run away?

"So, what now?" Genevieve asked, in an effort to understand what he was planning. "What will you do?"

"That largely depends on ye," he said, cupping her cheek gently and looking into her eyes.

"In what way?"

"Ye said before that ye'd wait for me to be a free man. Well, I choose to be a free man now. If ye can forgive me for what I've done, and still want a life with me, then we will have one."

"How, Cameron? No one knows about you and Deverell, but you've run away and broken your contract. You're a fugitive and will be severely punished if they ever find you. How can you speak of a future when we have none should you be caught?"

"I wilna be caught. I'll make my way back home and

reclaim my life. Give me a year, Jenny. I will send for ye; I promise. Will ye wait for me?"

Genevieve gaped at him. How on earth did he expect to get back home? Jamestown was the only port in the colony, and there was no conceivable way that Cameron could get on a ship bound for England without anyone stopping him. Even if he had money to pay for his passage, he was a fugitive, and they'd have him before the authorities before the ship so much as left port. She could see from his face that he'd considered all that because he was smiling at her tenderly, giving her time to think it all through.

"I have a plan," he said, "and it just might work."

"The risk is too great," Genevieve replied as she rested her head against his shoulder. It was suicide.

"I ken that, lass, but the risk of me staying here for another six years is nae less. I want a life with ye, and I'm willing to take the chance." Genevieve nodded. It was too late to change his mind. He'd run away and sealed his fate. There was no way back.

"Will ye wait for me, Jenny?" he asked again.

"What would I tell my uncle? This is the only family I've ever had, and I don't want to lose them, but I don't want to lose you either. You're giving me an impossible choice." Cameron leaned in and kissed Genevieve softly, his lips merely brushing hers, his hand warm on her cheek.

"Ye'll miss me when I'm gone, and ye'll be willing to give up everything to come to me," he said with a wicked smile. "I ken ye will. But in the meantime, go home and pretend ye've never seen me. Ye'll know what to do when the time comes, and it will come sooner than ye think. I promise ye that, Mistress Genevieve Whitfield."

"If you are so certain that you'll come back, then marry me," she said. "I've heard of handfasting. We can do it right here, right now." Her gaze held his as she waited for him to respond.

"Jenny, I'd like nothing better than to wed ye, but what if I die and ye didna know? Ye wilna be able to remarry and get on with yer life, and I wouldna want that for ye." Genevieve put a hand to his stubbled face and looked into his eyes.

"I don't want to marry anyone else—ever. If anything happens to you, then I will be your widow and cherish the memory of you till the end of my days."

Cameron nodded. His eyes were full of love as he reached for her hand. "Let's do it then. I'm no' sure how to do it proper-like, but I suppose it's the intent that matters." Cameron took both her hands in his and spoke the words in a solemn voice, "I, Cameron Brody, take ye Genevieve Whitfield to be my wedded wife. I promise to love ye, protect ye, and be true to ye for the rest of my life." He smiled at her to indicate that it was her turn.

"I, Genevieve Whitfield, take you, Cameron Brody, to be my wedded husband. I promise to love, honor, obey, and be true to you for the rest of my days." Cameron drew her close and kissed her sweetly, sealing their pact. Genevieve kissed him back, suddenly feeling a spark of hope. Maybe Cameron was right and it would all come to pass. She would go to Scotland and they would start their life together. She'd wait as long as it took.

"I'll wait for you, Cam," she said happily. "You just stay safe and find your way home. Here, take this," she said as she pulled a ring off her finger. It had been her mother's. Uncle Alec gave it to her when she arrived in Virginia, and she'd treasured it as she'd never treasured anything before, knowing that this very ring was worn by her mother until the day she ran away to join a convent and left it on her dressing table atop the letter to her brothers. She wouldn't need it where she was going.

Uncle Alec left all her mother's possessions behind when he and Aunt Valerie left England, but he'd taken the ring as a keepsake, something to remind him of his sister. The large, oval emerald was ensconced in a heavy gold setting, its surface almost dull until a ray of light hit it just right, and then the ring blazed with a green fire that drew the eye to its mysterious depths.

"Cameron, please take it. This ring is worth quite a lot, and it might save your life. It can pay for passage to England." She pressed the ring into Cameron's hand, but he shook his head.

"I canna take ye ring, lass. It's the only thing ye have left of yer mam, and I willna see ye parted from it. Ye keep it. I'll find my own way home."

"I want you to take it. You can give it back to me if you have no use for it, but I want to know that you have something to fall back on should you need to. Please, Cameron."

"All right, I'll take it, but I will return it to ye as soon as I see ye again. In the meantime, it will remind me of yer bonny green eyes," he replied softly, pulling her closer and sliding his warm hand up her leg beneath her skirt. "Now, come here, lassie."

SIXTY-ONE

WILLIAMSBURG, VIRGINIA OCTOBER 1779

The King's Arms Inn wasn't overly elegant, but it was cozy and clean, and the dining area downstairs was full of respectable-looking customers, men with money, not just laborers coming in for a jar of ale or a quick meal. It was a fine place to start, should she choose to stay on in Williamsburg and put her plan into action. Situated on the Duke of Gloucester Street, it was right in the heart of Williamsburg, and at the center of the social and political seat of the town, directly between Parliament and the campus of William and Mary College, where countless young men strove for academic excellence and suffered silently at night for the lack of female companionship so absent in such a place of learning.

Diana rose from the tub and reached for a towel as rivulets of warm water ran down her stomach and legs. She hadn't had a proper bath in ages, not one where she could luxuriate for a while rather than just wash the grime off as quickly as possible and return to the never-ending chores set forth by General Hannah Mallory, as Diana thought of Sam's mother. What a pleasure it was to be alone at last with a bed all to herself and an actual hip bath full of steaming hot water. There were no annoying questions from the girls or constant demands from Nat to be fed, changed, or cuddled to sleep.

Diana thoroughly dried herself and gazed at her reflection in the small oval mirror hanging above the washstand. She'd been on a downward spiral for so long that she'd forgotten what it was like to be pleased with one's reflection in the looking glass. Her hair was lustrous, her cheeks in bloom, and her eyes sparkling with merriment. It was nice to feel like herself once again. All in all, things had turned out for the best, despite the setbacks that had plagued her for the past year. She'd known as soon as Finn returned from wherever he'd been that her days were numbered.

He'd seen Jonah, so it stood to reason that he knew the truth and would reveal it sooner or later. Jonah was a bit of a dolt, but even he wasn't thick enough to believe that he'd sired a child without so much as sticking his prick into her. No immaculate conception here. It was time to resort to her backup plan, which she'd concocted after Sam's hurtful rejection.

Come to think of it, she was now glad that Sam turned out to be married and oh-so-devoted to his prissy English wife. Life on a farm wasn't for her, and the thought of bearing any more children didn't particularly appeal either. Sam had his wife full in the belly just as soon as the other sprat popped out, and birthing baby after baby wasn't what Diana had in mind. She'd leave Sam to his domestic bliss and get on with her life, which Nat couldn't be a part of either. She had to admit that she'd miss the boy, but it wasn't fair to drag him into the life she planned to lead. He was better off where he was, surrounded by good, kind, God-fearing folk, the type she hoped to avoid from now on.

She particularly hoped never to clap her eyes on Hannah's brother, Alfred Hewitt. The man had eyes that just bored into the soul, pushing past all the sentimental fodder straight to the heart of his victim, able to see their every wicked thought and desire. He'd been charming and polite to her, but her skin prickled with gooseflesh after he'd shaken her hand in greeting, making her want to run and hide from his piercing, unforgiving gaze. Diana suspected he was a highly placed member of the Committee of Correspondence, but no one ever said so out loud. She did know, however, that whatever information Finn brought back went directly to Mr. Hewitt, and then quite possibly to George Washington himself.

Diana sighed as she turned from the mirror. Finn's return had marked the end of her time with the Mallorys and a beginning of a new chapter in her life, one that promised to be a more pleasant one than the one she just finished.

Everyone had been overjoyed to see Finn, especially Abbie, who clung to him as if he'd been gone for years, not weeks. She'd sat next to him at the supper table, her eyes shining with happiness and her hand constantly straying to his as he recounted his adventures and made light of his near capture by the British. To everyone's great relief, Finn had brought news of Jonah, who'd been ill after the disaster at Brier Creek. Finn's eyes had held Diana's as he spoke of Jonah, letting her know that he was aware of her deception. The charade was over, and it was time to acknowledge defeat and rethink her position.

She'd gone to bed as usual, lying still and waiting for the soft snoring of Hannah Mallory and the even breathing of the girls, only then did she get out of bed, throw a shawl over her nightdress, and made her way quietly outside. John Mallory rarely went to bed early. He liked to stay up long after everyone was asleep, smoking his pipe as he leaned on the stile and looked up at the stars, so abundant in the pitch-black heavens above the isolated farm. Tonight, Alfred Hewitt had gone outside with him, but thankfully he was long gone, leaving John alone to enjoy the peaceful silence of the autumn night. He didn't turn as Diana approached, but continued to look up as if she weren't even there.

"Good evening, John," Diana began, her voice silky and low

despite the butterflies in her belly. Everything hinged on this conversation, and she had to stay in control and not let him dissuade her from her goal.

"And good evening to you, Diana," John replied, never turning to face her. "I suppose this is the part where you tell me the truth and throw yourself on my mercy," he guessed, but Diana shook her head.

"No, John, this is the part where I ask you for money and disappear from your life."

"Really?" he asked as if she just said she'd come out for a breath of air.

"I'm sure you already know that Jonah isn't really Nat's father," she began.

"The thought has crossed my mind," John Mallory replied, finally turning to face Diana in the darkness. She didn't like the look on his face, but at this point, there was no backing down. She had no choice.

"I think it would be best if I left quietly, don't you?" she asked, smiling at John in her most winsome manner.

"I'm listening."

"I think Nat is better off with his family, but I don't belong here, not anymore. I have plans of opening my own brothel, one where I'm the mistress and I don't have to work on my back and give fifty percent to some madam. I have the expertise to make such an enterprise a success," she announced proudly. "However, I need funds to make a start, and that's where you come in."

"And why, pray tell, should I finance your establishment?" John looked bitter in the moonlight, his lips compressed into a thin line, his eyes black holes in his shadowed face.

"Because I have the power to harm you and your family, John. I've no doubt Major Weland would be most eager to find out where a certain spy named Abigail Whitfield resides with her husband and brother, who are guilty of the murder of two

British soldiers. He might be willing to pay for the information most handsomely, don't you think? If you give me enough money to start my business, you will never see me or hear from me again. I will never ask for more, nor will I ever try to reclaim my son. He's your grandson and should be with you and his natural father. I don't care what you tell him about me; just take good care of him. I do love him, you know."

"Yes, I can see that," John Mallory replied, his voice dripping with sarcasm and his eyes glinting in the darkness. "You're a clever girl, aren't you? Was this the plan all along, or did Sam reject your advances and force you to come up with an alternative?" Diana didn't reply, but her face was answer enough.

John Mallory turned away from her once again and puffed on his pipe in silence, the smoke curling and dissipating into the night and leaving a sweet, pungent smell in its wake. Diana waited patiently for him to speak as her stomach launched into an acrobatic performance, nearly making her sick.

"I'm not a wealthy man, Diana, but I do have some money put by. I will give you enough to start your business on one condition. You will return to New York and stay away from my family now and forever. And if any harm befalls either my children or Finn, I will hunt you down, and I will kill you with my bare hands. Is that understood?" Diana had expected nothing less from John, so she nodded in acquiescence, agreeing to the deal. She had no intention of betraying the Mallorys. It was only a gamble on her part to get the money.

After all, she needed leverage against someone as canny as John Mallory. Once she had the money, she'd be free at last, and the Mallorys would be a distant memory, along with Nat. She could set up in New York and go back to her clandestine activities – spying for both sides. It was a lucrative trade in more ways than one. No matter which side ultimately won, she'd be right where she needed to be—safe and comfortably off.

"Get your things and be quiet about it. I will take you to

Williamsburg tonight. There's a coach heading north in two days' time and you will be on it." With that, John walked away from her.

The ride into Williamsburg had been silent and tense, John's disgust clearly visible on his face as he let her off in front of the inn and threw down her satchel. He didn't say goodbye or wish her well, just rode off into the night, back to his family. Diana didn't care; there was a comforting weight of a money pouch against her thigh and the jingle of coins as she walked up the stairs to her room was music to her ears. She had what she wanted, and life was full of promise once again.

SIXTY-TWO

The house was blissfully quiet for a change, leaving Abbie feeling somnolent and lazy, but there was work to be done, especially since Diana had finally gone to sleep and Nat was with her parents and sisters visiting Martha. They'd taken Ben as well to give Susanna a break. Abbie usually went too, but today she just wanted to be alone for a bit.

She took the pot of hot tallow off the hook in the hearth and started to pour the liquid into the candle molds. They were running short on candles and with the days growing shorter, they'd be using them faster than during the long summer hours. Abbie ran the wicks through the candles and left the tallow to cool, her mind working overtime.

Diana hadn't returned, and at this point, no one really expected her to. Whatever prompted her to leave had to be serious enough for her to leave her child behind. Finn said that no loving mother would ever leave her son, but Abbie had her doubts. Diana loved her son; she'd seen it in the way she looked at him when no one was watching. The boy was the only real family she had, so to leave him behind so suddenly must have been heart-wrenching for her. What had happened to make her bolt? Had Finn said something to her after seeing Jonah?

Abbie poured herself a cup of cider and went outside to continue her deliberations. It would be at least a half-hour till she could take the ready candles out of the molds and start another batch, and the day outside was too glorious not to take advantage of. She sat down on the bench and took a sip of cider, surprised to see Susanna appear in the distance. She was carrying Rachel in her arms and walking purposefully toward the house, her brow creased with tension. Had she quarreled with Sam? Abbie gave a tentative wave and saw Susanna's face relax somewhat as she got closer. Rachel was fast asleep, her little face cherubic in slumber.

Abbie held out her arms and Susanna placed the baby into them, putting her hands on her back and stretching before sitting down next to Abbie and accepting the cup of cider. Rachel was only two weeks old, but Susanna already looked much like her old self, her waist not as narrow as before, but tiny compared to the huge belly she had only a few weeks ago. She looked tired and worn, probably from feeding the baby at all hours.

"Where's Sam?" Abbie asked carefully. Susanna looked like a thundercloud on a summer day, and Abbie wasn't sure she was ready to bear the brunt of the storm.

"Chopping wood," Susanna answered curtly. "I just felt a need to get out of the house and talk to someone other than Rachel. She's a good listener, but I'm afraid she doesn't usually answer back," she supplied with a smile, suddenly looking less upset. "I've forgotten how much work a baby is. Can't imagine having another one."

"Are you...?" Abbie asked carefully. It was too soon after the birth to be having relations, but with Sam, who knew?

"God, no," Susanna giggled. "I'm sure Sam is eager to, but I need a bit more time." Abbie nodded in understanding. Men would like nothing more than to get back in the saddle right after the birth, but they had no idea what a woman's body went through, or how long it took to feel normal again.

"Actually, there's something else I wanted to talk to you about." Susanna's smile disappeared and she looked pale and tense again, suddenly recalling the purpose of her visit.

"What is it, Sue? Is everything all right between you and Sam?"

"In a manner of speaking. I wanted to get your advice before bringing this up to Sam, or the rest of the family." Abbie turned to face Susanna, unsure where this was going. She looked awfully serious as she clasped her hands in her lap and glanced away toward the horizon.

"I know, you see," she finally said.

"Know what?"

"What everyone knew from the day Diana showed up. Nathaniel is Sam's son, not Jonah's. They only said it to spare my feelings, but deep down, I always knew." Abbie put a hand over Susanna's in a sign of silent support.

"We don't know for sure."

"Oh, but we do. I've seen the way she looks at Sam, and how tense he gets, desperate to get away from her. They've been together, I'm sure of that. You all know Jonah is not the type to go to a brothel. Besides, she left the same night Finn came back and said he'd seen Jonah. Jonah must have told him the truth, and there was no longer a reason for Diana to stay."

"No, I suppose not. If Nat is not Jonah's, he'd never marry her, so the most practical thing would be to leave the child with its grandparents and father and flee." She supposed it made sense, but she could never fathom leaving her own daughter, no matter the circumstances.

"What advice were you seeking?" Abbie asked carefully. Did she resent Nat being there, or was it something about Sam?

"Abbie, I know that Sam met Diana long before he met me,

so it's not as if he were unfaithful or disloyal. He never meant to get her with child; it just happened. And it's certainly not Nat's fault. He's so sweet, and he looks just like Ben, don't you think?"

"He does. They could be twins if they weren't four months apart."

"Nat looks much healthier since he's been here. He's gained weight and his complexion has improved," Susanna added, smiling at the thought. Abbie had to admit that she was perplexed. What was Susanna thinking?

"Abbie, I want to suggest to Sam that we take Nat. I don't think Diana is coming back, and it's only right that a child should be with his father. He needs a loving home, and how will he feel once he gets older and finds out that Sam is his father but doesn't want the care of him?"

"Sue, that's very generous of you, but I'm not sure you can take him without Diana's permission. She's still his mother, and she's living, so she can reclaim him at any time, should she choose to."

"Hmm," Susanna said, "I suppose you're right. But he can still live with us, and if she doesn't come back, he'll just be ours, won't he?"

"Yes, he will." Abbie handed Rachel to Sue as she woke up and began to fuss, ready to be fed no doubt. She looked at Sue with admiration, unable to believe that she loved Sam so much that she was willing to accept his bastard. Abbie wasn't sure that she'd be willing to take on a child of Finn's had she been in the same situation. Maybe it was uncharitable, but she wanted Finn all to herself and the thought of some woman having a baby by him filled her with a jealous rage.

Funny how a scoundrel like Sam wound up with such a saintly wife. *The Lord works in mysterious ways*, Abbie thought as she rose from the bench, ready to make another batch of candles. She hoped Susanna hadn't made her decision on the spur of the moment and would come to regret it later. Hannah and John Mallory were more than willing to raise Nathaniel, so maybe it was best to let them.

"You're a saint, Sue," Abbie said, giving Susanna a brilliant smile, "a saint whom my brother doesn't deserve."

"I won't argue with you there," Susanna said, returning the smile and putting Rachel to her breast. "I do love him though, more than I ever thought possible, and I'll do anything to make him happy. I know having his boy with him would make him complete."

"Then that's the right decision. You're a better woman than I am, Sue, and I admire you for it." Susanna smiled, obviously much happier now that she'd reached a decision.

SIXTY-THREE
PRINCETON, NEW JERSEY OCTOBER 2010

Valerie slowed down as another group of students crossed in front of her, deep in discussion of some lofty topic recently covered in class, each one arguing an opposing point of view. Over the past several weeks, the number of young people on the streets of Princeton seemed to have multiplied a hundredfold as students returned to the dorms for the start of the school year. What had been a peaceful suburban town only a month ago was now a beehive of activity with young people sitting on lawns, their books propped open on their laps, tapping away at their laptops in cafes, and showing school spirit as they prepared for football games against other schools.

Valerie stepped into Starbucks to get away from the mayhem and ordered herself an iced cappuccino, which she took to a table by the window where she could watch life go by. Getting back into twenty-first century mode had been so easy. She'd forgotten how accessible and convenient everything was, designed to simplify the life of the people who took it all for granted. She didn't need to struggle with tinder and flint to start a fire or go to the well to heft back a heavy bucket of water, half of which usually spilled by the time she finally managed to get it to the kitchen. The supermarkets were bursting with anything and everything, and all she needed was money. Back at home, there was virtually no money. Everything was paid for in bags of tobacco or bartered, but for the most part, they were self-sufficient. They produced their own food, lumber, homespun for clothes, and even furniture.

Valerie took a sip of her drink, enjoying the cold, bitter taste of the cappuccino, the foam leaving a thin line across her lip, which she licked off with pleasure. How nice it was just to sit and not have to do a hundred things to facilitate the running of the household. A wave of sadness suddenly washed over her. She didn't miss the hard work, but oh, how she missed everyone back home, especially Tom. She'd give anything at this moment to feel his sturdy little arms around her neck as she lifted him from his cot, or the butterfly brush of his eyelashes as he rested his head on her shoulder, tired from playing and ready for his nap. He didn't look much like his mother, but he still reminded Valerie of Louisa in so many ways. He had the same single-minded determination once he set his mind to something, and the same sweetness when he hoped to get his way. How she missed her girl. Did any mother ever get used to living without her child?

Louisa had been headstrong, and at times puzzling, but she was still her beloved daughter, and Valerie felt the loss of her every single day, trying to block from her mind the unbearable pain and suffering Louisa must have endured in her final hours. Valerie had grown accustomed to people dying of ailments that could easily be cured in the future and had learned to live without medicine or proper nutrition, but she still couldn't get used to the fact that young women died in childbirth every single day, their babies often dying with them. What a cruel world it was in which an act of love that resulted in conception was ultimately the instrument of death and sorrow.

Thoughts of death inevitably brought her to her parents.

She'd promised Alec, well, sort of, that she wouldn't seek her parents out or make herself known to them, but not a single moment went by when she wasn't acutely aware that not an hour away, her mom and dad were still very much alive, but out of reach. She felt a tell-tale squeezing in her chest as she mentally counted how long they had left before a random accident killed them both on a street corner in Manhattan. If only she could do something to prevent it, but of course, Alec was right; she couldn't stop destiny, nor could she interfere with something that would have a domino effect on her sister's life, as well as her own. She had to let it be. That made her remember the Beatles song which her mother sang to her so often when she was upset or frustrated with some minor teenage drama. Her mom would hold her close and sing into her hair, frustrating Valerie beyond belief that her mom couldn't understand the suffering she was going through. How could she let it be when it had the power to destroy her life?

Valerie sighed, wishing she had appreciated her mom more while she had the chance. How right she'd been on those occasions, and how minor the crises that left her feeling so crushed actually were. If only life could be that simple again. Valerie finished her drink and rose to leave, reluctant to return to Isaac's house. She was growing more terrified with each passing day that he wouldn't be able to send them home, and Alec's forlorn expression and listlessness didn't make things easier. Things he'd enjoyed on their first visit to the future were no longer as exciting when weighed against all that would be lost if they failed to return to their own time.

He didn't complain or burden her with his feelings, but she knew him well enough to know that he was thrumming with anxiety and fighting a sense of overwhelming desperation that mounted with each day that passed by. Isaac kept assuring them that he was close, but Valerie had her doubts. If something didn't happen soon, they would very seriously have to consider an alternate plan, in which they would have to remain in the twenty-first century for good and relinquish all hope of ever going home.

Valerie got to her feet and walked out of the café, her feet carrying her across Nassau Street, through the FitzRandolph Gate, and toward the Princeton University Chapel. She'd gone to church every week back in Virginia, but that had been a forced ritual necessary to maintain good standing in the colony. She usually sat through the sermon, her mind full of other things and plans for the rest of the day, but today was different. She wanted to pray, and she would do it in her own way.

Entering the cool interior of the church, Valerie was grateful to be alone in the cavernous space that reminded her so much of Notre Dame. To call it a chapel was an understatement, since the place was nothing less than a cathedral. The vaulted ceiling soared overhead as sunlight filtered through countless stained-glass windows, casting muted, colored shafts of light onto the wooden pews and the stone nave flanked by the massive stone pillars that formed symmetrical arches. Valerie slowly walked to the front, her footsteps echoing in the empty church until she stopped in front of the ornate, elevated pulpit situated just to the left of the organ. She liked that this chapel held multi-denominational services, which made it truly accessible to anyone who wished to pray.

Valerie stepped into the nearest pew and sank to her knees on the kneeler in front of her, clasping her hands and closing her eyes. It had been a long time since she prayed in earnest, but today the words came easily, the need to ask for divine help overwhelming her usual indifference to religion. She beseeched God to allow them to return to their own time, and soon, praying for Alec and everyone back home, as well as her parents, who were so close, yet light years away, and Louisa who was about to embark on the rollercoaster ride which began with Valerie's disappearance from the antique shop. Valerie remained on her knees for some time, her head bowed and her hands clasped in front of her, listening to the silence of the chapel and trying to find some semblance of peace in her soul. A sense of hope slowly began to steal over her as she finally rose to her feet and walked out into the brilliant October afternoon. Something would happen soon. She could feel it, and she was eager to share her newfound hope with Alec.

Valerie picked up her pace as she exited the campus through the gate and turned left. She was suddenly eager to go back home. The streets got quieter as she left the campus behind and turned off Nassau Street. Here, the beautiful houses and manicured lawns basked in somnolent peace, their occupants either away at work or inside, hiding from the unseasonable heat of the afternoon. Valerie eagerly turned the corner, her heart nearly stopping in her chest when she saw an ambulance pull away from Isaac's house, the siren coming noisily to life as the colored lights atop the cab began to flash. She ran the last few feet, erupting into the foyer and looking around in panic. "Alec?" she called out.

Alec came out of the kitchen, an unfathomable expression on his face. "Isaac's had a heart attack," he said, opening his arms to Valerie as she walked into them before her knees had a chance to buckle. Poor Isaac, and poor them.

SIXTY-FOUR

Valerie followed Alec into Princeton University Medical Center, grateful that he'd had the foresight to wait for her rather than go in the ambulance with Isaac. She would have been frantic had she come back and found them both gone, with only a note telling her they were at the hospital. At least this way they could go together. She managed to put one foot in front of the other, but her mind felt muddled and hazy, almost as if she were underwater, the activity around her culminating into a muffled wave of sound rather than individual words and actions.

How had this happened? Isaac had looked the picture of health just that morning, planning to play a game of tennis with one of his retired friends from the university later that afternoon. He'd gulped down a cup of tea, as he did every morning, before disappearing into what he referred to as his lab, a room that neither Alec nor Valerie were permitted to enter.

Valerie wrapped her arms around her middle to keep herself from coming apart. She'd grown to care for Isaac, and the thought of losing him left her gutted, but of course, there was more to it than that. Isaac was their only hope of getting back home, and if he failed to recover, they were trapped in the twenty-first century forever--displaced, financially strapped, and utterly heartbroken. The wonderful sense of hope she'd felt only an hour ago had given way to despair and terrible fear as the reality of what happened finally sank in, nearly making her knees buckle. She snuck a peek at Alec and noted that he walked like an automaton, his eyes fixed on the floor in front of him and his shoulders hunched with tension. Valerie slid her hand into Alec's, and he squeezed it gently, acknowledging everything she was feeling. There was no need for words—he knew.

An unnatural hush hung over the Cardiac Unit as nurses floated by on silent feet and doctors disappeared behind closed doors to examine their patients and then move on to the next room. Several people sat in the waiting area, their eyes glued to the doctors as they emerged from the various rooms in the hope of hearing something positive about their loved one. Valerie sank into the nearest chair as Alec went up to the nurses' station to inquire about Isaac. He returned a few moments later and sat down next to her.

"The nurse said he's stable, but they're running some tests and will know more later. We just have to be patient."

Valerie nodded and rested her head against Alec's shoulder. She was too emotionally drained to reply.

SIXTY-FIVE

WILLIAMSBURG, VIRGINIA OCTOBER 1779

The dining room was almost full by the time Diana made her way downstairs. She'd dressed her hair and dabbed on a little scent in the hope that she might make her stay in Williamsburg a profitable one. Maybe she'd even stay here for good, close enough to the Mallory family to remind them of the power she had over them. She'd promised John never to ask for money again, but what was there to stop her? Would he gamble with the safety of his children? She highly doubted it. He was sure to have more money stashed away somewhere, and if he didn't, perhaps there was something he could sell, like that handsome pistol with the silver handle that he kept on hooks mounted above the hearth. That would fetch a pretty penny.

Diana cast her gaze over the dining room and took a seat close to the window, the slanting rays of the setting sun casting a rosy glow over her face and making her look almost ethereal. She liked the idea of being lit up and showcased for all the men in the dining room to see. One, in particular, couldn't tear his eyes away as he lifted his tankard to his lips. He was handsome, she'd give him that. His dark eyes looked like chunks of coal in his bronzed face, and the forelock of dark hair that fell onto his forehead gave him a slightly rakish appearance. The man set down his tankard and gave her a slow smile. Diana's heart nearly skipped a beat. That smile reminded her so much of Sam as did the way the man cocked his head to the side, studying her as if she were a priceless work of art to be admired and adored. He rose to his feet and strolled toward her table, his drink in hand.

"May I join you?" he asked as his eyes smiled into hers. "A beautiful woman should never dine alone. Unless you're waiting for someone and I'm making an utter fool of myself."

"No, you guessed correctly, and I'm on my own. And I do hate to dine alone. I would be very pleased to have your company, sir," she answered demurely. The man was so handsome, she might just forfeit a fee and do it purely for pleasure.

"Then you will be my guest tonight," he said, signaling the innkeeper. "May I know your name?"

"It's Diana," she replied, smiling prettily.

"No surname?"

"Surely, we don't need surnames. Just Diana."

"Then I'm just Ralph. At your service, Madame." He smiled that lazy grin again and Diana melted inside. This stay promised to be very pleasant. If Ralph proved to be unmarried, it might even need to be extended, Diana thought as she took a sip of her drink and smiled back. What a stroke of luck. She quickly took stock of the man from beneath her lashes. He was immaculately dressed, in a dark coat that bespoke of quality, and a shirt that clearly wasn't homemade. His boots gleamed in the candlelight, and he smelled of soap and boot polish. Diana glanced at his hands. She hated men with dirt under their fingernails, but Ralph's hands were elegant and clean, the nails finely rounded, not jagged and torn by hard work—clearly a gentleman.

Diana hardly noticed what she ate as Ralph regaled her with stories of his exploits in the Continental Army. He was a high-ranking officer who was in Williamsburg to visit his widowed father. He was witty, charming, and oh-so attractive. She couldn't wait to get him upstairs. It'd been a long time since she'd been so drawn to a man other than Sam. Or maybe it was because he reminded her of Sam. It was time to move forward and put Sam out of her mind forever. There were plenty of men out there, and she intended to fleece as many of them as possible while enjoying herself.

Diana smiled in gratitude as Ralph paid for the supper and gave her a questioning look that she returned with an almost imperceptible nod. She was taking him upstairs, no question about that. Judging by his capable hands and strong physique, he promised to be a fine lover, one who knew how to please a woman and not just himself.

"You go on up," he said very quietly, "I will join you in a few minutes." Diana was disappointed but smiled and began her ascent up the stairs. Maybe he changed his mind and didn't want to be with her, or perhaps she was just being overly suspicious. He might be married despite what he said and didn't care to be seen following her upstairs and entering her room.

Diana pulled the pins from her hair and unlaced her bodice. She would prepare for bed and hope that she didn't end up in it alone. Maybe Ralph was just giving her time to take precautions. Diana pulled out a small bottle and soaked a piece of rag in vinegar before pushing it deep inside herself. It never hurt to be prepared. She opened the window a crack to air out the acrid smell of the vinegar and began to brush out her hair, her ears straining for any sounds coming from the corridor outside her room.

She was already in her nightdress by the time a soft knock sounded on the door. Ralph was smiling as he leaned against the doorjamb and held out a small bouquet of wildflowers. "I picked these for you from the neighboring garden," he whispered as he entered the room. "I couldn't come empty-handed."

"You're a wicked man," Diana giggled, happy with this romantic gesture.

"You have no idea," he said as he pulled her close and kissed her. She could see he wanted to take things slow, but she couldn't wait. Diana was on fire, desire choking her as she unlaced his breeches with urgent fingers. He didn't protest but pulled her nightdress over her head and cupped her breasts as he kissed her again and pushed her toward the bed. She couldn't wait another moment and gasped with pleasure at the solid feel of him inside her.

She'd been right about his prowess as a lover. He brought her to the heights of ecstasy before pulling back and moving slowly and deliberately, teasing her, before changing tempo and finishing her off with a few urgent strokes that left her panting and quivering inside. Then kissed her tenderly as he brushed the hair out of her face with gentle fingers, his eyes never leaving hers.

"You really are beautiful," he said wistfully, a strange expression on his face.

"You don't have to leave," Diana whispered. She hoped he'd make love to her again and again, but Ralph was already pulling on his breeches and reaching for his coat.

"I'm sorry, Diana, but I must go. My father is expecting me, but I do hope I may return tomorrow," he asked shyly.

"I'll be waiting." She was already tingling with anticipation, thinking of all the things she would do to him when he came back the next day. They would take things slow and she'd make him beg for it as she teased him as mercilessly as he had teased her today. She knew how to bring a man to his knees, and she intended to show him. No other woman would ever be able to measure up to her after she was done with him. There were things she saved for only her best clients, but for him, it would be at no charge. She pictured herself on her knees between his legs as he looked down upon her. Most men nearly unmanned themselves at the sight of their cock in her mouth, and it made her feel all-powerful and in control. She couldn't wait for tomorrow.

Ralph finished dressing and sat down on the edge of the bed to give her another kiss. His lips were soft and tender as he kissed her, his eyes locked with hers. Diana barely registered the thin blade that slid just under her ribs. She froze with shock as unbearable pain sliced through her, stealing her breath away. She tried to call for help, but her scream was swallowed by Ralph's mouth over hers, still so tender. Diana thrashed for a few horrible moments before the life drained from her, leaving her lying like a rag doll tossed away by a bored child.

Ralph withdrew the knife, wiped it on her nightdress, and pulled the coverlet over Diana's body. He kissed her forehead and made a sign of the cross over her dead body before washing the blood off his hands and letting himself quietly out of the room. He stealthily made his way down the back stairs and into the night, where he walked for a few minutes before returning to the inn by the front door. He took a seat across from an older man who was nursing a tankard of cider and silently observing the other patrons. "A tankard of ale for my son," the man called to the barkeep as he studied the younger man's face.

"Well?"

"It's done, Father," the young man said as he took a swallow of his drink.

"You didn't actually lie with her, did you?" the older man asked. His mouth was pursed in disapproval and his eyes cold as he regarded his son, who shrugged, his meaning obvious.

"Did anyone see you with her?"

"They saw us having supper together, but then I left for

twenty minutes and came back by the back door. No one saw me go up or enter her room. No one saw me leave."

"Good. Now, after you finish your drink, go to the Mallory farm and tell Uncle John that he no longer has a problem. And give him back the money."

"Yes, Father." Ralph looked up at his father, his nonchalant expression slipping to reveal one of remorse lurking underneath. "Did she really have to die?" he asked quietly. "She was so young and beautiful. There's a difference between killing a man in battle and stabbing a young woman between the ribs. I feel like a murderer."

Alfred Hewitt's face softened as he looked at his son. He didn't go so far as to smile, but he laid his hand over his son's wrist, his voice low but soothing. "Ralph, I would be in fear for your mortal soul if you felt no remorse at killing a young woman, especially one who's a mother, but you were not the cause of her death—merely its instrument. Diana not only threatened our family, but our cause, and that's treason. If she thought it, she as good as did it. She sealed her own fate, son."

"I know everything you're saying is true, but I never hope to be put in that position again. Killing on the battlefield is honorable. Killing a defenseless woman in her bed is cowardly and beneath our cause, as it's beneath me. Please, don't ever ask anything like this of me again." Ralph looked away for a moment to hide the moisture in his eyes, and his father suddenly understood why he'd bedded the girl. He wanted her last hour on earth to be beautiful, filled with passion and love, not dejection or loneliness. He gave Diana a gift, but at the same time compromised his own feelings in doing so. Alfred's way would have been quicker and cleaner.

"What happens now?" Ralph asked.

"Tomorrow morning the chambermaid will find Diana's body. She will be buried and forgotten. And you, my boy, will be long gone, returned to your regiment from your furlough to fight for the cause of freedom."

Alfred Hewitt finished his drink and rose to leave, patting his son on the shoulder. Ralph smiled back, a hint of sadness lurking in his eyes. He looked remarkably like his cousin Sam when he smiled.

SIXTY-SIX
PRINCETON, NEW JERSEY OCTOBER 2010

The bright light of the autumn afternoon changed to the golden glow of early evening as the shadows lengthened along the linoleum floor and the harsh florescent bulbs lit the shadowy corners of the waiting room. People came and went, some overjoyed at getting a good prognosis, others devastated by the news softly conveyed by sympathetic doctors. Alec sat straight as a rod, his gaze fixed on some distant point behind the nurses' station. Valerie must have nodded off, but something woke her and she sat up, looking around in confusion. The smell of hospital food filled the corridor as a smiling orderly wheeled around a food cart, handing out trays to people who were able to eat. He nodded in greeting to Alec and Valerie, and walked right past Isaac's room, which wasn't a good sign.

"Are you hungry?" Alec asked as his gaze followed the cart.

"No, just thirsty," Valerie replied, but made no move to get up. Her legs felt like jelly, and she couldn't even articulate what she was feeling without bursting into tears. She had to admit that despite everything that happened, she'd still harbored a hope that things would somehow work out and they would return home. Sure, there would be a lot of explaining to do, but within a few days everything would be back to normal again and everyone would forget that they'd been gone for months with no explanation. They would once again be in the bosom of their family, surrounded by the people who made life worth living and safely returned to their rightful place in time. They would no longer be in limbo.

But she hadn't really considered that they might be in hell. Living the rest of their lives in the twenty-first century, torn from everything and everyone, never knowing what happened to them or able to let them know that they were all right was a thought that left her breathless with agony. They would be lost in time, unable to go back, and equally unable to make a life for themselves in the here and now.

Valerie would never be able to return to her family. How could she? The woman who left had been in her mid-twenties, but the woman who stared back at her from the mirror now was twenty years older, with tiny crow's feet around her eyes and strands of gray hair that became more abundant after the death of their daughter. No, there was no going back for her, and then there was Alec...

If she felt hopeless, Alec probably felt even worse, but he was doing his best not to show it. She could see it in the set of his shoulders and the grim look in his eyes. He was scared. Valerie sighed and got to her feet. She walked to the bathroom, brushed her hair and splashed a little water into her face to revive herself. The woman who gazed back at her looked terrified. She could put on lipstick and pinch some color into her cheeks, but she couldn't do anything about the desperate look in her eyes, or the feeling of hopelessness gripping her chest like a steel band. There was nothing worse than the death of hope.

It was nearly dark outside by the time the doctor came out to speak to them. He was fairly young, although the look in his eyes was that of a much older man, one who'd seen a lot of death. Valerie noted the lines of fatigue on his face, but instead of sitting down for a moment, he remained standing as he spoke to them.

"I'm sorry it took so long," the doctor said as he ran a hand through his unruly hair. "We wanted to be sure."

"Sure of what?" Valerie asked with trepidation.

"Sure that it wasn't more than it appears to be. It was a minor cardiac event, not a full-blown heart attack. Of course, it could be a prelude to one, so we ran numerous tests to rule out that possibility. Mr. Bloom is going to be just fine. We will keep him overnight, but he can go home tomorrow. He needs quiet and lots of rest for a few days, but otherwise, he can resume his normal activities."

"Thank you, Doctor," Alec said, the relief evident on his face. "May we see him now?"

"Only for a few minutes. We gave him a mild sedative. He was agitated and kept talking about some watch he needed to get, but he was wearing a wristwatch when brought in," the doctor added as he shrugged his shoulders in confusion. "Anyhow, he'll be a little drowsy, so it's best to let him rest."

"Thank God," Valerie breathed as she followed Alec down the hall. Isaac looked deathly pale, his white hair in disarray, eyes closed, and mouth somewhat slack. Several machines beeped over his head, and an IV tube stretched from his right hand to the clear bag of glucose solution hanging off a metal rack just to the right of the bed. The heart monitor beeped reassuringly as Valerie pulled up a chair and took Isaac's left hand. She didn't expect him to open his eyes, but he did, looking straight at her, his lips twitching in an attempt to smile. Valerie opened her mouth to say something, but Isaac cut her off, his expression suddenly agitated.

"You have to go," he whispered. "You have to go today."

"You mean you want us to leave your house?" Valerie asked, confused. The nurses had probably contacted Isaac's sons, and perhaps he didn't want his boys to find two strangers residing with their father. It was understandable, but Valerie felt a pang of panic at the request. Where would they go? What would they do?

"No," Isaac shook his head vehemently, trying to make her understand. "You have to go home. You must go today."

Valerie squeezed Isaac's hand, unsure of how to respond. He was under the influence of medication, so it was normal to be somewhat muddled.

"All right, Isaac, we'll go," she said soothingly so as not to upset him. He seemed to be very agitated, as if he needed her to understand something.

"It's in the study, in the top left drawer of my desk. Destroy the notebook." Isaac was looking at Alec, who nodded, although he appeared to be as confused as Valerie.

"Isaac, what's in the study?" Valerie asked gently.

"The time-travel device. It works. I tested it on myself several times already. That's what brought this on. I went back to see my wife. I suppose it's more than the old ticker could take. I thought I'd be happy to see her again, but it opened up all the old wounds, and I felt as if I'd lost her all over again." He closed his eyes once more, obviously tired.

"Isaac, we can't just leave you this way," Alec said, looking at the old man with undisguised affection. "We'll wait until you're better and can come home."

But Isaac shook his head. "My boys will be here within a few hours, and there'll be hell to pay if they find out I'd been working on time travel again. I'd promised their mother, and they know about it. If they see the device and the notebook, they might destroy it, thinking I was planning to use it for myself, which I did, technically," he said with a rueful smile. "I don't want anything to go wrong for you."

"Isaac, we can't thank you enough for everything you've done for us," Alec said.

"You've done much for me too, dear boy. I felt so lost after my Nancy died, but you gave me a purpose, and a respite from my solitude." He suddenly looked sheepish, a glimpse of his old self in the face of illness. "I must confess that I completed the device about two weeks ago, I just didn't want you to leave yet. I didn't want to be all alone in that empty house again. Forgive me. I know how desperate you are to return home. It was selfish of me."

"Think nothing of it," Valerie replied, patting his hand. "We are happy to have been able to repay you, even in this small way. God bless you, Isaac. We'll remember you for the rest of our lives."

"And I'll remember you. Now, listen. I tried to make the device based on what you told me of Fred's time-travel watch, but I wasn't able to duplicate it exactly. You can set the year and the coordinates, but you can't set the day. You won't be able to return to the day you left, but you will be able to return to today's date in the correct year."

Valerie nodded, the reality of what he was saying finally sinking in. They could be home today. TODAY! Her heart began to pound with the realization that their ordeal might be truly over and they would be able to return to their proper time. Oh, to see Louisa, Kit, and the children, and to hold Tom as he fell asleep tonight. Valerie felt Alec's excitement as she looked up at him. They were going home.

Valerie leaned in and kissed Isaac's wrinkled cheek. "We'll miss you, Isaac, and thank you again."

Isaac smiled, his eyes already closing with fatigue. Valerie waited until he fell asleep before letting go of his hand and getting to her feet.

"Alec, there's something I must do before we go," she said, her tone brooking no argument.

Alec rolled his eyes, having expected this from the start. "All right, but you can't speak to them."

"Deal."

SIXTY-SEVEN

JAMESTOWN, VIRGINIA OCTOBER 1626

The wood shivered beneath Cameron's feet as the heavy rode chain attached to the anchor creaked and groaned in protest as it was slowly wound by the members of the anchor detail. It wasn't long until the anchor was pulled up alongside the hull, bumping against the wood and causing the ship to rock from side to side as it was hoisted to rest against the bow of the vessel for the duration of the voyage. The sound of running feet and shouts of men reverberated all the way to the hold as the ship finally cast off from Jamestown, moving very slowly toward the open sea.

Cameron crouched low behind a large crate and rested his back against the wall of the hold to keep his balance. A small bundle of food lay at his feet, his only possession in the world besides the knife and the ring Jenny had given him, which hung on a string around his neck. He had to last at least two days before allowing himself to be found on board. That was his only chance. If discovered within the next few hours, he would be forced to swim back to shore, but once the vessel was in the Atlantic, that would no longer be an option.

He'd been on board since last night, having boarded the

Mary Celeste while the crew was loading the last of the cargo. It'd been easy enough to hide his face behind a large cask that he'd hoisted onto his shoulder and carried up the ramp and down into the hold. He never came back out, hiding behind this crate in the furthest and darkest corner of the crowded space.

The hold was full of crates, caskets, and sacks of tobacco bound for England, the cargo wedged in to utilize almost every inch of space. He hoped the heavy crate wouldn't suddenly shift and pin him to the wall, but that was unlikely. The hold smelled of spices, wood, and mildew, but thankfully, not of human misery. This vessel had not been used to transport human cargo. Cameron would have known, since the smell of people held captive below decks for months left a lingering stench, one that couldn't be washed away by sea water or even lye soap. There were no manacles attached to the walls, or tiny holes bored into the ceiling to allow air to flow into the stinking space. At least he wasn't at the mercy of slavers.

Time seemed to stand still as impenetrable darkness enveloped Cameron and made him drowsy, but he had to stay alert and keep to his hiding place. His stomach growled with hunger, but he banished thoughts of food from his mind. His meager supplies had to last him for as long as possible, for the further they got from Jamestown, the better his chances, slim as they might be. He understood the risks.

Cameron sat down, wrapped his arms around his knees and rested his head against the rough wood of the wall. He'd been living rough for many weeks, hiding by day and hunting by night, permitting himself to make a fire only in the dead of night when he was sure no one was about and it was safe to cook his kill and enjoy a few hours of sleep warmed by the embers of the dying flames. He'd been sure the search for him had been called off a while ago, but he couldn't afford to be seen by anyone until he was ready to try and stow away on one of the England-bound vessels. He'd had no idea what day, or even what month it was, but it was getting colder during the night, and the multicolored leaves that reminded him of autumn in Scotland were drifting down to cover the earth in a soft blanket and signaling the approach of winter. He'd known he had to get on board a ship before they stopped sailing for the winter, or he'd be trapped in Virginia and might not survive till spring.

Cameron closed his eyes and pictured Jenny's face as she had been the day they wed. She'd been so happy and so sad all at once, torn by her desire to be with him and devastated to lose him, possibly forever. She didn't believe he could get back home, but he'd promised to send for her and he would, just as soon as he managed to get out of this godforsaken colony and get back to Scotland, where he could pick up the thread of his former life.

Thinking of Jenny gave him the courage to do what he must, but it also pained him to acknowledge that he might never see her again, or his home. The success of this venture depended entirely on the nature of the captain and the timing of the sailing. Even if the captain proved to be a sympathetic man and allowed him to live, he could very easily have him shipped right back to Virginia as soon as they reached Europe, which is why it was imperative to make sure that no more vessels were leaving for the New World by the time the ship docked in England. Even if thrown in jail, Cameron would have some time before sailing resumed in the spring to make his escape, if such a thing were indeed possible, but he had to try. It was his only chance.

Cameron's stomach growled again, so he allowed himself a small piece of bread and cheese he'd stolen from an isolated farmhouse a few miles outside of town. He left a few rabbit skins as payment, hoping that was sufficient. He couldn't take any rabbit or possum on board since the meat would quickly go rancid and make him sick, but the bread and cheese could last for a few days at least. Cameron savored his meal, took a sip of water from a wooden bottle he'd carved for just that purpose, and settled in for the wait. There seemed to be much less activity on deck, so maybe it was night and the crew had retired to their quarters. He didn't expect anyone to come searching the hold in the dead of night, so Cameron allowed himself to curl up behind the crate and get some sleep. He needed rest and a few hours respite from his thoughts.

SIXTY-EIGHT
NEW YORK CITY OCTOBER 2010

Valerie pulled a cap low over her eyes as she scanned the crowd of workers spilling through the revolving doors of the Manhattan high-rise. It was 5pm on a Friday afternoon and everyone was eager to get home and begin their weekend or stay in the city a little longer and have dinner or drinks with friends. People chatted happily as they walked past Valerie and Alec, their faces alight with the knowledge that they were just starting their weekend.

Yellow taxi cabs wove in and out of traffic on Madison Avenue, horns blaring and tires screeching as they tried to make the light. A bus rumbled past, and a wave of people left the sidewalks on both sides, eager to cross the street before the light changed again. The sound of conversation, mixed with the cacophony of rush-hour traffic, made Valerie feel slightly overwhelmed. She never used to notice the noise or the crowding before, but after two decades of living in the seventeenth century, Manhattan was like a sea of humanity, pulsating with a rhythm all its own and powered by an unimaginable amount of technology. They'd come into New York several times over the past few months, but it still amazed her how busy the city was at any given time, and how many people flocked to it every single day to fill the office buildings, stores and restaurants, eager to enjoy everything the city had to offer.

They'd returned to Isaac's house to collect their meager belongings before taking the watch and the notebook and leaving for good. Isaac's sons might not arrive until the following morning, but they couldn't take the chance of being found in his house. They'd spent the night in a small B&B Valerie had spotted on her walks around town and left Princeton for good in the morning. Valerie knew Alec was eager to go home, but she couldn't leave without seeing her parents just one more time. It would mean they'd have to spend the whole day in New York, but what was one more day compared to never seeing them again as long as she lived? She prayed that her mother still came to New York on Friday afternoons to meet her father after work and have dinner together. It was their date night, one that they kept to religiously for years and looked forward to all week.

Valerie grabbed Alec's hand as she spotted her mother strolling down Madison Avenue, her pace unhurried. She stopped in front of a store window to admire the fall shoes and boots already on display, but the look on her face told Valerie that she wasn't really seeing them. She wore a pair of tan slacks and a light sweater in fall colors of brown and rust that picked up the coppery highlights in her hair. Valerie's heart gave a squeeze as she catalogued the changes in her mother's beloved face. She was still an attractive woman, but the lines had grown deeper, and the mouth that had been so quick to smile had a downward cast to it, the lips pursed. The woman who had been so vibrant and full of life was now crippled with grief, unable to bury a daughter whose body had never been found but mourning her disappearance every single day.

Valerie stood absolutely still, her eyes glued to her mother. She wanted nothing more than to push her way through the crowd and hurl herself into her mother's arms, to assure her that she was alive and well, and introduce her to Alec. It would have been painful to tell her about the children, but she would have still wanted to share with her mother, to beam with pride over Finn, and to cry over the loss of Louisa and baby Alex. There was so much she wanted to say, but most of all, she just wanted to tell her mother that she loved her and that her parents were in her thoughts every single day, never forgotten, never unloved. Valerie wished she could tell her of Louisa's children and Kit, and of the great-grandchildren they would never see.

Alec held Valerie closer as he felt her body tense with the need to make physical contact, but she leaned against him, taking a deep breath as her mother passed within a few feet of her and stopped in front of the building where her father had worked for the past twenty years. Valerie wiped away the tears as she watched her father walk out the door and kiss her mother on the cheek, taking her hand in his as they walked away together, probably heading for one of their favorite restaurants on the Upper East Side.

They looked so much older than she remembered, the strain of the past few months etched into their faces, but they were still the same, still her mom and dad. They probably continued to hope that Valerie would turn up and put an end to the nightmare, but that wasn't to be. By this time, she was already firmly installed at Yealm Castle, pregnant with Finn, and ready to embark on a life with his hapless father, Alec suffering silently and waiting in the wings.

Valerie let out a shuddering breath as her parents turned a corner and disappeared from view. She was happy to have seen them, but the pain of not being able to reveal herself to them left her emotionally drained and eager to leave.

"Was it worth it?" Alec asked, fully knowing the answer. Valerie nodded as the bitter tears flowed down her face and blurred her vision.

"Yes," she whispered as she buried her face in his chest, her shoulders quaking with silent sobs.

"Let's go home," Alec whispered into her hair after the crying had subsided. "It's time."

Valerie was ready to go. Alec slung their duffle bag over his shoulder and turned Valerie in the direction of Central Park. They would find a nice place to have dinner, their last in this city and this century, and then wait till darkness to find a place to change and use the device. The streets of Jamestown would be deserted after ten o'clock, all the inhabitants already in their beds, the shutters firmly closed against the night humors. It would be safe then. Somewhere at the back of her mind there was the nagging thought that the device might not work, but Valerie pushed it out of her head. This was their one chance to get back home, and she wasn't going to think negative thoughts. It would work—it had to.

SIXTY-NINE

The pungent smell of decomposing leaves filled Valerie's nostrils as she walked along Central Park's famed Poet's Walk. She used to love coming here when she was a student and just walking around the park for hours, enjoying the seamless combination of country and city. Where else could you find leafy deserted walks, statues, fountains, and numerous artists and musicians, performing for the multitudes strolling along the walkways in the hopes of being noticed, their talent appreciated and rewarded with a few dollars?

So often she would bring her books to the park and study for a few hours before heading uptown and meeting Louisa in front of the Metropolitan Museum where she worked as an art restorer. It had been Louisa's dream job, one that she worked hard to get, starting at the very bottom as a lowly assistant who prepared solutions and brushes and working her way to restoring some of the world's most valuable artworks. Louisa might even still be there, working late in a studio that was tucked away in one of the off-limits corners of the museum.

She often stayed late into the night, unable to walk away from a challenging bit of canvas, her eyes red with fatigue, but her hands as steady as a surgeon's. Valerie often wondered if Louisa missed her work, but she never asked. As the years passed, they spoke less and less of their old life in the twenty-first century, the connection to the past growing more tenuous by the day. Their life was there now, and there was no point constantly looking back, especially since there was no one left in the future whom they pined for.

Valerie sighed. Seeing her parents that afternoon had opened up a lot of old wounds, but it also gave her a little bit of peace. She'd never had the chance to say goodbye, and thoughts of her parents' suffering tormented her for years, as it would have tortured her had they never found Finn when he disappeared several years ago. They had been lucky enough to be reconciled with their boy, but her parents had never found closure, never made peace. Valerie couldn't approach them or tell them all the things she'd wanted to say to them since the day she vanished, but at least she got to see them one last time and say goodbye in her heart. It was time to let go.

Valerie was startled out of her reverie by Alec, who gently took her by the arm and steered her down the steps, beneath the arches, and toward Liberty Fountain. The winged statue looked demonic in the darkness, and the waters of the lake beyond flowed black in the autumn night, fallen leaves merely dark blotches floating on the surface. There were still some people in the park, but they were few as it was a dangerous place to be traipsing around at night, especially on the less-lit avenues and underpasses.

"I reckon we've come far enough," Alec observed once they passed the fountain. He peered into the dark lane that climbed uphill. It was leafy, lined with benches, and eerily silent. It would do. It was unlikely they would be disturbed as they changed into their seventeenth-century garb. Valerie unzipped the duffle bag and pulled out her chemise, bodice and skirt, stockings, shoes, and linen cap. She'd gotten used to her summer dresses and jeans over the past few months, and God knew she'd miss underwear and bras, but the clothes still smelled of home, and she donned them happily, praying she wouldn't have to change back should the device fail to work.

Alec was already wearing his breeches, linen shirt and doublet. He looked like an actor preparing for a play, and Valerie smiled at him, happy to see him looking like himself again. She loved seeing him in jeans and T-shirts, but it wasn't until this moment that she realized how wrong they looked on him. This was her Alec, the Alec she knew and loved, the Alec of the past. He hadn't said as much, but he'd had enough of the future. He longed to go home. Valerie folded their modern clothes and stowed them in the duffel bag before zipping it back up and hanging it off a bench. Maybe some homeless person would find them and have some use for them. If not, someone would just toss them in the trash since they wouldn't find any trace of its owners. They'd take Isaac's notebook though. Fred would want to see it and appreciate a memento from his old friend.

Alec unstrapped the watch from his wrist and gazed at Valerie. "Are you ready?"

She opened her mouth to reply, but her heart was hammering against her ribs, her breath coming in short, shallow puffs. She'd been a bundle of nerves the whole day, but now she was simply terrified.

"Your hands are like ice," Alec said as he took her hands in his and rubbed them gently. "Come, there's no point putting this off any longer." He let go of Valerie's hands and set the year and coordinates before taking Valerie's hands once more and pressing the green button that would activate the device. She felt a momentary dizziness, and then an odd sensation that felt as if gravity became suspended and she was weightless and insignificant, falling, falling through time and space, Alec's hand the only thing anchoring her to reality. She must have lost consciousness, because when she came to, she was lying on the ground, Alec sitting cross-legged next to her, talking softly and asking her to wake up. Valerie sat up slowly and looked around.

If Central Park had been dark, this place was way darker. There was no glimmer of lights visible through the trees or the sound of traffic filtering through the green darkness. No snippets of quiet conversation or bursts of laughter reached their ears. All was silent, except for the angry meowing of a cat somewhere not too far off, and the gentle lapping of water coming from the James River. The nearly black outline of houses was barely visible against the night sky, and several tall masts poked at the heavens, their sails furled.

Alec helped Valerie to her feet and adjusted her cap before gently kissing her. "I do believe we're home, my dear," he stated as he took her arm and turned in the direction of the plantation.

"Thank God," Valerie breathed, her heart swelling with joy.

SEVENTY

VIRGINIA OCTOBER 1626

The dark clouds parted, revealing the bright sliver of moon that cast a silvery light onto the dirt road. The wind moved through the trees, causing a shower of leaves to flutter to the ground in a silent dance that only Valerie and Alec could see and appreciate at that time of night. Everything was eerily quiet and still. Valerie shivered in her chemise and dress, wishing she had her woolen cloak to keep her warm. It'd been June when they left, but now autumn was well under way and the wind was biting as it blew through the homespun fabric and left her skin prickled with gooseflesh. Alec wrapped his arm around Valerie when he noticed her shivering, and she leaned against him, absorbing his comforting warmth and support. One more bend in the road and the house would be there, bathed in the moonlight and surrounded by maple trees that would be painted in the vibrant shades of yellow and crimson with the approach of winter.

Valerie's heart nearly burst with happiness at the sight of Rosewood Manor. They'd been gone for just over three months, but it felt like an eternity, and she saw the house as it might appear to a stranger. It looked small and terribly old-fashioned compared to the homes they'd just seen in the twenty-first century, and it was hard to believe that so many people lived there all year round, several to a room, with no bathrooms or running water. All they had was a well, and lots of candles, since even the oil lamps had yet to be invented. But it was full of people she loved, and Valerie had never been as content as she was at that moment. She wanted to break into a run, but Alec held her back, silently reminding her that everyone was asleep. Well, maybe not everybody.

All the windows were dark and shuttered, except for the parlor window, which glowed with candlelight. Kit liked to stay up and read, or just have a peaceful drink after the household finally quieted down and the children were in their beds. Sometimes Charles joined him for a drink, but most days he was alone, since Annabel preferred Charles to retire at the same time as her. Valerie smiled happily at the thought of seeing Kit. She'd go wake Louisa as soon as she could and tell her everything that happened over the past few months, especially about seeing Mom and Dad.

Alec was already knocking on the door, his face breaking into a huge grin as a surprised Kit threw open the door, letting them in. The two men hugged, and she noted the look that passed between them. It was a silent conversation, but it was all they needed.

"Are you all right?" Kit's eyes asked Alec.

"We are now. And how have things been during our absence?" Alec inquired without saying a word.

"That's a conversation for another time, but I have much to tell you." Kit clapped Alec on the shoulder and poured him a brandy as Alec sank into his favorite chair and smiled at Valerie with a look of pure joy in his eyes.

"Go, wake Louisa, I know you're dying to," Kit suggested, noticing her impatience. Valerie gave Kit a quick hug and raced up the stairs, desperate to see her sister. She would go look in on the children later and bend over Tom as she kissed his smooth cheek and inhaled his childish scent, but first she had to see Lou.

Louisa was fast asleep, her golden hair fanned around her face and her arm flung across Kit's side of the bed. Valerie would've liked to have said that Lou looked peaceful, but there were lines of tension around her mouth and her eyes moved quickly beneath the closed lids as if she were seeing something that made her anxious. Maybe she was just having a bad dream, or maybe she'd been wearing herself out with worry over the past few months, desperate to know what happened to them.

Valerie sat on the edge of the bed and took her sister's hand in her own, whispering her name softly, so as not to startle her. It took Louisa a moment to fully wake up as she looked at Valerie in the darkness of the room, her mouth opening with shock before she finally understood that she wasn't dreaming. Louisa sat bolt upright and threw her arms around Valerie, a sob tearing from her as she drew Valerie even closer.

"I thought I lost you," Louisa whispered urgently, "I thought I lost you for good. I had no idea what happened to you, and I was so scared. I thought Alec..."

"He's all right, Lou. We both are, but I lost the time-travel watch while Alec was in the hospital."

"What?" Louisa pushed Valerie away and stared at her in horror. "You lost it? How did you get back?"

"I'll tell you later. I can't bear to relive all that now. Just tell me about everything that's been happening here. I want to hear every minor, boring detail. I've missed everyone so much." Valerie wiped her tears away as she reclined next to Louisa, ready to hear all the happenings of the past few months.

"I'm not so sure I want to relive all that either," Louisa suddenly giggled as she turned toward Valerie, her head supported by her arm. "Oh God, Val, you wouldn't believe everything that's happened. It was awful. Kit was on trial for murder, thanks to Annabel, and one of the indentures ran off, and Jenny..."

"Murder? Who was he meant to have killed?" Valerie gasped in shock. "And what did Annabel have to do with it? And what happened to Jenny?"

"Oh, where do I begin?" Louisa said with a smile as she gazed at Valerie. "Oh, Val, how I wished you were here. Please, don't ever leave me again; I couldn't bear it." Valerie nodded, her head spinning with everything Louisa mentioned and what it implied. She assumed that Alec and Kit were having a similar conversation downstairs.

It was nearly midnight by the time Louisa finally finished her story. Her account had been detailed, but Valerie felt that her sister was holding something back. She didn't quite understand what led to the animosity between Kit and Deverell, but Lou seemed reluctant to explain and Valerie didn't press her for more information. All that mattered was that Kit had been exonerated and set free. Alec would be very upset about the situation with Charles and Annabel, but she would leave it to him to work things out with his brother. She hoped Annabel's meddling wouldn't destroy the relationship between Alec and Charles. They didn't always see eye to eye, but they loved each other despite their differences, and Valerie hoped that wouldn't change. It seems that no one had seen Charles since the trial, but Valerie was sure Alec would be paying him a visit in the coming days.

"Will you talk to Alec about Jenny?" Louisa asked.

"Is it as bad as that?" Valerie sighed. Alec would be upset to know that his niece had been so unhappy. Louisa shrugged and shook her head.

"She refuses to say anything, but I think she's pining after that Scot who ran off. She hasn't been the same since. I know she developed a friendship with him, but I now believe it must have been something more. She's so hard to read, that girl,"

Louisa said. "I tried talking to her, but she just tells me everything is all right and she's content with the way things are. She prays a lot, and seems to feel somewhat more at peace after, but then the melancholy returns."

"Do you think she might be pregnant?" Valerie asked, desperately hoping she wasn't. Alec would be devastated and feel that he let his sister down once again in failing to protect her daughter from harm and shame. He took his responsibility to Genevieve very seriously, in some way also projecting his feelings about his failure to protect their daughter onto his niece. He could no longer help their Louisa, but he could do everything in his power to make sure Genevieve was happy and safe.

Louisa shook her head. "I don't see any signs of pregnancy, and I'm fairly certain the girl is still a virgin, but who knows? Anytime anyone mentioned Cameron Brody after he ran off she practically jumped out of her skin. For the first week after he'd gone, she went around in a daze, sometimes smiling serenely and others just sobbing her heart out, but then she just sank into a depression."

"She was probably in love with him, poor thing. He was a good-looking lad, I'll give him that." Valerie thought of the big Scot. She could see how he might appeal to a vulnerable young girl and hoped he hadn't done anything to hurt Jenny. "Any idea what happened to him?"

"No one has seen him since his escape. Kit had Master Worthing organize a search party, but they found no trace of him. They searched for two days but could hardly afford to take more time since it was just before harvest." Louisa shrugged her shoulders, her expression hard to read in the darkness of the room.

"Where could he have gone?" mused Valerie. "There's only one port, and to go deeper into the woods is to risk being taken prisoner by the Indians."

"He might have walked to one of the other settlements, I suppose," Louisa replied, "but he'd be taking a risk of being detained and sent back here. Word does get around, so people would know he was a runaway."

"I hope he's all right," Valerie whispered into the darkness. "There was something about him that just pulled at my heartstrings. I would hate to think that he's lying dead out there somewhere with no one to even bury him or say a prayer for his soul."

"You're getting awfully sentimental in your old age," Louisa observed as she studied Valerie. "I didn't know him well, but I got the impression that he was no fool. He must have had some plan when he took off."

"I hope so."

SEVENTY-ONE

SOMEWHERE IN THE ATLANTIC OCTOBER 1626

The sun was blinding after the darkness of the hold and Cameron closed his eyes against its merciless rays as the two sailors dragged him across the deck and toward the main mast. They tied him securely in place and sent a young cabin boy to fetch the captain as the rest of the crew assembled to watch the entertainment. It wasn't often that a stowaway was discovered on a ship and the reckoning could be the most fun the crew could ask for on the long voyage.

Cameron rested his head against the mast and sucked in lungfuls of fresh, ocean air as the seagulls circled over his head, their calls muted by the sound of jeering men and the waves crashing against the hull. Cameron was almost glad he was tied up since he surely would have fallen, unaccustomed as he was to the rolling of the deck beneath his feet. The food had run out the day before, and the water yesterday, making it impossible for him to hide any longer. He was weakened by hunger and thirst, having allowed himself only a few bites of bread and cheese twice a day and a few sips of water. Cameron's stomach felt permanently empty and his tongue stuck to the roof of his mouth from being so dry. He hadn't taken a piss since the day before, which was a sure sign that time wasn't on his side. Cameron allowed himself to be discovered a few minutes ago by a sailor who regularly came down to the hold to inspect the cargo, and now it was time to face the consequences of his actions.

As his eyes finally adjusted to the light, he was able to look out over the water, noting the vast expanse of ocean and sky all around the vessel. They were far enough from land that he couldn't be returned to Virginia, but still many weeks away from the shores of England. Cameron silently prayed that the captain wasn't a cruel man, but he hadn't known much kindness from strangers and didn't expect miracles. He tried to focus on the faces of the sailors to distract himself from the clenching of his stomach muscles and the pounding in his head. His heart was hammering against his ribs, making it almost impossible to breathe, but he forced himself to take slow, measured breaths until he was able to achieve a modicum of calm. It never helped to show fear.

The jeering stopped, and the crew parted like the Red Sea to allow the captain to pass. He was a stocky man of medium height with hair that must have been black once but was now faded to the color of ashes left over from a roaring fire. His eyes appeared to be much the same color, as was the beard that hid the lower part of his face. Cameron noted the lines around the eyes, which could be a sign of someone who enjoyed a good laugh or a man who spent countless days squinting at the horizon as he sailed his ship. The captain stopped in front of him, his expression difficult to read. The murmuring of the crew had stopped, a dead silence enveloping the deck as everyone waited for something to happen.

"Identify yourself, sir," the captain said at last, his voice gravelly and cold, but full of authority.

"Cameron Brody, stowaway."

"Yes, I gathered that, Master Brody. Do you know what we

do to stowaways?" the captain asked in a conversational tone, making the sailors snigger as they eagerly watched Cameron for signs of panic.

"I cannae begin to guess," Cameron replied, knowing full well what the captain was talking about.

"Then I take it you're not a seafaring man. We throw stowaways overboard. If they are lucky enough to be close to land and can swim, they might have a chance of survival, but this far out to sea, they become food for the creatures that live in the deep and feast on human flesh. What have you got to say to that, Master Brody?" The captain was watching him, amusement playing about his lips. It made Cameron angry that the man was enjoying himself at his expense.

"I say that's a terrible waste of an able-bodied man, sir," Cameron replied. "Throw me overboard and ye'll have a few moments of entertainment as ye watch me drown but allow me to stay on board and ye'll have an extra pair of hands working for no wage and not uttering a word of complaint. I only need enough food to survive the voyage and can sleep in the cargo hold."

"And do you have knowledge of boats or sailing?" the captain asked, his head cocked to the side as he studied Cameron.

"Nae, sir, but I'm quick to learn and stronger than most men." Cameron glanced meaningfully at the members of the crew, who were mostly thin and sickly-looking from months spent aboard a ship and living on salt pork and dry biscuit.

The captain didn't say anything in response, just studied him in silence for a few minutes, weighing his options. At least he was considering it, Cameron thought as he lowered his eyes respectfully. Some of the sailors looked disappointed, having no doubt expected the captain to order him tossed overboard immediately, and angry to be cheated of their entertainment.

The captain finally stirred as he came to a decision, "Master

Brody, I can only assume you're a criminal, a runaway slave, or both, and likely deserve no mercy. Had you been older or less brawny, I'd have consigned you to the waves immediately. As it happens, two of my crew died on the previous crossing and I haven't been able to replace them during my stay in Jamestown. I will allow you to stay but will work you to the bone with no pay. You will be fed, however, and will sleep below decks with the rest of the crew. I will decide what to do with you once we reach England."

Cameron's shoulders sagged with relief, but the captain wasn't quite finished. "Don't congratulate yourself just yet. I said you can stay; I didn't say you wouldn't be punished for your transgression. Twenty-five lashes, Master Sewell, if you please," the captain commanded the tall man who stood to his right, possibly the quartermaster.

"Yes, Captain," Master Sewell replied, turning to the nearest sailor. "Untie him, remove his shirt, and turn him to face the mast," he ordered. "Bring me the cat o' nine tails, Jones, and make sure all crew members are on deck."

Cameron sucked in his breath as two sailors quickly untied him, ordered him to remove his shirt and tied his wrists to the mast above his head. He was glad he'd had the foresight to hide Jenny's ring in the hold before allowing himself to be found. If anyone had seen it hanging around his neck, they'd assume he'd stolen it and would most likely take it from him. He would retrieve it later, once he was free to move around the ship. Cameron closed his eyes and rested his stubbled cheek against the cool, smooth wood of the mast. He'd gotten off fairly easily, but he still had to take his punishment.

The captain had been merciful in sentencing him to only twenty-five lashes, but they were to be administered by The Cat, which made the punishment considerably worse. The whip had nine separate tails, rather than one, and turned twenty-five lashes into more like two hundred. Still, it was a small price to pay for being allowed to live, and he would take it like a man—silently.

A ripple of excitement went through the crew as Jones brought the whip and handed it to Master Sewell, who was to act as Master at Arms. "Ready, Master. Brody?" he asked, a note of amusement in his voice.

Cameron wasn't sure that anyone could be truly ready for a flogging, but he kept his voice calm as he answered. "Aye, Master Sewell, proceed." The sooner it started, the sooner it'd be over.

Cameron thought he knew pain. He'd been beaten savagely during his time in prison and on the voyage to Virginia, but this was something different entirely. All air left his lungs as the first lash struck his back, the multiple tails of the whip whistling through the air ominously before making contact with bare flesh. It felt as if a hundred hot pokers were applied to his skin, stinging and burning, tearing and savaging. He had just enough time to draw breath before the second lash came, and the third. The pain multiplied with every stroke, driving all thought from his mind. Cameron's already raw back was torn apart by the knotted ends of the whip which was now dripping with his blood as the crew cheered Master Sewell on. The captain watched from the side, his face a mask of bland indifference.

Cameron tried to count the strokes, but he was unable to focus after the first few, the lashes coming with barely any time to recover and leaving him gasping for breath and unable to see as salty tears stung his eyes.

"Jenny," he whispered to himself. He tried to conjure up her face but couldn't as another lash came down on his back with agonizing brutality. Had it even been twenty yet? Cameron hardly even noticed when the lashes stopped. He was in a state of semi-consciousness, the only thing holding him up the rope tying his wrists to the mast. Someone untied him and walked him from the deck to a small cabin below. It was dim, the only light coming from a small lantern. Cameron stumbled and nearly fell as he was laid on his stomach atop the dirty linen. Someone, he couldn't see the man, began to administer ointment to his flayed back. Cameron closed his eyes and allowed himself to float, the pain washing over him in hot waves that left him breathless and shaking.

"You got off lucky, my boy," a gruff voice said somewhere above his head. "Other captains might have ordered as many as forty lashes. I've seen it done, I have. Captain Doyle is a good man, and 'tis a privilege to sail under him."

Cameron didn't feel particularly privileged at the moment, but no answer was expected as the sailor continued to gently dab a poultice on Cameron's back. "You just work hard and prove your worth and the captain will see you right. I know he will. Now, try to sleep. 'Tis the best thing for you."

Cameron felt as if someone had dumped burning coals onto his back and fanned the flames, but he tried to breathe evenly and relax. His thoughts were jumbled, and his cheeks covered with dry salt, either from tears or seawater that had sprayed his face when he was on deck. For some reason, his muddled brain turned to his grandfather's funeral. His granddad had died when Cameron was six. It had been during a particularly hard winter, and the old man had been outside for hours chopping wood for the fire. They had just sat down to supper when the old man made a gurgling sound as saliva frothed from his mouth, grabbed his heart, and fell to the floor, writhing in agony. It lasted only a few moments, but it felt like hours as Cameron and his sisters watched their beloved grandfather die. Cameron's mother began to weep, but his father was strangely calm as he made the sign of the cross over his father's forehead and sent Cameron to fetch the priest.

Cameron couldn't remember the actual funeral, but he remembered the sin-eater. His mother had insisted on getting one since granddad had died suddenly and wasn't shriven. The sin-eater was a thin, miserable-looking man who was no more than a beggar. He looked to be very old, but underneath the dirt and rags, he might have been no more than fifty, which was still old to a boy of six. The sin-eater nodded to his parents as he came into the house on the day of the funeral, ready to do his job.

The girls hid in the loft, terrified of the strange man, but Cameron wanted to watch and remained in the corner. Cameron's father placed a crust of bread on granddad's chest and passed a cup of ale over the corpse before handing it to the beggar. The man drank the ale and ate the crust of bread off the corpse before collecting his payment and disappearing into the wintry landscape. Cameron had been fascinated and repelled at the same time.

He didn't think he was dying, but he suddenly wished that a sin-eater would come to him and relieve his soul of the terrible sin of murder. He'd confessed to Jenny, but she didn't have the power to grant him absolution, and he wanted to be shriven in case he died during the voyage. He wanted to be forgiven for his sin, he thought wearily before sinking into blissful oblivion.

SEVENTY-TWO

Cameron decided that Captain Doyle was merciful after all since he'd allowed him several days to recover before putting him to work. The old sailor known as Gimp, who tended to him, brought him food and water every day and fed it to him so that Cameron didn't have to sit up unnecessarily, but eventually the reprieve was over and he was ordered to report to the quartermaster.

The first few hours had been pure agony as the newly healed scars tore open and blood seeped onto his shirt and dried in the cold wind, sticking to Cameron's back. As he moved, the fabric was torn away from the wounds, which began to bleed again. By the time he was finally allowed to return to the cabin his shirt was a bloody mess, as was his back. But he was healing, and after a week the bleeding finally ceased, and he was able to ignore the soreness and itching as he worked.

Surprisingly, the captain and the crew made no mention of the flogging or his stowaway status and accepted him as one of their own, some even glancing at him with grudging admiration and clapping him on the shoulder in a gesture of camaraderie. It was odd that the same men who were baying for his blood only a week ago were now treating him as a friend, but that was human nature for you, Cameron reasoned as he went about his work.

The weeks passed in a blur of exhausting days and cold nights. Cameron stumbled to his hammock at night and fell into a dreamless sleep which seemed to last only a few minutes before it was time to get up and face another day. The captain had been true to his word and worked Cameron to the bone, assigning him the lowliest tasks and the longest hours. Cameron was either sweating profusely or shivering with cold since he had no coat to keep him warm against the bitter breath of the Atlantic. The clothes on his back were the only things he owned, aside from Jenny's ring, which he kept safely hidden and wouldn't sell for anything. At least he had a thin blanket to cover himself with while he slept, but it did little to keep out the biting chill of the autumn wind. The weather grew stormier and colder as they neared England, and the weak sunshine that sparkled on the water offered no warmth or comfort.

Cameron didn't complain. He was lucky to be alive, and as long as he was dutiful and hard-working, he had a chance. The captain never spoke to him, but there were times when Cameron felt the captain's eyes on him, watching silently as he stood on the bridge, one hand on the wheel, and the other holding the pipe that rarely left his lips. Master Sewell, on the other hand, went out of his way to single Cameron out for his displeasure, but Cameron wouldn't take the bait, replying only with "Aye, sir," "Nae, sir," and "Right away, sir." If Sewell hoped to find a reason to punish him, he wouldn't give him the satisfaction.

A few of the crew members tried to befriend him. Cameron answered politely when spoken to but kept his distance. What was there to say? He wasn't interested in their stories and didn't care to share his own. Every day he survived brought him closer to home and closer to his future, if he had one. He was sure the captain would inform him in due time what he'd decided to do with him, or perhaps he would just turn him over to the authorities as soon as they docked and Cameron would be sent back to Virginia to fulfill his contract and face his punishment. All he could do was wait and hope.

After about eight weeks at sea, Cameron began to sense excitement among the crew. They were days away from docking in Liverpool, and the sailors were anxious to get home, hopefully in time for the Christmas celebrations. The crew would be dismissed until the first sailing of the spring and the men longed to see their families after many months at sea. Some would be coming home to children who'd been born in their absence, while others would learn of the passing of loved ones, having had no word from home since they left the previous spring to sail to the New World.

As the day of arrival drew nearer, Cameron found himself unable to sleep. His body was worn out, but his mind wouldn't settle down and allow him to rest. He'd managed to escape the plantation and actually get to England, but now all his efforts might be thwarted if the captain chose to be spiteful. Cameron tried to put the thought from his mind and go to sleep, but after an hour of trying to get comfortable in the narrow hammock he gave up.

Cameron suddenly felt as if he couldn't stay in the dark, smelly space any longer. He was surrounded by snoring men who hadn't bathed in weeks and farted constantly in their sleep, mostly due to the severe constipation caused by their diet. He needed some air. Cameron grabbed his blanket and went up on deck. The bitter wind chilled him to the bone in a matter of seconds, but Cameron couldn't bear to go back down. He wrapped the blanket around himself and stared up at the crescent moon, hanging in the heavens at a jaunty angle and surrounded by a sprinkling of stars. The moon painted a sliver of silvery light on the black waters of the Atlantic, a magical pathway that beckoned to him like a siren song. If only he could get off the ship and make his way home. He was so tired of being at the mercy of others.

Cameron barely noticed as a dark figure materialized next to him, only the smell of the pipe identifying his companion as the captain. Cameron stiffened and was about to take his leave, but the captain put a hand on his shoulder bidding him to stay. He had no idea what to say, so he remained quiet, looking at the moonlit path and wishing himself anywhere but where he was.

"We dock tomorrow, Master Brody," the captain said at last.

"Aye, I ken that, sir." Cameron's shoulders and neck tensed as much from the frigid wind as from the uncertainty of his situation. Was the captain toying with him?

"Master Brody," the captain said, his gaze drawn to the moonlit water, "I'm not without compassion. I can only imagine how desperate a man must be to put himself into the position I found you in. You knew when you came aboard my ship that you would have a much greater chance of dying than surviving." The captain grew quiet, waiting for Cameron to say something.

"Aye, sir, I did, but I had nae choice." Cameron's voice sounded gruff, almost defiant. He had known, but he'd done it anyway because that was the only path to freedom, at least for him.

"I'm not going to ask you what you were running from or what you're running toward. As long as I'm not aware of your crime, I'm not duty-bound to report it. You're worked very hard, and as far as I'm concerned, you've earned your freedom. I wish you Godspeed, Master Brody."

"Thank ye, Captain," Cameron whispered, amazed that the man was willing to let him go. Was it really possible that as soon as tomorrow he would be on his way north? The captain drew something out of his pocket and held out his hand to Cameron. "Here, you've earned this."

Cameron stared at the coins in his hand, unable to believe his eyes. He gazed up at the captain, overcome with gratitude. Cameron opened his mouth to speak but had no idea what to say to convey the depth of his feeling, so he shut his mouth again and bowed to the captain.

"Master Brody, I can only assume that you're on your way to Scotland. You'll need food, a coat, and a horse. This will help." The captain clapped him on the shoulder and walked away, leaving Cameron agape with shock.

"Thank ye," he whispered to the heavens, not sure if he meant the captain or God. He couldn't believe he might actually be home within a few days. Cameron opened his palm and stared at the coins. He wasn't sure exactly what they would buy, but he intended to find out. He knew he must be frugal, but he didn't want to show up at home looking like a convict. A new shirt and a coat would go a long way to improving his appearance, as well as a hat. He must have a hat.

SEVENTY-THREE
VIRGINIA BOXING DAY 1626

Valerie pushed a lock of hair out of her face as she helped Genevieve pack several baskets of food for the workers. They'd had their Christmas dinner and service yesterday, but traditionally, Boxing Day was a day for giving gifts to the workers and servants, and Alec liked his traditions. He gave everyone the day off as well as some freshly baked bread, ham, cheese, and dry apple slices, which Valerie insisted on since the workers needed vitamin C to prevent scurvy.

In addition to the food, he also gave each man a small bag of tobacco, which could be used to trade for other goods in lieu of cash. The men were allowed one day to walk into Jamestown and trade their tobacco for whatever consumer goods they needed. Most men opted for a new shirt or a coat to keep them warm during the winter months. Some men asked Alec to hold on to their share for them until their contract was up, and they could trade the accumulated tobacco for a new suit of clothes or household goods.

Christmas this year had been a somewhat subdued affair. Charles had come by to offer his felicitations, but no one had had any contact with Annabel since the trial. Evie, Robbie, and

Tom were upset that Harry and Millie weren't there for the holiday, and Jenny floated around like a ghost, lost in her own fug of melancholy. Fred and Barbara Taylor had joined the family for Christmas dinner, as had Minnie, but the mood was less than merry. Valerie tried not to think of Finn and Abbie as they celebrated Christmas in their own time with the Mallory family. She missed them desperately, but in view of their long absence from home, the chance to visit hadn't presented itself yet.

Alec had toyed with the idea of telling Charles the truth about where they'd been, but Valerie implored him to reconsider, and he had. After Annabel's treachery, it was difficult to trust Charles with something as explosive as their secret. If Annabel found out she could have them arrested on charges of witchcraft, and although no one could prove anything, suspicion was often enough to convict. So the truth had to remain a secret.

Valerie fastened her woolen cape around her shoulders and slung a basket over each arm. The day was cold and gray, the afternoon light strangely flat beneath the low-hanging clouds. She walked cautiously on the frosty grass, careful not to slip. Genevieve walked silently next to her, her face rosy from the cold, but her eyes like shuttered windows. She'd never been particularly talkative, but now she was downright taciturn. The only time she smiled seemed to be when she was around the children, although a look of pain often crossed her features when she held Tom.

Valerie set down her basket, brushed the snowflakes off the bench and sat down on the bench by the pond, patting the space next to her, but Genevieve stared at the bench is if it were covered with hot coals. She finally set her basket down and sat next to Valerie, her eyes glued to the pond as if she could see something that was invisible to Valerie.

They weren't often alone, so this was a good opportunity to

talk. Both Alec and Valerie had tried to gently find out what was wrong, but Genevieve had learned to avoid being alone with them, and always had one of the children hanging on her skirts, preventing any kind of serious conversation.

Valerie took a deep breath and plunged in. "Jenny, I lost my daughter, and you've never had a mother, so we are both longing for someone to take their place. Won't you let me be that person? I know you're hurting, and it kills me that I can't help you. Maybe if Louisa had spoken to me, or to her aunt, things could have turned out differently. Won't you talk to me? I promise that if you want to keep our conversation secret, I won't say a word to your uncle. I only want to help."

Valerie hoped to break through the barrier the girl had erected around herself and get her to talk, but instead Genevieve dissolved into tears. She didn't make a sound as she cried, the tears sliding down her cheeks and dripping onto her cloak where they left little wet spots. Genevieve's face was contorted with misery, and Valerie opened her arms as Genevieve leaned into them and sobbed into her shoulder. This was the first time she'd seen Jenny cry, and she held her close as she shook with silent sobs, her arms wrapped around Valerie for comfort.

"Cameron, is it?" Valerie asked gently and was surprised to see Jenny's nod. She blew her nose and finally turned to face Valerie.

"Please, don't tell Uncle Alec; he'll be so upset. I know he wants what's best for me and keeps trying to find me a suitable husband, but I'm already wed." The tears began to flow again.

"Have you heard from him?"

Jenny shook her head. "Not since the day after he ran off, but he promised to send for me as soon as he was able."

Valerie didn't ask how he expected to get back home and with what money he planned to send for his bride. Maybe he'd said that to pacify her, or maybe he really meant it, but the reality of that happening was pretty slim.

"Jenny, are you pregnant?" Valerie asked carefully.

Genevieve shook her head again as she stared across the thin layer of ice covering the pond. How could she describe to Aunt Valerie the countless hours she spent praying, hoping, wishing, fearing, and finally accepting? Her monthly flow had never been regular, sometimes coming every month, and at others skipping as many as three months at a time. It had never been a great source of concern, but after Cameron left, the significance of that suddenly took on a new meaning.

She had no way of knowing if her menses were simply delayed or if she was with child. At first, Genevieve had been horrified by the possibility that she might be pregnant, but then the idea of having Cameron's baby filled her with such longing that she could barely draw breath. As the days passed, she went from praying for it to be true, to beseeching God to let her get her flow and not be put into a position where she would be shamed before all of Jamestown community, to longing for the baby despite everything. The weeks turned into months, and still she had no definite answer. She felt crampy and moody, her head ached, and her breasts felt tender, but that could only mean that her flow was coming. She'd felt that way before, and for lack of a midwife to tell her for sure, she was in Purgatory.

It was only a week ago that she finally saw blood as she wiped herself in the privy and knew that the dream of a baby was over. Her flow came with a vengeance, and she bled and bled, her body finally replying to the question and leaving no room for doubt. Genevieve had to admit that a part of her was relieved, but a bigger part of her was heartbroken, forced to accept that their baby was not to be, at least for the time being. She wished she could curl into a ball and stay that way until Cameron sent for her, but that was impossible in a household where so many people lived together and the children were constantly begging for her attention. She loved them all, but it was Tom, in particular, who broke her heart, for he was the youngest and the sweetest, the one who loved her unconditionally as her own baby might have.

"I thought I was, but then I wasn't," she finally replied, a faraway look in her eyes. "I was both relieved and devastated at the same time. Oh, Aunt Valerie, I wanted to have his baby so much. It would have been a part of him that was mine forever, but now I may never see him again, or know if he's alive or dead. I pray for him every day, and I try to close my eyes and feel him, but I can't. I just feel so empty inside."

Valerie took Genevieve's cold hand in her own and held it. What could she tell her that would make her feel better? It was a blessing the girl wasn't pregnant, but she could understand her desire to be. She clearly lost her heart to the young Scot, and she wanted to hold on to a part of him, but of course, in this day and age, having a baby out of wedlock would make her a social outcast and a woman of loose morals. No one would care that she and Cameron considered themselves married. In their eyes, she would be the whore of a convict and a runaway, and the only thing that would save her reputation would be to put about a story that she'd been raped by him, which Jenny would never allow. So, not being pregnant was indeed a blessing in disguise.

As to her husband, God only knew where he could be at this very moment. He'd managed to run away and avoid being captured, but where did he go then? He'd promised to send for her, which implied that he meant to go back to Scotland, but how did he propose to get there? He had nothing but the clothes on his back and would be instantly returned to Rosewood Manor if caught anywhere near Jamestown, which was the only port. The boy was most likely dead, but she couldn't say that to Genevieve, so she held her close and offered silent support, which was the only thing she had to give. Poor girl. She hadn't had a happy life, and now she would spend years pining for a man who was probably dead.

Soft snowflakes began to fall, twirling and dancing in the light wind that blew from the direction of the river. They settled on their cheeks and noses, melting within seconds and leaving their faces cold and wet. Genevieve suddenly smiled as a ray of sunshine lit up the heavy clouds and cast an unexpected glow on everything around them. She raised her face to the sky and closed her eyes as snowflakes fell on her eyelids.

"He's alive, Aunt Valerie, I know it. I wasn't sure before, but now I feel it in my bones."

She got up and went to fetch her basket and suddenly did a little twirl and dip that made Valerie smile. How volatile young people were, in any age. They could go from utter despair to shining hope in a matter of moments and could carry you along with their joy. Valerie smiled and picked up her own baskets. If Genevieve believed Cameron was alive, who was she to dispute it? Stranger things had happened.

SEVENTY-FOUR

JAMESTOWN, VIRGINIA SEPTEMBER 1627

The muddy waters of the James River sparkled in the brilliant sunshine, seagulls swooping down as they spotted a fish beneath the waves and coming up triumphant, their catch thrashing in their beaks. A gentle breeze blew off the water as puffy white clouds lazily floated across the dazzling blue sky. But Alec saw none of the beauty of the September morning. All he saw was the dark outline of a ship as it nosed its way out of the harbor and made for open water. He thought he could hear the snapping of the sails and the creaking of the wood, but the vessel was already too far away, and growing smaller by the minute. Alec was startled out of his misery by the touch of Valerie's hand as she gently tried to pull him away from the quay.

"She didn't give you much choice, Alec," Valerie reminded him gently, her eyes full of sympathy.

"I know, but I still feel as if I've failed her. And Rose," Alec added, finally turning to face his wife. "I was foolish to think I could protect her and give her security and comfort."

"But you have," Valerie protested, knowing they would have to go over the argument a few hundred more times before Alec finally came to terms with his loss. "You've given her a home, a family, and your love."

"What sort of life will she have in Scotland with that scoundrel?" Alec asked petulantly, sulking like a child.

"Alec, she loves him, and it stands to reason that he loves her just as much. He didn't have to send for her or repay you for the indenture contract he broke. You must admit that the man does have honor, and courage. You're just upset that she chose him over you," Valerie said playfully, pulling Alec along the dock.

"I suppose I am. I just wanted to keep her near, to see her get married and have children. I wanted to do right by her, and in doing so, do right by my sister. I can't protect her in Scotland."

"No, you can't, but Genevieve will have her husband to protect her, a husband who's strong, resourceful, and steadfast—all the qualities that I love in you."

Alec finally tore his eyes away from the receding vessel and smiled down at Valerie. "You're just trying to make me feel better."

"Is it working?"

Alec nodded and helped Valerie into the trap for the ride home. Genevieve's announcement that she was going to Scotland had come as a shock. He'd forgotten all about the runaway Scot and was focused on running the plantation and trying to put out all the fires that flared within the family from time to time.

Thankfully, the past year had been relatively quiet, especially with Charles and Annabel residing in Jamestown once more. Louisa resolutely refused to allow Annabel anywhere near the house after what she'd done, so Charles occasionally brought Harry and Millie to Rosewood Manor to visit with their cousins. It wasn't fair on the children, and they failed to understand why they were no longer all living together. Annabel, however, had gotten what she was after. Cousin Wesley made a will, in which he bequeathed the entire estate to Harry, the act appealing to Annabel's sense of justice. She seemed to forget that, strictly speaking, the estate should have gone to Tom, who was the direct male descendant of her brother, but Alec chose not to get involved. Tom would have his own inheritance when the time came, and he was happy that Harry would be well provided for.

Alec climbed onto the bench and took up the reins. He had to admit that he was looking forward to a game of chess with Fred Taylor after the midday meal. Those games had saved the day, and he was grateful to the old man for everything he'd done for them, especially his cunning ideas for freeing Kit. No one besides Louisa ever found out why Deverell was blackmailing Kit, so life was back to normal, at least on the outside. Relations between Kit and Louisa seemed a bit strained when Alec and Valerie finally returned, but they seemed to be on the right track, rebuilding their bond and healing the hurt.

Louisa would never completely forgive or forget, but she loved Kit enough to understand what drove him to submit to Buckingham and tried not to judge him. It was still difficult for her at times to understand that things were different in the here and now, and that a man could lose his head, as well as his title and fortune, on the whim of another. This wasn't the world she was used to where a person had rights and options. This was the seventeenth century, where a man of power could easily destroy his enemies without any consequences or guilt.

The countryside flowed past as Alec drove toward the plantation, his mind still occupied by his thoughts. He would miss Jenny dreadfully, but somewhere deep inside, if he were honest with himself, he was happy for her. She'd found love, and although he didn't necessarily approve of the man, he knew Cameron would take good care of her. He was one of those rare men who meant what they said and kept their promises at all cost. He'd never seen Jenny as happy as she had been the day the letter came, her face lighting up with joy and her hands shaking as she read and reread the message. Cameron Brody had somehow made it to Scotland, cleared his name, and managed to save enough money to get the farm back on track and repay Alec for his indenture. Alec knew it tore Jenny apart to say goodbye to everyone, but she had her life to live, and he had no right to stand in her way.

Charles had said his goodbyes the night before. He'd never grown as close to Jenny as Alec had, maybe because he was just a child when Rose ran off and could barely remember his sister, but Alec knew he'd miss Jenny. She was the only link to their family; all of them gone now. Thinking of family made him long to visit Finn and Abbie, settle Diana on his knee as he told her a story, and hold baby Edward in his arms. He'd been only a few weeks old when they last saw him, but Edward would be nearly three months old now. Alec's arms suddenly felt strangely empty as he thought of his grandson.

He was looking forward to seeing Ben and Nat as well. The boys were both thriving and looking almost the same age despite their four-month age difference. Alec had to admit that he had newfound respect for Susanna once he found out about Nat, but she was a wise woman, and had done the right thing. Sam was happy and content with his wife and children, confident in the knowledge that he no longer had anything to hide that would destroy his well-ordered life. He still grieved for Diana Littleton from time to time, but more so for Nat's sake. Her death had been sudden and brutal, but sadly, no one missed her much.

"Val, what do you say we go visit Finn?" Alec asked, turning to Valerie with a big smile.

"When?"

"Today."

"I thought you'd never ask, but this time we're bringing

Tom. It's time he met his family, and I will never, ever, be parted from him again," Valerie said, and saw the grin on Alec's face.

"And another time-traveler is born," Alec quipped as he hugged Valerie. "Only this time, let me hold on to the device." Valerie nodded into his chest so he couldn't see her smile.

EPILOGUE

Cory Hazard shook out the contents of the backpack onto his bed. Where the heck was that student ID? He was sure he'd thrown it into the pack, but then again, maybe he left it in the glove compartment. Cory began to put everything back when he came across the odd watch. He found it months ago while cleaning the women's fitting room in T.J. Maxx and had stuffed it into his pocket.

He'd meant to give it to the manager but had tossed it into his backpack that night and forgot all about it. God, how he hated that job. It only paid for condoms and cigarettes, but still, it was better than nothing. And he'd met Lindsay, hence the need for condoms. Being with an older woman was an education, to say the least, and he smiled as he thought of her as she had been last night when he left her happy and satisfied, sprawled naked on the bed.

Cory turned the watch over in his hand, really looking at it for the first time. It was a strange thing, almost as if someone took several different watches apart and combined the different bits into one complicated device. It didn't even show the time. Cory pushed the On button and the little screen lit up. He tapped it, but nothing happened, so he pressed a few numbers. 1,2,3,4. Two choices flashed on the screen 'BC' and 'AD'. Cory chose BC, then pressed a few more buttons just to see what would happen. He stared at the little screen as it suddenly read: "Giza, Egypt, 1234 BC" before the world he knew faded and disappeared altogether.

Cory opened his eyes to a brilliant blue sky awash with fierce sunlight. He was stretched out on warm sand, the patch he was lying on thrown into shade by the huge structure that rose above him. It took him a few moments to understand what he was looking at before Cory's mouth opened in a silent scream as he saw the stern face of the Sphinx directly above him, huge and frightening, and heard voices calling out in a language he didn't understand. Suddenly, he grew cold despite the blistering heat as a terrifying realization hit him—the Sphinx still had a nose.

A LETTER FROM THE AUTHOR

Huge thanks for reading *Shattered Moments*, I hope you were hooked on Valerie and Alec's epic journey. Their story concludes in the next book, *The Ties that Bind*. If you want to join other readers in hearing all about my new releases and bonus content, you can sign up for my newsletter.

www.stormpublishing.co/irina-shapiro

If you enjoyed this book and could spare a few moments to leave a review that would be hugely appreciated. Even a short review can make all the difference in encouraging a reader to discover my books for the first time. Thank you so much.

Although I write several different genres, time travel was my first love. As a student of history, I often wonder if I have what it takes to survive in the past in the dangerous, life-altering situations my characters have to deal with.

Thanks again for being part of this amazing journey with me and I hope you'll stay in touch – I have so many more stories and ideas to entertain you with!

Irina

KEEP IN TOUCH WITH THE AUTHOR

facebook.com/IrinaShapiro2
x.com/IrinaShapiro2
instagram.com/irina_shapiro_author

Printed in Great Britain
by Amazon